# The Big Picture

*A Katie Parker Production (Act III)*

Jenny B. Jones

**The Big Picture**

Katie's mother, Bobbie Ann Parker, is newly released from prison and wants to start a new life with her daughter—in a new town. Katie is forced to walk away from In Between, leaving the family she loves, an endangered town drive-in, and a boyfriend who suddenly can't take his eyes off his ex.

As life with her mom takes a serious nosedive, Katie must rely on her faith to keep it together. Yet God seems to be nowhere around. Katie struggles to keep it together, between taking care of her mother and spending time with a handsome new friend who makes her question everything. Will her big picture ever include a happily ever after?

**A Katie Parker Production Series**

In Between

On the Loose

The Big Picture

Can't Let You Go (Summer 2014)

**Other Books by Jenny B. Jones**

Save the Date

Just Between You and Me

So Not Happening

I'm So Sure

So Over My Head

There You'll Find Me

Print Edition
Sweet Pea Productions
Originally published by NavPress, 2008.



The Big Picture: a Katie Parker Production (Act 3)/Jenny B. Jones.

Cover design: Natasha Brown

[1. Foster home care—fiction 2. Theater—fiction 3. High schools—fiction 4. Christian life—fiction 5. Texas—fiction]

# Dedication

This book is lovingly dedicated to my grandmother Edith. Thank you for all the stories you used to tell me and for always naming the main character "Jenny." Though the best stories were the real ones from your life. Thank you for all you've done for me and your family. You've created an amazing legacy.

# Chapter One

"IF I EAT anymore popcorn, I'm gonna hurl."

I shove the bucket away, and Charlie Benson, my date for the evening, takes it and peers inside.

"In other words, you ate the top layer where the butter was and now you're done?"

I lean back in my chair and smile up at him. *Smart boy.*

The town of In Between doesn't have much to offer, but I will give it points for a cool hangout spot for Friday nights. The drive-in. There are very few left in the country but, much like the rusty water tower and home grown shops downtown, In Between hangs onto its classics, including Bubba's Big Picture Cinema.

Slurping sounds come from Frances's direction.

"Nash," I call to her boyfriend. "Get her another root beer so I can hear the previews."

Charlie's fingers intertwine with mine and he whispers close to my ear. "The previews are twenty years old."

And that's what makes them perfect.

The four of us sit beneath a sky crowded with stars and watch the screen pop and crack to life. Bubba's only shows old movies, and tonight is eighties night. And with our chairs arranged in the back of Charlie's truck, we settle in for the first flick of the evening, *Sixteen Candles.*

Frances spouts off some random trivia about Molly Ringwald,

and while my ears are trained on my best friend, my eyes are totally glued to Charlie.

Charlie Benson, Mr. Four-Point-Oh and quarterback for the In Between Chihuahuas, is some pretty fine stuff. He and I have been spending a lot of time together lately. And you'd think that would be great. I mean, he's hot, he's brilliant, and he has some well defined, 'roid-free muscles that make a girl want to just drool.

Sometimes I wonder if we're just friends.

Who occasionally hold hands.

"Actually"—I bat my eyes at the boy beside me—"I could use another drink myself."

Charlie steps toward the cab and digs into the cooler until he finds a Diet Dr. Pepper. He pops the top then places it in my waiting hand.

*Awww*, he's sweet like that. All the time. Except when he avoids me at school. Like he has this past week.

Did I mention he's *not* my boyfriend? But I want to rectify that tonight. You know, make him define what exactly we are. Maybe he *thinks* we're exclusively dating, and *assumes* I think the same? *Or* what if he thinks we're just really close friends and is under the impression that I know that's all we are? But let me tell you, Frances and I are close friends, and *she* doesn't open my cans and hold my hand.

As Charlie sits down, my green eyes lock onto his gray peepers. My expression says, *Thanks for the drink. You're so thoughtful. By the way, do you plan on kissing me anytime this century?*

Behind us Frances and Nash break out the cookies, as Frances continues her list of everything she knows about the movie. Which is too much.

"Did you know the cake at the end of this movie is actually made of cardboard? And it's interesting to note that when the girls are in the lunch line . . ."

Charlie looks over at the two of them then leans closer to me. "Frances still gets a little nervous around Nash, doesn't she?"

I inhale his light scent and smile. "At least she no longer requires her inhaler every time he's around. I'd say that's progress. We did pretty well hooking those two up."

His brown hair blows in the evening breeze. "Yeah, we're a good team."

See? He's always saying things like that. We're a good team? What does that mean? A good team as in Bert and Ernie? Or as in Spider-Man and Mary Jane?

The last few weeks Charlie and I have been hanging out. A lot. We're at that point where we call each other every night. And my foster mom told me if I didn't cut down on the texting, I was going to have to sell an organ to pay for the next bill. I love a good text message—but maybe not enough to sacrifice a kidney.

But lately Charlie's been acting strangely. I've barely seen him at all this week at school. A suspicious girl would wonder if he's avoiding her. But then tonight . . . he acts like there's no place he'd rather be than out here, with me, watching a girl from the eighties try to figure out her life while wearing hideous blue eye shadow.

"Um . . . Charlie?" That's it. I'm just going to put it out there. Lay it on the line.

"Yeah?" His eyes never leave the screen.

"I was wondering if maybe—"

He shifts in his seat. "Are you hungry?"

Hungry for us to move onto the next level? *Why yes! I am.*

"I packed some sandwiches for us. Er, for all of us."

I lay my hand on his arm and scoot closer. "I don't want a sandwich." *I want you telling the world I'm your girlfriend. I want to scribble your name on my notebook and have other girls look on with envy.*

"I know we just had popcorn, but I thought maybe—"

"Charlie, I think we should talk." I look behind us and make sure Frances and Nash aren't listening in. "I was wondering if you and I—"

The trill of my phone cuts off my big moment.

I hold up a finger, silently telling Charlie to wait. *I'm not through with you.* "Hi, Millie."

"Hi, sweetie. Are you having a good time?"

*Oh, yeah, sure. I was just about to break into song and declare my undying devotion to Charlie. Great timing.*

"Hon, I know you've looked forward to tonight all week, but I'm going to need you to have Charlie bring you home." My foster mother pauses. "Now."

The heart I was about to hand over to Charlie triples in speed. "Are you okay? What's wrong?" My foster mom has been doing intense chemo treatments in the last month for breast cancer. It kinda freaks me out.

"Nothing's wrong. No emergency. James and I just need you to come home. We'll explain when you get here."

I end the call and relay the message to my friends.

"Hop in the truck." Charlie's hand rubs my upper arm. "I'll take you home and come back for Nash and Frances later."

He opens my door as my best friend and her date set up their chairs on the ground. I wave good-bye and promise to call Frances later. Charlie pulls his Ford out of the drive-in lot and we head toward home.

"Sorry you're having to miss the movie." I tap my fingers on my knees. "You can just drop me off."

Charlie pins me with an intense look. "Katie, I'm staying with you. I want to make sure everything's all right."

"Oh . . . um." Now is *so* not a good time for this, but I blurt it out anyway. "Charlie, what *are* we?"

He frowns. "What do you mean?"

"I mean . . . are we friends?"

"Of course we're friends. You're a good friend."

"No." Boys are dumb. Boys are stupid. "I mean is that all we are? I don't know how to read you lately. Are we going out?" I feel my face flame.

He stares straight ahead at the road. Speechless. I feel my stomach sink to the floorboard.

"I think we're probably heading in that direction," he finally says. "What's the problem?"

"The problem is at school you've been pretty distant lately. But then we'll spend two hours on the phone and hang out on the weekends. Are you embarrassed by me at school?" It's not like *I* wear blue eye shadow.

"No. Of course not." His face clouds. "I like hanging out with you."

And here's where he sticks in the big but.

"But I just don't want anybody hurt."

"Who's going to get hurt?"

He turns on his blinker and navigates a turn. "I don't want to lose this—us. But you probably need to know something."

For the second time tonight, my body floods with panic. "Oh, my gosh, do you wear women's underwear?"

"No."

"You like boys too?"

"No."

"You secretly listen to polka and make up your own dance moves?"

"Katie, I've started spending time with Chelsea again."

Like Voldemort to Harry Potter, I suck in my breath at the mere mention of this name. Chelsea Blake—his ex-girlfriend. A girl born with a silver spoon in her mouth and pompoms between her ears.

He reaches for my hand, but I move toward the door. "Why?"

"She's going through some pretty tough times lately."

"Who hasn't?" Plus all she has to do is shop her troubles away. *I feel blue! Come to me, oh, MasterCard and Visa!* "Why does Chelsea need you?"

"I'm practically all she's got. She doesn't really have many friends."

"Because she eats them for dinner," I hiss.

"That's not fair."

"Need I remind you I was *with* you the day you saw Chelsea lip-locked with Trevor Jackson last month? She cheated on you. You don't owe her anything. Let Trevor help her."

"They were over before they started. She's just so alone. You don't know all the dysfunction she's got going on."

"Oh, what, did Mommy buy her a Dooney and Bourke instead of a Coach?"

"There's more to Chelsea than that."

Yeah, a couple hundred dollars worth of highlights. "What does she have to do with us anyway?"

"I need you to be okay with me hanging out with her. It's the right thing to do."

I study his face, honing in on his nose and consider tweaking it off his pretty face. "So we *are* just friends then. Because what you're *not* saying is that you're not sure your feelings for her are totally dead, am I right?"

I count the fence posts we pass until he answers.

"I'm not dating Chelsea."

"But you're also not dating me?"

"I do want to see where you and I—"

"You can't have both of us. What's wrong with Chelsea that she needs you so much?"

"I can't tell you."

I nod and process this. "Fine."

"You know I can't turn my back on Chelsea. That's not the right thing to do."

"And dating me is—while you sort out which one of us you like?"

"I said this wasn't about liking Chelsea."

The truck pulls into my driveway.

"And I don't believe you." I grab my purse.

He hops out to open my door, but I beat him to it, slamming it shut and stomping toward the front porch.

"Go home, Charlie. I'll talk to you later."

I hear him running to catch up with me. "I'll walk you to the door."

Yes, because that *would* be the polite thing to do after stomping on my heart. I speed up my pace, staying two steps ahead of him and race up the sidewalk.

"Wait. Please, I want to talk to you."

"Now is obviously not a good time. Go check on Chelsea and—" I halt in my tracks and Charlie smacks into the back of me, grabbing my waist with both arms to avoid a fall.

The front doors swings open and Millie files out. Followed by James. And the dog.

And one more person, who shoves past them all and holds her arms out wide.

"Hello, Katie."

Bobbie Ann Parker.

"I've come to take you home."

My mother.

# Chapter Two

MY MOTHER RUSHES to meet me, throws her arms around me, and squeezes tight. Soothing words come from her mouth, but I can't decipher any of them. Too dazed. Too numb. Instantly, overwhelmingly confused.

Mom steps back, her hands still clutching my shoulders. "Let me get a look at you." She smiles, revealing teeth that never saw the luxury of braces. "I can't believe it. You look so grown-up, so beautiful."

She pulls me close again, and as I rest my head on her shoulder, I look to the porch where Millie and James stand. James has his arm draped around my foster mom, who clutches her hands and frowns.

I clear my throat and step out of the embrace. "I didn't know you were coming."

My mom tucks a stray piece of hair behind my ear. "It was pretty sudden. I just got in the car and came to In Between." She leans in and whispers. "Did you know their mascot is a Chihuahua?"

"Yes. I believe I'd heard that somewhere."

Mom's eyes dart behind me. "And who is this nice looking young man? I'm Bobbie Ann Parker, Katie's mom." She sticks her hand out, and Charlie shakes it.

"Nice to meet you. I'm Charlie Benson. I'm a . . . uh . . ."

*Yeah, you're a what?* My non-boyfriend? My great disappointment? My let's-just-be-friends friend?

"He's a friend." I level my glare at him. "Just a friend."

My mom nods, setting her ponytail to swinging. "How nice." She focuses on me again, and unease prickles along my spine. "I met the Scotts. They seem real nice."

"They are." Millie's face is still pinched in a frown. So unlike her not to have her gentle pastor's wife face on. "They've taken very good care of me."

"And I'm glad. But it's time to go home."

"This *is* home." The words fly out my mouth before I can even fully process the thought.

My mother's face darkens. "No. It's not." She stretches her smile back into place. "Home is with me—your mother."

I nod mutely, as my thoughts swim in my head like sharks in a frenzy, yet none of them come to the surface long enough to grab onto.

Millie and James walk into the yard and join us. "Why don't we go inside—have some something to drink, sit down, and talk," Millie suggests, placing her hand at my back.

Everyone steps toward the porch. When I see Charlie following me, I stop. "Thanks for the movie. I'll see you later."

"I can't leave you right now." He tilts his head toward my mom. "Don't you want me to stay?"

I shake my head. "No." I walk off, but he catches my hand in his. It feels so right there, but I rip it out of his grip.

"Katie, wait. I—"

"I think Chelsea has first dibs on your help." My eyes burn into his. "I don't need you."

"Come on. Don't—"

I dare one final look back as I walk away. "'Bye." Part of me wants to totally unleash and tell him off. How dare he jerk me around? He led me to believe we were on our way to something great—together. Yet the other side of me wants to turn around, launch myself into his arms and just stay there forever, blocking out the reality that my mom is back, I'm probably leaving, and I can't stand the idea of losing the Scotts.

The screen door screeches closed behind me, as I turn off the porch light and step into the entryway.

*God, help me. I know I should be glad my mom is here. What normal person wouldn't be? But this place has become my home. And these people have become my family. I feel like I'm being torn in two. Show me what to do, what to say. I can't do this alone.*

Millie walks out of the kitchen carrying a tray of coffee and cookies. "We're in the living room, Katie." The blonde waves in her wig bounce around her face. Millie's not even through with her chemo. She needs me.

I follow my foster mom and join everyone in the living room. Rocky, the resident guard dog, who actually serves no real purpose other than shedding and taking up more than his share of personal space, plops down at my feet as I collapse into the couch. My mom rises from her seat and sits beside me. Rocky stares her down with his dark black eyes.

Millie hands my mom her cup of coffee and me a Diet Dr. Pepper. Now I know something is seriously wrong. Millie rarely lets me have diet drinks and only on special occasions—like Christmas or getting an A on a test, two events that don't come around nearly enough.

"Thank you, Mrs. Scott." My mom puts two sugars in her coffee, something that catches Millie's eye.

"That's a nice organic blend, so you might not need to add too much to it." Millie watches my mother pour in heaping amounts of creamer.

"Millie's into natural remedies and organic foods." I take a swig from my can. "She's a health nut."

"Oh, how interesting." Mom stirs her coffee and blows on it. "I tried organic gardening once a long time ago."

I'm not really sure marijuana crops count.

"Mrs. Smartly didn't tell us you were coming." James looks at my mom over the rim of his glasses.

"Yeah, I know I should've called, but I just couldn't stand to be away from Katie any longer. I've lived without this kid long enough." She pats my leg.

"Why didn't you write me?" I cross my leg away from her.

My mom swallows. "I did."

"I didn't get any letters. I've been here over nine months—not a single letter, card, or phone call."

"My letters must've gotten lost in the mail."

I reach down and pet Rocky, staring at his fur. "Right." Because between the United States Postal Service and my mom, the post office is definitely the most unreliable.

"So . . ." Mom sits her cup and saucer on the coffee table. "I thought maybe I'd get a hotel here in town, and we could head out in the morning. Thought you could come back with me—just for the weekend. You'll be coming to stay for good soon, you know."

"Whoa, now." James holds up a hand. "Nobody's going anywhere just yet. Ms. Parker, we can't just let Katie go with you. We are her legal guardians right now. There's a whole process that must be followed in order for you to take her with you." James's serious eyes meet mine, and I try to read them, but can't.

"Well . . . I . . . guess I didn't think that far." Mom selects an almond cookie and takes a small bite. "I suppose I just thought I would pick up my daughter—since she is mine. You *are* still my daughter, aren't you?" My mom laughs, but nobody joins her.

"Ms. Parker—"

"It's Bobbie Ann." Mom interrupts Millie. "Please call me Bobbie Ann."

"Bobbie Ann . . ." The line between Millie's brows deepens. "We understand you have been . . . er . . . out . . . since March. We even hoped you would come to Katie's last play with Iola Smartly."

Mom dabs at her mouth with a napkin. "Yeah, I heard about the play. I wasn't able to attend. I had a lot going on. It's a bit overwhelming to be back in the outside world."

My face flushes red. I can't believe we're all sitting in the living room chatting about my mom's incarceration like we're discussing the weather.

"Katie expected you there. It was upsetting to her that you couldn't make it." James levels his gaze on Mom.

"I do regret not being able to attend. And it was so nice of the director of the girls' home to invite me—Mrs. Smartie or whatever her name is."

"Mrs. Smartly," I snap.

"What has the last few months been like for you?" Millie touches a hand to her blonde wig. "Did you move back to your previous hometown? Where are you working?"

My mom's eyes dart to me then to the floor. "We lost our old trailer when I was . . . um, incarcerated. So I decided to just start over fresh." She grins and pats my leg again. "We'll be living in a nicer trailer park this time. You'll have your own room. And I'm working at a local beauty shop. I'm a shampoo girl. But if I like it, I may go back to school and get my cosmetology license." Mom beams with pride. "Things are gonna be different, Katie. You'll see."

Maybe she is making an effort to turn her life around. Maybe things will be better.

"Due to good behavior, there's a chance Katie could live with me sooner than we thought. Maybe in a few weeks."

"Well, we'll have to call Mrs. Smartly, of course. Arrangements will need to be made, the proper procedures followed." Millie twirls the wedding ring on her finger.

"And Katie only has three weeks of school left. You wouldn't want her to miss her semester finals. It could be detrimental to her grades."

Mom chuckles at James's words. "Grades were never Katie's

thing anyway, so I don't really see it would matter where she finishes her semester at."

"I have good grades." Ice shoots through my veins. "I've worked really hard. It just so happens . . . I'm smart." *Take that, Mother.* And I plan to grow up to be more than an entrepreneur of drugs.

"Katie has worked very hard. My husband and I are extremely proud of her."

James nods. "We are proud of her for many reasons. She's learned to drive and doing well."

Yeah, haven't hit anything in weeks.

My foster dad continues, "Did you know she got saved last month?"

"No, I don't believe I did."

"I told you about it in my last letter." You know, one of the many you didn't respond to. "Maybe the mailman lost that too."

"Katie is quite involved in our church. She did some mission work with the youth over Spring Break." Millie sends a wink my way. "She's just an absolute joy and—"

*Slam!*

"Everybody freeze!" Maxine's voice carries from the foyer into the living room. "Big news! *Big*, big news!"

"We're in here," James calls, then turns back to my mom. "My mother-in-law." James and I share a look of amusement. Mom's about to endure Hurricane Maxine. Only the strong survive.

Maxine runs into the living room, skidding to a halt on the hardwood floor. "Sam asked me to marry him." She grabs her daughter and gives her a shake. "Did you hear me? Sam asked me to be his Mrs. Dayberry!" Maxine plants a smacking kiss on Millie's lips.

"Oh, good. Mil, you'll have a daddy again." James sips his coffee. "Can I help you pack, Maxine?"

My foster grandma cackles. "*Bah*! Not so fast. Sam wants to get married next week." She turns a little green at the idea. "But I don't know. My schedule's pretty booked with a pedicure and a foil highlight."

Millie frowns. "Next week? Is there a reason for the rush?"

James coughs. "I could think of about seventy-five of them."

Maxine ignores him. "Millie . . ."

"Yes?"

"I'm pregnant." Maxine throws herself into a chair and chuckles. She wipes her eyes, surveys the room, and stops cold. "Who are you?" Her blue eyes narrow on my mother.

"Mom, this is Katie's mother, Bobbie Ann Parker."

Maxine stands up and instead of offering Mom a hand to shake, she paces in front of her, staring Mom up and down. "You can't take her."

"Mother!" Millie gasps.

"She can't!" Maxine clutches her chest. "How can I get married without Katie?" She grabs my hand. "You have to be my maid of honor."

I smile, despite the weird tension in the room. "Don't you have friends more your own age?"

"They're all dead."

I squeeze her hand back. "No butt bows."

"I wouldn't dream of it." Maxine returns her attention to my mom. "Are you staying in town long? I'm afraid all our rooms here are occupied. We had some storm damage from a tornado in February, and the repairs have yet to be completely finished. I'm Katie's roommate."

Mom shifts uncomfortably beside me. "I had planned to take Katie back for the weekend, but the Scotts pointed out it will have to wait a few weeks until I fully regain custody. I guess I was just so excited to have a weekend off and see my daughter, I didn't think. Is there a hotel in town I could stay at tonight?"

"We can find room for you here, Bobbie Ann." Millie stands and collects the coffee cups. "You can have our room."

"Their bed has lumps." Maxine runs a hand through her yellow blonde hair. "It's a good bed to jump on, but won't do much for you if you want a good night's sleep."

James rises and puts an arm around his wife. "Of course you can stay with us. Spend some time with Katie here."

"Supervised time you mean? With my own daughter?"

James nods, his eyes on me. "Yes."

Mom chews on her lip and watches me. Does she see all the confusion on my face? The doubts scrolling across my forehead?

"If you could direct me to a hotel, that would be nice. I think I've probably crowded you all enough today." She laughs nervously. "I'll see you in the morning though, Katie. Okay?"

My mom pulls me into a hug, and I catch the faint whiff of cigarette smoke. I guess I can't expect her to give up every vice.

We walk my mother to the door, and I stand there behind the screen and watch her drive away in an old Buick.

"Wow, who saw *that* coming?" Maxine slaps me on the back.

"I know. I had begun to believe she would never contact me."

Maxine frowns. "No, I meant this." She sticks her hand in my face and a giant diamond glitters on her left hand. Maxine walks upstairs singing an off-key rendition of "Going to the Chapel."

Hours later I lie in bed and stare at the ceiling in the dark. A million thoughts explode like fireworks in my head.

"Katie?" Maxine whispers from her bed across the room.

"What?"

"I can't do it. I can't marry Sam."

The knot in my stomach tightens as I add one more problem to my list. "Maxine?"

"Yes, Sweet Pea?"

"I can't go home."

# Chapter Three

SIX-THIRTY.

Saturday.

I'm awake at a time when most roosters are just thinking about crowing, and no self-respecting teen would be up.

I jerk the covers over my head and groan.

*God, what are you doing with my life? I hand it over to you, and then you totally detonate it?*

Tossing off the blankets, I swing my feet onto the floor and quietly tiptoe to the bathroom, careful not to wake up my newly engaged roommate.

I try not to focus on the sick feeling occupying space in my stomach as I wash my face, brush my teeth, and throw my hair into a ponytail. Nice bags under my eyes. The swollen, puffy, no-sleep look is *so* hot. But what do I care? Not like I have a boyfriend.

But I do have two mothers.

And one foster dad. One foster grandma.

One foster dog.

And one heart pulled in opposite directions like a tug-of-war.

After changing into some shorts and grabbing my iPod, I walk downstairs into the kitchen. I scribble a note for James and Millie and head out the front door.

The early morning Texas sun seems to hesitate in rising today, but

I know the gray clouds will burn off soon. Wish my bad mood would.

I scroll through the iPod until it blasts some up-tempo rock in my ears.

And then I run.

Soaring up the driveway and striding onto our road, I run like the wind.

A very slow, tired wind.

Okay, so running is not my thing.

I have a side-stitch, and I've barely made it past the mailbox. I suck in air and force it back out, desperate to drag up some energy from somewhere in this tired, sad body.

My Nikes pound the pavement, and I work to clear my head. To focus on the light breeze. The spring flowers. The glisten of the morning dew. The sight of—

*Ew.* The dog poo I nearly stepped in.

*Ring-a-ling! Ring-a-ling!*

I rip out an ear bud and look behind me.

Maxine. Doing figure eights in the street with her tandem bike.

"Hey, Toots!" She rings her little bike bell again and smiles big. "Thought you could use a little company."

I face straight ahead again and continue my determined attempt at running.

She pedals ahead then swoops around me in a circle. "You're up awfully early. Training for the Olympics?"

I had been so quiet when I had gotten up so I wouldn't wake her. Why did I even bother? It's like she has some sort of inner radar and knows where I am at all times. Like a few months ago when she caught me at a party I was *definitely* not supposed to be at.

"Since when did you start running?" She stands up on her pedals and the breeze ruffles her yellow bob.

I inhale. "Since"—exhale—"this morning."

"Is this supposed to be a stress reliever? Because I could think of a hundred better ways. We could sneak over and jump on the neighbor's trampoline again."

"Yes, this is a stress reliever. And I feel better already. It's clearing my head right up." I think I'm gonna hurl. I've had a lot of running experience this past year in PE, but I don't usually work out on an empty stomach, zero sleep, and the weight of the entire universe on my shoulders.

"Why dontcha get on my bike? We can take a ride."

"No, thanks." Six forty-five and I'm sweating like a pig. No wonder the birds aren't up yet. I'm scaring them away with my B.O.

"Aw, come on. Get on the bike. I won't make you do all the pedaling this time."

"How sweet." Why didn't I bring any water with me? "Look, Maxine, I just want to be alone. I want to run off some steam and be by myself."

"I think you need company."

"Well, I don't."

"I think you want to talk."

"You're wrong."

"Well, maybe *I* need to talk. And I'm on my way to buy donuts."

"I am committed to this run. Nothing you can say is going to deter me from my goal. I am powerless to your words."

"You can have extra sprinkles."

I screech to a halt. "Stop the bike."

And Maxine hands me my helmet.

A BOX OF donuts, two extra-large mochas, and an hour-and-a-half later, my foster grandmother and I return to the house.

My mom's rusty Buick sits in the driveway.

"It's only eight-thirty. What's *she* doing here?" Maxine asks as we pedal the bike to the front porch.

Good question. My mom is more a stay-up-all-night-and-sleep-all-day kind of girl.

We open the front door, and I inhale the coffee smell drifting from the kitchen.

"In here, ladies!" Millie calls.

Maxine and I exchange a look and walk into the kitchen.

Millie and my mom sit at the table in the breakfast nook and sip from steaming mugs. In the kitchen, James waves at me with his spatula, then flips a pancake.

"You hungry?" He wiggles his eyebrows like this is a cute, happy moment.

Well, it's not. I have two worlds colliding in my kitchen right now. I'm hurt, confused, and scared. Not to mention I clearly forgot to apply deodorant before my early morning jog.

"Everything okay, hon?" Millie pats the seat beside her then gets up and heads toward the coffee maker.

"Sure." I paste on a smile and make eye contact with everyone. *See, people. I'm smiling.* Smiling at Mom. Smiling at the Scotts and Maxine. Like this is *totally* normal to be having coffee and flapjacks with the mom who's ignored me for the past year and the people who have changed my life. Yes, I'll have butter with that.

"We called your mom to see if she'd have breakfast with us. I think we'd all like to get to know one another better." Millie smiles and hands me a cup of coffee as she sits back down.

She slides the skim milk and sugar toward me.

My mom takes it back. "Katie likes her coffee black."

Millie's smile freezes. She looks at me.

I look at my mom.

"Things have changed." I pour the milk in my coffee, adding a little extra because . . . well, I don't know why. Because for some reason this ticks me off. The woman hasn't contacted me in over a year and now she's telling Millie how to fix my breakfast?

My mom clears her throat. "I guess I never had the money for extras in the coffee, being a single mother and all."

*Yeah, and the fact you forgot to get groceries on a regular basis.* Like every day that ends in Y.

"Here you go, ladies. My special blueberry pancakes. Who wants whipped cream?" James arrives at the table bearing a two-foot tall stack of pancakes. My stomach lurches.

"I'm not really hungry."

He frowns. "You feeling okay?"

"Yeah, Maxine and I got a light snack this morning on our ride." Maxine called it a snack. I call it six donuts. And a few éclairs. All right, and half a Danish.

"Bring on the whipped cream. Yes, sir. Pour it on." Maxine parks herself in a chair next to my mom and rubs her hands. "I pedaled myself into a good appetite."

"So, Bobbie Ann. . ." Millie picks up her fork and cuts into a piece of cantaloupe on her plate. "I was saying that Katie has a home here for as long as she'd like. As long as you'd like."

My mom looks up from her plate, her faced scrunched in confusion.

"I mean, if you didn't feel for certain you were ready to return to full-time parenting, then that would be totally understandable. I'm sure pursuing . . . recovery can be a huge responsibility all on its own."

"Huh?" My mom swallows a bite.

"What Millie's trying to say is, we don't want you to rush your recovery process. Katie is thriving here with us." James lays his big hand on mine. "So if you feel having Katie with you right now would add to your stress, then we'd love for her to stay with us longer."

Millie blots her mouth with a napkin. "And I'd also like to know what you're doing in terms of drug rehab."

I choke on my java.

My mom blanches. You *know* she's dying for a cigarette right now.

Mom's mouth opens then closes. "Er . . . um . . . I . . . " She runs a hand through her brassy hair. First thing we're gonna do when we get to her trailer is touch up those roots. "I had some recovery classes in . . . prison."

I wince at the word and imagine my mom in an orange button-up suit and handcuffs. A total fashion don't.

"And I'm in a support group back home."

Millie slowly nods. I can tell she's not impressed. The Scotts' twenty-five-year old daughter Amy has drug issues, so Millie's familiar with the road my mom's on.

"Mrs. Scott, I know I have not been a model parent. But over the course of this year, I have realized things need to change." My mom sniffs. "And I'm ready to make that change." She reaches across the table and grabs my hand. "For my daughter."

An awkward silence descends on the room.

I hate awkward silences. I'm always overcome with the urge to hum. Probably not appropriate though. Humming solos rarely are.

"I appreciate breakfast, Mr. and Mrs. Scott." My mom scoots her chair back and stands up. Rocky leaps to attention, eyeing her like she's a potential source of danger. "I have to check out of the hotel by ten, so I guess I better go." Harsh lines fan around Mom's brown eyes as she studies my face. "I don't have a phone yet, but I'll try and call often. I'll keep you posted on coming back home. I guess I need to contact Mrs. Smartly."

"You didn't finish your breakfast." I drop my gaze and stare at her hands. "You don't want to spend the day with me? I have some play videos I've been wanting to show you."

Mom fidgets with the watch on her wrist. "I think the best thing is for me to just get back home. I didn't think this through very well. Besides, I have to be at work in the morning."

"On a Sunday?"

"I clean the shop on Sundays." She smiles. "See? Your mom's got a job. A real one."

*Real* meaning one that doesn't involve making deals behind a dumpster in the trailer park. Still, it's progress. And there's hope in that.

"I was kinda hoping we could hang out." *I was hoping you'd* want *to hang out.*

"We're gonna have all the time in the world for that—time for just you and me. I've got to go home and get the ball rolling and get my kid home. But I am glad you're being well taken care of."

She pulls me into a hug, and slowly I wrap my arms around the new and improved Bobbie Ann Parker.

My brain is absolutely numb, but one thought manages to form.

She doesn't smell like Millie.

"Okay, kiddo, I'll see you soon." She kisses me on the forehead, a move totally unlike my mom.

James and Millie shake Mom's hand, and we all migrate toward the front door.

"You take care of my girl now." And Bobbie Ann, former inmate number 19840981, slips outside and back out of my life.

But for how long?

"You all right, Katie?"

James rests his arm on my shoulders.

"Sure."

"Well, I'm not okay," Maxine barks. "Katie's not going anywhere. Millie, tell her she's not going anywhere."

Silence. Again.

I look at Millie. Who says nothing.

"Don't stress over this yet." James pulls me close. "You know my motto."

"God is in control." I parrot the words my foster dad has tattooed on my brain. "I'm not stressed." I look him square in the eye. "Really."

"You're not?"

"Nope." I brave a smile. "I am cool as ever."

"Oh, really?" He grins. "Well, if you're so cool, then why do you still have your biking helmet on?" He raps the top of my headgear.

"All I know is something smells."

"Mother, we will all reserve judgment on Katie's mom. Keep your comments to yourself."

"No." Maxine swats me on the behind as she sails past. "I mean your foster kid needs a shower. Woo-wee!" She laughs as she hits the stairs. "Race you to the shower, Sweet Pea."

I follow in the trail of Maxine's perfume, but stop when Millie calls my name.

I turn around. "Yeah?"

James drapes his arm around my foster mom. "We love you, kid."

I nod. "Same here."

Yet I know—nothing will ever be the same here.

# Chapter Four

MAYOR THREATENS TO *Condemn Bubba's Big Picture.*

My spoon of Cinnamon Toast Crunch halts midway to my mouth as I catch a glance at the front page.

"What is that?" I thrust my finger into James's Sunday paper.

"*Hmmm*?" With his mind already on the sports section, my foster dad doesn't even look up.

I grab the paper out of his hands and scan the article. "It says unless improvements are made on the drive-in, the city is gonna shut it down." Above the article is a picture of the current owner, Buford T. Hollis. Looks like he pulled out his best white Hanes T-shirt for his big moment.

Millie refills her coffee mug. "This has been going on for years. Mayor Crowley threatens to shut down the drive-in, Buford touches up some paint and gives the mayor some movie passes, and then the whole argument is dropped. It's nothing to worry about."

"That man's a tyrant. Who voted for him?" James growls.

Millie laughs. "We did."

"The article says Buford has three months to make fifteen thousand dollars' worth of repairs. That doesn't sound like an idle threat."

Millie pats me on the back. "I'm sure it will be fine. The mayor's just full of hot air."

Their nonchalant attitudes do little to calm me. I text Frances as soon as I hit my room and fill her in. If anyone can get more information about this, it's Frances.

An hour later, I walk into the youth building at church. I allow myself the luxury of basking in my friends' hugs and hellos. If I go home with my mom, I won't ever have this again. Not like my In Between church friends. I'll miss their smiles, the house band, and Pastor Mike and his bald head. These people brought me to Christ. And now I could lose them forever. I'm sure I can find new friends in a new church, but it won't be the same.

"Hi, Katie."

I turn around and there stands Charlie. Looking totally yum in khakis and a polo. "Hey." I take a deep breath. "Charlie, I just wanted to apologize for—" My mouth shuts and my eyes narrow to slits. "Hello, Chelsea." *Grrrr.*

My non-boyfriend's face pinkens.

"Charlie brought me to church this morning." Chelsea looks at him like he just saved her life instead of giving her a lift. "Isn't he the best?"

Oh, he's the best all right. The best at walking all over my heart. The best at being a total jerk. "Yeah, very nice of him."

"I'm gonna go save us some seats, okay? Don't be long." Chelsea flounces off in her cute pink skirt that probably cost more than my entire week's worth of outfits.

Charlie leans in and I catch a whiff of his shampoo. I may be mad at him, but that boy smells *gooood.*

"Chelsea's car got taken away." He frowns.

"Oh, what happened? Let me guess, it was time to change the oil in her new Beemer and Daddy just bought her a new one instead?"

"No . . . I mean her car got *permanently* taken away."

"What are you talking about?" I lower my voice to match his. "What's going on with her?"

"Chelsea's dad—"

"Hey, Charlie. I forgot my Bible." Miss No Car appears between us. "Get me one from the back, would you?" She pats his bicep and smiles.

*Okay, God, I'm sorry, but I cannot stand this girl. I know the Bible says you love all of us, but seriously, don't you sometimes just want to make some exceptions?*

"Er . . . right. I'll get that now." Charlie smiles sheepishly. "I'll talk to you later, Katie."

"Uh-huh. Sure." He hasn't even asked me about my mom. I roll my eyes and go off in search of Frances.

I find her standing in a corner surrounded by a motley crew of friends. She jerks the front page of the paper out of Nash's hands. "Can you believe this?" She pushes her trendy black glasses up on her nose. "This is an outrage! This demands action."

"James and Millie say it's gonna blow over." I stand next to my friend Hannah, who twists her hair, deep in thought.

"Blow over? Like they think there will be another tornado?" Hannah pops her gum.

Frances and I stare at our friend, then continue our conversation. We're quite used to these Hannah moments. There's a big blank spot in her head where things make sense only to her.

"We have to do something." Frances jabs her finger in the air. "I know. We'll start a petition."

"A petition for what?" I ask.

"To save the it. We'll get people to sign it. If we have a lot of signatures in support of preserving the drive-in, then the mayor will think twice about shutting it down. He won't want the whole town mad at him."

"I don't know, Frances." Couldn't she come up with anything better? She's the brains among us.

"It's a start," Nash chimes in.

"Um . . . Katie?" Frances looks beyond her boyfriend and glares. "Is that Chelsea Blake sitting with Charlie? *Your* Charlie?"

I follow the path of her stare and see Chelsea giggling at something Charlie's said. She whispers in his ear and he smiles. My hands ball into fists. "Yes, on the same night my mother rolls back into town, Charlie tells me he's decided to renew his connection to Chelsea."

Nash shakes his head and sends his long hair dancing. "What? Dude, that stinks."

"Yeah." I purse my lips. "He said something about how he couldn't really explain, and he just needed me to be understanding. But—" Chelsea's lilting giggle carries over to our corner. "I think I'm all out of understanding." That skinny little Dooney-and-Bourke-carrying, feather-brained—

"Charlie's a good guy though. I'm sure he has a good reason for hanging out with her again," Nash says.

Frances gasps and throws her arm around me. "Men! You're all clueless. Your friend has left Katie abandoned and alone." She pulls me closer. "Destitute and distraught. Crying out for help as the vultures swoop and circle around the decaying remains of her dying relationship."

Hannah twirls her hair. "Huh?"

"Charlie's a jerk, Hannah. That's all I'm trying to say." Frances lets me go and motions us toward some seats.

Right behind Charlie and Chelsea.

I shake my head in spastic jerks. *No!* I would rather go sit alone in the church basement than sit here.

Frances takes her seat and clears her throat. "So, Katie, you were telling me Joey Farmer asked you out?"

I blink. "Huh?"

Charlie swivels around in his seat. "Who?" Seriously, boy is even hot when he scowls. When I scowl I just look constipated.

Frances's dark eyes laser into mine. It's that "smile pretty and just go with it" look.

"He's *such* the catch." Frances elbows Nash. "You hang out with him sometimes, don't you?"

"I have no idea who—*oomph!* Right. Love the guy," Nash says. "An absolute . . . um, stud. If I wasn't a dude, I'd date him myself."

Charlie's gray eyes lock onto mine. "You have a date?"

I open my mouth to deny it, but Frances stops me.

"He's so cool. He taught Nash everything he knows about music. Isn't that right, Nash?"

Frances's boyfriend glares. "Yes, Johnny Filmer is a genius in the music world."

"Joey Farmer," Charlie corrects.

"Right. Well, sometimes I forget . . . and use his stage name."

No, this has got to stop. It's dishonest! We're lying in the house of God. Lightning bolts are going to shoot out of the ceiling at any moment.

Must put an end to this. "Actually, Frances was just—"

"I think it's sweet you have a boyfriend, Katie." Chelsea's cat-who-just-ate-the-canary smirk unravels all my righteous intentions.

"He's not a boyfriend." I smile right back. "He's just a . . ." I pretend to consider this. "Friend." *And you know all about those special "friends," don't you Charlie?* Jerk face.

"You should invite him to go bowling with us after church," Charlie suggests, his expression unreadable.

"Uh . . . I can't. He's . . . he's . . ." I send a silent message to Frances for help. "He's . . ."

"Doing trigonometry." Frances nods.

I openly gape at my normally bright best friend. She didn't just give me an imaginary boyfriend, but an imaginary *dork* boyfriend. He's doing trigonometry? *Who* says that? How about he's lifting weights? Or he's volunteering at the local soup kitchen? Or he's home waxing his chest for his next modeling gig? *Anything* but he's home crunching numbers on his graphing calculator!

"Nash's band is playing at my birthday party next weekend. Invite him. I'd like to meet your new *friend*." A challenge gleams in Charlie's eye.

"You say that like I'm lying." Suddenly I'm mad he would think I would be dishonest. Even though I am. The *nerve* of that boy.

"I didn't say that." Charlie shrugs. "If he exists, then I'll meet him Friday night."

"Oh," Chelsea says. "You should have him play with Nash's band, Charlie."

"Yeah. Great idea. Tell him we'd love to hear him."

I swallow. "He's pretty busy."

Charlie lifts a brow. "With all his trig homework?"

"Right. Er, no. With his music. And . . . stuff." Sometimes when you dig yourself in a hole, your only option is to just keep shoveling.

"If he's such the musical genius, then he'll love the opportunity to play. Can't wait to meet him." And I'm totally dismissed as Charlie turns around.

Pastor Mike jumps on the stage and the room settles into silence. My head buzzes with raging thoughts.

"Welcome to church, guys." The pastor's diamond earring sparkles under the stage lights. "Today we're gonna talk about honesty."

I reach into my purse and pull out a pen.

I should probably take notes.

# Chapter Five

MY BOWLING BALL lands with a thud and careens down the lane. Right into the gutter.

Again.

I turn around and my team cheers for me anyway. Nothing like pity claps to make you feel even more like a loser.

Next to us, Charlie, in perfect form (and I do mean that in every sense of the word), throws a strike. Again. Chelsea jumps up and throws her arms around him. I have to turn my head.

Nash stands up and puts a hand on my shoulder. "Hey, Charlie, maybe you could give Katie some tips. She could really use the help." His hand squeezes twice. I glance at Frances and she nods. Total conspiracy.

"No, really, I'm fine. Just bad luck today. Maybe my shoes are too tight." Or the hand squeezing my heart as I watch Chelsea throw herself on the guy who was about to be my boyfriend!

"It's *not* fine." Frances picks up her bowling ball. "Katie's only bowled a few times in her entire life, so she's kind of at a disadvantage."

Charlie, now completely disentangled from Chelsea, looks my way, a question in his gray eyes. Like he's afraid I'm gonna try and throw him down the lanes instead of the ball. Even if I wanted to, I couldn't get him any further than the gutter, so it would be a completely wasted effort.

"I'd be glad to help you out. Give you a few tips."

"Sure." I lift an indifferent shoulder. "Whatever."

I pick up a ball and follow Charlie to the lane on the other side of my team, left vacant mid-game by fellow churchies who decided to try their luck at pool.

"First of all, this ball is eleven pounds." Charlie takes it from my hand.

"So?"

"So, Miss Attitude, it's probably too heavy for you."

"Yeah? Well, I like it." My chin lifts. "It's pink."

"Katie, you can't pick a bowling ball because it's cute. You pick one you can adequately lift and guide down the lane."

I inspect my fingernails.

"Are you even listening to me?"

I turn my head, only to discover our noses are now inches apart. I take a step back. "Yes, I'm listening."

His eyes darken. "Katie, I—"

"Yes?"

Charlie's gaze drops to our crazy bowling shoes. "Why didn't you return any of my calls this weekend? I texted you a hundred times."

"I guess I was busy." You know, worrying about how my life was falling apart. "Besides, you had Chelsea to keep you company."

His expression clouds and he walks away, returning with a new bowling ball. He shoves it into my hands. "Here."

I slip my fingers in the three holes. I notice I've totally broken my thumbnail. This game is stupid. Knock down some pins and lose all your fingernails. Great fun. Buy me a T-shirt and sign me up for a league.

"You're holding it all wrong." He picks up another ball and demonstrates. "See? No, no . . . here, let me show you."

I hand the black ball (such an uninspiring color) over and before I can say PDA violation, Charlie stands behind me, his arm extended. "Like this, see?" His arm brushes my side as he demonstrates his technique. "Got it?" He looks down into my face.

Our eyes linger for a moment as I look up.

"Katie—"

"Charlie—"

"What's going on with us?" He asks, his voice deep and low in my ear.

"I don't know. You're the one who backed off." Do I need to replay Friday night for him? Because I have it memorized *word for word.*

"I asked for your understanding." Turning me around, he then drops his arm.

"I can't be that girl who trusts you blindly. I'm not going to let you walk all over me."

His brows snap together. "What does that mean?"

I jerk my head toward Chelsea, two lanes down. "Your renewed *friendship* with your ex-girlfriend."

"What if that's all it is? A friendship."

"You expect me to stick around until you figure it out? I don't think so. How is it that suddenly this girl who . . . who *cheated* on you is now your BFF, and the three of us are all supposed to hang out?"

"She needs my help. Chelsea needs friends right now."

I shake my head. "What she wants from you goes way beyond friendship and you know it." I remove his hand from my arm. "You can't have us both. I'm not gonna date you while your *friend* throws herself at you at every opportunity."

Charlie runs his hand through his toffee hair. "Oh, yeah, and what about you, huh? Joey Farmer? Who is this guy? Friday night you're on a date with me, and by Sunday this dude's asked you out? Have you been talking to him this whole time?"

"This whole time? This whole time we've been *not* dating? Because I've never really been sure what exactly you and I were. Were we a couple? Were we good friends?"

Charlie checks the area to make sure no one is within earshot. "Is this because I never kissed you?"

"No." Well, maybe. I don't know! After so long a girl does have to wonder: am I someone he really likes or just someone to share his popcorn combo at the movies?

"I wanted things to be different with us," Charlie says. "I wanted us to have this solid friendship and take it from there. Like Pastor Mike talks about. Chelsea and I just jumped into our relationship."

"And it's a great idea. What's *not* a fabulous idea is bringing Chelsea back into the equation and expecting me to believe it's all about friendship. Are you going to tell me what's going on with her?"

He opens his mouth. Then shuts it again. "I can't."

"Fine." I slowly nod. "Then I hope you guys will be very happy." *You, Chelsea, and your big fat secrets.*

"It's not like that." He reaches for my hand, but I pull it away.

"Charlie!" Chelsea's petite hand waves him over. "It's getting lonely over here, and it's your turn to bowl!"

"It's not like that?" I laugh. "Tell that to her."

* * *

"WHAT'S THE MATTER, gloomy pants?" Maxine belly flops onto my bed, where I sit Indian style, staring at my phone. I read Frances's latest text.

> CHARLIE ASKED NASH ABT J FARMER AGAIN. C SAID IF HES GOING 2 DATE U, HE WANTS 2 CHECK HIM OUT. YIKES.

"Nothing."

She crawls closer to me. "*Awwww*, you can tell ol' Maxine." Her smile dims. "Besides, nothing could be worse than my life."

"My mom is out of prison and wants to take me back home forever. I might never see you guys, my friends, or In Between again. I'll be leaving while Millie still needs me. Charlie no longer wants to date me. Instead he wants to focus on his friendship with Chelsea Blake.

And by Friday night, I have to produce a fake boyfriend who's hot *and* excels in trigonometry and is a musical virtuoso." I glare at my foster grandmother. "And your problem is . . .?"

She grabs one of my pillows, fluffs it, and sticks it under her chin. "Sam still wants to marry me."

"Of course he does."

"Well, *duh*, I mean I know he *should* want to. Who wouldn't?" She rolls her eyes. "But I've dropped hints lately we should wait and not rush into anything. That maybe a nice, long, well thought-out engagement would be wise."

"Maxine, he's been in love with you for two years. Why would he want to wait? You aren't getting any younger."

"Ha!" She pats her face. "Tell that to my plastic surgeon." Her face sobers. "I don't know what's wrong with me. I thought marriage was what I wanted. But now . . . am I ready to marry some old geezer and settle into a boring domestic life as a wife?"

"He's younger than you."

"Not according to the fake birth certificate I got off eBay."

"Maybe you should have a fake boyfriend too. I'll have Frances come up with one. She's good at that."

"Shame on you girls." Maxine clucks her tongue. "That is so deceitful." She rubs her hands together. "And I like it."

"James and Millie wouldn't."

Maxine nods. "No, they wouldn't. But you can get out of it, can't you? Does this Joey Farmer really have to make an appearance?"

"Yes. Charlie insists on me bringing him to his birthday party Friday night so he can meet him. And he was so smug about it, I want to prove there could be another guy."

"Joey Farmer . . . Why didn't you girls come up with a better name? Like Enrique or Sebastian? Something hot and foreign."

"Yeah, because it would be *so* much easier to find a guy who's good looking, brilliant, a master guitar player, *and* has an accent."

"So find a guy to pose as Joey for one night, and be done with it.

How hard can that be?"

"Uh, next to impossible? Is that really all the advice you have for me?"

"I'm in a crisis myself here! I'm sorry, kid." Maxine taps her French manicured nails together. "I might have an idea . . ."

"Am I gonna like it?"

She smiles. "Most definitely not."

# Chapter Six

"ARE YOU INSANE?"

I shut my locker door and face Frances. "Maxine says she's going to take care of finding me a Joey Farmer."

"Katie, Mad Maxine is *not* to be trusted."

Frances and my foster grandmother don't exactly have the closest relationship. Maxine loves to torment Frances, and my best friend falls for the bait every time.

"What other option do I have?" I grab my English book and a binder. "You came up with this ridiculous idea and totally left me hanging. Maxine talked to Mr. Diamatti, her old neighbor at Shady Acres, and he's going to introduce me to one of his gorgeous Italian grandsons who live nearby." But not too nearby. Close enough to make an appearance Friday, but far enough away so that Charlie has probably never laid eyes on the boy.

"This is unacceptable." Frances stuffs books into her backpack. "You don't know this guy from Adam. He could be a murderer. A serial killer. Or even worse"—she zips her bag—"a total dork."

"Mr. Diamatti showed Maxine a picture of his three grandsons. They all belong on Abercrombie bags." Well, actually she said it was a picture of them at a ski resort. The oldest two grandsons were "delish," but my soon-to-be Joey Farmer was too wrapped up in snow gear to tell. But come on, if two of them are amazing, I think it's a safe bet brother number three will be super fine too.

"Relax, Frances. I'm the one who should be stressed, not you. I'm going over to Shady Acres with Maxine Thursday to meet him. If he's a Greek Adonis, then great. And if he's a total freak job, then he will not get the role of Joey Farmer, potential love of my life."

Frances squints behind her trendy black glasses. "This just seems very wrong."

"It was wrong the moment you gave me an imaginary boyfriend. It's too late now."

"Hi, Katie."

Charlie.

Almost six feet of ooey-gooey off-limits boy. *Why* is everything going wrong? I feel like the world is plotting against me. It's like I'm Britney Spears or something.

I set a cool gaze on Charlie. Be smooth. "Hey." My voice cracks like a twelve-year-old boy.

He greets Frances, then his eyes settle back on me. "I've got two tickets to see *The Sound of Music* at the Valiant Theatre for Tuesday night. Know anybody who might want to go?"

I feel my resistance melting at his reluctant smile. He knows I can get tickets to any show at the Valiant since my foster parents own it, but I also know he hates musical theatre. He would suffer through singing nuns and tunes about lonely goatherds just for me? I am powerless to resist this new tactic. Charlie is hard to resist. But Charlie together *with* yodeling Von Trapps? Impossible.

"I don't know . . ." Translation: pick me up at six.

"It will be fun. We can go eat at the Burger Barn, then catch the show." He leans down. "Besides we need to talk. About you and me."

I consider this. "Do you promise not to make fun of the children's matching outfits?"

He flashes his mega-watt grin. "If you promise not to sing along with every number."

And then we're laughing, Charlie and I. The Monday morning crowd disappears around us, and it's just me and this boy who is confusing, maddening, and yet everything I could want in a boyfriend.

"Katie—" Charlie speaks and breaks the magical bubble around us. "I'm sorry about everything. I don't want to fight, and I don't want to stop hanging out with you."

*Hanging out with me?* In the friend sense? Or as in you Brad, me Angelina?

"I need you to believe me that there's nothing going on between Chelsea and me."

"Yet." I shake my head and become more aware of the crowded hall. "I don't know. I want to believe you." In the sixth grade I wanted to believe Tommy Parks when he said that lighting a box of matches in the Jackson Middle School ladies' room wouldn't turn the sprinklers on, but one flooded bathroom and a week's suspension later, I realized Tommy had lied. I don't want to miss the obvious again.

"Let's just go have a good time Thursday night. No pressure. No worries. No—"

"Chelsea Blake?"

The guarded mask returns to Charlie's face. "Give it a rest. Can't you just try to avoid the topic of Chelsea?"

*It's kind of hard when she's been attached to you like a perfectly highlighted, Siamese twin.* "Okay, sorry." I hold up a hand in surrender. "We'll just avoid that topic." I give my strawberry-blonde hair a slight toss and fix Charlie with my glossy smile. "I would love to go to the theatre with you. It sounds fun."

He opens his mouth to respond, but the first hour bell cuts him off. "See ya at lunch."

I wave as he walks away.

In English class, Ms. Dillon assigns us our end of the year project. When she announces it will take the place of a final exam, everyone cheers. When she adds we have to write a ten-page life autobiography, the groans nearly rattle the windows.

The young English teacher hands out rubrics. "For bonus points, you have the option of writing an additional three pages, giving us a view into your future. Perhaps in a decade. Where will you be? What will you be doing?"

In a decade? I don't even know where I'll be next month.

Hannah leans into my row. "This is totally lame."

No, lame is having to write an essay in which you detail the events of living with your druggie mom, moving from town to town, and being shipped from girls home to foster home, then back to newly released mother. I'll call it "The "Sweet Life of Katie Parker." Or "The Life and Times of a Girl the World Continues to Chew Up and Spit Out." Or maybe "I'm Katie Parker. Sure There Are People Worse Off Than Me. But I've Never Met Any."

I glance across the room at Angel Nelson, a nemesis of mine and resident bully of In Between High. I can imagine her essay. "Sixteen Years of Beating People Up." Or "I Skip School, Therefore, I Am." That girl seriously needs some God in her life. And some deep conditioner—major split ends.

At lunch I grab our usual table and set my bag down. Ever since Millie's cancer, she's been on this psycho health kick, so I've started packing my own lunch. It was either that or eat tofu and bean sprouts every day.

"Can I sit here?" Charlie places his tray of nachos and fries across from me.

I arch a brow. "What would your baseball coach say about your menu choices?"

He grins, and for a moment it feels like the good old days. "He'd wonder why I didn't get pizza too." He bites into a fry. "So tell me about your mom."

And just like that, my appetite is gone. "Um . . . I dunno." I push my lunch bag away. "I guess I'll be going back home sometime." The words are acid on my tongue. Shouldn't there be at least *some* joy in the thought of living with my mom again? At least I won't have to eat Millie's tofu burgers anymore.

Charlie reaches across the table and pulls my hands into his. "What? What are you talking about?"

I try to focus on the question, but all I can think is *He's holding my hand! In his inner battle between Chelsea and me, did he just pick me?* "Yeah, that's why my mom was here. She's been . . . um . . . free for some time now, so she decided she would stop by for a visit and take me with her for the weekend. The Scotts wouldn't let her, but pretty soon they won't have a choice."

"She can't just take you like that, though, can she?" Charlie's frown is fierce. "You want to stay with the Scotts, right?"

My chest tightens. Yes, I want to stay with the Scotts. And yes, I want to be with my mom. At least I'm pretty sure I do.

"I'll finish up the school year here. Millie says my mom is in the process of being evaluated by the state to see if she's fit to regain custody, and apparently things are moving quickly." Too quickly. By the time summer break starts, I could be on my way back to my mom.

"What can I do?" Charlie asks.

*How about never let my hands go. Tell me there is no other girl you'd rather gaze at than me. Never look at Chelsea again.*

*And offer me half your fries.*

"Nothing." I force a smile. "There's nothing any of us can do."

"How do you feel about all of this?"

I lift my shoulder in a shrug. "It doesn't matter, I guess. If the state says I go, I go."

He leans in. I want you to know no matter what—"

"Hey, Charlie." Chelsea sashays our way, stopping next to Charlie. Her eyes narrow. "Hi, Katie."

Charlie drops my hands, and I rest them in my lap. "Hey." Perfect timing. It's like she has some homing device that goes off every time

Charlie takes a step in my direction.

"I was wondering if I could talk to you." Chelsea strikes a tragic pose, clutching her Aquafina and her Coach bag. "Please?"

Chelsea holds a quiet conversation with Charlie, as if I'm not even there. *Hey, Chels, I'm sorry you broke your nail and all, but I was just telling Charlie how I have real problems.*

She straightens. "I'll call you later, okay?"

She walks away before Charlie can answer. He faces me, a light blush on his cheeks.

I hold up my hand. "I don't even want to hear it."

"No, it's not what you—"

"Forget it. I don't want to know."

"Come on, don't be like that."

My mouth drops. "She is *so* manipulating you. Are you blind?"

"She's not manipulating me. She really does have some major stuff going on."

I snort. "Then tell me about it."

He pauses, as if he's considering it. "I promised her I wouldn't."

I stand up and throw my food back into my bag. "Well, I'm glad she has such an honorable *friend*." I walk off, with one last glare over my shoulder. "See you later."

* * *

I WAVE AT Frances as she drives away, leaving me in the parking lot of the Valiant. I work here some days after school. I used to work here for punishment, but now I hang out at the theatre because I love it. It's like my home away from home. Er, away from home.

I open the door and step into the Art Deco lobby. I can't imagine not being able to see the Valiant as often as I want to. Can't imagine life without any more chances of performing on the stage beyond those double doors. Sometimes I feel like I was born to the wrong parents. Like the Scott's kooky daughter should've belonged to my mom. And I should've been raised a Scott. Life here just seems to be such a good fit. So right.

*God, why do I have to leave? Why did you even bring me here, just to jerk me back out again? It's going to be so painful leaving James and Millie, Maxine, Sam, my friends. Why are you doing this to me?*

I fling open the doors and step into the theatre. I inhale the scent that *is* the Valiant—a mixture of wood polish, set paint, and a distinct smell that comes from something only as old and historical as this building. A cool old, you know? Not great-grandma's mothball collection old.

Walking down the center aisle, I notice Sam Dayberry sitting on the first row. He's talking on the phone. His voice gets louder. Angrier.

"I've called you all day long. Where have you been?"

I stop in my tracks. Should I stay? Should I go? I don't want to eavesdrop.

Oh, who am I kidding? Of course I do.

"Now, Maxine, you hold on just a minute, there . . . Now, see here . . . *Forcing* you into marriage? Where did you get that blasted idea?"

I hold my breath, frozen in my spot. I strain to hear every word, even the ones bursting through the phone from my foster grandmother.

"*What?* Well, I *never* said I expected you to cook and clean for me. Where is this coming from? Now, just a minute . . . I've had about enough of your dramatics. Yes, I said dramatics! You've been hinting for months you wanted an engagement ring. I buy you one and propose, and you go stone cold loco. Yes, I said *crazy*!"

More shouting erupts from the phone. Sam holds it away from his ear.

"What do you mean you didn't get a proper proposal? We're in our seventies, what do you want me to do, skydive? I'd break a hip!"

Sam's neck is red and splotchy. I hope he doesn't get so worked up he has a stroke or something. I had CPR in health class, but I totally don't remember it.

"If you think I'm no longer good enough, then go find someone else. Nobody else will put up with your craziness like I do."

*Oh, no. No, Sam. Do* not *issue Maxine a challenge. You do not want to do that.*

"What do you mean you were doing me a favor by agreeing to marry me? I happen to be the catch of Shady Acres. What?" Sam pauses and listens. "Now that's just insane. You don't mean that."

I step closer.

"See other people?"

What? *No, Maxine! What are you doing?*

"Fine. We'll see other people if that's the way you want it. Good luck finding someone to date you. You and all your split personalities."

Though a shrill voices still emanates from his phone, Sam pushes a button and shoves the device in his pocket. He stands up, grabs his handkerchief and swabs his forehead. He rips his cap off his head and swivels around.

And sees me.

Standing there like a total idiot.

"Uh . . ." I search for the right thing to say. Something intelligent. Something comforting. "What's new?" *So* not it.

He shuffles out of the row and stomps his way to me. "What's new? I'll tell you what's new. The world Maxine wakes up in every day is new. I don't know what I'm gonna get from her from one day to the next. I've had it."

"Now, Sam—"

"I mean it, Katie. I'm too old for her soap opera tactics. I can't take it."

"But you love her."

His mouth stretches into a grim line. "She doesn't care. She's got some bee in her bonnet, and until she realizes I'm the best thing that's ever happened to her, it's hopeless."

"No, it's not hopeless. You guys are such a cute couple. You've been chasing her for years. Don't give up now. You know she's just having one of her fits. She wants you to pull out the big guns, romance her, woo her back, make a big fuss over her." I hear the panic in my voice. Everything is falling apart—even Maxine and Sam.

"My fussing days are over, kid." Sam tries to step around me, but I throw out my hands and halt him.

"She's just scared. You gotta talk to her."

"What's *she* afraid of? I'm the one marrying Mad Maxine. If anybody has the right to be running scared it's me."

He's got a point there. Maxine is infamous in this town for her antics.

"Sam, please, call her back. Say something sweet to her. Take her out to dinner. Buy her some chocolate."

"It's too late."

"No, it's not, it's—"

"She brought me this today." Sam digs into the pocket of his worn khakis. His rough hands pull out a diamond ring. "Maxine broke off the engagement." He hangs his head. "It's over."

I close my eyes and seethe.

Katie and Maxine—two losers in love.

# Chapter Seven

TUESDAY AFTERNOON, TWO hours before Charlie is supposed to pick me up for our evening out (I hesitate to call it a date, much like I once hesitated to call him my boyfriend), Brian Diamatti, a.k.a. Joey Farmer, my mystery man, sends me our first text.

*Hey, Katie. My grandpa gave me your e-mail addy. Wanted to introduce myself and say I'm sorry, but I'm going to have to cancel for Thursday night.*

I feel a mix of relief and alarm.

*OK,* I type. *Nice to sorta meet you. Are we still on for Friday night?*

His reply is instant. *I can't wait.*

Funny, I can't say the same. *How will I know you?*

*Sending you a pic right now. Don't judge me too harshly. :)*

As I wait for his picture to show up in my in-box, we make some final plans to meet at my house instead of the party so we can do our first meeting in private, and not under the scrutiny of Charlie and Chelsea. Plus, I'll have Frances and Nash meet us, so we can all ride together—in case he is an ax-murderer, I want to be in good company. Or as Frances warned, in case he's a total dork.

I click open his email attachment. *Ohhh, very nice.* No dork here. In fact, my Italian stallion looks a lot like Orlando Bloom. Score! Eat *that*, Charlie Benson. Maybe Frances's ploy wasn't such a bad idea after all.

*See you Friday night.* I know any other girl on the line with Orlando's stunt double would keep him talking, but I just don't feel like it. Maybe when I meet him there will be some spark, some flare of attraction that will capture my attention and erase all thoughts of Charlie from my mind.

Not that today wasn't nice. Charlie sat with me at lunch again. Chelsea had some appointment and checked out (probably had to get her brows waxed), so she wasn't around. It was just Charlie and me, laughing, talking about school and people at church. No weird tension, no bubbling anger over his secrecy and Chelsea-allegiance. Who knows, maybe it's the start of a new era in our relationship. Maybe there *is* a shot at a relationship. I have to admit, I'm still totally head over ballet flats for him.

Guilt tugs on my conscience.

I should text Brian Diamatti and cancel for Friday night. I can't bring another guy to Charlie's party. *Especially* someone posing as a date.

I pick up my phone and just do it.

*Hey, Brian, I've had a change of heart. While I appreciate—*

My bedroom door opens and crashes into the wall, rattling on its hinges.

Maxine enters the room, grabs the doorknob on the rebound, and with a slam, closes us in.

She speeds to her bed in her red high heels and slides across the comforter like it's home plate. Maxine flops over with a dramatic sigh, scoots around 'til her legs are propped up on the wall and her head hangs over the edge.

I study her upside-down face. "So. How was your day?"

She lifts her ruby lip in a snarl. "As if you don't already know. Sam told me you were standing right there in the theatre, listening in on our conversation."

I delete the text and put down my phone. "Maxine, you were yelling so loud, I could've had my music cranked up full blast and standing next to an army of roaring B-52s, and I still couldn't have avoided hearing you."

"Well, no matter. Sam and I are done with. Finished. Kaput." With her yellow bob grazing the floor, she stares at the ceiling. "You got cobwebs you need to sweep down."

"You've got cobwebs in your—"

"I just don't understand what's wrong with that man."

Um, he has a psycho girlfriend?

"Engaged a matter of days and the romance is already dead and gone."

I push away from my desk in my rollie-chair. "Is that what this is about? You just want him to send you flowers more often? Write you love sonnets? Because that sounds like a stupid reason to kick someone like Sam Dayberry to the curb."

Maxine's heels do a little tap dance on my wall. "You don't understand. I've waited a long time for Mr. Right Again. Mr. Simmons has been gone for fifteen years. He would want me to be with someone who cherishes me and adores me."

"And Sam doesn't?"

I watch Maxine study her French manicure; her face pinkens as the blood rushes to her head. Maybe it will reengage some brain cells, and she'll come to her senses. I love Maxine. I love Sam. And I love them together.

"I just don't think he truly appreciates me. Anymore I feel like I'm just somebody he watches TV with. I'm someone to cut his chicken-fried steak. I don't want that! I want to be the hot mamma who blows in his ear and—"

"Okay!" I throw my hands over my ears. "Too much information here. Children present." I mentally shove the image out of my head. "Sam is a good man. And he's crazy about you. He worships you. Some people will go a lifetime and not have that. You've had that opportunity twice—with Millie's dad and now with Sam."

Maxine shrugs. "It's probably just too soon since Mr. Simmons to get married again."

"Fifteen years?"

With a grunt, she hoists herself upright and sits Indian-style on her bed. "Fifteen short years. It seems like only yesterday . . ." Her voice trails off as her mind wanders to some bittersweet place. "I don't know, Katie." She rights the strands of hair out of place. "I don't know what's wrong with me."

I smile. "Just give it some time. Pray about it." Whoa, that sounded weird coming from my lips. "At least Sam isn't hanging out with old girlfriends or anything."

Maxine lounges back against the wall. "Like Charlie, huh? That rascal. Well, you show him what he's missing tonight, Sweet Pea. You get all dolled up and smokin' hot, and he'll forget about Chancey . . . Cheesy . . . Shirley . . ."

"Chelsea. Her name is Chelsea. I don't know that he's capable of forgetting her. And I suspect he doesn't want to."

Maxine stands up and rubs her hands. "I guess you'll have to convince him otherwise." She winks. "Come on. Let's do hair."

And like a willing—yet desperate—victim, I follow my foster grandmother into the bathroom.

* * *

"YOU LOOK GREAT tonight." Charlie opens the door to the Valiant and I walk through, unable to contain my triumphant smile. His eyes again sweep my red and white retro sundress. And even though he's probably oblivious to the finer details like my cool fifties-style headband and my red wedges, I know he appreciates the total package.

"Thanks." He holds out his arm and I loop mine through it, always excited to be amongst the buzz of the theatre crowd, but especially pumped to be spending alone time with this boy-wonder.

"You're looking quite fetching yourself." Tonight he wears a crisp pair of khakis, just lightly faded, and a blue long-sleeve button down, his cuffs rolled up to reveal his muscular forearms.

I bask in my happiness, blocking out all thoughts of my mom. Of leaving. Of Millie's cancer. Of Sam and Maxine. And of She Whose Name I Will Not Utter Tonight. I wave and toss out hellos to townspeople I know and to fellow Valiant regulars like me. I pretend all is perfect in the world, and imagine behind everyone's smile they think to themselves, *What a lovely couple. How lucky they are. Oh, to be that girl.*

Across the lobby I spot James and Millie and throw up my hand in greeting. They are in their Sunday finest for the opening night of the musical. The theatre is like their baby, and I've grown to love it as much as they do. It's so much a part of us. I can't imagine leaving it.

No, not gonna to think like that. Not this evening.

I lean into Charlie and breathe. Because tonight I'm this pretty boy's girl, and I'm going to sweet-talk him into some popcorn.

Fifteen minutes later the lights flicker, signaling it's time to make our way in.

"I hope you got us good seats." I grin up at my date and make a grab for the tickets. "Wow, box seats. My favorite." But pricey. The seats that hang out over the sides in their own suspended box are reportedly where the old In Between elite would sit. The dignitaries and old money of the town. And it's rumored Charlie Chaplin himself once sat in one of the boxes.

"Love to make you smile," Charlie says. And for a moment our eyes lock and everything stills. He moves in like he's going to kiss me.

"Oh, excuse me." A rotund man in a three-piece suit invades our space, our seconds of possibilities, and the spell is broken.

Charlie takes a step back. "After you." His hand at my back guides me up the stairs and to our seats, where we have a bird's-eye view of the stage and all the theatre.

We sit down, smiling at those around us. His arm nestles next to mine on the armrest as the lights go down, and the opening chords of "The Hills Are Alive" trill from the orchestra pit. Chills race up and down my spine, and I sit up straighter, not wanting to miss a single thing when the curtains rise. There is no greater time in a play than the moment the curtains lift, revealing the beginning. There's no feeling like it. It's when everything comes together, and this whole world opens up right before your eyes.

"This better be good." Charlie's voice teases my ear, bringing me back to reality, where I realize his hand has slipped over mine. He gives it a squeeze.

I sit back, relaxing into my seat as Maria sings to her hills. I scan the faces of the audience in the glow of the stage lights. Looking back, I see the four seats behind us are empty. "That's odd," I say, my voice low. "Millie said the show was a sell out. I wonder why our box is half full?"

Maybe it's a trick of the light, but I think I see something flash in Charlie's eyes. He moves toward my ear as the singers' volume rises.

I shake my head, unable to hear him. He opens his mouth again, but my hand on his shoulder stops his words. "Thank you." I beam and my eyes travel to the stage and back to him. "Thank you for tonight."

His teeth look even whiter in the darkness of the theatre as his mouth spreads into a warm smile. Charlie rubs his thumb over my hand, then lifts his arm. I lean in so he can wrap—

My head jerks behind me as people shuffle into the empty seats, and I catch a whiff of a familiar floral perfume.

I twist all the way around in my seat, dread seeping through my body.

Chelsea Blake.

I swallow hard and face forward, pulling my hands into my lap and scooting as far away from Charlie as my seat will allow.

I think I hear him whisper my name, but between the blasting trumpets and the roar in my head, I can't be sure. I'm suddenly grateful I didn't text Mr. Diamatti's grandson and cancel his Friday night appearance. Bring on Mr. Italian Beefcake. If I even go to Charlie's party, that is.

Chelsea leans down, her face between us. "Hey, guys." She smacks her gum, and it's everything I can do not to grab her long blonde hair and pull her over the seats and into the floor. "Charlie, thanks for the tickets. My dad really appreciates the night out."

I turn my head where she is not in my peripheral vision and focus on the stage. I would bawl, but it's just not worth it.

He can have her.

But he can't have both of us.

At the end of the play, Captain Von Trapp holds his Maria close, and together, with the children, they sing. One couple finally reunited.

And another . . . definitely over.

# Chapter Eight

*DING-DONG!*

My stomach does the rumba, followed by a quick cha-cha.

He's here. Brian Diamatti, my Joey Farmer, is here.

*God, forgive me. I know this is dishonest. But what could I do? Frances opened this can of worms.*

I jump off my bed and race downstairs. I have to get to the door before James or Millie. I mean, they know he's coming. Well, that is, they know I'm riding to the party with Frances, Nash, and a *friend.* If they don't meet this friend, though, then they won't ask questions, like "Is this a double date? I thought you liked Charlie—why are you taking a boy to his birthday party?"

After Tuesday night, I ignored Charlie for the rest of the week. He texted me and tried to talk to me at school, but I just shut him down. I don't even want to know. Don't care.

But if Brian is as cute in person as he is in the picture, then it will be a good dose of "in your face" for Charlie.

Halfway down the stairs, I hear the door open and Maxine's voice.

"Why . . . hello, young man."

I halt at the bottom step.

"Do come in." Maxine's voice takes on an airy, odd quality. He must really be something to look at. "My granddaughter will be down shortly."

I'm torn between savoring the moment of Maxine calling me her granddaughter—like I'm the real deal—and charging into the living room before she continues talking and says something embarrassing like, "Katie still secretly watches *Hannah Montana* reruns." Or "She has yet to pass all of her driver's test, but third time's a charm!"

I ease into the kitchen and head toward their direction in the foyer.

Can't wait to see what my Date of Duplicity looks like.

"So . . . you're Italian?" I frown at Maxine's odd tone.

"Yes," a voice replies in a high-pitched squeak. *Aw*, how cute, he's nervous.

"Do you know George Clooney? I hear he has a villa in Italy."

I roll my eyes and round the corner as my date comes into view.

"I don't live in Italy. My grandfather is Ital—Oh, hello. You must be Katie."

And unfortunately, I am.

My feet freeze to the floor. The room spins and tilts around me as doom, imminent doom, closes in.

Doom as in Jesus take me *now*.

"Um . . ." My palms sweat. "Hi?"

Before me stands Brian Diamatti, in all his five-foot, double chin, two hundred and fifty pound glory. Dark eyes squint behind glasses as thick as a car windshield.

He steps forward and grabs my hand to shake. "Nice to meet you in person."

My tongue, heavy in my mouth, refuses to move. I can only stare.

*Seriously, God, I'd like to order up one big rapture. Or maybe one ticket just for me to the Pearly Gates because I'm looking at phase one of my own dating apocalypse right now.*

I look down, a full ten inches down at this perspiring boy, and take my hand back. "Uh . . . uh . . . nice to . . . meet you." *Forgive me for lying. Sooo lying.* "I'm crazy, er, I mean Katie! I'm Katie."

He tosses his head back and laughs, the noise coming out in nasally honks. His lips part, revealing oversized teeth held together by shiny braces and crisscrossing rubber bands.

My eyes laser into Maxine, who for once in her life appears to be speechless. I could strangle her. But what did I expect? I can't be mad at her for her part in something already so corrupt. I have no one but myself to blame.

*You're totally laughing right now, aren't you, God? Great. Thanks. Glad to give you this Holy Knee Slapper moment.*

Maxine clears her throat, her blue eyes still wide as bike tires. "So . . . young man . . . you're Antonio Diamatti's grandson?"

"Yes, ma'am."

Maxine steps closer. "Are you sure?"

He runs a small hand through his orange hair, not-so-artfully parted down the center. "Last time I checked Papa Diamatti was my grandfather, yeah." He giggles.

Silence hangs as Maxine and I both stare and nod.

Nod and stare.

I look at her.

*Help me!*

She looks at me.

*I don't do miracles.*

Maxine clasps her hands behind her back and pastes on a smile. "I've seen pictures of your brothers, Brian. You don't . . . er . . . that is to say . . ."

"Oh, you mean we don't look alike. Is that what you're getting at?"

Maxine jumps on this. "Yes! Exactly."

"Yeah, my nose is a bit smaller than my brothers, but other than that, we might as well be triplets." More snorts. "Which is wild because I was adopted from Canada."

Maxine's lips thin.

Brian throws up his hands. "Shocking, I know."

I nod. "Totally. Unbelievable."

Somewhere there has to be a camera on me. Am I on *America's Funniest Home Videos?* A YouTube prank?

This cannot be real.

"Well. . . I guess you should be going." Maxine jerks her head toward the back door where just beyond James and Millie work in the yard.

I swallow hard. "You know, I don't feel so well. I've been trying to fight it all day, not wanting to miss this opportunity to spend time with you, but there's this tickling in my throat and—"

Brian grabs my hand and sticks a warm cough drop in my palm. "Probably your allergies." He sniffs loudly. "I've been having lots of drainage too."

There is no way on God's green earth I am walking out that door with this boy.

"Katie, tonight means so much to me."

I can hardly find my voice. "It does?"

"See . . . my precious Felicity died last week." He bows his head. "Killed tragically by an out-of-control car."

I suck in my breath, shame roiling through my body.

"She was my everything. I never thought I'd be so lucky God would bring me together with someone like her."

"*Oh*, Brian. I am *so* sorry." You have no idea *how* sorry.

He wipes a lone tear from his cheek. "We only met last year, but she became my best friend. She loved me for who I was."

Maxine sniffles. "You dear boy." Her gaze latches onto mine, a look that says, *Only the lowest life form would cancel this date.*

"So you see . . . when Papa Diamatti called me, it was like a ray of hope. I put down my advanced soduku puzzle and said, "Brian, Superfly Math Stud—that's what I call myself."

"Of course." I nod.

"Brian, this is like a sign. A sign from Felicity it's okay to move on."

He steps closer. "Tonight I have hope. Tonight . . . I return to life and living—and I want to thank you for that."

Somewhere in my head violins play. Oh, the drama. How can I tell him it's off? I am so stuck with this. My life—ruined. I will never recover from this.

"This is for you." He holds up a corsage the size of a small shrub.

"How . . . nice." *Okay, God—lesson learned. Now let's rewind to last Sunday. I won't choose this path. This social-life-imploding-path.*

I feel like Jonah in the whale—full of ick and desperate to get out.

Brian's voice squawks. "The carnations match your skin."

They're pee yellow.

He stands on tiptoe, and his hands aim straight for my—

"Okay!" I grab the corsage—before he commits his first date foul. "I'll just put this on in the car." I smile through clenched teeth.

"Actually I brought my dad's van tonight." His fingers run under the collar of his starched, short-sleeve button down. "It has a rockin' bass."

"Grrreat." And the last nail in the coffin of my reputation hammers home. "Nash and Frances should be here any second."

The back door creaks open, and I hear my foster parents' voices.

Maxine flings open the front door. "You kids have fun. Out you go. Scoot!"

"Katie?" Millie calls from the kitchen, and the sound of her sandals follow.

She walks into the entryway, a smudge of potting soil on her cheek and a confused expression on her face. My foster mom adjusts the scarf covering her head and offers Brian her hand.

"Hello. I'm Millie Scott." James appears behind her. "This is my husband, James. You must be Katie's new friend."

"Yes, I'm . . . Brian, er, I mean Joey Diamatti . . . No, I'm definitely Joey Farmer."

Oh, here we go.

Millie quirks an eyebrow and turns to me and Maxine. "Why do I smell trouble?"

My date flushes a shade of purple. You can tell he's a total novice at mayhem.

"This is Brian Diamatti." I shrug and laugh lightly. "It's a long story, but believe me—" I pin Maxine with a heavy stare. "This *is* Brian." Every nerdy inch of him.

James zeroes in on his mother-in-law. "I'd like to hear this story."

"Uh . . . you see . . ." Maxine is saved by the bell as Frances and Nash knock on the door right on time.

"I'll have her home by eleven, Mr. Scott." Brian pushes his grandpa glasses up his nose.

"James would prefer I come by ten. He's strict like that."

"Actually, your curfew is—"

"See ya!" I silence James and push Brian towards the door, opening it to greet Frances and Nash.

"Let's go," I growl at my best friend. "No time for chitchat. Keep moving, keep moving."

We reach the porch when James calls me back to the door. I leave my friends openly gawking at my "hot Italian" date.

"I know you and Maxine are up to something." He hands me some blankets for the drive in.

I sigh. "You can trust me on this. Frances . . ." I stop myself from blaming it on someone else. "No, I wasn't exactly honest last Sunday with Charlie about my date for this evening. It's a huge mess. It was dishonest." I watch the trio load into the ugliest brown van the 1970s ever created. "And it has *so* backfired."

James rubs a hand over his evening stubble. "Lying tends to do that."

"I know." I silently implore him not to intervene. "But now I can't get out of it. It's just snowballed."

He peers over his own perfectly normal glasses. "Can't get out of it?"

"The dude's girlfriend died last week. He said I was like hope from heaven." Or something like that. "Believe me, I'm about to commit social-life-suicide here. If I could get out of this, I would."

He lays his hand on my shoulder and gives a squeeze. "I am relying on you to do the decent thing and make this right by the time you get home."

"Okay."

"And that boy better see nothing but kindness and friendliness from you and your friends."

"I know. Promise." I pat his hand. "See you at ten."

"Eleven." James steps back into the house. "I have a feeling you're going to need that extra hour."

# Chapter Nine

I SLAM MY van door shut. "You totally Photoshopped your picture."

"What do you mean?" Brian revs up his engine. It may have a fine sound system, but who could hear over the choking noises of the motor?

"I mean your picture looked a lot like Orlando Bloom."

Brian beams. "I am proud to say that picture was me."

"Yeah, morphed with the photo of one very famous actor." This is so what I deserve. "You know, maybe this wasn't such a great idea. Perhaps—"

"I can't thank you enough for asking me to this party. Even if it is under dubious pretenses, I'm thrilled to be going."

I glare at my date, who drives his van to Bubba's Big Picture as cautiously as any senior citizen.

"Just to have a few hours in which I won't think about . . . Felicity. You'll never know. It's a huge gift."

With a sympathetic nod of my head, I focus on breathing through my mouth so his dangling air freshener doesn't asphyxiate me. Number one, those things *never* smell anything remotely like pine. And two, why would you *want* your car to smell like a big, tall, sappy tree?

With longing and regret in my eyes, I watch in the mirror as the familiar scenery of my neighborhood get further behind us. Maybe I should've stayed home. Millie's been wiped out with her intense chemo this week. Probably needs my help.

For the next few minutes, I steam. And think. And inwardly freak out.

Every time I get brave and open my mouth to call off this ill-planned charade, Brian launches into another tale of Felicity. Seriously, I think the poor guy needs some grief counseling.

Frances leans forward from the back seat. "Okay, Brian, er, Joey, I should say. Just to review, be vague about how you met. Say something about Maxine and your grandpa. No elaborate stories though."

Yeah, because we wouldn't want to lie.

"And you and Katie are just friends—but you want to make it clear you are really into her."

Brian's eyes rove my way. "I can do that."

"Do you have any last minute questions?" Frances asks.

"No. I think I've got it. My name is Joey Farmer. We met through our grandparents. And we're friends, but I should subtly make it known I'm interested in her."

*Right. And no snorting.*

"I think he's going to do just fine, Katie."

Of course. Now if only I could snap my fingers and turn him into a six-foot-tall hunk. I glance over at him. He tries to engage Nash in a conversation about a computer game, then sticks his hand out the window to signal a turn. A half-mile before the street.

Yeah, Charlie's really gonna be jealous of this. Look out. He'll probably feel so threatened, he'll want to fight Brian for me.

"Sure, I play some video games. My favorite is Guitar Hero. Love that one. How about you?" Nash calls from the back.

"Never heard of it," Brian says.

"How about some Madden?"

My date shakes his head. "Who?"

I sink into my brown seat. Let's just get this over with. Quickly.

Brian navigates the beastly van down the drive that leads to Bubba's Big Picture. We wave at Wanda Carlson, who has worked the ticket booth since before she had grandchildren, and she signals us on through. I'm glad Charlie rented out the drive-in tonight so there's no awkward "who pays" moment.

We cruise on in, and I fight to catch my breath as something clutches at my chest.

I think it's humiliation.

"Brian, when Charlie asks about playing in Nash's band, just tell him you're off duty tonight."

He turns off the engine and pushes his door open. "Fear not, my fake date." His smile does nothing to soothe me. "I happen to be able to rock out with the best of them."

"That's great, but I don't want you to—" With the slam of his door, I'm cut off. I reach for my door handle, but it won't budge. My breath catches. I'm stuck in here. I'm stuck in this stinky, carpet-lined van. Get me out. Must . . . get . . . out . . .

"Push on the door." Brian yells from the other side.

I lean into it, but nothing gives.

"Push harder!"

I push until I'm grunting like a body builder.

Then I rare back and heave myself into the door, pulling the handle with all my might. "The stupid thing won't—"

I feel myself dropping as the door releases, emptying me to freefall.

Right on Brian.

We both tumble to the ground.

"Well, aren't you two cute?"

I lift my head and see Chelsea Blake standing over us. And next to her—the birthday boy himself, Charlie.

I shove myself off Brian as Chelsea's giggles echo in my ear. "I um . . . uh . . ." I can't think of a thing to say. I turn to my left and see Frances, and I beg her with my eyes to intercede.

"Happy birthday, Charlie!" She engulfs him in a friendly hug as I help a stunned Brian up from the ground. "This is our friend . . . Joey Farmer. Joey, meet Charlie and Chelsea."

Brian dusts his hands off on his black jeans, rights his glasses, then smiles his rubber-bandy smile. "Nice to meet you. Hey, you two are a cute couple."

My face falls. What?

Chelsea giggles some more. "Oh, that's so sweet. Did you hear that, Charlie?" She tosses her blonde hair. "I'm so glad you're here, Joey." Her words are for my date, but her eyes are on me. "You guys are cute too."

Oh. My. Gosh. If she were a cat, she'd be purring.

Charlie frowns.

At least I think he frowned. Please tell me that was a look of unhappiness that crossed his face at the mention of Brian, er, Joey being my boyfriend.

"We're just friends," I gush. "Totally friends. Just two amigos here. Compadres. Platonic companions, just—"

"But that's how all the great romances begin, right?" Brian throws a meaty arm around my waist and hoists me to him. I look down and find him beaming at me. "I think it's okay to tell these two our little secret, Snookie-Doo."

*Snookie-Doo?* "I—"

"Have you two known each other long?" Charlie's face is neutral.

"Uh . . . no, not really, I—"

"In our hearts, it feels as if we've known each other a lifetime." Brian winks at me.

"No, it really doesn't." I grit my teeth. "We've barely—"

"Had time to process our feelings." He makes a grab for my hand. "Yet they're so strong, so true. Words cannot describe what this lady right here means to me. I can't imagine letting this one go. No way."

And for his finale, Brian snorts in a guffawing crescendo.

"We're just gonna get the blankets." I jerk Brian by the arm and lead him behind his van. "You!"

"What? Not enough? I can amp it up a bit."

I clutch my hands to keep from strangling him. "Not *enough*? Too much! Too much, Brian." *Inhale. Exhale.* "Look, I appreciate you coming tonight, but I was very clear you were to pose as my friend. Not my . . ." A chill chases up my spine. "Ew! Just nothing. Let's just drop all the acts, okay? Continue being Joey Farmer, but just be yourself. No more embellishments."

"But I could—"

"No." I jerk the van doors open and reach for the blankets. "Just be you—with a different name."

His head bobs in a nod. "Okay. So that was too much?"

"Just a bit." I hand him a blanket.

"Everything okay back here?"

I slam the door shut to find Charlie standing near.

"Uh . . ." *Other than the fact I'm trapped inside a dating nightmare, yeah, things are pretty good.* "I forgot to tell you happy birthday. So . . . happy birthday!"

"Thanks. I'm glad you came. Katie, I've been wanting to talk to you about—"

"This town has the coolest drive-in." Brian steps between us. "I heard it was going to be shut down though. Such a waste."

"Maybe we can talk later?" I stare at Charlie, willing him to give me an indication that Chelsea means nothing to him, that he's ready to tell me what all the secrecy is about.

Chelsea, in her tiny khaki shorts, walks herself to where we are. "Hey, sweetie," she coos. "You have lots of guests to greet before they start the movie."

*Sweetie?* Make me vomit.

Without thinking, I link my arm through Brian's. "Yeah, we should get settled. We don't want to miss a thing."

"Katie, wait—"

"See you later." And I pull my date along and join Nash and Frances.

"I knew you'd come around." Brian pats my hand. "Few can resist my charms."

I glare. "Is this before or after you send them the Orlando Bloom picture?" I jerk my arm back and pass a blanket to Nash and Frances.

Ten minutes later a young, feather-haired Michael J. Fox struts his stuff as *Back to the Future* begins.

"Hey, Charlie said the snack bar is open and it's all on him tonight. Wanna go get something to eat?" Frances glows in anticipation of endless, free popcorn.

"Definitely." I jump up, grateful to get away from Brian, if for just a few minutes.

"I'll go too!" My date is on his feet, moving faster than a superhero.

"No, that's okay. Just tell me what you want, and I'll get it." Of course it could take me a while. Like a few hours.

"I insist on going. I'll help you carry stuff."

He walks ahead, and Frances and I follow, resigned to our fate.

Buford T. Hollis greets us from behind the snack counter. "Well, if it isn't my favorite kids." Buford says that to everyone. But it always makes me smile.

"I love tonight's movie choice." Frances grabs some napkins in anticipation of her popcorn, heavy on the butter.

"Yeah, you come back next week, and it's *Karate Kid*." His big, chubby hands do a perfect wax on, wax off.

"Don't you ever show anything more modern?" Brian asks, and everyone freezes. Even the popcorn maker slows.

"We love Bubba's Big Picture just like it is. Old movies are what make it so cool," Frances sputters. "Bubba's captures the essence of yesteryear and family values, when people would slow down and spend time together. When life was simple and the world was innocent. When America—"

"We can all get in for five dollars a car." I grab my popcorn. "It's the best deal in town, especially for those times when you're grounded and without allowance. Not that that happens to me often." Unless you call once a month often. "Plus," I pop a kernel in my mouth. "It's the best popcorn in town. Buford is not stingy with the butter." Though I now probably have the arteries of an eighty-year-old.

"Well, enjoy it while you can, kids." Buford sighs. "The Big Picture will only have a few weekends left if the mayor gets his way."

Frances slams her hand on the counter. "But he won't! We won't let him. He can't take the drive-in."

"I'm afraid he can. He has a mile-long list of things to fix or else he'll condemn it." Buford wipes his hands on his white T-shirt. "I can't possibly do everything he's requested. The old place just isn't worth it."

"It's worth it to me!" Frances cries. "Whatever it takes, Buford, we will help you. I promise you."

The owner shakes his head. "Sometimes you just have to let it go, kid. I've fought this fight for the last decade. The mayor wants this land for a strip mall, and he's going to see he gets it."

"But it's ours!"

I put an arm around my friend. "You've got that petition going, right? We'll just have to get more names."

Beside me Brian snickers. I would glare at him, but it's getting a little repetitious at this point.

"I appreciate what you're doing, girls. But the mayor doesn't want signatures. He wants money—from me. And I ain't got it."

"I'm going to pray about this, Buford. I will not rest until I feel a peace in my heart that it's time to let Bubba's go."

Buford wipes down the counter. "You do that, Frances. I'll take all the thoughts and prayers I can get. 'Cause I think a stinkin' miracle is all that can save this place now."

Frances leans in. "Then a stinkin' miracle is what I'll pray for."

We grab more drinks and popcorn for Nash, hand it all to Brian to carry, and find our way back to our spots.

Even though my date bemoaned the antiquated movie, he totally enjoyed it. At least I think he did, based on the sheer volume and quantity of snorting I had to endure.

"I think that's my cue." Nash gets to his feet as the credits roll. "Time to set up."

He climbs into the van to get his guitar, then takes off toward the screen.

Beneath the movie screen is a small stage area. Sometimes they use it for outdoor concerts or speaking events. Like last year, when the mayor was reelected and made his big speech. To a crowd of five.

"Let's move closer to the stage so we can hear the God Wads." Frances picks up her blanket, then stills. "Here comes Charlie."

"Did you guys enjoy the movie?"

"I love me some Michael J. Fox," I say, like lusting after someone in a decades-old movie is going to make him jealous.

"Buford says he's made a fresh batch of popcorn if you guys want to grab some before the band plays their first set." Charlie smiles at each one of us, and I scrutinize his every blink to see if his eyes linger on me a little longer than the others.

"Thanks, but I'm all popcorned out. I think Joey ran his little legs off refilling my bucket," I coo. "Er, not that you have *little* legs, Joey. I just meant . . . well, it was a figure of speech. Because you don't. Have little legs, that is. Well, I mean they're smaller than mine." *Shut up, shut up, shut up!* "But I'm unusually tall for a girl. You wouldn't want to be me. Oh! Not that you've given me any reason to think you'd want to be a girl. 'Cause you haven't. You're totally masculine." I grab his arm and squeeze his nonexistent bicep. "Feel the power."

I hang my head. I'm a disaster. A rambling, deceitful, disaster. Not only am I *not* making Charlie jealous, but I'm probably reminding him how smart he was to set me free.

Charlie stares at me for a moment longer, then turns to Brian.

"So . . . Joey, Frances mentioned you are quite the instrumentalist."

Brian chortles. "My good man, I must say . . . I rock."

"Well, you are welcome to join the God Wads up there." Charlie's lips lift in a partial smile. "My dad brought his guitar and is probably going to play in at some point. Feel free to join."

Brian holds up his fingers in a rock on sign and shakes it in the air. "Righteous!"

I turn around and face the snack bar, as if something has caught my attention. But honestly if I don't get this one big eye roll out of my system, I think my head is going to explode. Charlie walks away, mingling with other guests, and I murmur a good-bye.

"Brian, don't worry about playing with the band. Just hang out with us and enjoy the show." *As in no way are you getting up there.*

"I hate to pass up the opportunity to jam."

Frances intervenes. "They'll have one too many guitarists tonight anyway. Maybe another time."

"Guitar?" Brian shakes his dark head. "Oh, I didn't bring my guitar."

Well, then why are we all stressing? I breathe a sigh of relief, confident now there is zero chance of seeing my date trying to shred it onstage.

The God Wads play some Tomlin and Crowder before switching it up to some classic Aerosmith and bringing everyone to their feet.

I point to Nash. "That bass player's kinda dreamy, Frances. You should totally get his autograph."

"He is kinda cute. I might let him have my phone number."

I waggle my eyebrows. "Just don't get any ideas about tossing your bra onstage."

The band continues to play, and I scan the crowd for Charlie. He's nowhere to be found. Neither is Chelsea. Where are they?

Brian taps me on the shoulder, jarring me from my focus. I turn around with a start, and the drink in my hand tumbles down my shirt.

"Oh, I'm sorry. I—" He makes a lunge, like he's going to pat me down.

"No!" I jerk back out of arm's length. "I'm fine." I clench my teeth. Why don't these things ever happen to Chelsea Blake?

"I'm so sorry, Katie." He wrings his hands, his head drooping.

"Um . . . it's okay." My millionth lie for the night. "I'll just go to the bathroom and try to get this out. I'll be back."

Great. Diet Dr. Pepper all over my new Abercrombie T-shirt. I picked it especially for tonight. I thought it clearly said, "Check me out, Charlie, cause this is what you're missing." Now it just says "Large drink makes extra large stains." Could this night get any worse?

I stomp into the bathroom and daub at my shirt with a wet paper towel.

Two minutes and one hopeless shirt later, Frances bursts through the door. "Katie! Come quick!"

I drop my towel in the trash. "What's wrong?"

"It's Joey . . . er, Brian. He's onstage. Playing." She drags me outside.

"What? He said he didn't bring his guitar."

I clutch my ears as an offensive sound blasts through the air.

"He didn't."

My mouth drops, and Frances gives words to the nightmare before me.

"He brought his bagpipes."

# Chapter Ten

WE RIDE BACK to the house in a heavy, awkward silence.

Brian, obviously having enough of the quiet game, pipes up. "I wasn't sure I could hit that high note in 'Jesus Take the Wheel,' but I totally nailed it." He has the audacity to touch my arm. "Did you catch that?"

"Yup." Every wheezing second of it. As he played, I saw my social life flash before my eyes, knowing that was the bitter end.

"Hey, Nash, maybe I could hook up with you guys again. When's your next gig?"

I twist in my seat, and pin Nash with the stare of death, hoping he can see it in the darkened van.

"Uh . . . I don't know."

"Well, let me know, 'cause tonight was just killer."

Dude, you have *no* idea.

Brian pulls into my driveway, puts the vehicle in park, and Frances and Nash spill out.

"I'll just walk you to the door."

I gulp. "*No,* not necessary, but thanks. I had a gr—er, I had a . . . um . . . .that Michael J. Fox sure is funny, eh? Okay, g'night." I fling open my door and all but run to the safety of the porch.

I breathe a deep sigh of relief, put my hand on the knob, and—

"Katie—"

I jump.

Brian.

Like Lindsey Lohan in the tabloids, he's everywhere.

He sticks his hands in his pockets. "I know tonight wasn't the best night of your life."

No, I'm just having an off night. Because normally I really like my dates to haul out an instrument that sounds like a pack of screaming kitties. "Ice Ice Baby" never sounded so good.

"But it was amazing for me." His eyes flutter just slightly.

If he moves in for a good night kiss, I will take him out like Jackie Chan. "I . . . I'm glad you had a good time." Me? I think I'd rather have some molars pulled.

"I know I'm not exactly your type, but it was still fun hanging out with you and your friends. The people I met tonight were really nice."

I smile despite it all. "Yeah, I do have some cool friends." *And there's one named Chelsea. Why don't you take her as a parting gift?*

"I know you're going to find this hard to believe, but I don't get asked out much." He shrugs. "And when I was up there playing, it was like I was somebody, you know?"

I think of standing on the Valiant stage. "Yeah, I do know."

"Tonight I got to meet some new friends. And I got to forget about my troubles, forget about Felicity for a while. It was good to just have fun and not be reminded of my heartbreak."

Guilt is a vice-grip on my heart. I fight it with all my might, but the words tumble out anyway. "You'll have to hang out with us again sometime soon."

Brian's bands stretch as he grins. "You mean it?"

No.

Yes.

No. "Yeah."

He pulls me into a brief, sisterly hug. "Thanks."

I smile as he pulls away. "No problem. Oh, and Brian?"

"Yes?"

"I really am sorry about your girlfriend."

"My girlfriend?"

"Yeah—Felicity?"

"Felicity wasn't my girlfriend." He snorts and slaps his leg. "She was my gerbil."

* * *

"HAVE A GOOD time?"

I shut the door behind me and follow James's voice into the living room where he's watching a replay of *SportsCenter*.

Collapsing into a chair, I lean back and close my eyes. "It was . . . interesting."

James watches me, a spark of both uncertainty and amusement in his eyes. "Did Brian have a good time?"

"Time of his life." Can't say I'll ever forget it either. "Where's Millie?" I check the mantel clock. Eleven-oh-three. "Did she already go to bed?"

James grabs the remote and turns the volume down. "Yes, this week's chemo treatments caught up with her. I think she did too much today."

Thoughts of leaving assault my mind yet again. I want to be here for Millie's bad days. And for her good days. And when she starts radiation in a few months. But I'm going to miss all of that.

James takes off his glasses and folds them into his hand. "So are you doing okay?"

My head bobs in a nod. "Wonderful." As terrific as a bagpipe solo of a Clay Aiken song.

"Your mom called tonight."

My eyes pop open. "What did she say?" Dread punches my chest. And then the guilt.

"She wanted us to know she had some evaluations from child services today, including a drug test." James turns his attention to the TV. "She passed."

Great. One step closer to regaining custody.

"I guess that's good," I say lamely. Of course it's good, right? My mom drug-free. Why wouldn't I want that for her? Why wouldn't I want to live with my bio-parent like most kids. Isn't it the dream of every kid in foster care?

James flicks the TV off and gives me his full attention. "I know this isn't easy for you. But Katie, the state isn't going to let you live with Bobbie Ann until they're confident she's rehabilitated. And neither are we."

Rehabilitated. They're checking for drug-abuse, but who's going to rehabilitate her for her poor mothering skills? Hello, I'm sixteen and I'm just *now* learning Pop-Tarts are not a major food group. And it's not normal for mothers to be out past midnight every night. And rings around the toilet are not halos angels left behind.

I sniff and run my hand over my nose. "I'm home here, you know? But at the same time, I need to be with my mom. I don't know . . . I just don't know. I think part of me doesn't understand why God would bring me to In Between, get me settled, and then rip me back out again." I smile, desperate not to give into the tears pressing at my eyes. "Besides it's not fair to you guys. You fall head over heels in love with me, dedicate your lives to catering to my every whim, then I just leave? I know it's going to be devastating."

James doesn't smile in return. "I can't say it's not going to be devastating, but no matter what happens, we will be here for you. We'll call, we'll visit. Millie and I will work out something where we get to see you and spend time with you."

One tear drops.

Then another.

I bow my head and avert my eyes. I simply nod and sniff. "Okay. Thanks." I needed to hear that.

"But we're going to cross that bridge when we come to it. Right now we'll just enjoy each day and let God take care of the future."

I can't help but taste a little bitterness over this.

I got saved over spring break. I asked Jesus into my heart and gave him my life. But I thought membership had some privileges, you know? When I rose out of those baptismal waters, I was told I was a new creation. I was hoping new meant improved. I mean, I wasn't expecting to shoot out of the church baptismal with double D's or anything, but I thought I would have some perks being in the family of God. So far—not really working out for me. Where is God in this? Maybe God plays favorites—and I'm in the bottom ranks. Maybe the Chelseas of the world are more his style. And the Katies? Well, they get tossed around like a volleyball. Slung into the net and spiked to the ground.

I stand up and step toward the doorway.

"He hasn't forgotten you, Katie."

And I keep walking. Up the steps and into my room.

Where Maxine sits in the dark, under the window sill.

I turn on the light. "What are you doing?"

"Turn that blasted light off! You'll blow my cover."

I flick the switch again. "Who are you hiding from, the nursing home? I told them as long as you were still wearing big girl undies, you could stay."

"Very funny," she hisses. "Sit down." She pats the spot next to her on the floor.

And like it makes all the sense in the world, I park myself beside her.

Where we wait.

And wait.

Outside the crickets serenade and the bullfrogs harmonize.

Though I've learned it's usually best not to ask, I throw caution to the wind and do it anyway. "What are we doing?"

"Waiting." Her voice stays a steady whisper. "Sam and I had another big row today, and I'm waiting for him."

". . . Because you're afraid he's going to sneak in here and strangle you?"

Maxine plants her nose to mine. "I don't need your sass." She turns her head back toward the open window. "I just thought he might do something romantic and apologize. You know, like throw some pebbles against the windowpanes, wake me up, and shout out his undying love for the whole neighborhood to hear."

I cover my mouth, stifling a laugh. "Yeah, like that's gonna happen. Where would he get an idea like that?"

"Because he has the potential to be romantic?" Maxine drums her nails on the floor. "And because the last thing I shouted was, 'Maybe you should throw some pebbles against the windowpanes, wake me up, and shout your undying love for the whole neighborhood to hear.'"

In all the chaos that is my life, I do have one constant I can be grateful for. One idea that is steady and true.

Maxine Simmons will always be crazy.

# Chapter Eleven

MY LIFE STORY takes up four lines on my paper. Wide ruled.

The next Monday in school, Ms. Dillon is nice enough to give us almost the entire class period to work on our autobiographies. Here's what I have so far:

*I was born in Texas.*

*I still live in Texas.*

*I wish Millie would let me eat cold pizza for breakfast.*

Seriously, that's all I have. I don't know, it's like on one hand I have too much to say about my life, and on the other, I haven't really lived much. Aside from moving around a lot with my mom, I've never really traveled. I don't think stealing off in the middle of the night so you don't have to pay rent qualifies as a vacation or anything. I've never been on an airplane. Aside from some stray cats, I've never had a pet (and no, Rocky doesn't count). I don't have a lot of family, so no thrilling stories about summers with grandma or zany family reunions.

Ms. Dillon, wearing a cute, summery dress from the Gap, sweeps through the rows and checks our work. She pauses at my desk.

She clears her throat. "Having trouble focusing?"

"I'm just brainstorming."

"You should be past that stage. We brainstormed last week."

I strike a reflective pose. “Ms. Dillon, can you really put a time limit on the outpouring of thoughts?”

She cracks a smile. “Are you stuck?”

“Like a thong bikini.”

“Well, every life has defining moments. What are yours? What are the things you’ll want your grandchildren to know?”

I’ll want them to know if you skip brushing your teeth just one night they won’t fall out. That if you cross your eyes, they’re not gonna freeze that way. And that chocolate will never do you wrong.

“I don’t know. I don’t really have any highlights or anything. Can I just make some stuff up? You know, give it a creative, soap opera flare? I mean, nonfiction is so dull.”

Ms. Dillon leans down, pulling her shoulder-length blonde hair to one side. “I *know* you’ve had your moments.”

“Leave my disciplinary file out of this.”

“I’m talking about moments that shaped you. Made Katie Parker who she is.”

“But I don’t know who I—”

“Yes, you do.” She taps her pen to my paper. “Now just have the guts to put it on paper.”

* * *

AT LUNCH THE gang decides to eat outside in the commons. Commons is just fancy talk for “We’re taking our Frito pies and tater tots to some picnic tables outside.”

I set my Millie-packed lunch down at a table marked “Donated by the class of 1993.” Dang, that is old. But it has a nice view of the parking lot. I like to see who’s sneaking off campus for lunch.

“Hey, Katie. Looks like it could rain.” Hannah slides in next to me, then Nash parks his tray in front of us.

“Where’s Frances?” I pop a carrot in my mouth.

“Sneaking a call to her mom. She said it was important. So how about that history test today? Heinous, huh?”

Hannah cocks her head at Nash's question. "I don't know about that, but I thought it was really, really hard."

"Yeah," I sigh. "I have got to do really well on the final in next week and bring my grade up."

"I can help you study."

I turn at Charlie Benson's voice.

"Can I sit with you guys?"

Hannah scoots over, making a space just for him. A month ago this would've sent my heart into orbit. Now . . . I'm not sure what to think. Part of me just wants him to go away and leave me alone. Let's just call this done. Another part of me wonders if it's stupid to toss away a good friend just because he'd rather hold someone else's hand besides mine.

I scoot down even more until I have one cheek practically hanging over the edge. Charlie notices my distance and raises a single eyebrow.

"Seriously, you know history is my strong area. I'd be glad to help you study. We could review together."

The boy is a total genius. His strong area is any class that comes with a book. My area of expertise? Study hall.

"Um . . . that's okay. I just need to sit down and make myself some flash cards, go over our old tests, that sort of thing." *I probably couldn't study and look at you at the same time anyway.* Something would be too distracting, and it wouldn't be the War of 1812.

He steps closer, and I smell the scent that is his alone. Eau de Hot Boy. "Come on. Give it some thought. We'll get some pizza, quiz each other . . ."

Be still my heart. Just what every girl wants to hear from a guy: I want to quiz you.

"I'll . . . think about it." I just can't stay mad at this guy. Am I becoming a doormat? Are the words *walk here* tattooed on my forehead yet?

I hear Frances before I see her. Breathing like a rabid rhinoceros, she stomps through the gravel, her shoes crunching a mean path to our table.

"We have a crisis!" She slaps her phone on the table next to Nash.

I take in my friend's flushed cheeks. "Oh, are they out of bean burritos again? It's really for the best, Frances."

"No." She exhales loudly. "I'm not kidding. I just spoke with my mom. She said the mayor heard about my signature campaign to save the cinema. He called my mom and told her I had until seven o'clock tonight—that he would be waiting in his office."

We all stare at each other, not really sure what to say.

Nash tugs on Frances's hand. "So how close are we?"

"We have to have five hundred signatures." Frances lets that sink in. "We only have one hundred and seven. No, make that one hundred. My brother took it to school last week and got seven signatures."

"That's great. We'll take all we can get," Nash says.

"They were kindergarteners. Plus I don't think the mayor is going to accept any signatures in Crayola."

"Then we'll have to go out tonight and get what we need."

Frances looks at Charlie. "Yes, we have to. We'll cover this city from every direction. I'll make maps, charts, come up with some strategies."

Nash tosses a tater tot in his mouth. "Make sure you pack me some snacks. Sounds like this could take a while."

Frances punches her first toward the overcast sky. "We will launch a door-to-door assault on In Between! I will not sleep until I have my five hundred signatures."

We hash out a few details, but leave most of it to General Vega. Agreeing to meet up after school, the topic drops. Hannah takes her tray in, and Frances and Nash become engrossed in talk about his band.

Leaving me and Charlie.

Not alone. But pretty much.

"How was your date with Joey Farmer?"

I look up from the gluten-free cookies Millie packed for me. "It was fine." These things don't even resemble cookies. And I don't know what glutens are, but I miss them.

"I have to be honest with you . . ."

He angles his body to where our knees are touching, and he's totally facing me, blocking out the remaining sun, Frances and Nash, and what's left of my self-control.

"Yes?" Did I just imagine it, or did he just move his face in closer?

"He seemed like a really nice guy."

I feel my face fall. I think my smile is somewhere around my ankles. "Um . . . he is. Very nice."

"And uh . . ." Charlie's mouth quirks. "Quite the musician."

And I don't know why, but for some reason, this ticks me off. It's like family—I can talk about them, but *you* can't. Same way with awkward, blind dates of convenience secured through retirement home connections. I can say the bagpipe thing was awful, but *he* can't.

"He's just different. And I happened to think his serenade of Fergie's "My Humps" was . . ." I search for words. "Captivating . . . enthralling . . . unique." And so off-key, it was everything I could do not to roll on the ground and clutch my ears in agony.

"Katie—" Charlie moves his hand closer to mine on the table. Not touching, but just a whisper away. "I'm sorry. That was rude. It's just that you went out with that guy."

I blink. "Yeah?"

Charlie opens his mouth, then snaps it shut. "I . . ." He runs his hand through his hair. "It bothered me you were bringing some dude to my party. Then when I saw him, I was just . . . so relieved. I thought I could enjoy the rest of the evening, knowing he wasn't a major threat." Charlie holds up a hand to halt my oncoming protest. "I'm not saying there's anything wrong with him. But I know he's not your type."

Yeah, the distant, lead-you-on-type is more my thing apparently. Because I love the adventure of never knowing where I stand. It's some crazy fun.

"But yet it did bother me—seeing you two together. All night I kept thinking, why isn't that you and me sitting on that blanket? Things were going so well, and now it's a good day if I can even get you to talk to me."

"That wasn't my decision."

"Wasn't it?"

I chunk my cookie substitutes back into my lunch bag. "You know what I think?" I pin him with my stare. "I think you *know* you messed up. Chelsea came sniffing back around, waving her Marc Jacobs bag in your direction, and you dropped me like a stale donut. Then your Charlie-do-gooder conscience set in." I poke his chest with my finger. "And I think your conscience tells you that you didn't handle that situation right. You didn't treat *me* right."

He grabs my finger and holds it captive. "I told you the truth. I told you Chelsea was going through something major and needed a friend. I didn't mean she just needed someone to IM her every once in a while. I meant she needed a full-time friend. Did I not lay that out for you?"

Interesting how you can feel heat radiating off of someone. *Ugh, focus, Katie!* "But at some point, the line between friend and *more than friend* has blurred, am I right?"

Charlie's left eye twitches. "Chelsea and I are just friends. Maybe you're just too insecure to handle my being friends with a girl."

I jerk my finger back. "Number one, big boy, this isn't just any girl—she's your ex-girlfriend. And number two, you're just friends? Does Chelsea know that?"

"Yes."

"Yeah? Really? Then why did she call you sweetie Friday night?" I could vomit just recalling the memory. Seriously, who *says* that?

Charlie gives a dismissive eye roll. "She called me that? Chelsea calls everyone that."

"Oh, really?" I crane my neck around him. "Hey, Frances! When's the last time Chelsea called you sweetie?"

"Never."

I nod. "Nash?"

"Uh—"

I look behind me. "Hey! Boy in hoodie and saggy pants with safety pin in your lip. Yeah, you. Has Chelsea Blake ever called you sweetie?"

"Nope."

I jerk my face back to Charlie. "You were saying?"

He crosses his arms as growing anger tightens his face. "We're just friends. That's all."

"Correct me if I'm wrong," Frances stands up and peers into the distance. "But isn't that your *friend* right now, throwing herself at that tow truck guy?"

We all rise and walk to the edge of the gravel to get closer to the parking lot. Charlie takes off in a sprint.

"Come on," Frances waves us on. "I don't want to miss this."

I hesitate, but follow. Honestly, do I care?

". . . and this man says he's going to take my mom's car away." Chelsea shrieks like she's on fire, clinging to Charlie's shirt. "Don't let him. Please don't let him!"

Charlie, with his arm around his ex-girlfriend, steps away from us with the driver.

I whisper to Frances, "Either they are talking really low or Chelsea's screeching is too loud, but I can't hear a word they're saying."

She nods. "Very inconsiderate of them."

A few minutes later, the tow truck drives away, carting Chelsea's mom's BMW.

I watch as the boy who could've been my boyfriend wraps both arms around Chelsea, pulling her close, as she cries against his Abercrombie polo.

I hope she gets snot all over it.

# Chapter Twelve

PER MILLIE'S INSTRUCTIONS, I catch a ride with Frances to the Valiant. Now that my foster mom has started chemo, she's working a little less at the theatre, so I've been picking up some of the slack and helping her out.

"See you in about an hour." I shut the door of Frances's station wagon, oddly named Sally Ann. A few raindrops fall on my head, and I look up to see the sky getting darker. Not good.

I step into the Valiant where George Strait blasts from inside the theatre. Sam is obviously still here.

You know things are bad when a senior citizen has the cheatin' songs cranked up.

"Where's Millie?"

Sam jumps at the sound of my voice, and his hammer shoots across the stage. "Dagnabbit!"

I take a step back. "Sorry."

Is it safe for a child to be around a cranky old man who is listening to depressing country tunes and throwing tools?

He pulls out his red handkerchief and swabs his brow. "No, no, I'm sorry. Didn't see you standing there."

I pull myself on stage, sitting on the edge, letting my feet dangle. "So . . . how's it going?"

"Fine. Just fixing a loose board here. Can't have a performer tripping now, can we?"

"I meant with Maxine. With the ol' love life." Maybe we can swap war stories here. Because both of us have totally been shot down in the romance department.

Sam stuffs the handkerchief back into the pocket of his faded khakis. "I have no comment."

"None?"

"No. I don't want to talk about it."

"Oh." I lean back and let my back rest on the cold floor. I stare up at the ceiling, where a whole world of lights, pulleys, and other magical items are tucked neatly away. "Okay, well, I just thought you might want to vent a little."

He sniffs. "I have no need. I'm a grown man. I certainly am not going to stand here and share my feelings with a teenage girl like some love-sick puppy."

"Right. Of course, I—"

"What is *wrong* with that woman?" Sam slaps the stage and his nails scatter. "I know I'm not Mr. Excitement. I know I'm not the richest man in Texas. And I'm not exactly . . . er . . . who's the It-Guy these days? Tom Cruise?"

"Not so much."

"I know I'm not perfect. But neither is she!" He begins to pace. "She's crazy. She's an expensive date. She eats enough to feed the Dallas Cowboys. She wears way too much perfume, and I'm always sneezing around her. She has a weird obsession with Frank Sinatra, and she's *always* running over some poor neighbor child on that ridiculous bicycle of hers."

I stifle a laugh. And these are Maxine's good points. "But Sam, isn't this worth fighting for?"

"Fight? All I've done is fight for her."

I sit up. "She says she just wants some romance. Maybe you need to bring out the big guns."

"Believe me," he growls, "I've been tempted daily to bring out some big guns."

A chuckle bubbles out of my mouth. Sam stops pacing and his eyes narrow.

"This funny to you? You think you're an expert on love?"

"Oh, come on. Don't get mad at me." I smile at this man who has become like a grandpa. "Sam, I want to see you and Maxine work this out. You two belong together." Number one, because I love this guy. And two because no one else will take her.

Sam slowly shakes his head. "It's over. I can't fight this battle or play her games. I am what I am. And I can't be some Romeo for her."

"Maybe she really is just scared."

Sam's barking laughter echoes through the theatre. "Maxine isn't scared of anything." He laughs some more. "I thought you knew her."

"Every girl's afraid of something." My list of fears could circle the globe at least twice.

He stills and seems to consider this. "Nahhh." Then walks away.

I jump down and go into the office where I find Millie hunched over the computer, chewing on a pencil.

"Is that an organic, pesticide-free pencil?"

She startles and makes a grab for her wig resting on the desk. "Hey, sweet girl."

"You don't have to put that on for me."

She smiles sheepishly. "It was itchy." She places it on her head anyway, then holds out an arm. I step into her hug and give her a squeeze. "Good day at school?"

"Yeah." Minus the Charlie drama. Minus the English project hanging over my head. "Can you take me back up to the school in a bit though? We're meeting up to go around town getting signatures for Bubba's Big Picture."

Millie clucks her tongue. "That mayor. He has no sense of tradition."

"Let's go toilet paper his house."

"Ah, no." She pats my hip. "You know I only do that on weekends, and today, my dear, is only Monday."

"Tucker's Grocery has a great deal on some double rolls."

"So tempting, but—"

A pop song sings from my back pocket, and I grab my cell phone. "Hello? Oh . . . hi, Mom."

Millie stands up, mouths something, points toward the door, then leaves.

"Um . . . yeah, I'm okay. How are you?" This is the first time my mom's called me since I landed in In Between. I should probably write this down somewhere. A calendar, a journal. The *Guinness Book of Records*.

"Yeah, that's great. James told me you passed the test. What?" My heart thunders in my chest. "What do you mean I'll be home in a month?" I sit down in Millie's rollie-chair. "Oh, really. No, I guess the Scotts forgot to mention they'd talked to you again." Or kept it from me. What is up with that? I thought we had worked all this stuff out—I am not to be kept in the dark about anything that went on this family anymore. *Especially* when it has to do with me. The Scotts are tight-lipped people, but they *promised* me they wouldn't shut me out anymore.

"No, of course I think that's . . . good. You know, it will just be sad to leave the Scotts and everyone." *I have a life here, Mom. Because you bailed on me. Remember that?* "Yes, I know *you're* my mother." Believe me, I've tried to blot it from my memory many times, but it never worked. Like that time I had to go throw clothes on her when she was passed out, spread-eagled on hole number four at the local putt-putt course in her skivvies. Just my mom in her underwear and bra under a three-foot windmill, as "Wild Thing" piped out of some fake rock. She was too heavy to move, so all I could do was cover her up until the police got there and did their thing.

"Yeah, I know you're having to make big adjustments too. What? You met a guy at your addiction meeting?" How romantic. My love life, or lack of, is all starting to make sense now. I clearly inherited a bad relationship gene. "Um . . . don't you think that's moving a little fast?" *And couldn't you find a boyfriend somewhere a bit safer? Like at a Star Trek convention or something?* Who gets out of prison and dates a fellow recovering addict? I thought there were rules against that.

"I realize you're the mother, and I'm the daughter. Right, you know best." I would laugh at this, but she really believes it. "Look, Mom, I gotta go. Just . . . be careful, okay? Focus on getting back on your feet." We exchange some final good-byes, and I hang up the phone.

And sit there.

Unmoving.

My days at In Between are numbered. I mean, I knew they were, but no, they *really* are. Unless my mom screws this up, I have about a month left here. The Scotts had to know about this.

"Millie!" I rush out of the office and run into the theatre.

My foster mom stops her conversation with Sam and turns around, her brow furrowed. "What is it?"

"My mom says I'm going home in a month."

Millie sends Sam a meaningful look. "Will you excuse us, please?"

Sam gathers his tools and leaves us alone.

"Katie, we didn't want you to—"

"Worry. Yeah, I know the line. I've *heard* it a few dozen times." I stomp my foot like I'm five. "When you hid Amy and her crazy life from me, you said that was the end of secrets. When you hid the breast cancer from me, you said that was the end of secrets. Why do you do this to me?" My words break on a sob. "I deserved to know this."

"Honey—" Millie reaches out, but I step away. "This time was different, really."

"How?" I'm practically yelling.

Millie just shakes her head, looking at the ground like she's searching for words. ". . . It wasn't about keeping things from you. It was about protecting you."

I give her my best *whatever* face.

"Katie, James and I have been keeping track of your mother ever since you came to stay with us."

My eyes widen. What?

"We had no reason to think she'd be released from prison. And honestly, no reason to think, given her track record, she would . . ."

"Come back for me?" I swipe away a tear.

"That she would pass her drug tests or be given custody so soon. For most people it doesn't work that way, but your mother's case got bungled up, and the evidence couldn't be used. Bobbie Ann started the process of regaining custody as soon as she got out, apparently."

"And you didn't think I, of all people, needed to know that?"

"She never contacted you until a few weeks ago." Millie's eyes fill with her own unshed tears. I look away, unable to see her pity pool. "I just couldn't believe a mother would never pick up the phone and call her child. Couldn't believe a mother who was serious about getting her daughter back would miss out on seeing you onstage." Millie pulls a Kleenex out of her pocket and dabs her nose. "I guess I didn't want to believe."

Her words are like Kryptonite, and I'm almost powerless to them. But still, this was my future, my entire world we're talking about. I deserved to know what was going on in it.

"I need to go to the school now," I whisper. "Can we please just go?"

# Chapter Thirteen

IT'S EVERYTHING I can do not to slam Millie's car door. The hurting brat in me just wants to have a total Veruca Salt meltdown.

I watch her sedan drive away, and I stand in the school parking lot, feeling totally alone, even though I seem to have an overabundance of parents these days.

"Katie?"

Charlie comes up behind me, and with a hand on my shoulder, he turns me toward him. His gray eyes seem to assess every detail of my face.

"What? Is Chelsea Blake the only girl who gets to have a bad day?" And I stomp off to stand next to Frances and Nash.

Frances, whose nose is buried in a clipboard, briefly glances my way. Her head drops, then immediately shoots back up. "*What* happened to you?"

"What?"

"Your face. It's all splotchy. And you have mascara . . ." She trails her fingers under her eyes.

I wipe at my face. "It's nothing. Let's just get this over with, okay? The sooner we get started, the less likely we'll get rained out. A storm is moving in later tonight." I feel like one's already hit. A stinkin' tsunami.

I ignore Charlie as we wait an additional ten minutes as Hannah and about ten other classmates show up.

"This is it?" Frances asks, surveying our group. "I invited practically the whole school. Where is their Chihuahua pride? Where is their loyalty to Bubba's? Where is their heart, their—"

"Hey, Frances?" I tap my watch. "Burning daylight."

She sighs. "All right, while we would cover more ground by traveling solo, my dad will kill me if we don't use the buddy system, so I will partner you off."

She consults her hot pink clipboard and assigns pairs. "Bowen and Harris. Valentine and Marshall. Parker and Benson."

Charlie and I together in his truck? Fabulous. Less than five hours ago I watched this boy wrap his long arms around skinny little Chelsea as she sobbed into his shoulder, and *now* I have to ride with him?

I approach my friend. "Frances, I—"

"It's an order, Parker."

I shut my mouth. "Okay." I'm too tired to fight anyway.

She leans in, her voice low. "That was my Coach Nelson impression. How'd I do?"

"Pretty convincing."

"You okay?"

My smile wobbles. "Fine."

Her eyes narrow behind her glasses. "That *wasn't* convincing."

"Let's just get going. I'll explain everything later. And I will be plotting my revenge later too."

She smiles. "For what?"

I jerk my head toward Charlie Benson.

As he unlocks my door, Charlie casts a cautious glance in my direction. "I know you're mad at me."

I climb in and stretch for my seatbelt. "Actually, though it may bruise your ego, you're pretty low on my list of concerns right now." And this door I slam.

We drive to the first street Frances has highlighted for us on our map of In Between. When Charlie puts the car in park at the first house, I bail out, leaving him in my dust. I knock on the door, and it swings open, revealing a small, old woman in a muumuu. She looks like someone's grandma who bakes cookies and mends socks.

"Hello, I'm Katie Parker, and I wanted to—"

*Slam!*

*Hm.* So that's what it feels like.

"No luck?"

Charlie steps behind me.

"Did you see me get a signature?"

With hands on my shoulder, he stops me from stepping off the porch. "I didn't see anything except your tail running out of my truck. We're a team here, Parker. Don't go off by yourself."

"Whatever."

"You either work with me, or I'm taking you back home. It's not safe to be running up to doors by yourself."

My mouth hangs open like a hooked catfish. "What did you just say?"

"I said, you either—"

"I heard you! I cannot *believe* you are pulling this gentleman crap on me. Next you'll be throwing your jacket over a puddle for me to step over." Okay, now I'm babbling. Seriously, I probably do need to just go home, but Frances would kill me. Not to mention that wouldn't help Bubba's Big Picture in the least.

I brush Charlie's hands off. "Don't tell me what to do."

"Look, if you're mad at me, just say it. We have work to do, and I don't want to disappoint everyone. Let's just clear the air. You're mad because of today at lunch."

"I don't care about today at lunch. You're like underwear to my Lindsay Lohan—I don't *need* you."

"Well, if you don't care, then why are you so mad?"

"Because I have PMS?"

"Because you care about me."

I throw up my hands. "Because I'm upset over the Middle East?"

"Because you're so jealous you can't stand it!"

I match his raised volume. "Because girls don't need a reason to be mad!"

"Or because you can't get me out of your mind!"

"Oh, you wish, don't you? You'd love that. Well, too bad, big boy. You are so out of my mind that—"

"I haven't left your mind, and you know it! And that's what's driving you crazy because—"

"My mom is coming to get me!" I yell.

A raindrop plinks on my nose.

For what seems like hours, minutes, we don't move. The only sound is our worn-out breathing.

And the sound of a door. Granny Rudeness pokes her head out. "You two are really entertaining and all, but I'm trying to watch *CSI* in here."

I nod. "Right then."

"Off we go." Charlie's hand at the small of my back guides me to his truck.

"When are you moving?" Charlie's truck crawls down the road.

"I don't want to talk about it right now."

"But—"

"Drop it."

We finish up the street, and thirty minutes later, we head for our next neighborhood.

And the bottom falls out of the sky. Charlie's windshield wipers race back and forth, but it does little good.

I lean my head back on the seat and sigh. He pulls his truck off to the side of the street, and puts it in park.

Silently, we both stare straight ahead, watching the pelting rain and the darkening sky.

"You ready?" I pick up my clipboard.

"It's practically flooding out there."

"Then I guess we better run fast." I jerk open the door and jump out.

Charlie and I race to the first house. The rain beats at my skin, and I clutch the clipboard to my chest, trying to keep the signatures as dry as possible. My shoes and pants are instantly soaked through, and my feet squish with every quick step. *Ew.* I hate that feeling. Where your feet are swimming in your socks.

A woman I recognize from church opens the door before we make it to the final step. I shove the clipboard and pen in her hand.

"Petition. Drive-in. Sign!" I yell over the weather. Without asking questions, she grips the pen and scribbles her name. "Thanks!" I yank my clipboard back, and Charlie and I run to the next house.

We manage to get signatures from ten houses on the street when the rain picks up even more and lightning cracks across the sky.

"Katie," Charlie yells as we leave 112 Sycamore. "We have to go back. This is pointless!" Thunder reverberates around us, and we take off running again—back to the truck.

My feet are slow moving as I seem to hit every water-filled pothole in the street. I'm mad at my mom, mad at the Scotts, disgusted with Charlie, and we barely have any signatures. Yet all I can think is *I'm so glad I'm not wearing a white T-shirt.*

I giggle the rest of the way to the truck, even as rain beats my skin.

I jump in place (which makes me very aware of the wet padding in my Wonderbra), as Charlie fumbles with his keys to unlock my door.

"It won't work!"

I shake my head. "What?" I yell.

"The lock. It's been sticking lately. You'll have to get in on my side and climb over."

We jog around to the other side, and in three wet seconds, Charlie is holding the door open. I step in and leapfrog over his seat and the console, trailing water everywhere. *Please don't let my underwear be visible through my wet capris! Today* would *be the day I wear my retro Hello Kitty panties.*

Charlie shuts the door, starts the truck, and cranks on the heat.

"Do you have a blanket in here?" My teeth chatter.

He runs a hand through his sopping hair. "Yeah, I keep blankets in the truck. For all those times I get caught in rainstorms." His adjusts the temperature. "Nice hair, by the way."

"Nice . . . uh—" I can't think of a comeback.

"Yeah?" He knows I've got nothing. A corner of his mouth lifts.

I smile. Then laugh.

Then we're both laughing.

"We look like drowned rats."

"Yeah, but now I can go back to school and say I steamed up the windows with Katie Parker." He turns the defrost on. "If I get pneumonia, I am so blaming you." He lays his hand on my headrest.

"I'll send you a box of Kleenex."

His eyes lower to my lips, and I feel my stomach flutter. "If I'm gonna get pneumonia with anyone, I'm glad it's you."

Our eyes meet, and I'm powerless to look away.

He leans in.

I lean in.

*Why* am I leaning in? Stop leaning! *Stop* leaning!

With his hand, he lifts a stray strand of hair and tucks it behind my ear.

"We didn't get many signatures," I blurt out, breaking our spell. "And some of them are smeared off."

He nods his dark head slowly. I notice his hair is curling at the ends. "Some things just don't work out. Even though we want them to."

Are we talking the petition drive or us?

"Some things are worth fighting for, Charlie. And I'm not giving up. Some people give in too easily, and I'm not one of them." I flip my hair for effect, but it only sticks to my ear.

"No, you're not." His voice is deep and low.

I tilt my head and look at him. "Are you really ready to give up?" On the drive-in? On me?

He grabs my hand. "No, I'm not. I'm not ready to give this up."

His thumb rubs over my wet palm, moving in lazy circles, lulling me—

I jerk my hand back. "I can't do this anymore! One minute you're hot, one minute you're cold." *And one minute you're soaking wet and I can see the outline of your six-pack beneath your clinging shirt.*

"Can't you just be patient with me? Have I ever purposely hurt you? I don't think asking for a little trust is too much."

"No. This isn't fair to me. Don't jerk me around and then make me the bad guy by saying I'm not trusting you."

"It's not that simple."

"It can be."

Lightning cracks and illuminates his face in the darkened truck. "You don't understand."

I grit my chattering teeth. "Try me."

Silence.

"Is it because of where I come from? Who I am?" Hello, Insecurity just climbed in the truck.

He scowls. "No."

No as in sorta? As in no way? Or no as in I love girls with shady pasts?

"Is it because I'm probably leaving?" Sooner than I thought. I feel a lump forming in my throat at the thought, and try to breathe it away.

"I have to admit that doesn't help matters, but no."

"I know I don't fit in with your country club life. My mom has a reputation a mile wide, and I know it's not the coolest that I'll be in summer school." I feel my temper rise along with the heat in the truck. "But I'm not trash, Charlie. And there's nothing wrong with coming from a trailer park just because you—"

"Chelsea's dad embezzled a lot of money."

"And yeah, my mom's done time, but don't judge me before you walk a mile in my—"

"He's probably going to prison."

"—shoes, and . . . What?" Lightning cracks. "What did you say?"

Charlie rubs a hand over his damp face. "Chelsea's about to lose everything. They will probably lose their house, all their possessions, and every friend they've ever had."

They have friends?

"There will be an indictment, it's going to be all over the news, it's going to be messy, and she just has no one."

I suck in my breath. "You're telling me Chelsea has a parent who has committed a crime, he's going to prison, and they're broke."

"Exactly."

I close my eyes and rub my temples.

*Dear God, it's a scary, scary day when Chelsea Blake, my nemesis, my opposite in every way, has a life story that sounds tragically . . . just like mine.*

We could be twins.

Except I'm not a size zero.

# Chapter Fourteen

I SNAP MY phone shut.

"Frances says we're to meet them at the mayor's office in five minutes." I glance at my watch. Ten 'til seven, and the rain is just now letting up enough to see the road. Charlie and I have spent the last hour in awkward silence, him refusing to talk anymore about Chelsea. And me counting raindrops, regrets, and what ifs. All endless.

"We only have twenty-five signatures. It's not going to be enough." Charlie starts his truck up, his windshield wipers lurching into action. "Did she say how many she or the others had?"

"No, but she wasn't happy." Join the crowd.

We cruise downtown, and Charlie pulls into a spot next to Frances's station wagon. Before I get out, my eyes meet Frances's and she just shakes her head. We didn't do it. We didn't get enough. Frances jumps out of her car, her umbrella bucking in the wind, and she stomps across the street into city hall.

We all follow. Sad. Wet. Defeated.

The mayor's assistant lets us into the office and shoos us inside, watching our muddy feet leave tracks on her carpet.

"Right this way, children," she says primly. *Children*. What is *that* about? Hello, I wear a bra and buy Clearasil. You cannot call me a child.

Frances grabs my clipboard, does a brief count, and trods on down the hall.

"Mr. Mayor? Your visitors are here."

We all file in, as Mayor Crowley removes his boots from his mahogany desk. "Well, now. I see you made it by the deadline. Did you get all your signatures?" The smirk under his handlebar mustache tells me he *knows* we weren't able to pull it off.

"No. Sir." Frances's words shoot out like bullets. "We tried, but then the rain . . . we couldn't even drive in it for a while. Most of us have spent most of the evening in our cars, waiting out the weather."

"Aw, that's a real shame. Just a shame." He grabs his computer mouse and continues a solitaire game. "So if this little project is over, it's past my dinner time. And it's pot roast night at Ida Mae's House of Vittles."

Frances moves in front of his desk. "No, it's not over. We just need seventy-five more names on this petition."

"Not my problem, darlin'." The squatty mayor reaches for his cowboy hat and places it on his balding head.

"But it is," Frances sputters. "The closing of an In Between institution is everyone's problem. You're going to deny us the opportunity to save it on seventy-five measly signatures? Why would you do that?"

He leans over his desk. "Two words. Strip. Mall."

"What about Buford Hollis's career?"

The mayor throws back his head and hoots with laughter. "Miss Vega, the man operates a rundown drive-in. He pops popcorn two nights a week. You call *that* a career? This"—he holds his arms out, indicating his office—"is a career. Selling tickets to *Top Gun* is not."

Hannah stands beside Frances. "This isn't fair."

"Then not only have I settled this ordeal tonight for you, but I've also taught you a lesson. Because life *isn't* fair, girl. So get used to disappointment." The mayor stands up, drawing himself to his full five-foot-four-glory, his paunchy belly stressing the pearl buttons of his western shirt. "Now, I agreed to stay until seven o'clock for you kids. I've been more than accommodating, but it's time we all went home."

Frances dashes to the door, her arms planted inside the frame. "No! We can't. You can't!"

Charlie and I exchange worried looks. I glare at Nash. *Do something.*

Nash shrugs.

Ugh, boys. Useless!

"Can't we have one more day, Mr. um . . . Mayor?" I ease my way to Frances, where I whisper, "You are not blocking the mayor in his own office. Move!"

"No. You may not. Bubba's Big Picture Drive-In will come down. We cannot get in the way of progress." He shuts his briefcase and maneuvers out from his desk. His beady brown eyes narrow on Frances.

"Young lady, you'd better remove yourself from my doorway."

"Not until you give us another chance."

The mayor's face reddens. "I'll have you know I've been giving Buford Hollis second chances for the last decade! Enough is enough! Now there is nothing you can do, so I suggest you get out of my way."

"Or what?" Frances demands. "You'll hit me?"

The mayor does a double take. "Of course not."

"You'll swear at me?"

"Hadn't planned on it."

Frances frowns. "You'll charge through and mow me down?"

Mayor Crowley reaches into his pocket and pulls out his phone. "I'll just call the police." His voice drops sarcastically low. "I sign their checks, you know. We're rather tight."

"Come on, Frances. Let's go home. We'll talk to an attorney or something for Mr. Hollis." Charlie steps closer, but she only increases the tension in her arms, as if her strength is all that's holding up the doorframe.

"Please, Frances. We'll figure something out." I'm just plain worn out. The whole day has been one battle after another. "I've got to get home and write a paper."

"Miss Vega." The mayor waves his phone. "You have five seconds to leave my office or else I'm calling the police."

I turn to Nash. "You know what you have to do."

He nods, walks toward the door, and without missing a stride, scoops up a hollering Frances, and doesn't let her down until we're all back in the parking lot.

"How could you do that?" Frances yells at Nash, but sending accusing stares at all of her friends. "We could've had a sit-in protest. Started a picket line. Burned our bras. Something!"

Nash rubs his neck. "Because I think your dad would get a little mad if he had to pick you up from jail."

Yeah, been there. Not a good time.

"We can't just give up." Frances's glasses slide down her nose, unnoticed. "We can't, guys."

"Let's just go home," I say quietly. "And pray about it." That really just came out of my mouth again, didn't it? I'm an official churchie now, aren't I? I sound like Millie. I sound like Frances (well, minus the hysterics). But it's all we've got. The reality is we are a group of teenagers going up against a strip mall and an overinflated poser cowboy. God is all we're gonna have. Unless we can come up with fifteen thousand dollars. And last time I checked my piggy bank, I think I was at least a few dimes short.

"I guess." Frances mopes the rest of the way to her car. "Good work, team."

"What's our next move?" someone calls out.

Frances stops. "Get a miracle." And she shuts herself in her car, her boyfriend jumping in just before she peels out and tears down the road.

Everyone disperses to their own vehicles, grumbling and rain-drenched.

Charlie opens my door, but when I go to close it, he doesn't budge. Just stands there next to me, filling up the space.

I look up, a question in my eyes.

"Katie, I'm not into Chelsea."

I study his expression, desperate to find some truth there. "Okay." My voice is neutral, but my heart ever hopeful. Like an idiot.

"And I can't stand this weird tension between us. If you're not willing to hang in there with me and try to make this work, we should at least continue to be friends."

I twirl the big silver ring on my left hand. "Friends . . ." Awful, detestable, dirty word! Did Romeo ever say, "Hey, girl, let's be friends?" No, he downed some Grade A poison! Did Spider-Man say, "Mary Jane, let's be buds." Nope, he said, "Wanna go for a cobweb ride and make out?" What if Adam had asked Eve to be his friend? Um, I'm thinking civilization would've ceased to exist. No good can come from Charlie and I being friends, I tell you. None!

"Yeah, I'd like for us to be friends."

"Sure. Friends would be . . . great." My plastic smile hangs heavy on my face.

And I watch in horror as this boy who only a few weeks ago was holding my hand now offers his hand again—to shake. Like you would shake someone's hand at church. Like you would shake someone's hand upon first meeting him. Not as in, "My next step is to smash my lips onto yours."

And yet I put my hand in his and pretend like just being friends is the niftiest idea ever.

"So you're leaving In Between?" Charlie asks as he starts his truck.

"Yeah." Pal. Amigo. BFF.

"When?"

"Not sure." I glance his way to see if I can find any hint of sadness, desperation, or signs of a boy on the verge of begging me not to go.

His face is annoyingly passive, a blank mask. "Are you okay with it?"

*Are you kidding me?* I'm about as okay as I'd be crashing into a semi right now. And it would probably feel about the same. "I'm fine."

"Seriously, Katie." He touches my arm for a moment, and I just want to yell, *"We're friends! Don't touch me!"*

"Is your mom able to take care of you?" He turns his windshield wipers back on as a light mist covers the glass.

"I guess." Who knows. She has passed a few drug tests. That's a serious accomplishment for her.

"I know the Scotts will miss you."

I close my eyes to block out the image of a Scott-free life. "Yeah, I'll miss them too." I wonder if they'll really visit like they said. Or will they forget me as soon as I'm out the door? Will they just get a new foster kid? They can replace me—but I can't replace them.

"I'll miss you too." His voice is so low I'm not sure if I hear him right.

"What?"

"I'll miss you too." And then he smiles, making me doubt his intensity. "You're the best actress the Valiant's ever seen."

I release a reluctant laugh. "I don't know about that." *Tell me more.*

"No, seriously." His lopsided grin has me reminding myself to breathe. "I don't know if I ever told you this, but I was in the audience for your first play."

"Get out."

"*Romeo and Juliet*, right?"

I nod my head, remembering that magical night. The night I learned my life was possible. And I had talent. I had a purpose, and I was genuinely good at something.

"And you were Juliet. And you did an amazing job."

Charlie wheels the truck into my driveway, and I sigh, wishing we were still miles away from home. I want to keep driving. Keep talking. If we could just stay in this bubble, we wouldn't have to settle for being just friends. We could be Katie and Charlie.

But outside this truck lies the real world. And that world includes Chelsea. And my one-way road trip back home.

I stare at the front porch, where the light has been burning for me since last September. A reminder that a family lives in that house, one who cares about me and loves me. And who will hopefully wait a respectable amount of time before they get a newer model of a foster kid or turn my room into a place for crafts and scrapbook supplies.

Charlie puts the truck in park. "I'll walk you to the door."

"No." I ease the door open. "I'll see you later."

"Katie?"

I turn around, forcing all traces of hope off my face.

"I mean it—we're going to do this friend thing right."

"Great." Sounds fabulous.

"We're not going to lose touch when you leave. That's not going to happen."

"Right. Okay." And Charlie drives off, leaving me standing there staring at the spot where his truck was.

Wondering if my life could possibly stink any more than it does right now.

# Chapter Fifteen

"PICK UP YOUR lip. It's dragging the floor." Maxine turns a magazine page. "You know what else drags that floor? The dog's butt."

I walk into the living room, where my foster parents and Maxine sit. Each one with a book or magazine, yet I get the distinct impression they've been waiting on me. If Millie's posture got any straighter, her spine would snap.

"Just wanted to tell you I'm home." I sail through and head toward the kitchen.

"Katie, wait."

I stop at James's voice.

"We want to talk to you."

I knew it. Something's up. Or maybe they just want to talk about the fact I'm mad at them, and they totally dropped the informational ball again.

I plop myself on the couch next to Maxine, who smells like pickles, but I probably don't even want to know why.

James rubs his eyes behind his glasses. "I know you're upset right now."

*Oh, eensy, weensy bit.*

"But we haven't been keeping things from you. We've talked to you lately about everything we know about Millie's cancer and treatments. About Amy. We just didn't have a whole lot of information ourselves about your mom's situation."

"You had more than I did." I cross my arms and stare at my flip-flops.

"When we knew something definite, we fully intended on telling you," Millie says, her tired eyes intense. "We've had to watch you suffer through disappointment after disappointment with your mom in the last year. James and I wanted to be sure this wasn't another opportunity to get your hopes up, then be let down."

"Is that what you think? That the idea of going home is something I'd be hoping for?"

Millie blinks. "Well, isn't it?"

"It's not even home. It's just another new town, a different trailer, and possibly the same Mom." My eyes fill like the rain gauge outside. I put my head in my hands. "I don't know!"

Maxine's arms surround me, and she pulls me to her. "It's okay, Sweet Pea."

"It stinks!"

"I know. But things will get better."

I lift my head. "No, your shirt. You smell like a giant dill pickle."

Maxine's eyes dart to the left and right, then down. "Er . . ."

"What did you do?" I move to the opposite end of the couch and breathe through my mouth.

"Might've had a little accident at Tucker's Grocery Store today."

"Mom, what kind of accident?"

Maxine clears her throat. "The kind where you stand on a barrel of homemade pickles in order to see who your ex-fiancé is strolling with down aisle number four."

James rolls his eyes. "And?"

"And the lid gives and you fall in. But back to Katie and her desperation—"

The three of us stare at Maxine, our eyes boring into her, trying to make sense of her.

Millie busts into laughter first, her cheeks puffing as she loses her struggle to contain it. Then James. And then I'm laughing—holding my nose and laughing.

"You are so not sleeping in my room tonight."

"What?" Maxine cries. "I'm clean. I've had two showers already. It's just going to take a little while for the vinegar smell to wear off. It's good for you—cleans out your sinuses."

"Katie—" Millie leans forward in her chair, back to the original subject. "If you don't think your mother is capable of taking care of you, if you think your life is endangered in any way, we'll fight for you."

*We'll fight for you.* Magic words if I ever heard them. Even though I know I have to go back with my mom, maybe it's enough the Scotts would be willing to do everything they could to keep me.

"I want to stay here. But part of me wants to go live with my mom too." Either way, I'm hurting someone's feelings it seems. If I willingly go with my mom, will the Scotts think I don't care? And if I ask to stay with the Scotts, my mom would be devastated. And I can't live with the idea I might cause a relapse, and she'd go back to drugs or back to prison. Or worse—on the streets.

Millie and James look at each other, their eyes meeting and some silent communication takes place. Some of that husband-wife telepathy stuff.

"What?" I ask, dread sinking deep in my stomach. "Did my mom call again?"

Millie looks at her hands, but James meets my steady gaze. "Iola Smartly called an hour ago."

No.

It's happening. It's really happening. Iola Smartly, director of the girls' home I lived at before the Scotts, doesn't just make calls to ask about the weather or if I happen to know anyone who smells like pickles.

"What . . . what did she say?"

James steeples his fingers, his face grave. "She said you have five weeks. Unless something goes wrong—and it could—you'll be returned to your mom."

"But—" Millie holds her hand up. "We're going to ask that you come back for a Fourth of July visit. You don't want to miss the fireworks display. Then there's Chihuahua Days after that. You'll have to see that."

"Last year I had four sparklers in each hand." Maxine slugs my shoulder. "Accidentally set old Norman Foster's toupee on fire. Well, he shouldn't have gotten in the way of my impromptu dance routine."

James ignores his mother-in-law. "Mrs. Smartly says your mom has been the picture of cooperation and rehabilitation."

I withhold my information about her new boyfriend. That doesn't exactly scream out responsibility and common sense. "I guess anything's possible." Except for the chance for my life to be normal—definitely not happening in this lifetime. Kinda like the odds of my growing boobs.

"If we hear anything else, we will let you know." Millie moves to sit between me and Maxine. "My gosh, you do reek, Mom. What did you do, stay and swim in the barrel a while after you fell in?"

"Of course not," Maxine snaps, her lips pursed. "You know I would never swim without my Floaties."

Millie's hand combs through my hair and returns her focus to me. "I'm sorry we made you mad. We had to be sure we were giving you accurate information. I don't want to see you hurt anymore, Katie."

I close my eyes and lean into her. Her arm wraps around me, and we stay that way for a long while—me hanging onto the best mom I've ever had. And trying not to breathe through my nose.

After I explain our Mr. Crowley experience, I head upstairs to get ready for bed. I take each step slowly, the stress of the day sitting on my shoulders like a five-ton elephant.

I rush through a shower, and though it's well after ten, I pull out my English homework and climb in bed.

"Aw, you're not gonna do schoolwork, are you?" Maxine yawns and turns her bedside lamp off. "What is the point?"

"Not all of us can rely on our long legs and showgirl skills."

"What are you working on?"

"English."

"*Bah*! Who needs it? Rap stars obviously didn't take it, and look how well they've done for themselves."

I open the screen of my laptop.

And wait.

Five minutes later, still no inspiration.

*This is my life story.*

*This is the life story of Katie Parker.*

*This is the story of Katie Parker. Guaranteed to put you to sleep or make you want to read something more entertaining. Like a cell phone manual. Or the instructions that come with a box of tampons.*

I fall back into my pillows and sigh like the stage diva I am.

"Problems, Snookums?" Maxine doesn't even open an eye.

"I'm supposed to write my life story."

"Write mine instead."

"I thought I'd write something that *wasn't* rated R." Or C for crazy. "I just don't know what to say. It's not like I have a lot of warm, fuzzy Christmas memories to share. Or fun family vacations. My life isn't exactly the stuff of sweet Hallmark movies."

My foster grandma lifts her head. "Write your truth, girl. You should be proud of your story, proud of how far you've come. Though we both know I alone am personally responsible for you no longer being a street hoodlum, you could give yourself a little credit, too, I suppose. Talk about the things you've overcome."

"Like the time I overcame hypothermia after crashing into a pool last year when you made me spy on Sam?"

"Not really what I meant."

"Or the time you made me pedal fifteen miles to the hospital to see Millie after her surgery."

"You needed the exercise."

"Or how about a few weeks ago when we were taking care of the toddlers in the church nursery, and I spent an hour soothing that kid whose juice box you swiped."

"He didn't need the sugar."

Eyes back on the screen, I roll my shoulders back and give it another shot.

*Last year I sat in church, one of the few times in my life at that point.*

*And a bald-headed youth pastor told me God had a purpose for my life.*

*I had hoped that might include fewer zits, more time with the Scotts, and cute boys.*

*I was so wrong.*

I rip the paper out of my notebook and crumble it up, and give it a toss.

The assignment sinks into the trash.

Kinda like my life.

# Chapter Sixteen

I SPEND WHAT'S left of May in a daze—mad, hopeful, scared.

And as I sit in English class and count the hours until school is over (six hours and fifty-one minutes), it's totally bittersweet. In three weeks I will go live with my mom. We have an official date and everything. And I have yet to figure out how I feel about that. I wish I could live with my mom *and* the Scotts. Sounds like the makings of a really bad reality show.

"All right, students, pass your autobiographies forward. Since this is your final, you get the privilege of sitting here and entertaining yourselves while I begin the fun task of grading them." Ms. Dillon stands at the front of my row and waits.

I reach my hand into my backpack and pull out my essay. My life story. My own *Odyssey*. The Declaration of Katie. The Magna Parker.

"Thank you." Ms. Dillon takes the stack out of my hands. She smiles then leans down. "I'm looking forward to reading this."

As she tucks the essays close, I feel some relief at the giant assignment being over. "You didn't do the extra credit assignment and write about where you'd be ten years from now?" Ms. Dillon asks and flips through my work.

"Um . . . no." I lower my voice. "See I have this top secret plan for world domination, and telling you would really throw a kink in things."

She bestows her famous wry grin upon me, then moves on to the next row.

I almost call her back, just so I can look at her kind face one more time, tell her I'm going to miss her, miss our literature conversations, miss our poetry slams, even miss her research papers and her obsession with MLA format. Okay, so maybe I wouldn't go that far. But still, she's tutored me, she's always written encouraging notes on my writing, and she usually let me read the juicy parts when we got to the play portion of our lit book. It's kind of cool having a teacher on your side—on your team. Team In Between.

During lunch the tater tots never tasted so good. I savor each bite, knowing they are my last bite of deep fried, overly processed, saturated fatty goodness here. I skip the ketchup, just so nothing will stand between my tongue and the potato crispiness.

"What are you wearing tonight, Katie?" Frances takes a bite of her sandwich.

I think of the new outfit Millie got me for tonight's last-ever movie at the drive-in. "A totally cool skirt and this eighties-retro shirt. I love it." Probably the last new clothing I'll have for a long time.

"Have you talked to Charlie lately?"

My eyes automatically scan the cafeteria at the mention of his name. "No, he's been really busy with Chelsea." I say the name without choking on it. If that doesn't get me a treasure in heaven, I don't know what will.

"He asked about you yesterday."

I drop a tot. "What? When? Where?"

"Nash and I saw him in the parking lot. He wanted to know how you were doing, if finals were going well."

"Oh. That's nice." Charlie and I e-mail a few times a week, but the phone calls have stopped, and other than church and biology class, we really don't see much of one another.

Frances adjusts the chopsticks in her hair, a messy-updo that probably took her an hour to create. "I think he still likes you."

"You do? Er, I mean . . . no, he doesn't. He's got Chelsea." The jerk made his choice.

"Katie, he watches you all the time. Don't tell me you haven't noticed."

"Guess I'm too busy not watching him, because I haven't noticed." I wipe the grease off my fingers. "But it doesn't matter. I'm leaving. I'll be living four hours away, so there's no point in getting anything started."

"But it's not going to change the fact that we're best friends. So why couldn't you have a long distance boyfriend too?"

I stick a few grapes in my mouth to avoid a response. Frances has mapped out a whole strategy she calls "friendship maintenance." It involves a certain number of phone calls per week, daily e-mails, and continuing our mutual TV viewing habits of *Gilmore Girl* DVDs. But I've moved a lot in my life. I know how it usually works. You hang onto that distant friend because until you really settle in, she's all you've got. But then your old friend still has all of her other friends, so she doesn't need you nearly as much and eventually the calls and e-mails stop. I know one day Frances won't call to remind me of the new Johnny Depp movie. Or text me when Judge Judy blows a gasket on a particularly good episode. Life will go on for her. Without me.

When Millie's car pulls up to the school at three o'clock, I'm surprised to see James behind the wheel.

He leans over and opens my door. "Hop in, kid."

"What's up?"

He lifts a conspiratorial brow. "We're going to take the driver's test today."

I gulp. "*We?*"

"As in you."

"*Today?*"

"As in now."

"No! I can't. I can't suffer that humiliation again. Those people laugh when I walk in. They point and stare. They talk about me on their CBs. There's a poster of me in the office so they automatically know to fail me."

"You've been hanging out with Maxine too much."

"Yeah? How'd I do?"

"Oscar-worthy. But seriously, there's no shame in failing the driver's portion of the test twice. You were just stressed out last time."

"I pulled out in front of a man on a horse."

"He should've heard you coming. They had four ears between them."

"I—"

"Katie—" James pulls the car out of the parking lot. "It's important to me that you leave here with your driver's license."

It's like everything now relates to my leaving. All conversations go back to it. Last night Millie gave me a lecture on making my mom buy organic fruits and vegetables. Yeah, like that's gonna happen. And when we shopped for tonight's outfit, Millie ended up buying me a suitcase full of new clothes to take with me when I leave. If my mom doesn't have a washing machine, I'll still have enough clean undies to last me through next Christmas.

Fifteen freak-out-worthy minutes later, we're at the Department of Public Safety. James rests his hand on mine and prays over me. He should probably pray over everyone in the opposite lane. Or the sidewalks.

Officer Willy Sampson puts down his paper as we walk in the office.

"You here to take your test?"

No, I'm here to hang out. "Yes, sir. The driving portion." I finally passed the written last month—proof that miracles still happen today. See atheists, God exists because Katie Parker passed her written, thank you very much.

His eyes narrow. "You look familiar."

*Yes, I'm the kid who let you see your life flash before your eyes.* "I've already taken it once." And twice. "And I'm ready now." Ready to throw up.

Officer Sampson wallers a big piece of gum in his mouth. "All right." He sighs as he stands. "Let's go."

James gives me two thumbs up as we leave him waiting and walk outside.

I climb into Millie's Honda and pull the seatbelt across my shoulders, singing under my breath. "Jesus take the wheel. Take it from my hands . . ."

"Start the car." Smack, smack, bubble.

Maybe I should try breaking the ice. Get to know Officer Smacks-A-Lot. Appeal to his human side. "Would you like to listen to the radio, sir? Some pop hits? Some uplifting Christian music?"

He stares at me and crackles his gum.

"You like some gangsta rap. Am I right?"

He pulls out his clipboard.

"It's okay. I can appreciate some Snoop Dogg every once in a while. Of course, not his drug references. Because drugs are illegal, and I am a law abiding citizen and—"

"Quit stalling." Smack. "Either start the car or I'm leaving. I have a crossword puzzle to finish."

Okay then.

I twist the key until the car rumbles to life.

"Pull out of the—"

Parking lot and take a left turn at Smith Street. I've taken this thing so many times, I could administer it myself. I'd tell him his presence isn't really necessary, but I don't think he'd appreciate it.

I turn down Smith and offer up a brief prayer.

*Dear God. I'm not gonna close my eyes like I did last time. I'm pretty sure I got points taken off.*

*Lord, please put compassion and mercy in this man's heart. And give me wisdom and skill.*

*And the ability to avoid all pot holes, red lights, fender benders, and kamikaze squirrels.*

"Turn right at the four-way."

I turn my blinker on early, then plaster a smile on my face. I want to give the illusion that I'm calm and tranquil. That my heart isn't hammering like a drum in the Chihuahua marching band, and my sweaty palms aren't slipping off the wheel.

Officer Sampson jots down a few notes.

I wonder if now would be a good time to offer some fashion advice. He could write down my tips instead of his little driving criticisms. I sneak a peek at his hand. No wedding ring. Well, duh. Not dressed like that!

Ten minutes later, I'm still sweating, but I'm still driving—with no casualties! I think the fact I haven't run over anyone and the front bumper is still intact says "driver's license" to me.

"Pull into this driveway with the red mailbox." The officer scratches his chin stubble. "Good. Now back out onto the street."

With a shaky breath, I put my foot on the brake and the gear in reverse. I check the rear view and the side mirrors. I look over each shoulder. All clear.

I repeat the process two more times, stopping only when my copilot clears his throat.

"Any day now."

I force air into my lungs, inhaling deeply (and I think I smell my own armpits). I lift my foot off the brake . . . slowly . . . .slowly . . .

So far so good. I can almost taste that driver's license. How should I wear my hair for the picture? Definitely I will need to flat iron my—

"Look out!"

I catch a blur out of my peripheral vision and hit the brakes. Officer Sampson covers his head as we screech to a shrieking halt.

"Oh, my gosh! Wh-what was that? It looked like—"

"A crazy lady pedaling like a demon on a bike?" He pops another piece of gum in his mouth.

"Yes."

And then I catch sight of the hot pink helmet in the blur as it sails into the distance.

Maxine.

She honks her bike horn as she continues to tear through yards, plowing through flower beds and waylaying a few gnomes. Through the trees I can see her goal—the next street over. She stands on her pedals as she gains speed, breaking through the neighborhood and onto Persimmon Lane.

Right as Sam Dayberry's truck goes by.

That lunatic. That nut! She's chasing Sam—during *my* driver's test!

I grip the steering wheel and face Officer Sampson. "It was clear. There was nobody coming. You had to see that, right? I mean, you saw me checking my mirrors. I all but pulled out a telescope. She exploded out of that yard, and I—"

"Kid?"

Inhale. *Ahhhh.* Exhale. *Whewwww.* "Yes?"

"You pass."

"I what?" I shake my head. Maybe I did hit her. Maybe we had a seriously bad wreck, and I'm in the hospital, but I'm dreaming or in a coma. Maybe I'm fighting for my life right now and this is just a dream. *I'm not walking toward any light, God. Do you hear me?*

"I said you passed." Officer Sampson scribbles something at the bottom of the clipboard. "That lady ought to be locked up. She's caused more accidents than the time the circus broke down off Highway 12. That was some good defensive driving on your part."

"I passed?" I'm not dreaming? "I passed!" I grab the officer in a hug.

"Hey, now. Don't smudge the badge. Okay, that's enough. Very nice. Just back off now . . . *Let me go, kid!*"

I clap my hands in glee and grin. *Thank you, God!* First Moses parted the Red Sea. Then Jesus turned water into wine. And now let it be known Katie Parker passed her driver's test!

I am now among the chosen. The few. The proud.

The street legal.

# Chapter Seventeen

GUYS HAVE IT so easy.

To get ready all they do is shower and swipe on some deodorant (if we're lucky). But girls? Our required routine takes an hour of planning, an hour of execution, then no sudden movements all night so the look is not disturbed. It's so not fair. Women bear the burden of PMS *and* primping. What do guys deal with? Um, hairy arms and chin stubble. Big whoop.

Determined to maximize our remaining month together, Frances came over to my house to get beautiful for our night at the drive-in.

"Maxine bought me this new lip gloss. Wanna try it?" I scoot my makeup bag down the bathroom counter to make room for my friend. "It's called Hot Tamale."

She laughs. "That's from Maxine? Probably should be called Lethal Lips or Vampy Vixen or—"

"I'm not deaf, you know." Maxine jumps off her bed and stomps into the bathroom to join us. "And hurry up, would you? I need to get gorgeous, too." She pats her hair. "Not that I have to do much to get there."

I pat her cheek. "Then why does your makeup bag weigh more than my backpack?"

My hair hangs in loose waves past my shoulders. It's taken nearly a year, but I think my locks have finally forgiven me for my pre-In Between home color jobs. With the help of a curling iron, frizz potion, some gel, and half a can of spray, my tousled strands look natural and free-flowing. And it only took forty-five minutes to make it happen.

I take in my reflection in the mirror. I'm no exotic beauty like Frances, but tonight I don't exactly feel like Ugly Betty either. Plus there's just something about a new outfit that gives a girl a boost of confidence. I grab my fitted blazer hanging behind the door and slip it on over my vintage eighties T-shirt. My Audrey Hepburn-style flats go perfectly with my new miniskirt. For a finishing touch, I add a funky ring and my industrial-sized pink hoop earrings. *Look out* Vogue. *I got me some style tonight.*

"You look great, Katie." Frances applies some blush. "Retro-preppy-punk."

I smile at my best friend, then turn away to dig into my makeup bag as tears push at my eyes. Frances is my first *real* best friend. Not just somebody I hung out with because it was the best I could do. Not somebody I hung out with because we both had tattered jeans and got free school lunch. Not somebody I was friends with because our moms partied together. Frances likes me for me. She gets me. My neurotic tendencies. My moodiness. My math handicap. All of it. And I could lose her forever. There might never be another Frances Vega in my life. It's like it's still not real to me. Like I'm going to wake up and discover I don't have to walk away from all of this. That life can go on as it was before my mom was sprung from prison. Well, minus the totally rockin' driver's license part.

"You do look pretty fab, Katie. Both of you girls do." Maxine applies a powder puff to her nose, her face consumed in a cloud of talc. She twists up a tube of lipstick. "Did Sam Dayberry mention if he would be there? Not that I care, mind you."

"Not care?" I wave her powdery dust out of my face. "I nearly killed you this afternoon on your bike. Ripping through a neighborhood going Mach ten on your tandem doesn't exactly scream 'who cares' to me."

"Well, you're just a child. What do you know? I was simply getting some exercise today."

I turn away from the mirror and face her. "Maxine, you ramped some kid's slide to catch up with Sam. I don't think that was about burning some calories. Why don't you just tell Sam you got cold feet but you still love him, and put us all out of our misery."

"Who says I still love him? Is that what he thinks? Is that what he says?"

"Admit it," Frances chimes in. "You are just afraid of love. You've been a widow for a long time now, and you're running scared."

Maxine goes nose to nose with Frances. "This from the girl who couldn't even form a single sentence when you first began talking to Nash? Who giggled like you had voices in your head and said things such as, 'I like water,' while drool dribbled out of your mouth? Yes, please, give me some more love advice."

"She's just trying to be helpful, Maxine. And you know she's onto something."

"And you, Little Missy." My foster grandmother jabs me with her blush brush. "Who are you to be spouting romantic wisdom? You're so insecure the second your boy starts hanging out with that blonde again, you call it off."

"I didn't call anything off. He did." Well, not exactly. "He was never my boyfriend anyway." I'm not really sure what Charlie was. "Besides, he can't have me *and* Chelsea. Is he studying polygamy or something? I'm not that type of girl."

Maxine sucks in her cheeks and applies a pink tint. "He told you to trust him. And what do you do?"

"I did trust him!" I feel my face warming. "And every time I looked up, Chelsea would be there with her arms wrapped all over him. And hey, we're talking about *you* here, not me. You are the one who had a diamond ring on your hand, but gave it up because you were afraid Sam would expect you to bake a casserole once a week."

Like she could even identify an oven.

Maxine gasps, her ruby lips forming an O. "That is not fair. This is so much more complicated than that."

"Then what is it?" I stare at my foster grandmother and watch her eyes lose some of their fire. "You tell me why you broke it off with Sam."

"I . . . I . . ."

*Ding-dong!*

"My date is here." And Maxine grabs her purse and sails downstairs.

Date? No, Maxine *has* to get back with Sam. I can't leave In Between with things like this.

"Come on." I wave my hand and motion Frances to follow. We ease down the steps, our ears peeled for the sound of the visitor at the front door.

"Why Maxine, you are a vision," a squeaky voice says. I hear Maxine giggle like a middle-schooler.

"Thank you, William. So nice to be appreciated," she purrs.

Frances and I tiptoe through the kitchen. I step into the entry way with Frances at my heels.

And freeze.

Frances plows into my back.

"Oh, my gosh," I hiss.

"Well, hello there ladies." Maxine's date tips his cowboy hat and smiles bigger than Dallas. "Fancy meeting you here."

Behind me Frances sucks in her breath. I throw out my hands to hold her back.

"Girls," Maxine says, tucking her hand into the gentleman's arm. "I'd like to introduce you to my date, William."

William twists his handlebar mustache. "But you can just call me Mr. Mayor.

# Chapter Eighteen

"I CANNOT BELIEVE your foster grandma is dating the mayor. That's a lot of nerve—even for her—to bring him *here*." Nash sets his chair on the gravel next to his car.

"Unbelievable," Frances fumes. "She's dating the enemy. After all we've been through, and she's snuggling up with Mayor Crowley—the dream killer."

I know she's probably just doing it to make Sam jealous, but couldn't she have picked someone else? Someone who doesn't wear a belt buckle the size of a hubcap. Someone who doesn't think Wranglers are business attire. And someone who isn't planning on bulldozing Bubba's Big Picture tomorrow.

Like I have a built-in radar, I look up as Charlie wheels in five spots down. My heart constricts a bit at the sight of his copilot, Chelsea. I should be used to it by now, though. Where he is, there you'll find her. Needy never looked so cute.

He gets out of his truck and goes straight for his lawn chairs in the back. I rejoice over the fact he doesn't open her door first. He always opened my door. And while it annoyed me at the time, I miss it. Miss him.

The two of them make their way over to our group. He saunters closer in his cargo shorts and blue T-shirt. He could pass for a surfer.

Our eyes meet and hold.

Then he smiles.

And reluctantly I do too.

I still totally dig this boy, but I know we'd never make it long distance. Not that it wouldn't have been fun to try. It would be nice to be that new mysterious girl in town who says things like, "My boyfriend back home . . ." And "Gotta take this call. It's my boyfriend . . ." But now I'll just be the loser new girl who stays home on Friday nights watching Lifetime marathons and drowning my sorrows in boxes of Twinkies.

Everyone greets the two. I do my best to smile at Chelsea like she doesn't bother me, but it comes out more like a grimace. Or like I have gas.

"I heard you got your license today." Charlie pats me on the shoulder, his hand spreading warmth up and down my arm.

"Yeah." I beam. Seriously, like my face hurts from grinning over this. "It's been quite the day."

"I didn't see you much this week. How were finals?" His hand drops back to his side.

"I survived them. Frances helped me study for algebra and history. How about yours?"

"I thought biology was a little tough. I almost called you last night to get help with the study guide."

Help. *From me? Surely you jest.* "That's funny. I almost called you too." And I did. Last night I wanted to pick up the phone so bad. I miss talking to Charlie. Miss just hanging out. Charlie's eyes wander across the parking area. "It's gonna be sad to see this go. I watched my first movie here."

"Yeah, but I think Buford picked a great flick to end with—*Star Wars.*" For Halloween once I twirled my hair into buns like Princess Leia. They were in knots for the next two days. It wasn't attractive. And my mom's only advice was, "Get the scissors."

"Well, Little Darlings. How are we tonight?" Maxine strolls by on the arm of the mayor. I pierce Nash with a look that says, *Don't let Frances loose.*

"Fine, Mrs. Simmons," Charlie says. "Just enjoying our last night at the drive-in."

"Forever," Frances grunts, as she's nestled quite tightly into Nash.

"Kids, don't look at this as good-bye. Look at it as hello," the mayor says. "Hello progress. Hello growth for In Between. Hello—"

"Capitalistic Nazi dictatorship."

"Now, Miss Vega," Mayor Crowley coos. "One day you'll thank me for this. And you will be grateful I didn't let you stand in the way of progress. Sometimes we have to tear down to grow."

The only things Frances wants to tear would be his eyeballs.

"Maxine, I think I see James and Millie over there waving for you to join them." I jerk my head to the left. "They're probably missing you by now."

"Missing me? They've sent me to the concession stand five times already." Maxine takes two steps away from us, pulling her date along. Then freezes. "Oh, no, he didn't."

We all turn. Sam Dayberry. Walking with Betty Lou Lawson.

"That two-timing, back-stabbing, overall-wearing gigolo. How dare he come out here tonight on the arm of—Well, hello there Betty Lou. So nice to see you." Maxine steps closer to the mayor. "Oh, why hello, Sam. Didn't notice you there. Lovely evening, isn't it?"

Charlie whispers low. "Looks like we're going to get fireworks with our movie."

"With Maxine, it's more like pistols and brass knuckles. This could get ugly." And embarrassing. Betty Lou, seventy if she's a day, sports one of those fake ponytails, and I know that will be the first thing Maxine goes for if a catfight breaks out.

"That's a lovely hair piece you have there, Betty Lou. *So* natural." Maxine pats her own perfectly coifed do. I watch my foster grandmother narrow her eyes and no doubt scrutinize how hard it would be to grab it in one yank.

"Mayor Crowley, many in the town feel like we didn't get ample opportunity to sign that petition to stop the closing of the drive-in,"

Sam says, tearing his eyes away from his ex-fiancée. "I would think the neighborly thing to do would be to let us have another week or so. Give Buford Hollis a fair shake."

The mayor laughs. "I've been more than fair. I've given him years to clean this place up. Enough is enough. As I was telling the kids here, when progress rolls into town, nobody will miss Bubba's Big Picture."

I don't really care about progress, but I have to admit a McDonald's on the corner would be nice. Just not in this location.

"Betty Lou," Maxine says, stepping toward her competition. "I thought you were seeing old Donnie Blevins."

Betty Lou takes a bite of her popcorn. "He died."

Maxine's eyes widen, then she settles her gaze on Sam. "See what you have to look forward to."

"Let's go, Betty Lou. You don't have to listen this." Sam pushes a bewildered Betty Lou along.

"She's a man-eater! Is that what you want? I danced for Sinatra, Betty Lou. Can you top that? Whatchu got?"

"Maxine?" I sigh with relief as Sam and his lady friend walk on.

"I can still do the splits!"

"Maxine?"

She retreats and reigns her temper back in. "Yes, Snookums?"

"As much as we have all enjoyed the geriatric version of *Bring It On*, you probably need to go back to your seats before you scare everyone off." I lean in and my voice drips with disdain. "I am making a memory here tonight, and you trying to pick a fight with that poor woman is not what I want to recall."

"He brought another woman here." Maxine crosses her arms over her ample chest.

"You brought a man." And the town pariah at that.

"That's different."

"Yes, it is different. In *Crazyville*—in your head! Now move on," I whisper. "Your date is upsetting Frances. And I don't exactly like to look at him either." Or his outfit. If it was winter, we could sled on the man's belt buckle.

Maxine clears her throat. "Good-bye, children. William and I will be returning to our seats now. Enjoy your evening, keep your hands to yourself, and no swapping spit."

"Oh, and Miss Vega," the mayor stops. "Time will heal your wounds, my dear. You'll see."

Frances's hands are balled into fists. "It's not over yet, Mayor. I'm not giving up until the final hour."

He chuckles and pivots to leave. "Oh, the things kids say." And walks away in his lizard skin boots.

"It's not over yet, though. Right?" Frances looks at all of us, her black eyes fierce.

"Frances, I think we have to admit defeat here." I stand shoulder to shoulder with my friend. "We tried. We did everything."

"Not everything." She nods and stalks back to her chair. "What if we *didn't* do everything? I don't think I can live with that. My father's family left Mexico for freedom and a better life. My ancestors would roll in their graves if they saw me giving up like this." She plops down. "And I won't do it. I will not back down."

"It's just a stupid drive-in." Chelsea's whiny voice is like nails on a chalkboard.

Frances leaps up. "Stupid? *Stupid?*"

"Yeah." She pops her gum. "I don't get why you're throwing such a hissy and—"

"Okay, let's go get something to drink, eh?" I grab Chelsea's arm and drag her away from Frances. "We'll be back soon!"

Chelsea jerks her arm back as we hike toward the concession stand. "What are you doing?"

*Saving your life before Frances rips your face off. And you're welcome.*

"Frances is really upset about the drive-in. Most people are. You could be a little more sensitive to that." I know, I'm a snippy hag. I can't help it. But if the snack bar were selling clues, this girl would need a double order.

"I just think it's a dumb thing to get worked up over. Some people have *real* problems."

Wait a minute. I have Chelsea Blake telling *me* about *real* problems?

We settle into line at the busy snack bar. With tonight's crowd, Buford's selling a lot of popcorn.

"I know you know about my dad, Katie." Chelsea locks her eyes onto mine.

I say nothing, not sure how to tread. Did Charlie tell her he told me? Or is she just taking a guess?

"Daddy will get out of it."

"Okay."

"He's totally innocent. It's just a clerical error."

I don't think they usually haul away cars for clerical errors.

"He belongs with me, you know."

I struggle to focus. "Your dad?"

"Charlie. You're not his type."

Her transition could use a little work. You know, a little warning before her whiplash topic change? Wait a minute—not my type? "What is *that* supposed to mean?"

"You know." Her indulgent smile has me seeing red. "He just doesn't have the heart to tell you that he's fallen for me again. He doesn't want to hurt your feelings during this hard time for you. He's such a good guy."

*Yeah, which makes him* so *completely wrong for you.*

"He wants to send you off with a smile and not mad at him. Or me."

I laugh. "Oh, I'm not mad at you."

"You're not?"

"Why would I be mad at you?" *I thoroughly dislike you. Maybe you're getting the two confused.*

She steps closer to me, and the scent of popcorn mingles with her expensive perfume. "Because we're pretty much back together."

My heart takes a nosedive, but I keep my face as expressionless as Maxine's after a Botox injection. "Chelsea, I really don't care."

"I know you do. It's okay. If anybody knows how hard it is to let Charlie Benson go, it's me."

"You didn't seem to have too much trouble letting him go a couple months ago when you were lip-locked with Trevor Jackson." She blanches. "Remember him? The boy *I* was dating?"

Chelsea's pink mouth drops. "That was just two actors caught up in a moment."

"Really? Well, your hands were caught up in—"

"That was then. This is now. And you have to accept the fact you and Charlie are never going to happen," she snaps. "He and I are so much more alike. I'm his kind."

"His *kind*?"

Though I'm taller than her, she still somehow manages to look down her nose at me. "You come from a different place. And there's nothing wrong with that, but—"

"You're right, there's nothing wrong with it. And let's get one thing straight here, Chelsea. If you think Charlie dates girls because of their pedigree, then you don't even know him. Unlike you, *he* isn't that shallow. He cares about the person, not her background or how much money she has."

"That's not exactly what I meant. And I think I know Charlie. He was my boyfriend after all." Her voice drips with possessiveness. "But you need to totally walk away from him, so he can move on. He feels sorry for you, that's all. Do you really want him hanging around for that reason?"

I step out of the line. "I wish you and Charlie the best. I hope you're very happy. But next time you start counting off the ways you're so much better than me, you think long and hard. I don't know about you, but when my momma went to jail, I got a whole new perspective." I shake my head in disgust. "Oh, but that's right.

You won't have to deal with that. Because your daddy just made a clerical error."

Shaking, I walk away.

* * *

"CHELSEA IS CRYING."

Thirty minutes later Charlie looms over my chair.

I peel my attention away from the light saber duel onscreen. "What?"

"I said, Chelsea is crying." His whole body is tense, his gray eyes cold.

I already regret what I said to her earlier. It was wrong, and I know it. But now, seeing him all steamed up and defending her like he's her man, my regret seems far away.

I can tell my bland expression is ticking him off.

"Aren't you going to say anything?"

With a glance at Frances and Nash, who now think we're the main attraction, I get up and walk out of hearing range. Charlie follows, his hands stuffed in his pockets.

He glares. "Well?"

"What do you want me to say?"

"That you're sorry?"

"Okay . . ." Yeah, I *could* do that.

"I can't believe you." Charlie runs a frustrated hand through his hair. "I specifically asked you not to say anything about her dad. I *trusted* you with that information. I told you not to tell anyone. And what do you do? You throw it in Chelsea's face."

Dude, there's a whole list of things I'd like to throw in Chelsea's face.

"She was baiting me. I wasn't going to stand there and take it."

He gets eye level with me. "Did you or did you not basically tell her her dad would be going to jail?"

". . . I guess, but—"

He holds both hands up and steps away. "I cannot believe you."

Yes, I think we've established that. "Did your little princess tell you what she said to me?"

"Does it matter?"

That stops me cold. "It used to. I guess now that I have a one-way ticket out of town, you don't care, right? Chelsea can just say anything she wants. Be a witch to anyone she wants."

"You have no idea what she's going through."

I can't help but laugh. "Okay, Charlie." I nod and smile. "Okay, you win. Yes, I said something hateful to Chelsea. I'm sorry. She didn't provoke it at all. I just did it to hurt her—just for the fun of it. Because that's who I am—who I really am."

"I never said that."

I glance over his shoulder at the In Between moon, not really seeing it, but looking right through. "Somehow in the last few weeks you've changed your opinion of me—and of Chelsea. I'm not going to stand here and fight with you to try and change your mind. I'm better than that." I drag my gaze back to his. "I said too much tonight, and for that I'm sorry. You can tell your *girlfriend* that." I wince at my own jealous tone. "But I won't be dragged into her petty little world." I turn around. "I'll leave that for you."

"That's all you're going to say?" He calls after me.

I pause. And turn around. "You know me, Charlie Benson." I shake my head, a trace of a bitter smile on my face. "And I thought I knew you."

# Chapter Nineteen

"COME ON, SUNSHINE. Wakey, wakey, eggs and bakey!".

I lift one heavy eyelid and see Maxine sitting on my bed, with Rocky panting beside her.

"Upsy daisy!"

"Get that dog out of my room." I don't want him drooling on my rug.

"What's that?" Maxine raises her volume like *I'm* the senior citizen. "You want Rocky to give you a big, wet kiss. Okay. Up, Rocky! Up!"

"No!" I raise my hands to block my face, but not before the nine-hundred-pound bag-of-slobbers wets me down with his giant tongue. *Ewww.* Bathed in dog spit.

Maxine flips my blanket off. "Come on. Family breakfast downstairs. You don't want to miss it. James is fixing waffles. Real ones. Not gluten-free, wheat-free, nasty organic cardboard ones."

"Just go away." Normally the lure of real food with all its additive and preservatives would have me sliding down the banister. But not today. Not after last night. It's like I have a fight-with-Charlie hangover.

"Aw, why so glum, Sweet Pea? Did the big, bad blonde sit too close to you last night?"

I yank my sheet over my head, desperate to get away from Rocky's Milk Bone breath. "I don't even want to hear Chelsea's name."

Maxine snorts. "I was talking about me." She scoots in closer and leans over me. "Trouble in sophomore paradise?"

"I want to sleep. It's only seven-thirty." And Bubba's Big Picture goes down at eight. I find this a dark day and one that would best be observed from the comfort of my bed and my pj's. And maybe a little Netflix later. And Diet Dr. Pepper.

"Somebody's got her Victoria's Secrets in a wad."

"Spare me the details of your wedgie."

Maxine chuckles. "I meant you. What happened last night? You know I hate to be left out."

"Does it matter? You'll just read it in my journal later."

"True. But I like to hear it from the source. Saves me a lot of time."

I raise up and spill out last night's details. "Besides . . . I'm mad at you."

Maxine studies a manicured nail. "Is this about borrowing your shoes last night?"

"You did?"

"Is this about using your Abercrombie T-shirt to wipe up my spilled nail polish?"

"What?"

"Or are you mad because I used the last of your perfume as air freshener in the bathroom?"

I rub my eyes. When I fully wake up, I have a lot to be mad about. "You and the mayor, Maxine."

"Oh. That."

"Yeah, *that*. What is that about? What are you thinking?"

"That ten-gallon hats are kinda sexy?"

I sit up, grab a ponytail holder from my bedside table and bundle my hair. "No, they're not. You know who is hot? Sam." Ugh, my stomach turns. "For you, that is. Maxine, what are you doing pushing him away like that?"

"Me pushing *him* away? He's been seen around town with that . . . that . . . tramp."

"Betty Lou wears Velcro shoes. That doesn't exactly scream slutty vixen to me."

Maxine snorts. "You'd be surprised."

"Look, I know this is just about making Sam jealous. But couldn't you pick someone else?"

"William is a man of culture. A man of class."

"His Cadillac honks 'The Yellow Rose of Texas'."

"Mind your own business."

But this *is* my business. I can't leave with everything so unsettled. I need to know everyone is okay, and life is as it should be.

Schlumping behind Maxine, I follow her downstairs to the kitchen. James mans his post at the stove, whistling a happy tune.

"Morning, ladies."

"Where's Millie?" And does she know James is fixing food that is neither natural nor gross?

"She went back to bed for a bit. Thought she'd catch a few more z's."

I frown and grab a juice glass. Lately Millie's getting worn down by her chemo. She's even been going in for fluids to keep her up and running. Just another loose end for me to stress about when I leave. Millie needs me to stay around and help her. At some point the contractors in town will get caught up with all of the tornado destruction and fix Maxine's senior apartment. Then she won't be around to help Millie as much. Of course her help consists of dusting the remote control and getting the mail.

"Are you okay, Katie?" James flops two waffles on my plate, and I inhale their sweet aroma. Oh, sweet bread product with absolutely no nutritional value—how I have missed you.

"Yeah." I drench my plate in syrup. "Just tired." Tired of worrying. Tired of my brain being on permanent rewind and watching last night over and over. Tired of this constant feeling of being pulled in too many directions.

"Buford Wallis will be okay. He'll find other work." James serves his mother-in-law.

"But the drive-in makes him happy. Bubba's Big Picture is his dream." I stab a bite of waffle and put it in my mouth. *Yummm.* Heaven. "And your *boyfriend* could stop it all."

Maxine lifts a shoulder. "When that man's made up his mind, there's no stopping him."

*Ring! Ring!*

James steps into the kitchen to answer the phone. "Katie, it's for you." He eyes the clock with a scowl. "It's a boy."

I pick up the phone as Maxine makes kissy noises from the table. "Hello?"

"Katie, it's Charlie."

Charlie? It's seven-forty-five. On the house phone? What's going on? But I push down any fear and remind myself I'm mad at him. "Yeah?"

"Katie . . . I need you."

*I know that's right.*

"It's Frances. She's climbed up to the top of Bubba's Big Picture snack bar. She refuses to come down."

"*What?*"

"I came out this morning to . . . well, to take one last look at the drive-in. And Frances was here. Katie, you've got to talk her out of this. The demolition crew will be here any minute."

"I . . . I . . . " Oh, the dilemma! I have waffles waiting on me—and who knows when we'll be together again. "I'll see you in five minutes." I run back to my plate and inhale the rest of one waffle. "Gotta go."

"Where?" James sets his morning paper down. "What was all that about?"

"Frances is on top of the drive-in concession stand. I need to get to her before she does something crazy. Can you take me?"

James does not get the urgency. "I really don't want to leave Millie this morning. She's not feeling so great. And you're not even dressed yet." He points to my saggy pajama bottoms and "Nerds Are Hot" T-shirt.

"I'll take you, Toots. Just let me get my helmet."

"There's no time to ride your bike, Maxine. I want to get there before the demolition crew." And then an idea hits me. "James . . . can I borrow the car?"

He chokes on his juice. "Excuse me?"

I engulf him in a loose hug and lean my head on my shoulder. "Please? I'll be extra careful. I am a licensed driver now."

"Katie, I don't know. You're still so new to driving. And you have to drive with an adult for six months. And I'm not leaving Millie right now."

I sigh. "So I guess I'm out of luck."

"Hey, what am I?" Maxine chirps.

"It looks that way, hon. Sorry."

"Yoo-hoo! Adult, right here." Maxine waves her hand in my face.

"Maybe one of the neighbors could go with me."

"Hellewww, I ain't swigging prune juice because I like it. I'm an adult." Maxine stands up. "Get the keys and let's go. We have to save Miss Advanced Placement."

James and I share a look, then he shrugs. "I suppose she'll do. But you are changing first, right?"

"Nope. No time to lose." Thank you, Frances. Nothing like parading myself in front of Charlie with morning breath, bed head, and pants that make me look like I have a full diaper. A little warning about her freaking out would've been nice.

James follows us outside to the car, spouting a litany of driving reminders and handing me my flip-flops. I grab the keys from my foster dad, give him a smacking kiss on the cheek, and put Millie's Honda into motion. My first voyage as a licensed driver! I guess there is something good about Frances's freaky-psycho meltdown.

Maxine cranks up the radio, her grin wide across her face. "You with a license—I like it. I like it a lot."

I turn onto Main Street. "I am not going to be your personal chauffeur." I don't trust that gleam in her eye.

A few minutes later I pull through the entrance to Bubba's Big Picture. I drive straight to the snack bar area and park next to Charlie.

"Frances!" I yell, jumping out of the car. My best friend perches on the flat roof of the concession building, arms crossed, chin in the air. "Frances Vega, I know you can hear me!"

"She refuses to budge." Charlie stands next to me, and the scent of his shampoo carries my way on a breeze. "I called Nash. He should be here any minute."

"Yeah, and so will the police. What are we going to do?" I stand with my arms crossed so he knows I'm still steamed.

Maxine looks up to the roof. "A day in the slammer might do her some good . . . What? Never hurt me."

I walk closer to the building. "Frances, listen to me."

Nothing. No response.

"Zhen Mai Frances Vega—" She winces as I use the name only her parents call her. "This is crazy. Your dad is going to kill you! Does he know where you are?"

She might as well be a statue for all the reaction I'm getting.

I hoist myself onto the snack bar then with every ounce of strength I've got, pull myself onto the roof. I lie there, trembling and out of breath.

"You could've just used the ladder." Frances points to the backside. "I brought one with me."

I close my eyes, sigh deeply, and walk toward her. "What are you doing out here? You know this isn't going to solve anything."

Frances shakes her head, her black hair shining in the morning sun. "I can't give up. Progress robs a town of its history. First it's the drive-in. Next it will be a supermarket in the place of Tucker's. Then what—they'll change our Chihuahua mascot?"

Oh, life couldn't be that kind.

"The wrecking crew is going to be here any minute, you know."

"So? I'm not moving."

I try a new tactic. "Harvard doesn't accept incoming freshmen with rap sheets."

Frances blinks behind her glasses. "Then I'll go to Yale."

"You're gonna be grounded so long, you won't even be able to go to the junior college."

"That's the price I'm willing to pay." She tucks a runaway piece of hair behind her ear.

"Grounded so long you can't even go to the junior college and will have to work in a plant."

"For this, I would pluck chickens."

I sigh and shift my legs beneath me. "You can so kiss dating good-bye."

"I hear prom is overrated." Frances looks into the distance.

I study my friend, the set of her face, her crossed arms. The Goldfish crackers and juice box beside her. This girl ain't going nowhere. "There's nothing I can say?"

Her black eyes meet mine. "Katie, I have to do this. I can't let the drive-in go without a fight."

I nod and take a step back, the boards creaking beneath me. "Okay, then. I'll visit you in prison." I've got a little practice with that. "You know they're just going to physically remove you from this roof."

Frances shrugs. "If that's what they have to do. But I called the paper, and they should be arriving in another ten minutes, so let them get the story of the big bad mayor having a young girl roughed up and dragged off a building."

Wow. "You should've been the one in theatre." I walk toward the ladder, deciding to take the easy way down this time. Not that heaving my full body weight onto the roof wasn't fun. And probably really attractive too. "I'm going to be down there if you need anything." I give Frances a thumbs-up sign and a bolstering smile, then walk toward the edge.

I frown as the roof wobbles a bit. "Kinda weak over here. Be careful, okay?"

"What?" she calls.

"I said there are some weak boards and—"

*Crash!*

I stumble onto my knee as my right leg rips plunges through the roof.

"Oh my gosh!" I yell. My body hits the flat surface, and my brain whirls, as if trying to locate all my body parts.

Frances dashes over to me. "Katie! Are you okay?"

"Yeah . . . I think I'm okay." Sweat beads on my forehead. "I . . . um . . ." I move my right leg. All toes work. Ankle—*ow*. Not so good. Just gonna pull it back up and get out of here.

"Katie?" Charlie bellows from below. "What's going on?"

"I know mouth-to-mouth!" Maxine hollers. "Do you need me?"

"It's nothing! I'm fine!" I inject some attitude in my yell for Charlie's sake.

"Are you sure you're okay?" Frances asks, her brow knit with concern. Her gaze travels over my head, and I turn to follow her stare.

Oh, no.

The demolition crew is here.

Racing toward the back, steering clear of me and the hole, Frances grabs the ladder and manhandles it until it slides up next to her.

"Put that ladder back down, Frances."

She ignores me.

I lift my leg, desperate to get both legs in the same place and on level ground.

"I can't pull my leg up."

"What?"

I double my volume. "I said, I can't pull my leg up!"

"I heard you! What do you mean?"

I balance my body weight on my arms and give a few good tugs. Nothing. "My pajama bottoms are caught on something. I think it's a nail." This could only happen to me. I know God's up there with his angelic posse saying, "Come here. You gotta check this girl out. She's at it *again!*"

"Maybe if I . . . um . . ." Frances wraps her arms around my upper body and pulls.

"Ow! I need my leg out, not my torso detached!" My heart beats wildly in my chest. *Don't freak out. Do* not *freak out.* What if I fall all the way through? I don't want to die in my ratty pajamas.

"Hey!" A gruff voice echoes from below. "What are you two doing up there?"

Frances tiptoes to the other side. "Hello, sir. How are you this fine morning?"

"Yeah, great. Whatever. Get down. *Now.*"

"No."

"Frances," I hiss. "Tell him I'm stuck. Tell him I'm seconds away from busting through and doing a cannonball into the popcorn machine, and I need some help."

"No."

"Help!" I scream. "Help me!"

"What's going on up there?"

"My leg is stuck! It fell through the roof!" And I should never have gotten out of bed this morning.

"Katie?" Charlie calls. "Are you okay?"

"Yes! My leg is stuck in the roof, I can't move it, Frances hauled the ladder up, it's a million degrees up here, and I'm having the time of my life. *Thanks for asking!*" I snarl.

Frances *tsks.* "Kinda crabby this morning."

"The project manager just went to call the mayor." Charlie's voice grates on my every nerve. Even the ones dangling midair below. "He said they have instructions to demolish the place no matter what."

"Oh, well, great. Let me just gnaw my own leg off, and I'll be right down." *Where* are these people's brains today? Unlike Frances, *I* am not up here to make a statement. My statement right now? Get me *down!*

I tug my right leg to no avail. Buford Hollis and his stupid rotting building. It's probably eaten up with termites, and they're going to swarm in on my trapped limb at any second.

"Frances, let the ladder back down, so I can come up and help Katie!"

"No, Charlie!"

My head spins toward my best friend. "Are you nuts? Give him the ladder. You can stay up here, but I want down. This place is a time bomb. It's probably going to cave in before the bulldozer gets it anyway. We both need to get down from here."

"Katie," Frances rushes to my side, spies the hole again, and backs up a step. "I can't. I'm sorry. I didn't ask you to come up here."

"You're going to sacrifice me for the sake of this drive-in?" I squawk. "Have you been drinking?"

Charlie pleads with Frances again.

"No, I'm not giving you the ladder. Those men in the big yellow trucks will just storm the roof and make me come down."

I close my eyes. My body hurts from this awkward position. Legs were just not meant to go in these two different directions.

"Hey, kid!"

Frances runs to the edge. "What do you want?"

Oh, yeah, big talk from the girl not tooth-picked through a roof.

"You have five seconds to climb down or else I'm calling the police. The mayor's on his way. I got clearance to call the fire department, the sheriff, and the drug dogs."

Frances gasps. "I don't have drugs up here!"

No, she took them all *before* she came.

Turning back to me, Frances evaluates my situation. "If you could just get free, I think I could distract these guys long enough to get you down."

"Great. Fabulous. Thanks for caring. But Frances?" I pant, weary of holding up my own body weight. "I am stuck until someone gets into the snack bar and detaches me."

"Could you just take your pants off?"

"No!" Though the thought did cross my mind. But James would have a cow.

"It's okay." Frances sits ten feet away from me. "I think I'm just going to sit here and pray."

"Pray? Pray for me some help." *You freak job.*

I hear a few more vehicles pull up to the snack bar, one of them sounding especially close. *Dear God, please don't let anyone plow into this building. That would kinda complicate things. And cut me in two.*

"Frances Vega? Katie Parker? Keep driving, Tom. A little closer."

I frown at this new voice. Now what?

Doors slam, voices mingle. *Thud! Thud! Thud!*

Leaving her meditative pose, Frances slinks to the edge again. "Oh . . ."

"What?" I could really use that juice box about now.

"Oh, no . . ."

And then I see a head pop up. And another one.

"It's two guys on a van," Frances whispers.

Yes! Some help. *Thank you, God.* "Looks like your prayers were answered, Frances." At least for me.

"Uh . . . I don't think so."

"Frances Vega and Katie Parker—I'm Rick Saldano."

"Who?" I blanch at the TV camera lifted high.

"Channel Five News."

# Chapter Twenty

"LADIES, IF YOU could come closer to the edge, I could get you on the mic."

Frances leaps toward the TV newsman. Dude, that girl's *already* on the edge. She's one step away from crazy town.

"I'm Frances Vega." She lifts her chin like she's royalty. "We're protesting the destruction of Bubba's Big Picture, an In Between institution."

"No, *we're* not. I'm just stuck up here. If you would be so kind, sir, as to—"

"Miss Vega, is it true you and your friends started a petition to keep Bubba's open?" Rick's face looks like mine when Millie gives me an extra ten in my allowance.

"Yes, we did. But we got caught in last week's rainstorm and couldn't safely get out and obtain all the support we needed—all the support we know we would have received. This town—"

The roof shakes with force. Now what?

Metal scrapes the building as a gray ladder appears. "Miss Vega! You get down this instant!"

Mayor Crowley. He huffs with every step up the ladder.

I'll take help from anyone. Even this weasel. "Mayor, please help me out, I—"

"Frances Vega, you and Katie Parker have thirty seconds to make your way down this ladder and get off that roof."

"No!" Frances's voice overlaps mine.

"Be glad to. What I've been *trying* to tell everyone is that my leg is—"

"Mayor Crowley!" Walking on the top of his van, Rick Saldano inches closer to the mayor. "How do you feel about these two girls protesting the fact you are forcing Buford Hollis out of business?"

"I'm not protesting anything here. I simply want someone to go in the snack bar and just—"

"I'm not forcing anything, young man." The mayor's face reddens. "The drive-in is an eyesore and is crumbling around Buford."

"Actually it's crumbling around me." Hello, girl with dangling leg here. Anybody care that I have roof parts sticking into places that are totally inappropriate and uncomfortable?

"Miss Vega does not believe she was given ample opportunity to obtain signatures."

My neck aches from following the bouncing conversation and holding my weight up.

"Those kids were given a fair deadline!" The mayor's cowboy hat bobbles as he shakes his head. "It is absolutely not my fault they couldn't rally enough of the citizens to back them."

"That's not true!" Frances shouts. "Mr. Saldano, it's not our fault it rained. Had we stayed out in the weather, someone probably would have gotten struck by lightning or hurt. I knew the mayor wouldn't want that on his conscience."

"Losing circulation here! Do you want *amputation* on your conscience?"

"Mr. Mayor, would you please tell our viewers what you plan to do with this property after you tear down Bubba's Big Picture?"

The mayor opens and closes his mouth guppy-style a few times. "I . . . I plan to—"

"Put in a strip mall." Frances crosses her arms and glares down at the mayor. *Oh, don't make her mad, mayor. One kick of her flip flop, and you and that ladder are headed south like a big, fat, Texas torpedo.* "He doesn't care he's destroying the livelihood of Buford Hollis and his family. Who cares if Buford's kids have food on the table, right, Mayor Crowley?"

"Now just a minute there, you little—" Rick's cameraman moves in for a close-up, and the mayor recovers. "I am not the enemy here, Miss Vega!"

"Well, we're not leaving this roof until you agree not to tear down the drive-in."

"You are out of your mind!" The mayor stabs a finger toward Frances. "Get off this roof or I'll—"

Her dark eyes narrow. "You'll what?" Rick Saldano follows their every word.

A siren whirls in the distance, and the mayor's face settles into a satisfied grin. "I won't do anything, my dear. The police can take it from here. You are trespassing on private property—a condemned piece of property at that."

Frances thrust out both arms. "Arrest me, if you must! I will not go without a fight! You will have to peel me from this rooftop!"

Yeah, if someone could just peel my pj's from a nail . . . I can't feel my toes anymore.

Rick's eyes widen. "Tom, he's going to arrest these kids. Let's get another camera out here quick."

"Now hold on! I didn't say I would have the girls *arrested.*"

"Yes, you did!" Frances growls.

"No, I did not!"

The rest of the conversation is lost on me as a new member is added to the roof.

Charlie. Crawling up from the opposite side.

"Charlie!" I gush, like he's the water in my drought. "Help me. Please!" His eyes take in my condition and he rushes to my side. "Be careful. The roof's rotten here."

"Nash brought a ladder. I thought I heard a weird noise earlier."

"Oh, that was just Frances doing her 'give me Bubba's or give me death' speech."

He tugs on the particleboard around my leg. "No, I meant the splitting sound."

"Oh." I glance toward Frances, still embroiled in a fiery conversation with the mayor. "Took you long enough then. Hey!" I yip as his hands get too close to . . . well, too close to mention.

His hands fly away. "Sorry. What can I do to help?"

"That ain't it," I droll. "Look, I think my pants are hung on a nail in the concession stand. You have to get in there and get me loose."

"I'll be right back. If I have to bust down that door, I will." He comes to his feet, his eyes intense on mine. "But don't move a muscle until I get back up here. It's not safe."

My rescuer steps back over the ladder and disappears.

My gosh, we've got more plots lines here today than an episode of *General Hospital*.

"I'm an honors student! I'm vice-president of the student council!" I tune in as Frances shouts her credentials to the reporter and mayor. The police sirens grow louder.

Below me I hear the pounding of what must be Charlie's body meeting the door of the snack bar. Followed by grunting.

Then the building quakes as the force against the door grows heavier. Louder. Nash's voice mixes with Charlie's.

"We can't get it yet, Katie, but we will. Just hold on and be patient!"

"Charlie!" I yell. "This place belongs to Buford Hollis, remember?"

"Yeah?" Comes his breathless response.

"So did you think about trying the knob?"

Silence from below me. "Oh." And then the blessed sound of a door opening. "We're in!"

Amen. Hallelujah. Praise and glory. And a woo-hoo on top of that.

"Are you in your *pajamas*?" Charlie's voice travels from beneath me.

"Yeah," I speak toward the hole my leg occupies. "I know my Tweety Bird pants are hot, but try to focus."

He laughs. And as freedom is seconds away, I realize we've both forgotten we're mad at each other.

There's a pull on my leg, then a small tug. "Nash has to cut you out of here."

"Don't take anymore than you have to, big boy." Nash carries a knife? Good to know.

I feel Charlie's arm on my calf. Or somebody's. Who cares whose it is. Whoever breaks me loose can touch my leg all they want.

"Gotcha!"

And my leg is free.

"Don't move, Katie. I'll be right up."

Charlie's shoes are quick and loud on Nash's ladder. "Hey." He smiles as he throws a leg over.

"Hey, what's up? Just hanging out, myself."

He steps near me, carefully as if I'm on ice that could break through. "I'm going to pick you up, okay?"

"What? Charlie, no. This is ridiculous. We'll both fall through. I'm getting up myself."

"Don't move, I mean it." His breath is warm on my cheek as he squats down. One hand weaves under my arms and the other cradles my left leg, then slowly, inch by inch, my right.

Oh, right leg. At last, we are reunited. How I've missed you. I shall never crash through a building and part with you again.

"Are you okay?" Charlie's face, so full of concern, quickens my heart.

"Yes, I'm fine. Seriously, just put me down." Did that sound convincing? Hope it wasn't too strong. Because right here next to his chest is a fine place to be. Yes, I know. So very weak.

"All right, I'm going to lower you to the ground slowly."

Drat. After all I endured, is a little cuddle time with my off-limits hero too much to ask for?

I feel the granite-hard contours of his fab abs as he slowly slides me down. My left leg lands solidly on the surface of the roof. I lower my stiff, right leg, stretching it beneath me, just a bit more, and—"Ow!"

Charlie clutches me as I lean into him. "What's wrong?"

I shake my head and sweat beads at my temple. "I don't know. Probably just sore from being in the same position so long." Unused to the movement, my right leg tingles as I touch my toe down then my heel and lower all my body weight. "Owwww!" I yelp and hop back into Charlie's waiting arms. "Something's not right!"

"You're telling me. Hold it right there, son."

With a worried glance at me, Charlie takes one big step backward away from the hole in the roof and swivels around. My arms tighten on his neck, and I suck in a breath.

Gone is the mayor. But in his place stands the In Between police chief. "I'm going to have to ask you kids to come with me. We have some talking to do." He spits to the ground below. "Downtown."

* * *

"SO CHARLIE *CARRIED* you in his arms?" Maxine clutches her heart and slumps into her seat at the kitchen table. "Why didn't the news crew get *that*?"

I lift a bite of meatless spaghetti to my mouth and readjust my propped foot on the chair across from me. "They were too busy zooming in on the mayor siccing the police chief on Frances." And Frances played it for all it was worth.

"Katie, are you ready for some more Advil?" Millie moves my crutches and settles into the seat next to me, her face tight with concern. "You're lucky you got by with a sprain and not a broken ankle."

"Well," Maxine harrumphs. "Even though your actions today got you a reprieve on the demolition, I still wish that Rick Saldano would've showed footage of you in the clutches of your hero."

I swallow my meds and try not to look at my ugly Aircast. "Why?"

"Maybe Sam would've been watching and could've seen what a *real* act of romance looks like."

I shift in my seat, my left cheek already asleep. "How do you think Channel Five News got there so quickly? How could they have known we were on the roof before the mayor?"

Millie shakes her head, her wigged tresses swaying. "Just another crazy element to the day, I guess."

"I don't know about *crazy*." Maxine lifts a perfectly shaped brow. "I prefer the word *strategic*."

My mouth drops. "*You!* You called them!"

She shrugs. "Who—me? I don't know what you're talking about. That would be a betrayal to my sweet admirer, the good mayor." She stands up, pushes her chair in and glides out of the room, her hips swaying like a southern belle. And her throaty laugh lingering behind.

# Chapter Twenty-One

HOW DO YOU make days and weeks pass slowly?

Crutches. Sore armpits. Time spent immovable and the captive audience of one Maxine Simmons. And some super fun summer school classes.

And yet, before I know it, D-Day is here. My departure day is tomorrow, when the Scotts will load me and my crippled carcass into their Honda and drive me to Middleton, Texas, to reunite with my mom.

The last three weeks have been like a school year—it goes so slow, and yet on the other hand, it's hard to believe the time has passed.

But it has. My time in In Between is over.

And I tear up every time I think about it, every time someone mentions it. Every time Millie gets that look in her eyes, like she's committing my face to memory. Or maybe she's worried I'll fall off the wagon of success, and she's learning my face in case she's expecting to see it on a Wanted poster some day.

"Katie?" Millie's voice draws my head up. She opens my door and pokes her head in. Her brown eyes assess my bedroom and the packing progress. "Are you sure you don't want any help?"

This is the same question she's been asking. All week. Yes, the only thing on my to-do list besides sit around and look pitiful with my propped-up leg, was to pack my belongings. And here it is, the night before I leave this room forever, and all I've managed to throw in a suitcase is my In Between High yearbook and a bottle of Midol.

Millie crosses the room to sit on the bed next to me. She pats Rocky on the head as he rolls over and snores beside us. "Honey, are you doing okay?"

"Yeah, I'm fine. Of course, I'm good." Perfect. Wonderful.

"You don't seem yourself today."

"What makes you say that?"

She points. "The dog is drooling on your bed, and not only are you letting him, but you haven't started yelling."

My tired eyes travel to Rocky.

And it crashes in on me—all of it. The sadness, the confusion, the hurt. The dueling need to stay and yet to go. The fear. But mostly just this unnamable ache that's been lodged in my chest ever since my mom showed up in In Between. I thought it would go away. But it hasn't.

Pressure builds behind my eyes, and I turn my head and sniff, then cover my mouth and pretend to cough as I choke with tears.

"Katie?"

I shake my head. All I can do is shake my head. There are no words. Hallmark doesn't make a card that addresses what I'm going through, what I feel.

Millie scoots closer, and I inhale her light perfume as her fragile arms loop around me with strength and pull me to her.

And the floodgates open.

We sit that way for what seems like hours, but could only be minutes as Millie strokes my hair and gently rocks the two of us. She then begins to pray over me, bathing me in her words of love, hope, and encouragement. And though I didn't think it was possible, understanding.

"And God, we know this is tearing Katie apart. It's tearing all of us apart."

I'm soaking Millie's shirt.

"But we know this is part of your plan, that you are at work here. And though we may not comprehend it now, your plan is unfolding, and you have Katie under your wing."

I have a Kleenex-box-worth of snot going on right now.

"Though it's one of the hardest things we've ever had to do, this family surrenders Katie to you, God. We know she is cloaked in your protection, and she has the strength and your guidance to see her through."

I can't see anything right now; my eyes filled to the brim.

"God, we love Katie, and know you do too. We pray you continue to grow her faith and reveal yourself to her daily as she returns to her mother." Millie closes the prayer, then presses a kiss to my forehead. "Love you, kid."

"I love you too." More tears. *Aw, stop it, stop it,* stop *it.* Millie and James are taking me out to eat tonight, and I don't want to hit the town with swollen eyes and a Rudolph nose.

"Sure you don't want me to help you pack? I know it can't be easy on your crutches."

"You mean my sticks of Satan?" Seriously, I hate these things. They're evil. The doctor said if I had a hard time with crutches, I could get a walker with wheels on it. Yeah, even better. Maxine said she had plenty of friends who'd loan me theirs.

I can't believe I finally get my driver's license and I can't even drive! Add that to the list of things unfair in my life.

"I want to pack, Millie." I just need some alone time in my room, with my things. Decide what to leave, what to take with me.

"Where's the new suitcase I got you?"

"Um . . . in the closet." Where you left it a few weeks ago.

"And the packing boxes?"

"Closet." Millie arches a brow at this. "I'll get to it tonight when we get back. It shouldn't take long. I'm mostly just taking my clothes. Mom said she doesn't have a lot of room in the trailer." Plus she needs the extra space for her coffee mug collection. Totally not kidding—my mom collects coffee cups. Mugs and drugs—that's what Bobbie Ann Mason was into about this time last year.

Millie hugs me again. "Well, if you're not going to fill your boxes, then start getting beautiful for dinner. You have an hour. Of course, if you get ready at the same rate you pack, we won't get to leave until midnight."

I force a smile. "Very funny."

"Where are we going?" Maxine sweeps into the room, her hair in curlers. "Somewhere fancy?"

Millie laughs as her mom joins us on the bed, parking her rump on my other side. "Only the best for Katie. We're getting out of In Between and heading to that steak house on the lake."

"Oh, dining on the water. How romantic." Maxine digs out more seating room by shoving the dog away with her butt.

"Has it ever occurred to you that your idea of romance is overrated and unrealistic?" I dare to ask.

My foster grandmother huffs. "Says the girl who's been alive a whopping sixteen years."

"Almost seventeen." My birthday's in August.

"Ohhhh, excuse me. Almost seventeen." She levels her nose with mine. "A little candlelight, roses, and sweet nothings whispered in my ear are not too much to expect from a man. Just look at William—"

*Ick*. "I'd rather not."

"He's not all that bad, Katie." Thought Maxine's tone doesn't sound like even she's completely convinced. "He did agree to let Buford Hollis have the rest of the summer to raise the funds to save his drive-in."

"Yeah," I snort. "Because he's been getting truck-loads of hate mail ever since the news ran the footage of Crowley cornering us on the rooftop." And my injury sealed the deal. The town really felt sorry for me. And instead of blaming it on Buford and his dilapidated building, they threw all the responsibility on the mayor. Not sure if four to six weeks on crutches was worth it, but it definitely made

Frances's year.

* * *

ASIDE FROM MY ankle throbbing, dinner is a totally awesome affair, with me eating more than my own body weight in shrimp and steak. And then the dessert cart arrives, and Millie lets us order one of everything.

As I swallow a bite of chocolate mousse, mixed with a bite of strawberry shortcake—okay, and a bite of tiramisu—I shut my eyes and savor the flavors. It will be a long, long time before I have good food again. I want to remember this moment of decadence. Maybe I should wrap up a piece of cheesecake and put it in my purse. Like Maxine's doing.

"We thought we'd stop by the Valiant—give you a moment to say good-bye." James looks at me over the rim of his coffee cup.

"Yeah . . . that would be nice." So many things, so many people to say good-bye to. Everyone says, "It's not good-bye. It's just good-bye for now." But yeah, it is. I know it's good-bye—for good.

"Open your present." Maxine claps her hands, her face intense on the box that's been sitting in front of me all night.

I glance at James and Millie, who nod in agreement.

"I didn't get you guys anything." Yet another thing for me to feel rotten about.

"You are our gift, Katie." The candlelight highlights Millie's warm smile. "Open it."

I slip my finger under a corner of the pink and brown paper, knowing it was lovingly wrapped by my foster mom, and that she was thinking of me even when picking out the paper.

The wrapping falls away and reveals my present. "A camera!" I rip into the box and pull out a small, flat digital camera. "I love it!"

"It's ready to go," James says. "It syncs with your laptop. Go ahead—take a picture."

I turn the power on and hold the camera up. "Something's not right. It's just a blur in the lens."

"Mom, get out of the way."

I lower my camera and see Maxine leaning over the table, her face a centimeter away from me. "I thought you'd want a close up."

"Not of your nose hairs." I lean back into my chair. "You guys get together." And I snap a few pictures.

"Oh, waiter?" Millie hails our server. "Would you take a picture of our family?"

We all lean toward the center of the table, and I smile—surrounded by the people who have created a home for me. Who have changed my life. Who know me better than my own mother. And who have made a mark on my life.

On the ride to the Valiant, I watch In Between pass me by, and it's everything I can do not to demand James stop the car and let me out, so I can photograph every building, street, and store I see.

I clutch my camera as James helps me out of the Honda and onto my crutches.

James holds the door open for me, and I run my hand down the wooden panels as I pass through into the darkened lobby. The Valiant and I go way back. It was here I met Sam Dayberry. It was at this theatre I worked my tail off when I first arrived—and got myself hauled downtown and in some serious trouble. And it was on this stage I fell into the part of Juliet and discovered myself in the Valiant spotlight.

"Let me get the door and the lights." James steps in front of me and swings the theatre doors wide.

"*Surprise!*" I teeter on my crutches as the lights flare to life, and I'm greeted by the voices of what must be half of the town. Cameras flash in my eyes, and I struggle to close my gaping mouth.

Frances steps forward and hugs me tight.

"For me?" I whisper in her ear.

She holds me at arms length. "For you, Katie Parker. Come on, see who all's here."

For the next forty-five minutes I hobble all over the theatre, receiving well-wishes and parting advice.

And every time someone hugs me or pats my back, I come that much closer to losing it—to throwing myself in the floor and begging these people not to let me go.

But it would just be really awkward with my cast, so probably not worth it.

I mingle through the crowds, laughing and reminiscing with the newly divorced Mrs. Hall, my drama teacher, who's here with a date—an artsy-looking fellow. I lecture Nash on taking care of my best friend in my absence. And I promise Pastor Mike and his wife I will find a church home in Middleton.

"Hey, remember me?" Brian steps forward, wearing a Frodo Rocks T-shirt, and engulfs me in a bear hug. "I wrote a special good-bye song for you."

"Oh." I smile. "How nice." Do *not* break out the musical instruments.

"It's called 'Katie is a Lady'."

I laugh. "Wow, and so . . . deep too."

"Katie—"

I turn around to find my favorite English teacher, Ms. Dillon. "Thanks for coming." I can't believe all these people are here. For me.

"I wouldn't have missed it for anything." She reaches into her giant purse and pulls out a stack of papers. "Your final. I thought you might want it."

"Oh. Okay." I guess.

She grins, revealing perfect, Jessica Simpson teeth. "It's not done."

"But I've already received my grade. It was totally done."

"Nope." She lays her hand at my back. "I want you to do the bonus point assignment—to write about your future. Even though it's too late for credit, I feel your story is not complete. There's still more to tell."

I roll the paper into a tube. "Six pages says done to me."

She adjusts her bag and waves at someone across the room. "Nope. Finish the assignment this summer and e-mail it to me."

I open my mouth to politely refuse.

"The paper isn't done—and neither are you." And with a wink, my English teacher dissolves into the masses and leaves me standing there.

Feeling a little fatigued at all the hugging and socializing, I go in search of a piece of cake at the refreshment table.

"Nice replica of a Chihuahua, eh?" Maxine puts her plate down and cuts me a slice. "Corner piece, right?"

I smile. She knows me so well. "I can't believe you were able to keep this a secret."

Her face contracts in outrage. "I beg your pardon? *Moi*? Of course, I could be counted on to keep this secret."

"When did they tell you?"

She stuffs a bite of cake between her lips. "About thirty minutes ago."

I kiss her cheek and we giggle—like the girls that we are. "Sam just got here." I look toward the door. "Maybe you should bring him a piece of cake."

Maxine snorts. "Yeah, like the Chihuahua's butt."

I grab her wrist. "Maxine, take him a piece of cake."

"What if he's with Betty Lou?"

"Maxine—"

"All right," she says on a sigh. "But that rat-tailed hussy better not be here tonight. I'm not in the mood to duke it out."

Oh, young love.

I peek into a galvanized bucket on the table and feel tears spring to my eyes. There in their iced-down-glory, are as many Diet Dr. Peppers as a girl could possibly want. This I need a picture of.

With piercing regret, I leave the drinks alone, knowing I can't carry a plate *and* a can, and amble my way backstage.

Setting my cake down, I place both crutches under my right armpit, and holding onto the rail, hobble my way up the steps. I take a resting breath or two at the top, then walk onto the stage, behind the curtains.

I look toward the ceiling, then find the location the spotlight would fall on.

This is it. This is the spot where my life became possible. Sure, I got saved at church, but on another level—I got saved right here. This place is like church to me. It's holy. I love the smell, the sounds. And I will cling to the memories of the Valiant for all my days. This is where I was the love of Romeo's life. And it was here I was in *Cinderella.* Okay, I was the ugly stepsister—with a hideous prosthetic nose—but still, I delivered an Academy-worthy performance.

And now . . . my time here is done. I look down at the scarred black floor and wonder if this is the last time my feet will ever touch it.

I jump as the floor creaks behind me, and there stands Charlie Benson.

"Hey. You scared me." I was having a moment here—with my stage.

He sticks his hands in his jean pockets. His lips lift in a cautious smile. "Sorry. Frances was looking for you a minute ago. I figured you'd be up here."

My eyes pan the stage area again, and I inhale deeply. "It's pretty, isn't it?"

Charlie steps closer, a hand resting on my crutch. His eyes pull me in. "Very pretty."

"Charlie, I—"

"Katie—" Our words mesh and overlap.

"You first." Tingles race along my spine. I can't believe he's not out of my system yet.

His gray eyes drop to the floor, and I think he's not going to speak. Then finally, "I know I overreacted at the drive-in a few weeks ago."

"Yeah, you did." I am not letting you off easy, dude.

"I don't want to end things on a bad note. I don't want you to leave and there be this dark blot on our friendship."

There's that F word again. But I guess I'll take friendship.

He runs a tanned hand through his hair. "I was upset you had told Chelsea what you knew about her dad." His voice drops. "I trusted you with that information. I hadn't shared that with anyone else."

"But I didn't—"

"I know you were mad at me. I get that now. We do stupid things when we're mad."

Oh, I can think of a few right now. "That's not how it went down, Charlie."

"It doesn't matter anymore."

"Yes, it does. Did Chelsea tell you what she said to—"

"We talked about it. She's forgiven you. I've forgiven you."

My face burns scarlet red. "How kind." My fingers itch to totally take him out with my crutch. "Look, I don't think you have the story straight, so—"

"I'm sorry I let you go, Katie."

I close my mouth on some gospel truth about Chelsea. "What?"

Charlie's hands move up my arms and onto my shoulders where they rest. His eyes lock onto mine. "I'm sorry I walked away from us. I did need to help Chelsea—still do. But I think I was just running scared too."

"You? Scared?" Great, now I'm reduced to single syllable responses.

"It's taking me a while to get it. But that morning I pulled you from the roof of the snack bar . . ."

"Yeah?" Am I drooling yet?

"I was standing below, and I was thinking about how mad I was at you, wondering why I was even there."

I nod my head as he rubs my arms. "And then I heard you scream and the wood split. I was panicked. But then I heard you yelling at Frances, and I knew you were probably okay."

"Uh-huh." He smells so good.

"And I realized none of it mattered—not our fights, not our past relationships, not even Chelsea."

Wait a minute—Chelsea doesn't matter? Can I get that in writing—like in blood?

"I made a huge mistake by shutting you out when I befriended Chelsea again. But when I pulled you off the rooftop, it hit me that you were different. Before I had just dated Chelsea. And before Chelsea—a girl who could've been her twin. But you . . . you were . . . you." He smiles and steps closer. "I realized I had never felt that way about a girl before—" Charlie leans in until our lips are a breath apart. His gaze travels to my mouth. "Until you."

Standing on my Valiant stage, Charlie Benson lowers his face to mine and holds me captive with a long, slow kiss.

Quite possibly better than any standing ovation.

# Chapter Twenty-Two

THE RIDE TO my mom's is filled with alternating stretches of silence and lengthy bursts of chatter. And the closer we get to Middleton, the quieter I become.

I didn't sleep at all last night, and I feel the effects today. I'm drained—of energy and of feeling. When I left this morning, I waved good-bye to friends standing in my driveway—Frances, Charlie, Nash, Hannah, Sam Dayberry, Pastor Mike, his wife, and a few others. I didn't even cry. It's like there's nothing left to cry. All dried up.

Except for my bladder. It's *so* not dried up. James has had to stop for me every hour. That's what I get for chugging Diet Dr. Pepper this morning like a marathon runner downing Gatorade.

Millie turns around in her seat. "Did you remember to pack your—"

"Yes."

"How did you know what I was going to ask?"

"Because we've gone through every possible item I've ever owned, touched, or seen in my life."

"Besides"—Maxine kicks off her flip-flops—"if Katie forgets something, that gives us an excuse to bring it to her." She levels her blue eyes at me. "Not that I'll miss you or anything."

At this I can smile. "Whatever."

"I won't." She pats her sunshine yellow hair. "Since the remodel on my apartment has been delayed *again*, I can enjoy all the space of your room all to myself. Have a few more sleepovers. Hang my pantyhose up wherever I want."

"You'll be missing my shoe collection by tonight." But I did leave her my newest pair of Converse. I stuck them under her pillow, along with a letter telling her that, along with Frances, she's my best friend. And instructions on how to run the DVD player in our room. Her room.

I left James and Millie letters too.

Rocky got nothing. Good riddance.

An hour and a half later James pulls the truck into a mobile home park. We drive past the sign that says "Happy Meadows." I glance out the window—rows and rows of trailers, a few trash dumpsters, some apartments across the street, and a rundown Quickie Mart. Where's the meadow?

And where's my happiness?

I'm coming home to my mom. Shouldn't I be excited? Content? Feel oh-so-complete?

Instead I feel oh-so-gonna-hurl.

And I need to tinkle. Again.

Millie unfolds a piece of paper and reads it to James. "Turn on Trail View, then on Wingard. Number sixteen."

We wheel into a small gravel drive, pulling up next to a beige singlewide trailer. A few stray cats scatter from the wooden steps leading to the trailer as James gets out and opens my door.

"Here we are," Millie says, her eyes fixed on mine.

Yes, here *we* are. Here's where I'll stay, and you'll leave. *God, help me to keep it together and not totally break down when they drive away.*

As everyone else heads to the back of the truck to retrieve my stuff, I'm pulled toward the trailer, where I simply stand in front of it. And stare. And remind myself to breathe.

And my mom flings open the door. "Katie!" She scrambles down the steps, knocking a bowl of kitty water to the ground, and races to me.

I'm engulfed in a hug, Bobbie Ann Parker's twig-like arms circling around me as I bear my weight onto my crutches.

"Hi, Mom." *This is right, isn't it, God? This is where I'm supposed to be? Granted, I think I cut out my heart and left it in In Between, but here with my mom—it's gotta be right. Right?*

She takes a step back, her hands on my shoulders and just looks at me, a smile turning up her mouth.

This is probably where I should be telling her how happy I am to see her, how glad I am to be back "home."

But I can't find the words. Can't make them come out.

It's not like she and I have talked much over the last year and a half. Even in the last month, she's barely called. And when she did, it was just to give me updates on her progress to pass on to James and Millie. She didn't even ask how my finals went or if I passed my summer school class. Or how I felt about all of this. My mom doesn't know my best friend at school is Frances, James sneaks me Oreos at least once a week from his private stash, science is my worst subject, and my favorite color is now green.

And my ankle hurts like a semi-truck is sitting on it. Or Rocky. Same difference.

"Hello, Bobbie Ann." Millie rests a small suitcase beside me. Her hand moves in small circles at my back as she stands next to me.

"Looks like you must've packed an entire Wal-Mart store." My mom laughs as she surveys my three suitcases and five boxes. "That's a lot of stuff." She casts a worried glance my way.

"A girl needs her necessities." Maxine rests an elbow on my crutch and flanks my other side. "I'm sure you'll find the room. If not . . ."

"Mother—" Millie warns.

"Where do you want me to put all this?" James heaves the last bag onto the steps by the door.

My mom toys with the edge of her Metallica t-shirt as she looks at looks at each one of us "Um . . . why don't we go in and put her things in her room and sit for a bit?"

I know my mom can't wait for the Scotts and Maxine to clear out.

And I don't want them to leave.

Maybe I could talk James into leaving Maxine.

The inside of Mom's trailer smells like stale cigarette smoke and vanilla air freshener. She shows James into my room, and I don't even bother following. I collapse into a faded blue chair as if sitting for the last four hours in that truck hadn't been enough.

I raise my head and find Maxine and Millie both studying me. I force a smile and hope it looks real. I am an actress after all.

"You okay?" Millie takes a seat across the small living room.

"Oh, sure." More smiling. "Fine." Mouth hurting.

Maxine snaps her gum. "Know what's going to get me through all this?"

I shrug. "Ben and Jerry's?"

"Know what *else* is going to get me through?"

"I dunno."

"The G.O.G., baby." She nods sure and slow. "The G.O.G."

I can't help but smile. The grace of God. Yep, I'll have a double order of that, please.

My mom and James reappear, Mom chattering away. "So we'll get her all enrolled in the high school here for next year." She swoops her faded red hair into a ponytail, tying it off with a rubber band from her wrist. "Guess what the Middleton mascot is, Katie?"

"I don't know." Couldn't get any worse than an In Between Chihuahua.

"A muskrat."

I stand corrected.

"How about we help you unpack and get all settled?" Millie's voice is hopeful.

I shake my head. "No. I'll do it later."

"We thought maybe we could all have lunch somewhere together." James stands in the kitchen area, which is open to the living room.

"There's not a restaurant for miles. Well, there's a hamburger joint, but it's closed on the weekends."

Maxine and I trade glances. Me without easy access to fast food? This does not bode well.

"But I made a casserole and a cake last night. I was going to save it for tonight, a little celebration for me and Katie." My mom plays with the silver ring on her right hand. "I guess we could eat it now." She doesn't look very happy about the idea.

"That would be great." I smile, though secretly I worry about my mom's cooking. A casserole? Since when could she even decipher a recipe? "You guys can stay, right?"

Millie watches my mom. "If you're sure it's okay."

"It's fine." Mom's unenthusiastic response tenses my shoulders. "I'll just preheat the oven. Katie, would you like to join me in the kitchen?"

James helps me out of my chair and back onto my crutches, my instruments of pain and torture. I step into the kitchen, as my mom opens the fridge.

She whispers low. "I know this is hard for you—"

"Do you?"

Bobbie Ann's brows snap together. "Don't take that tone with me. I'm your mother," she hisses. "I'm your family." She points toward the living room. "Not them." Mom pulls out a covered dish, places it on the counter, then inhales deep. Her face calms. "Babe, I know you think a lot of those people."

Kinda love them and stuff.

"And I'm grateful to them for all they've done. But I've waited a long time to have my daughter back."

"Mom, I want us to all have lunch together. It will be my last chance to be with the Scotts and Maxine for a while." At her frown I add, "And it will give you a chance to get to know them better." I lift the foil on the casserole. "What is it? Smells good," I lie. Smells . . . funky.

"Tuna casserole." Her face splits into a grin. "It's gonna be good." She pats my hair, then shoves past me to turn on the oven.

I hate tuna. I've always hated tuna. *This* was the special dish she prepared just for me? Some mayo, some chips, some noodles, and pieces of the stinkiest fish ever shoved into a can? My mom wanted to commemorate my homecoming with smelly fish?

An hour later, I help Millie clear the table of the paper plates, as my mom continues to avoid Maxine's relentless interrogation.

"I don't know who Marlena is, I'm sorry Mrs. Simmons. She sounds like a real nice lady though." Maxine continues to grill my mom, evaluating her worth based on her knowledge of daytime television. "No, I don't watch the *View*, so I wouldn't know if Barbara Walters got her eyes done this year or not . . ."

"I think I would like for you to help me unpack, Millie."

My mom stops mid-sentence, her hazel eyes snapping to me. "I can help you."

"I know. But if we all worked together, it would get done quicker." And keep my In Between family here longer. "My ankle is bothering me today."

"Oh." My mom puts our Dixie cups on the counter and straightens. "Well, let's get started then, huh?"

"That reminds me—" Millie sashays back into the living room for her purse. "I wrote down some instructions for Katie's ankle. She's not out of the woods yet, and so I wanted you to have the instructions. Like now"—Millie holds up her list—"is time for her Advil. And next week she has an appointment with a Doctor Bernard here. I made the appointment myself. He'll need to check her progress. I've already had her file faxed to him."

The clock ticks in the kitchen. Bobbie Ann stares at Millie for a few tense seconds, her mouth in a grim line. "Thank you." She clears her throat and forces a smile. "I appreciate the help. I will be sure and get her to the doctor, of course. I wasn't going to neglect her."

"I didn't think you would." Millie hands her my instructions. "I simply didn't want to take any chances with Katie. I mean her ankle."

My mom nods and lays the paper down on the counter, next to what's left of the tuna casserole.

"Okay, let's go unpack." I look between the two ladies. "Come on. I'm getting tired." Tired of the tension.

With Maxine still quizzing my mom on totally irrelevant facts, the four of us ladies walk to the back of the trailer and into my room.

My heart stops a beat.

My eyes tear, and I quickly dash it away with my hand. Why did I think I would walk in here and it would look just like my bedroom at the Scotts? My stuff is all here. I'm here. But this isn't it. By a long stretch.

Ivy printed wallpaper covers the walls in the small room. A twin bed takes up most of the space. My mom has a tan comforter on the bed and a single, white pillow. Over the bed hangs a poster of Orlando Bloom.

"Welcome home, Katie!" My mom squeezes my shoulders. "This is your new room! What do you think?"

I think I want to be someone else. Someone who isn't torn between two homes, two families.

Someone who isn't uncertain of every breath of her future.

# Chapter Twenty-Three

"I GUESS WE'LL go."

Three hours later, my In Between family is ready to leave.

Ready to leave me.

We've had a tour of town. (*So* not impressive. Smaller than In Between, which I didn't even know was possible.) We've eaten mom's version of homemade cake (Duncan Hines), rearranged my room (I now want the bed on the left . . . no, the right), and as a last stalling resort, I made Millie help me organize my underwear by color.

My mom shakes hands with everyone, then with a glance at me, walks toward her bedroom.

"Walk us out, Katie." James curls his arm around my shoulders, and we follow Millie and Maxine into the yard.

Where we dissolve into a group hug, awkward crutches and all.

I cling to these people like they're the last life preserver on the Titanic. *Don't leave me*, I want to say.

But I know I can't.

Moments pass and finally we pull away.

"You've got your cell phone, so we're just a call away. Anytime." Millie tucks a piece of hair behind my ears. When I see her eyes fill, my throat closes.

James digs into his pocket and pulls out his wallet. The one I got him for his birthday a few months ago. "This is for you. It's for emergencies." He hands me a debit card. "Just in case there's ever anything you need."

I sniff and swipe a tear. "Like some iTunes purchases or a new purse?"

"Not quite what I had in mind." He tweaks my nose. "You'll know when and if you need to use it." In other words, if my mom forgets to buy me food or other important things. Like deodorant.

"Here's some cash too." Maxine stuffs a bill in my hand. "Some Diet Dr. Pepper money." She winks, then blows her nose into a tissue. "Woo! Allergies are bad out here."

"We love you, Katie." I look into the eyes of my foster mom—the woman whose love I didn't want. But now I can't imagine life without it. "We'll visit. You'll visit. I talked to your mom about spending Fourth of July with us, and she wasn't too keen on the idea. But we'll work on it. And there's Chihuahua Days that next week. When we celebrate our mighty mascot. You'll have to come for that weekend."

"Just don't forget me, okay?" *Please don't forget me.*

"Forget you?" Maxine chortles. "Sweet Pea, you're like mold. Just because you can't see it, doesn't mean it ain't there." She smacks me on the butt, then pulls me close. "Better not be anybody else putting their hands on your tushie, you got it?"

I nod and cling like a dryer sheet on pantyhose. "You patch things up with, Sam." I raise my head and stare her down. "That man loves you, and you love him. Quit making it complicated. This isn't *Days of Our Lives.* So quit being a drama queen; tell him you're sorry, and you want him back."

Maxine sticks out a hand. "Whatevs."

James swabs his glasses with his shirt. "Why don't I pray—for all of us." We gather into a circle again, arms and hands connected. My head on Millie's shoulder. My heart somewhere back in In Between. "God, we come to you now . . . hurting and rejoicing. We are a family, Lord."

My chest shakes as the tears rise.

"We grieve over the separation from Katie, the daughter of our heart."

A sob escapes my mouth, and I am powerless to stop it. I'm pulled in tighter to the circle.

"But we know this is your plan, and we wait with anticipation and faith to see where you are leading Katie. Where you are leading this family. We ask for strength for Katie. For wisdom. And for growth. This is a hard time for her, and we pray she will fix her gaze on you and grow as a child of a king. We pray for healing in her relationship with her mother . . ."

Millie's strong voice takes over. "And we pray for protection. Lay your hands on Katie and keep her safe and protected. Watch her as only you can. We entrust you to her. We surrender her to you."

"God, this is Maxine Simmons." Her watery voice quivers. "I love this kid something fierce, and I pray for her to never lose sight of her importance in this world, her value to us, and the knowledge she is on this planet to do great things. Give her guidance and keep her on the straight path. Because I am *not* afraid to ride my bike Ginger Rogers all day long to bust up another party or tear her from harm's way. Jesus, the only person who has the right to put the hurt on Katie Parker is me."

James clears his throat then wraps up the prayer. "Amen."

I raise my head as Millie hands me a Kleenex from her purse. "Well, I guess this is good-bye for now," I say when I find my voice.

"We love you, Katie."

I bob my head. "I know. Love you too." I manage a wobbly smile. "I'll be fine here. I'll keep you updated. Who knows, before too long Bobbie Ann and I will be dressing alike and sporting identical tattoos."

I laugh at Millie's frown.

"I want to know if *anything* happens with you guys. Any cancer updates, reengagements, Amy contacts, anything. I want to hear it all."

"Are you sure you feel okay here?" James asks.

"Yeah. Things are fine. I can tell my mom's made lots of progress." Minus the tuna casserole. "I know this is where I'm supposed to be." Wow, that was mature. Totally did not sound like me.

Millie stands in front of me and places her soft hands on my cheeks. "If you need *anything*, you call. Do you understand? Day or night. We can be here in no time."

"Got it." I'm sure if I call every time I'm going to miss them, they'd have to leave In Between and move into my bedroom. "It's okay . . . you can leave me." Somehow, it will be okay. "You guys can go."

"You know we don't want to?"

"I know, Millie," I whisper, my voice broken. "I have to do this."

We hold onto each other one last time before my foster family climbs into James's truck. The sound of the engine tears into my heart. It's all so final. They're really leaving. And I can't go with them. How is it they will be in In Between, and I won't be there with them? How is it I'll exist in a world where I don't see them every day? No more Millie hugs. No more late night hot fudge sundaes with Maxine. No American Idol watching with James. No more organic, gluten-free waffles with tofu sausage and free range scrambled eggs. Who knew I could miss that?

"Bye!" I yell and wave my hand in the air. Maxine hangs her head out the window like Rocky would if he had been invited. She blows wild, frantic kisses until the truck disappears.

*Oh, God. Oh, God. Oh, God. Where are you in this?* I clutch my stomach and lower myself to the ground. I want to chase that truck. But they would stop. I know they would. And they can't.

I can't let them.

# Chapter Twenty-Four

I STALL A full thirty minutes before going back in. I am not one of those pretty criers, so it's important to wait until the splotches and puffiness goes away.

I almost sprain my other ankle, but I finally maneuver back up the stairs. The metal screen door squeaks as I step into the trailer. My mom sits on the faded couch, flipping through the channels on the TV. I hesitate before sitting beside her.

She pats my knee. "I'm glad you're here."

"Me too." I'm sure at some point I will be. I hope.

"You'll forget about the Scotts in no time."

I close my eyes. I'm too spent to be mad, even though her statement is yell-worthy. "I don't want to forget the Scotts, Mom."

A rerun of *Friends* blares to life. "Those people can't replace your real family."

I look at my mom, her eyes clouded with things I can't even comprehend. Her face etched with lines of a hard life, even though she's at least twenty years younger than Millie. Her hair struggles to stay in the ponytail. She reaches for her pack of cigarettes, now lying open on the scarred coffee table. Interesting how she waited until the Scotts were gone to pull out the smokes.

Her rough hands flick the lighter, and she inhales deeply.

"Mom, it smells like one big Marlboro in here. Could you maybe smoke outside?"

Bobbie Ann tosses her Bic, and it skids across the table. "Since when did it bother you?"

"Hello, secondhand smoke kills. Do you really want that on your shoulders?" On top of everything else.

"Then don't breathe it in."

I blink. "Where would you like me to acquire my oxygen then?"

"You know, I don't like your attitude. I picked up on it the minute I saw you in In Between that weekend."

"I don't have an attitude." Well, maybe the my-rehabbed-druggie-mom-smokes-and-it's-gross attitude. Or perhaps the you've-never-really-been-a-mom-to-me-and-now-we're-supposed-to-act-like-a-normal-mother-and-daughter attitude.

My mom whips her pointer finger in my face. "You have a snotty little attitude, and I will not put up with it. You're not better than me."

"I didn't say I was."

"You might as well. Just because I don't drive a fancy truck or I don't wear designer clothes."

"Millie doesn't wear designer clothes."

"I was talking about the other one."

"Just back off on the Scotts and Maxine, okay? They were very nice to you today."

"What is *that* supposed to mean?" Mom stands up and blows her smoke toward the ceiling. "You say that like I should be grateful they were kind?"

"That's not what I meant."

She paces the length of the living room, her eyes never leaving mine. "You just make sure your new uppity disposition is temporary. I can see it did you a lot of good, living with rich people."

"Rich?" I laugh. "A pastor and his wife—rich?"

"You don't think I saw the way your *pastor* and wife looked down their noses at me? I saw it." She takes another drag off her cigarette. Millie would freak if she knew I was on the receiving end of this nicotine pollution.

I prop my foot on the table, my ankle throbbing after my trek up the steps. "You've barely seen me in a year and a half." I swallow hard. "And *this* is how you want to spend our first day together? You didn't so much as pick up the phone until a few months ago, and *this* is what you most want to say to me?"

Her pacing stops and she plants a hand on one hip. "I've listened to enough of this. I don't want to hear anymore."

"You know what I want, Mom? I want us to get along. I want this to work. And I want you to want me to be here. I don't want to be here just because the state said you could have me back. I want to be here because you wanted your daughter—missed me, needed me." I hoist myself up and grab my crutches. "Because you love me and give a crap about me."

On shaking, sore arms, I lean into my crutches and hobble back to my room.

I settle onto the bed, grab the phone the Scotts gave me, and text Frances.

> TELL ME U R DOING SOMETHING MORE FUN ON UR SAT THAN DODGING CIG SMOKE AND FIGHTING W/ UR MOM.

In less than ten seconds, my phone beeps with her reply.

> WE MISS U ALREADY! NOTHING EXCITING HERE EITHER. A BBQ CHICKEN COOKOUT 2 RAISE MONEY 4 DRIVE IN.

I shut my phone. I was so busy this past week getting ready to leave and having mini-meltdowns, that I was totally out of the Bubba's Big Picture loop. I should be there. Selling chicken and stinking like cheap BBQ sauce. That would be so much fun. I wonder if Charlie is there.

I stay holed up in my room for another two hours. Headphones in, flipping through photo albums of In Between, reading, and just doing everything I can to avoid Mom-time. This is *so* not how I pictured my homecoming, you know? She barely acts happy to see me. We've been separated almost a year-and-a-half, so you'd think she'd be a little less bitter and a lot more joyful. I know *I'd* be glad to see me.

*God, how do I deal with this? You threw me into this mess. I guess I thought Mom would come out of prison and rehab all fixed. She's so not fixed. It's like you let me live on the green grass side, only to jerk me back to the side that's . . . um . . . grassless? Anyway, kinda need your help here. Are you even still on the job? I feel like you have totally forgotten about me. Like you gave me all the attention you could and now you're done. Well, I'm still here. And I need some serious God intervention.*

I startle at a knock at my door. "Katie?" Mom peeps her head in. "We're going to eat dinner in an hour." Her gaze flits across my room and takes in all the stuff I brought with me. Stuff the Scotts bought me.

She eases in and sits next to me on the bed. "We'll have a guest for dinner tonight." Her hazel eyes wait for my reaction.

"Your boyfriend?" It's everything I can do to keep a neutral tone.

Mom unwinds her hair from its ponytail and shakes it out. "Yeah." She smiles big. "You're gonna love him. He's very nice." She sighs. "Very cute."

I catch a glimpse of myself in the mirror behind the door. "Mom, I'm tired. I look like something the dog threw up, I probably smell, my makeup's disappeared, and I'm all out of politeness and manners."

"I noticed." She waves her hand. "But you'll love John." She clutches my knee. "He's amazing. He understands where I come from—he gets me, you know? I think . . . this might be the one."

I level her with a droll stare. "You've known each other a matter of months." And do you know how many "the ones" I've had to hear about over the course of my life?

"Love can't be measured by time."

"Yes, actually, it can. You're just now getting on your feet. This is so like you to just jump into something."

She stands up. "Now look, I don't know what happened to my daughter, but I sure wish you'd get her back. I will not allow you to speak to me like that. *I* am the mother. *You* are the child here."

Really? I'm almost seventeen and she *finally* gets that concept?

I run my hand over my face. "I'm just worried about you. Is that so bad? I can't take any more shuffling around, Mom. Remember that?" She blanches. "Remember when the police came and got me for the last time, and they didn't bring me back? Instead they took me to some state home and dropped me off. Do you want to know what that feels like?"

Silence descends on the room. The only sound is the hum of my laptop in the corner.

"I'm sorry," she whispers. "I know I haven't always been the best mother." Her breath hitches as she sits on the bed again. "But I have tried."

Yeah, tried to screw my life up. Tried to ruin my existence.

"I just thought you would be glad to see me happy. I was excited for you to meet John, but if it's going to bother you . . . then he doesn't have to come over tonight." She touches my cheek, her expression hopeful and ridiculous.

"Fine," I sigh. "He can have dinner with us."

She jumps off the bed and squeals like she's twelve. "Great! He'll be over in thirty minutes, so do something with that face."

I take a quick shower in the lone bathroom in my mom's room, and when I step out, I feel somewhat refreshed.

"Make sure you're dressed!" my mom calls out. "John's here!"

*Crap.* I clench my towel around me. It's a skimpy towel at that, covering the important stuff and that's it. I was barely in there ten minutes. This is so par for the course.

I gather my dirty clothes, suck in a deep breath, and fling open the door. I pogo on crutches through the master bedroom and hurl myself through the living room.

"Katie, I'd like you to meet—"

"Hi, nice to meet yoooou." My armpits thoroughly abused, I zip straight to kitchen and back to my bedroom. I slam the door and breathe again.

Clothes. Must get clothes. My mom's boyfriend just saw me half-naked. What if my towel was flapping? Perfect. I'm the teenager, yet *I* need to have a conversation *with my mom* about boundaries.

I grab some clothes, lie down on the bed, and slip into them. So much easier than trying to stand up and balance on the stinking crutches. I give my hair five minutes under the blow dryer, secure my locks in a knot, then shuffle back to the living room.

Where my mother's dream man sits—right next to her on the couch. I look him up and down. Surprisingly, not bad—for my mom's taste. She usually gravitates toward the overly tattooed, worn-out ponytail types. This guy wears jeans that are a tint of this decade. I find that quite redeeming. His solid polo shirt is nicely tucked in, and for the life of me, I cannot find a single tattoo. Even a simple "Mother" tattoo would be acceptable, but this guy's got nothing. Well, not that I can tell in a quick survey. It's not appropriate to stare at your mom's boyfriend for too long. Unless he has something hanging out of his nose, then he's just asking for it.

"Hi, Katie." He stands up and helps me into the chair across from them. "I'm John."

We shake hands, his grip calloused and less refined. Like he's used to manual labor. Hopefully not the drug-selling sort like my mom.

"So . . . you two met in your substance abuse support group?" My mom's eyes bulge. "Do you normally pick up chicks there, John?"

John sputters then coughs. "Er . . . uh, no. First time for me."

"First time to be there or first time to snag a girl in group?"

"Katie!" My mom, ready to leap from her spot on the couch, stills when John rests his hand on her arm.

"It's okay." He inhales deeply. "I've been going to group for almost a year now. I attend twice a week. And yes, that was my first time to 'snag a girl' there." His hesitant smile chips away at some of my resistance. "We didn't plan it. Your mom and I struck up a friendship the first time she came to the support group. You need friends in our . . . situation."

"And what is your situation?"

John interlaces his fingers and rests his arms on his knees. "I'm a recovering alcoholic."

"Uh-huh. And how long have you been sober? Five months? Five days? Five minutes?"

"Five years."

Oh.

Still, why would he jeopardize his sobriety by hanging out with my mom? She's not exactly a sure bet in terms of having it together.

"Katie, I think that's enough rude questions for now." My mom leaves us for the kitchen. "Save some of your obnoxiousness for later." She shakes her head and digs into the fridge.

"It's okay, Bobbie Ann."

No! It's not okay. *Nothing* is okay. There are red flags everywhere. Doesn't anyone see them?

My mom boils water on the stove and reaches into the cabinets for a bag of chips. "How many hot dogs do you want, Katie?"

"Are they all beef?" I ask like Millie just took over my body.

Mom frowns. "What?"

"Just one. Thanks." The Millie in my head tells me to read the hotdog package label, but I resist. The days of soy burgers and tofu dogs are gone. I've got to adjust to my life here—my overly processed, artificially flavored life.

We sit down to a dinner of hotdogs, pork-n-beans, Fritos, and tall glasses of fruit punch. Once the plates are filled, I bow my head.

Then remember I'm not at the Scotts. I peek through my lashes to find John and Mom staring at me.

"Is there something wrong with you?" My mom squeezes mustard up and down her bun, her eyes suspicious.

"Um . . . no. I was just . . . um . . ."

"Praying." John's easy smile catches me off guard. "Why don't we all pray?" He reaches for my hand, then my mothers.

Staring at the two of us like we're alien life form, she sets her hotdog down on the plate. "Well . . . fine. Sure. Whatever."

John lowers his dark head then thanks God for our food.

"When did you start doing that?" my mom asks.

My answer overlaps John's. "Since I lived with the Scotts."

"I always have. Just never have around you."

Mom shifts uncomfortably in her seat, narrows her gaze at me, then her boyfriend, and shrugs it off.

"So . . . John. Where's a good place to go to church?" If I don't find a church, I'll never hear the end of it from James.

He takes a swig of fruit punch. "I think Maple Street Chapel is a great church. Very small, but a good pastor." He daubs at his small mustache with a napkin. "It's where I go. Been trying to get your mom to go for weeks, but she won't."

"I work on Sundays. Got too much to do."

"You should go *this* Sunday, Mom. I'll go. We can have a little more mother-daughter time."

She considers it then shakes her head. "I have to work. I took today off. I don't get three weeks' vacation like the rich folk you know."

"You don't have to work in the morning, do you?" I prod. "Can't you clean the beauty salon after church?"

Mom's spoon clanks on the table. "I *said* I have to work. Surely God understands frivolous things like food, water, and electricity bills that need to be paid."

"You could ride with me tomorrow, Katie. I pick up a few of my elderly neighbors, but I have room for one more."

"I can drive my own daughter to church, John," my mother snaps.

His forehead wrinkles in a frown. "Well, of course you can. Just thought it would be easier on you if I picked her up, since I'm going that way anyway."

I feel an undercurrent here that has nothing to do with the earlier church tension. I lift my brow in question and lock my gaze on Mom.

She picks up her Kool-Aid and swirls her glass around, the ice clinking. "He's just being a worrywart. I had a little fender bender last week in my car. No big deal. Just wasn't paying attention."

"I'm just concerned, that's all." John folds his napkin in half, then thirds.

"People have little accidents all the time. I just dazed off. I was probably messing with the radio. I don't even remember."

"It's your second 'little accident' in three weeks."

"I said I was messing with the radio. I wasn't paying attention. I think I'm still perfectly capable of driving my daughter down the street to the church." Mom stands up and grabs her paper plate. "I need to run and check on some things at the beauty shop." She dismisses John with a nod.

He rises from his chair, his focus intense on my mom. "They'll be closing about now." My mom doesn't say a word. John nods, then moves toward the door. "It was nice to meet you, Katie. I'll be seeing you around."

"Yeah, I guess I'll see you at church tomorrow." Awkward. Weird. Uncomfortable.

John lets himself out the door, as my mom grabs her purse.

"Where are you really going?" I know this woman.

She pauses, her hand on her bag. "I said I was going to run to work real quick."

"It's after six. Can't it wait?"

"No, it cannot. I need to check on next week's schedule and talk to my boss. I need to ask off for your doctor's appointment." She grabs her own cell phone and hustles to the door. "Don't go anywhere and don't open the door for anyone. And don't do anything stupid like jumping off the front steps on your crutches." She forces a smile. "Be back soon."

From the kitchen window, I watch her drive away in her 1990 Cougar.

Heading the opposite way of the beauty shop.

# Chapter Twenty-Five

WHO KNOWS WHAT time my mom got in last night. As they say in Texas, she must've stayed out with the dry cows.

I run my flatiron down the last section of my hair, and give it a small mist of spray. My stomach turns a small flip as I think of once again being the new girl at church, the new girl in town. Of course, it helps that this time I don't have a rap sheet that says breaking and entering. I didn't exactly make the best impression when I first landed in In Between. But still, I won't know anyone. Won't have anyone to sit with. Won't be able to look up at the choir loft and see Millie's sweet smile. Or glance behind me and catch Maxine sneaking bites of Cheetos during the invitation.

My crutches stab into the linoleum as I walk my way across the trailer and into my mom's room. I knock. Loudly. You never know. And in case her boyfriend came back with her last night, I don't want to barge in and see something that will scar me for life.

I finally hear her rustling around, then her feet thud onto the floor. "What?" She cracks open the door.

"I'm going to church, remember?"

"Yeah?"

"You said you wanted to take me." I wait for her brain to join us in the conversation.

"Oh, yeah. Uh-huh." She lifts a hand to push her tangled hair back. "Gimme a sec. I'll be right out."

The door shuts, and I limp back to my room to brush my teeth and beg God one more time for some confidence. Maybe I'm rushing this. I mean, do I really need to go to church the second day here? I'm sure James would understand my taking a Sunday off. I'm tired. I'm depressed. And my mom has satellite TV.

I brush my teeth over the kitchen sink, watching some kids do donuts on their bikes in the street.

"Do you want some breakfast?" Mom ties her knee-length robe closed and reaches for her coffee pot.

"Some of your turbo-charged coffee would be nice."

"You can't get that at no Starbucks."

We share a tired grin. "Nope. Nobody makes it like Bobbie Ann Parker."

"Got you some Pop-Tarts too."

"Aw, Mom. You do care." But I will have to reconsider if she serves me the s'mores kind. The taste of graham cracker does not belong in breakfast. "So where did you go last night?"

She doesn't bother looking up from the toaster. "Work. I told you."

I hope it's the legal kind. "You must've gotten in pretty late." Or early, if you want to get technical.

"I stopped by the salon then had some errands to run."

"What if Child Services had shown up?"

My mom stills. "Can we have one peaceful moment together? Is that too much to ask? Is it?"

"No." I pour myself some juice. "I worry about you, though."

"Well, don't." She snaps up my Pop-Tart and plops it on a napkin. "John's church starts in fifteen minutes. You better eat in the car."

I ask her one more time to go with me, but she refuses. She holds my breakfast for me, pours me a to-go cup of coffee, then helps me out the door and into the car.

The drive to the church is a quiet one. My eyes adjust to the sight of Middleton like I'm stepping from dark to light. Like they need to refocus. It's unexpected. It's unfamiliar. And it's not In Between.

"You've got your phone. Call me when you get done." She pulls up as close to the door of the small church as possible.

I hoist myself out and walk toward the building that's just crying for a new coat of white paint. Men in suits stand on either side of the walkway, greeting everyone who passes them by name. Sometimes it's a huge comfort how friendly church people can be. This is not one of those moments. I just want to slip inside, find a seat, and—

"Oops, dropped your Bible. Let me get that."

Before I can contemplate the challenge of bending over, a blond-haired guy jumps in front of me, reaches for my leather-bound NIV, and hands it to me with a Channing Tatum grin and a twinkle in his eye.

"You're new here."

"How'd you guess?" Boys. I'm so over them.

"I'm Tate Matthews." He continues to hold my Bible.

"Katie Parker." He looks a little older than me, but I can't be sure. He doesn't dress as GQ as Charlie, but not too shabby. Better than Nash.

"Just visiting or is Middleton home for you?"

My chest constricts and I have to look away. "Something like that." Will this place ever feel like home?

"Will you be going to Middleton High? Let me guess . . ." Eyes as blue as the ocean squint as he studies me. "A senior?"

At this I do laugh. "No, a junior."

"Ah, well, as a member of the Middleton Student Council, let me be the first to officially welcome you. We're the home of the Musk-rat." His voice drops. "Our mascot gets beaten up a lot."

My mouth tips upward, despite my sad mood. His student council status reminds me of Frances, and his easygoing demeanor brings my drama buddy Jeremy to mind. So he can't be all that bad.

"Are you meeting someone in here?"

I shake my head and move toward the door. "No."

"And if I said I had a seat saved just for Katie Parker?"

"I'd say Tate Matthews was full of it." But I let him walk me through the doorway and hold onto my Bible as I greet the men at the door.

"Look . . . Katie." Tate slows as we reach the sanctuary. "If you don't take me up on my offer of a seat—*just* a seat—all my friends will laugh at me. You don't want to shoot me down and ruin my reputation, do you?" He lifts a brow and strikes a barely tragic pose.

I pretend to scan the perimeter. "I don't exactly see any friends flocking around you. Unless you count that lady over there giving you the eye." I point to a woman who has poured her Rosie O'Donnell figure into a tube top, even though she could pass for somebody's grandmother.

Tate winces. "Old girlfriend. She'll get over me one day. Anyway, I happen to have a number of friends, which, I'm guessing you are in short supply of as the new girl."

His words sting, even though I know he doesn't mean them to.

"If you sit in my pew, I'll introduce you.

I chew on my lip and consider it. "Okay," I sigh. "But for the record, I think you might be trouble."

He holds up his hands in surrender. "My mom would agree, but you would both be wrong." His hand rests lightly at my back. "This way, Muskrat newbie."

Crutches and pews do not go together, so I let Tate take my hands and help me into our seats. He high-fives some people around us then introduces them to me. As Tate's friends make small talk with me, my eyes drift to the door, halfway expecting James to march through and take the pulpit. But this isn't his church. I just hope God shows up.

Across the aisle, I spot John, and I hold up a hand in greeting. He starts to get out of his pew, but the choir files in, and the pianist lights into the first few bars of a hymn.

Without asking, Tate helps me rise as the congregation comes to their feet for the opening song. His touch isn't creepy or intrusive. It's efficient and quick. Friendly. Reluctantly, I must admit I like this guy. *As a friend.* Totally as a friend. No dating for me. Not for a long time. My heart still howls for Charlie Benson. But I guess my heart wants a lot of things it can't have. Like a mom. And Keira Knightley's waistline.

We sing "Amazing Grace" with a contemporary flare, and I'm reminded of the moment I walked down to accept Christ. I was surrounded by my friends at church, as well as victims of the tornado that had hit town, and we were singing this song. The words, older than me and my friends put together, were so fresh and new to me that evening. That was the night I knew beyond a shadow of a doubt I was a child of God. That he had created me with a purpose. And I was in In Between for a reason. And I have to suck it up and remember I'm in Middleton with my mom for a reason.

*So here I am, God. Keep me focused. Keep me on your path. And just keep me sane.*

The same man who leads the choir walks to a microphone and welcomes the church. He reminds me of an older version of our youth pastor, Pastor Mike—muscular, bald, and his enthusiastic words twanging with their deep Southern roots.

"That's our preacher, Brother Jamie. He's really good." Tate points to the man who returns to direct the choir.

And Brother Jamie is good. At least he passes the keep-my-attention test. His sermon is over, and I realize I didn't look at my watch one time or draw hearts and deformed flowers all over my bulletin. He leads the church in a closing prayer, then dismisses us with a final serenade by the Maple Street Chapel choir.

"So . . ." Tate passes me my crutches and takes the Bible from my hands. "A group of us are going to Brother Jamie's house for pizza and volleyball. I dare you to join us."

"Let me guess, Brother Jamie is also the youth minister?"

"You're dodging my challenge, but yes."

"I don't think so, but thanks."

"Why? Are you allergic to pizza?"

I shake my head.

"Pastors? A good time?"

"No." I laugh. "I'm not exactly up for volleyball."

He glances at my Aircast. "Right. You're probably more of a synchronized swimming girl, anyway. But I still think you should come with us. You're not going to get to know anyone if you only share a hymnal every Sunday. Come hang out. I promise you, you'll have fun."

Everything in me says no—everything except this small voice whispering in a distant corner of my brain. "I . . . " I can't believe I'm going to do this. "Okay."

Tate sticks his fist out and I tap my knuckles to his. "I do want to warn you though—not everyone will be as cool as me. You're at the disadvantage since you happened to have met me first. The bar is now sky-high, but—"

"Tate?"

"Yeah?" His smile melts a little of the frost on my mood.

"I'm armed with crutches—and I know how to use them."

He shrugs and takes a step away. "Right then."

Outside, I call Mom. She doesn't answer, so after five more tries, I leave a message.

"Katie, hi." Mom's boyfriend walks my way. "I'm glad you came. Couldn't get your mother to join you, huh?"

"No. Maybe next week." And maybe my mom will sprout wings and fly like a 747 too. "Did you see her last night? After you left?"

John's puzzled expression unsettles me. "No. I went home after dinner and didn't hear from her all evening. Why?"

"Nothing." Tate moves away to talk to some friends nearby, so I decide to give the full court press to John. "Mom was out really late, so I thought maybe she was with you. She wouldn't tell me where she had been all night."

John only stares, then shakes his head. "I don't know what to tell you. Things have been going really well the past few months. Your mom has been doing great. But . . ." His eyes search the Middleton horizon. ". . . Lately she has been acting strange. She has a sponsor—a support person who she should be checking in with. I'll see your mom gets a phone call from her. I think things are basically all right. I mean, I don't think your mom is using again. But it's important we not let up on encouraging her and making sure she's supported."

"Okay." *I think you could be wrong and totally in denial.* "Good to see you." So if my mom couldn't have been at work the whole night, and she wasn't with John—where was she? What had she been doing?

"Hey, you ready to eat pizza and watch me spike it like a champ?" Tate returns to my side, still holding my Bible. The noon breeze catches his sun-streaked blond hair. "Did you get in touch with your mom?"

I could not be more out of touch with Bobbie Ann Parker. "Let's go." I paint on a semi-interested face and follow him and a few of his friends toward the parking lot.

"I hear all that unbridled enthusiasm in your voice, and I'm going to have to ask you to tone it down. This is a church event, and it requires maturity and composure. So in case you were on the verge of squealing for joy at the prospect of hanging out with us, and I suspect you were, rein it in." He takes my purse and hangs it over his shoulder. "Our coach awaits."

Tate and his friends Tyler and Ashley talk and laugh as they fill me in on previous youth group events, all punctuated with some tragically funny event involving banana peels, sleepless camping trips, or someone losing his shorts.

Tate's old Explorer pulls up to a brick home much like Frances's, except the yard is larger, and the nearest neighbor is a good half-mile away. He opens my door and helps me down. Tyler and Ashley run on ahead, still reminiscing over their last tale.

"Are you hungry?" His eyes connect with mine.

"Sure." *Not really.* More like stressed. Numb. Sad. Hollowed out. Like nuclear PMS.

"That wasn't very convincing. An actress you're not."

"Actually I am." *And I kick butt at it, thank you very much.*

"Oh, really?" We walk around the house to the back yard, following the sound of voices. "What have you done?"

I give him my acting credentials, and he nods in approval when I mention my run as Juliet.

He stops and extends his arms. "Lady, by yonder blessed moon I swear, that tips with silver all these fruit-tree tops."

"O, swear not by the moon"—the words trickle out of me, like I've found a long lost friend—"the inconstant moon, that monthly changes in her circled orb, lest that thy love prove likewise variable."

He gasps with all the melodrama of Maxine, and I laugh at his mockery of Romeo. "What shall I swear by?"

"Do not swear at all; or if thou wilt, swear by thy gracious self, which is the god of my idolatry, and I'll believe thee."

And we stand that way for a few moments—gaze to gaze, wordless, and me wrapped up in the love of the familiar words.

He inches closer, his face serious, thoughtful. "Let the record show . . . that Katie Parker just said I was gracious and she idolized me."

"That is not what I said! I was reciting—"

"Totally what you just said." He laughs and walks ahead of me, moving toward one of the picnic tables in the middle of the backyard.

About fifteen teens are gathered around, not nearly the numbers we'd have at Target Teen, but still not a bad turnout for such a small church. I look at the group and feel very . . . tired. Do I have the energy to make new friends? What if my mom just picks up and moves us again like she usually does? We never stayed anywhere for too long. I'm tired of being the new girl. Frances isn't in this group. And yes, maybe a new best friend is, but I don't want a new best friend.

"Are you coming?" Tate turns around, way ahead of me. My crutches dig into the grass, and I catch up. "Hey, Katie?"

I roll my eyes and look up, ready for more of his pseudo Shakespeare. "Yeah?"

"I don't know where you come from or what you have going on, but I know this isn't where you want to be. I just wanted to tell you I'm glad you came. And I think if you let yourself, you'd have a good time." The intensity leaves his face. "The preacher's son is a little nuts, but the rest of the guys in the group—they're pretty cool."

We share a slow smile, and I nod. "Okay." And with a heavy heart, I join him and the others at the tables.

Tate introduces me to more of his friends, and I'm bowled over by their instant acceptance and kindness. I scan the group, trying to find the Chelsea in the mix—you know there is one. Every group has one. But nobody stands out as the resident snob.

"What kind of pizza can I get you?" Brother Jamie reaches for a paper plate. "We have every kind—including pepperoni with anchovies." He drops his voice to a stage whisper. "That's my son's favorite. You probably want to avoid him and his fish breath."

A tall blonde woman, who introduces herself as Lisa, Jamie's wife, takes my drink order. "Here's a Diet Dr. Pepper for you, Hon. And Tate, what can I get for you?"

"Oh, you know. The usual."

The pastor's wife shakes her head, then mixes a drink concoction, pouring from a variety of two-liters like she's a cocktail waitress. "One root beer–Dr Pepper–orange–Sprite."

The preacher holds up a plate. "And three slices of pizza."

We thank them then take a seat with some others under a massive shade tree. Tate helps me to the grass then hands me my plate. And that's when I take a glance at his plate.

Anchovies.

"You're the crazy pastor's son?"

His eyes dance in the sunlight. "Don't worry, I have no intention of breathing on you." He steals a chip from my plate. "At least not today."

# Chapter Twenty-Six

THE PASTOR'S SON *is* crazy.

Two hours later, I sit in the Middleton heat, watching the last game of volleyball—or, as Tate calls it, extreme volleyball. The girls have long since surrendered and sit around me. Basically all rules are off in this game and anything goes, including body slams, vicious spikes, wrapping friends in the net, and too many chest bumps to be appropriate for my taste.

The game is finally called on the count of Mrs. Matthews running out of Band-Aids and Gatorade, and the sweaty boys join our circle in the grass.

Tate sits beside me. "Our ladies are wusses. I know you would've been out there with us, if it weren't for that cast."

"Right." Though I did learn some cutthroat moves in Coach Nelson's PE class this past year. He might be surprised. Tate slaps the guy next to us on the butt. Okay, then again, maybe not.

Tate's eyes fall to the phone in my hand. "Did you ever get a hold of your mom?"

"No. Still no answer." I feel my cheeks flush with heat. "I hate to ask, but do you think—"

"Let me grab a water and we'll go."

I say good-bye to the girls who've kept me company the past thirty minutes, promise to call Ashley, and wave to the guys. I survived this. I did it. There's no replacing my In Between friends, but I know I gotta have people here too. My mom's not the only one who needs a support system.

Mrs. Matthews gives me a side-hug, and the pastor invites me to the Sunday night service. But I know I've had all the church I can handle today. If I went to the evening service, and my mom didn't pick me up, I'd have to spend the night in a pew.

"You did a great job today." Tate shuts his door and starts the engine.

I shrug my shoulders. "A good job being a benchwarmer?"

He steals a quick glance. "You know what I mean. I know it was hard for you today—not knowing any of us. Not getting all the private jokes and the inside scoop. But everyone really liked you."

For lack of originality, I shrug again, like I care . . . but I do. "Your friends were nice." I shoot him a grin. "That guy who eats the fish pizza is a whack-job, but the rest of them are okay."

I give him directions for getting to the trailer as we drive, and within minutes he's cruising past the Happy Meadows sign. I push down the old shame of people seeing where I live. This place *ain't* Buckingham Palace, but it's where my mom is starting over. And it's where God planted me. So if this guy so much as curls a lip at Number 16 Wingard Street, then I will show him a super-convenient spot for a crutch.

We pull into the dirt drive, but Mom's Cougar is gone. I sigh and lean my head on the window. Where is she?

"Thanks for the ride." My hand stills on the door handle. "And for today. I did have a good time."

He props an elbow on the steering wheel and faces me. "And you didn't expect to."

"Right." I look toward the front steps, where Mom's cat collection lounges.

"Coming back tonight? I could swing by and get you."

"No. But thanks. Maybe next week. I've only been in Middleton a little over twenty-four hours."

"And you don't want to overdose on church. I totally understand." His grin is back, and I match it with one of my own and open the door. "I can manage it," I say as he starts to get out to help.

"Katie?"

I pivot on a crutch.

"You've got a friend in Middleton. Just wanted you to know that."

I reach for my purse and Bible. "Tell that friend I said thanks." And I shut the door.

I spy the cats eyeing me from the door, like they're thinking, *Her odds of doing a face plant coming up the steps are pretty good. Let's stay and watch.* I throw one last wave to Tate then hike it around the back of the trailer. Yes, I'm doing a lap until he's gone. My armpits will hate me for it, but my dignity will say thank you. My method of getting up the thin wooden steps is not attractive, so I will just wait 'til he's gone.

Two minutes later I shoo the strays away and unlock the front door. Aside from a loud-mouthed woman selling life-changing blenders on TV, the trailer is still.

I go back to my room, shut the door, and crash on the bed.

And then my phone rings. The screen displays Millie's name, and my heart thrills.

"Hey!"

"Hi, sweetie." I snuggle back into my pillow and let the sound of her voice work its soothing magic. "How's it going?" I hear James holler something in the background. "James wants to know if you went to church today and if you miss him yet." She laughs.

"Yes to both. Mom dropped me off at a small church here in town, and I actually stayed and had lunch with their youth group."

"Get out."

"No, really. You should be proud."

"Always."

We talk more, and I fill her in on Middleton and the people I met today. I leave out the parts about my mom and her bouts of weird. The phone is passed to James, then finally to Maxine.

"Sweet Pea?"

I laugh. "Yeah?"

"Did you get my last text message?"

"The one about the new prune juice you'd tried?"

"Shoot. Meant to send that to Dottie Nelson. But probably wouldn't hurt you either. I meant the one about . . ." Her voice is a light hiss. "Sam."

"No. What about him?"

"Saw him in town last night. I was at Ida Mae's House of Vittles with the good mayor and—"

"You went on a date with the mayor at *your* restaurant—the one Sam always took you to! Let me guess . . . you sat in booth number seven and ordered chicken-fried steak and a root beer."

Silence. Gum pops. "So?"

"So? You are baiting that poor man, Maxine. What did Sam say when he saw you?"

"Well, I was sitting in the booth alone at the time. And he came by and spoke to me for the first time since the big breakup. He wanted to know how you were. Things were going so well. For the first time we were talking, and nobody was yelling or insulting our mamas."

"Then?"

"Then my date came back from the john and sat down. Sam didn't even speak to him. Just looked at the two of us, adjusted his hat, and stomped off."

"Well, you got what you wanted."

"What is that supposed to mean, Sass Pot?"

"You went there in hopes he would see you, and he did. You're like the iceberg to your own Titanic. You're doing this to yourself."

"Is there a better time I could call and get some sympathy?"

"No."

"Maybe you could talk to him for me. He said he misses you at the Valiant already."

I squeeze the bridge of my nose, a headache beginning to force its way through. "And I miss him. But I can't make this right for you. You'd just jack it up somehow if I did, anyway."

"I gave him your number . . ."

"And I'd love to talk to him." That man's the grandpa I never had. "But I'm out on this crazy fiasco of yours. Out."

Maxine huffs. "Fine. I raise you and make you into the fabulous young woman you are today, and this is the thanks I get?"

Despite the pounding in my brain, I laugh. I don't even bother reminding her she's only known me less than a year. "Right. But if he does call, I might let it slip that you have mentioned him."

"Really?"

"*If* I decided to say something, it would be subtle."

She considers this. "Okay. I'll take what I can get. Low-key and understated. I don't really understand that approach, but whatever. Not that I'm not perfectly happy with William. He's a charming companion."

"His outlaw mustache is a nightmare. And his knuckles? *Ew*, have you noticed how hairy they are? Like *so* in need of a wax job or something. Maybe some Nair?"

Maxine clears her throat. "Anyway, Sweet Cheeks, I only miss Sam's friendship, mind you. I wouldn't reconsider his marriage proposal again if he shoved handfuls of George Washington's down my brassiere." Maxine covers the receiver and I hear Millie's garbled voice. "Millie wants to talk to your mom when we're done here."

I still and listen for any sound of life from the other part of the trailer. "Uh . . . she had to run out for a bit, but she'll be back later."

"What's that? Oh, she said she wanted to talk about your doctor appointment with her and go over some questions about your ankle."

"Well . . . I'll tell her to give Millie a call. She should be back anytime." Hopefully before I graduate from high school. "We ought to be able to handle the appointment though."

"Okay, Toots, we love ya and stuff."

I smile. "I love you and stuff." Two hours later I'm still lying on my bed, staring at the ceiling and clutching my phone.

*Okay, Katie. Get it together. Enough pouting for the day. You've reached the maximum amount of time allotted to feel sorry for yourself. Find something to do. Get your mind off all this craziness.*

I know. I'll make dinner. We have a stocked refrigerator for the first time in history, and there has to be something in there I could throw together. I've seen Millie cook a hundred times. How hard can it be?

I ease myself from the bed and move into the kitchen to investigate my options. Ground beef. Check. Buns. Check. Great! I'll make some hamburgers—burgers to rival the Golden Arches and make my momma glad to be home.

*Okay, here we go.* I gather everything I need and group it into one spot. If nothing else, being crutch-bound has made me more efficient. And crankier, but that's irrelevant.

I open the hamburger meat and press some into patties. *Ew.* Gross. This stuff is nasty. My mom doesn't have Extra Virgin Olive oil—which I've seen Rachel Ray use in everything on all her cooking shows, so I pick something that looks like it and pour a few inches into the heating frying pan. The vegetable oil pops and cracks to life.

Just going to put the burgers in now. One gourmet patty . . . two masterpiece patty . . .

Music busts out from my bedroom, and I grab my crutches and beat it back there to catch my phone. It could be Frances.

Reaching for my phone, my heart skips a beat.

Charlie.

"Hello?" I'm breathless—but maybe he'll find that totally hot.

His voice is as rich as dark chocolate. "I was hoping you'd pick up."

I laugh. "Why wouldn't I pick up the phone for you?"

He pauses and I take the moment to sit down at my desk. "I wasn't sure where we'd left things Friday night."

*Hmmm.* Me neither. Let's have a repeat. Like the part where your lips were on my mine.

"Katie?"

I jump. "Oh, yeah. I'm here."

"I was saying that I wasn't sure if we had really settled anything. If you were still mad at me . . ."

"No. I'm not still mad. I probably would be if you hadn't reverted back to the boy genius that you are and realized Chelsea's not right for you." I twirl my hair and sigh. "And I am."

Static-filled words from the other end.

"What's that? I can't hear you." I move my phone around to try and get a better signal.

"I . . . um . . ."

"Charlie?" I sit up straighter in my chair. "I know we can't really have much of a relationship with the distance. I don't even have a car. But . . . I don't know . . . I've had a lot of time to think since I've been here."

"You've been gone two days."

"It's been a long two days." What is this new attitude? "Anyway . . . I'd be willing to try and make it work . . . if you would." Please. I need something from In Between to hold onto.

"Katie, you mean a lot to me, and—"

The line mutes. I check the display. Call ended.

With a growl, I punch a button to redial his number. Ten tries later and ten messages of service not available, I give up.

Is there hope for us after all? Is he so into me he would be willing to put in miles on his car and tons of minutes on his phone and—

What is that smell?

Oh, my gosh! The hamburgers—I forgot about them. I hope—

*Beep! Beep! Beep!*

I slap my hands over my ears as the fire alarm screams in millisecond intervals, and hop, crutchless, into the kitchen.

*Oh crap, oh crap, oh crap.*

Fire. Flames. Smoke.

Gonna burn the trailer down.

Mom's gonna kill me.

Stop the fire. Grab some water. No, grab a towel. Many towels. Baking soda? Baking powder—think! What is it that puts these things out? Is there a fire extinguisher anywhere? *Help me, God! Help me.*

Hopping on one leg, I tear through Mom's cabinet drawers, yanking one after another open until I find tea towels.

And then I stare at the flames.

It's never going to work. It's too big. Inches away from the cabinets. I throw one on the skillet anyway.

*Help me.*

The fire consumes the material instantly.

*Help me.*

I take a deep breath and hold my hands over my erratic heart.

A lid. I need a big lid.

Grabbing the edge of the counter, I ease down and dig through the pots and pans. Lid, lid, lid. Come on. Be here . . . Yes!

With a towel covering my hand, I say another prayer and lower the lid down. So hot.

And I let it drop. Please don't explode. I take a step back just in case. Even more important than this trailer—my face.

The front door bangs open. My mom stands, mouth open, then jerks into action.

"What are you doing?" she yells.

"Cooking dinner!" Or the kitchen.

"Get back," she barks. "Get back." Her hand pushes me away from the remaining flames. I teeter back and rock on my good leg. Oh, no. My arms flail . . . and backwards I go.

On my butt.

In time to watch her pour a giant box of baking soda all over the flames. I stay put, my breath pushing at my lungs.

The fire diminishes. Slowly at first. Then down to nothing.

Bobbie Ann Parker turns on her heel and pins me with a look that could wilt a sumo wrestler.

"What"—she pulls her sweaty hair from her cheeks—"were you thinking?"

I lie back onto the cold linoleum and cover my face with my hands. "That I'd fix you dinner."

Her sigh could rattle the walls. She sits down beside me. "Are you okay?"

"Yes."

"Katie, look at me."

I spread a few fingers and peek through.

"Are you okay? Did the fire touch you?"

I shake my head. Just took some years off my life, but I don't suppose she really cares to hear.

Mom puts her hand on my leg. "What about your ankle? Are you good? Okay? Tell me."

I try to wiggle it around. "Could be better." It hurts. I must've twisted it during my fall. Or when I sailed through the kitchen like I was on a trapeze wire.

"You could've burned the house down." Her voice drifts back to angry. "We could've lost everything."

I swallow hard. "I know. I was just trying to be helpful."

"What if you'd hurt yourself?"

"I know." My butt probably is bruised, but I'll keep that one to myself. I lift myself up to a seated position and face my mother. "I didn't know where you were, though. I've been worried all day."

"I got called into work."

Why doesn't she look me in the eye when she says that? "You could've texted. How did you think I'd get home from church?"

She studies her ragged nails. "I figured John would give you a lift."

"He's a stranger. I don't want a ride from him. And what if he didn't? I couldn't walk home. Wasn't going to stick my thumb out. What did you expect me to do?"

Her eyes flash. "I didn't expect you to burn my house down. I had to work. It's not easy being a single parent, and we have bills to pay."

"You forgot about me."

She lifts her chin. "I tried to call."

"No you didn't. Your number would've shown up. You would've left a message."

"Well, I don't know what happened, but I did try to call. And I didn't have time to leave a message." Mom stands up and dusts off her jeans like we've been sitting in the dirt. "You're a big girl, Katie. I expect you to take care of yourself too. I can't do it all."

*No, but you could do the minimum.* "I don't know *anyone* in this town. I'm alone, I'm crippled." I hold up my Aircast. "Can you wait a day or two before you leave me to my own devices?" My voice shakes. "You can't just bail out on me." I gesture to the stove. "This happens."

"You're not an infant. I shouldn't have to worry about fires and falls!" She yells back, throwing towels in the sink.

"And I shouldn't have to wonder where you are all night. Or if you're coming home." I lift myself to my feet. "Or if you're going to leave me stranded at church."

Her face twists with bitterness. "Maybe you shouldn't have gone to church."

"And maybe you shouldn't have been a mom." The words burst out of mouth before I can pull them back. My eyes go wide.

Her eyes narrow. To slits. "Don't think I haven't thought of that." She stomps out of the kitchen, grabs the purse that was thrown down at the door, and pauses. "I'm not going to stand here and fight with you. I'm going back to work."

I raise my watch. "At five-thirty? On a Sunday?" My brows wrinkle in doubt. "You're lying. You're not cleaning any beauty shop at this time of evening."

Mom throws her bag over her bony shoulder then marches back to the kitchen. She stops near me and looms. "I don't care where you think I'm going. I'm leaving." Her voice sears through my head. "I won't be back for a couple of hours. If you want to think the worst, then go ahead. Everybody else does."

"Mom, I—"

"Open these windows and clean this place up." And back to the door she tramps. "You have two hours. Don't ruin anything else." And the door slams.

Leaving me alone.

Again.

I laugh and brush away a hot tear. Ruin anything else?

Like my life?

I think it's too late.

# Chapter Twenty-Seven

WHEN I WAKE up the next morning, my mom is gone.

I know she came home at some point because she's laid out the Pop-Tarts and some snarky instructions on how to operate the toaster without incinerating the neighborhood.

I don't even feel like eating, and I push the foil package aside. I was to have been at the doctor's office an hour ago. Millie is going to flip. I don't know whether Mom forgot or purposefully didn't get me up for the appointment. I don't know that it matters.

Frances calls and we catch up. I fill her in on my fire routine, and she gives me the update on the drive-in.

"We're having a date auction in three weeks. Isn't that a cool idea?"

"Yeah, any chance Jake Gyllenhall is going to show?" I'd give up my allowance, my cell phone, *and* my future firstborn for that.

"No, but there's still time."

And then I ask the question I told myself not to ask. "So what's the status? With Chelsea and Charlie, I mean."

Dead air.

"You there?"

"I don't know, Katie. Chelsea's family had to move out of their big home, and they're in a tiny rent house. The family's been coming to church. Chelsea's been pretty torn up."

"You didn't answer my question."

"Charlie's spending a lot of time with her. I've tried to get Nash to grill him, but you know . . ."

Yeah, I don't exactly see Nash willing to do the Barbara Walters routine.

Is that what Charlie had called me about yesterday? To tell me he was getting back with Chelsea?

A knock at the door cuts off any more Charlie thoughts. "Gotta go, Frances. Somebody's here."

I peep out the window and see Tate on the steps, talking to the cats. "Just a second!" I yell, and hop into my room and throw on a bra and some shorts. I one-foot-it back to the living room, yanking my hair into a ponytail.

When I open the door, he stands, wearing a slanted grin.

"Did you come to see the cats?"

"No, but Blackie here says he'd like filtered water from now on instead of tap."

"His name is Blackie, huh?" I laugh and hold the door open for him. "I just call him Stray Number Seven."

Tate smiles into my face as he passes. I offer him a seat and notice his eyes assess the room. That old familiar shame rolls in my stomach. Nope, not gonna care about that. Not today. Not ever again.

I sit on the other end of the couch. "So, you were cruising around town in your swimming trunks and thought of me?" His madras plaid trunks look like they came from Sam Dayberry's closet. Except on Tate, they're kind of cool.

"A group of us—most you met Sunday—are going to the creek over in Tuckerville. It's about a thirty-minute ride. Thought you might want to go."

"Um . . . I can't. I have a lot to do here." I cover a yawn with my hand.

"You just got up, didn't you?" He consults his watch. "It's almost eleven."

So sue me. I haven't slept a lot lately. "I'm on summer vacation. Who cares?"

"Exactly—summer vacation. A time of fun, sun, and eating a disgusting amount of junk food. Come on out with us. I have a cooler packed and a few Diet Dr. Peppers with your name on them."

I smile at that. Met me less than twenty-four hours ago, and he already knows my drink preference. I wonder if he'd be interested in my friend Hannah. Of course, he may have a girlfriend already. Who knows.

"I'm not in any shape to swim right now. I don't know if you've noticed, but I have this cast . . ."

His bronzed face startles. "Oh, I just thought you had one mutant foot. Come on, you can work on your tan on the bank, read a book, talk, listen to your music. I promise you'll have fun."

"You said that last time."

"And you did, right?"

I bite my lip. "Maybe."

"I'll take that as an 'Absolutely, it was the best day of my life. Don't you dare leave this house without me.'"

"I don't want to trip on the rocks and mess up my ankle." It's not exactly in tip-top shape after the gymnastics I did on it last night.

"Then I'll make sure it doesn't happen."

I blow out a loud breath and stand up. "I need to change."

"I can help with that too."

I laugh. "I'll be right back."

Ten minutes later we're on our way to pick up some of his friends and head to the creek. I left my mom a note, but I'm not worried about her lack of permission. She's not really into curfews and schedule approval. Millie, on the other hand, would want to know the life history of everyone I'm with, their contact numbers, and copies of their parents' Social Security cards.

"Okay, gang, lunch will be served in an hour." Tate sets down a monstrous red cooler when we arrive at the creek bed. "Only the best for my friends—fifty-nine-cent bologna with slices of cheese-substitute." Everyone groans. "Work up some appetites. I made dessert too."

"And that is?" Ashley walks next to me as I slowly descend the rocky hill to the creek bed.

"Fruit Roll-Ups."

"I'm glad you came out here with us, Katie." Ashley sets up two lawn chairs, one for each of us. "Tate usually chases off the new people in town." She leans in for a loud whisper. "They fear him."

Ashley looks a lot like Chelsea—tall, slender, blonde, ridiculously cute. But there's nothing about her to dislike. Kindness radiates from her blue eyes. And I've yet to hear her utter the word Prada.

At Tate's war cry, the seven other people with us tear off t-shirts, kick off shoes, and jump into the water.

"That creek is always freezing." Ashley laughs as she watches the group yell and splash around. "But it's some of the clearest water you'll ever see."

I slather on some sunscreen and roll up my shorts a few inches. I wasn't ready to strip down to my bathing suit for these people, so I just went with some cute denim shorts and a tank. I figured the combination of a two-piece and my cast was too sexy for anyone to handle.

I'm halfway through my second *People* magazine when Tate climbs up the bank, stands over me, and shakes off like Rocky after a bath.

Knowing he's expecting a girly-shriek, I continue my reading. "Thanks. I was getting a little hot." I grin over the magazine.

He quirks a brow. "Always looking for an opportunity to tell us you're hot." He rests his arm around Ashley. "Hey, Ash, it's now the portion of the day in which I work on my tan, so I'm going to need that chair." She gets up without protest and heads straight for everyone else at the river.

"That was nice of you to relieve her, but I don't need a babysitter. I'm perfectly content up here watching you guys."

He shakes his head and sighs. "You were watching me? I knew it. I try, Katie. I *do* try not to attract the ladies. But I can't help myself. What can I do to make myself less . . . irresistible?"

I hold my laugh. "I totally relate. I get so sick of the constant stares, the boys begging for my number. I'm more than just a pretty face, you know?"

"It's a burden, indeed." He reaches into a cooler, opens a water, then puts it in my hand. "Prayer is all that gets me by. God gave me this burden, so I know he will see me through.

"I knew you'd understand." My phone sings, and I check the display. Charlie. I glance at Tate then answer.

"Hey, Katie. How's it going?"

I smile at his voice. Ugh! Why does he still do this to me? Charlie could call and read the *Sports Illustrated* table of contents, and my heart would still do flips.

"It's going."

"How's your mom?"

"Okay." Not even going to discuss it. The day is too nice to ruin with talk of the anti-parent. "I heard you guys are getting ready for a date auction. That sounds fun."

Beside me Tate puts on his headphones and rocks out.

"Yeah, wish you were here to help."

What does that mean? He wishes I were there so we could be together? Or he wishes I were there because I could help hang up fliers in town?

"Frances mentioned Chelsea's been having a hard time." Hint, hint. *This is your opening to tell me once and for all where you stand with her.*

"Um . . . yeah. Things are . . . interesting, I guess."

Interesting? What does that mean? Are lips involved in interesting?

"So . . . we got disconnected yesterday when I called. I really wanted to talk to you about some things."

"I wish they all could be California girls!" Tate belts out a summer tune loud enough to scare the birds.

"Who was that?"

"Huh?" I focus on the phone call. "Oh, nothing. Er, no one. Charlie, I've really been thinking about our last conversation, too. I wasn't sure if—"

"Hey, guys! You about ready for lunch?" Tate yells out toward the water.

"Who is that? Where are you?"

"I'm at the river. With some new friends—church friends."

"You ready for my special bologna sandwich specialty? The secret is the corn chips under the—oops." Tate notices the phone and gives me some space.

"Who's that guy?" Charlie's tone is as friendly as a pit bull.

"That's my friend Tate. He's the pastor's son."

"Your friend? Wow, you work fast."

No, God does. "He's a friend, Charlie. Am I supposed to stay holed up in my mom's trailer and not make a life for myself here?"

"No . . . no, of course not. That's . . . um, great you're making friends. Yeah. Well, anyway, I guess now's not really a good time to talk."

I can tell even if it was, he's done. "Can I call you later?"

"Yeah. And Katie . . . I'm sorry. Things have just been kind of wild here."

Like flaming kitchen wild? No, I don't think so.

"Everyone misses you." Charlie's voice deepens.

"I miss everyone too." Could we be any more vague?

"Do you think—never mind. I gotta go. Have a good time with your new friends. Just don't forget your old ones." And the line is dead.

I sigh and snap my phone shut.

"Let me guess—boys are stupid?" Tate hands me a sandwich, and I inspect the contents.

"Something like that."

He waves his own sandwich as he sits back down. "It's okay. I'm not offended. We're genetically destined to screw things up—especially with the ladies." He stops talking, his eyes intense on mine until I take a bite.

"Mmmm." Was that convincing? Millie would rip this processed meat sandwich out of my hand if she were here.

"It's the Fritos. My special touch."

I crunch and nod.

"So you have a boyfriend?"

I look out toward the water. "I don't really know if . . . No, I don't have a boyfriend."

"That was good—all that certainty. One of *those* relationships, huh?"

I take another bite. "I think we're just friends. We live too far away from each other anyway."

"*Nahh.* If a guy likes a girl, distance doesn't matter."

I consider this. "Really?" I shift in my seat to face him better. "Tate, do you think a guy can like two girls at the same time?"

"Only on *The Bachelor*." He grabs a Coke out of the cooler. "Not that I watch it." He hides a smirk behind the can. "The guy in me wants to say what a lucky dude, but no . . . I don't actually think you can like two people at once. It's not fair to the ladies, and it's a jerk thing to do."

I take a drink of my water and replay his words in my head.

"But you're not the type of girl who would let a guy play you, right? I totally don't see that. You've got too much fire for that."

Yeah, I'm all about the fire.

Tate shakes his curly mop. "Wow, getting deep over here. Anyway, remember yesterday when you mentioned you were a drama queen?"

I laugh, grateful for the lighter subject. "Yeah?"

"My dad has me teaching Sunday School now. I've been trying to spice it up. You know, make it more exciting, but it's not working. So

I had this idea. I wondered about you and me putting our heads together and writing some skits."

"Like Bible stories?"

"Yeah, and acting them out. You know, some Jonah and the whale. Or maybe the story of Jesus walking on water—I'd play our Lord and Savior, of course."

"Of course."

"What do you think?" He sees my reluctance. "Come on. God gave you those talents for a reason. Use them."

It does sound kind of fun. And my theatre muscles do need a good stretch. "Okay. I'll try."

"Cool." He nods and smiles. "Maybe we could start with a little Adam and Eve, Garden of Eden business? I'm all about realism, so for a costume I thought maybe you could—"

I douse him in my water.

"Or not. Totally okay. Clothes are good too. I'm game for both of us wearing clothes."

* * *

DESPITE MY PROTESTS, Tate helps me up the steps, around the cats, and to the door of the trailer. Mom's car is parked out front, so when I step into the living room, I expect to see her there. But the room is empty.

I walk back to her room and find her sprawled out on top of her bed. I guess when you only sleep a few hours a night, a nap might be in order. I definitely relate.

In the kitchen I mix up some tuna salad, and breathing through my mouth so not to ingest the nasty fish fumes, I stick it in the fridge to chill for Mom. Then I go to my room and pull out my Bible. My finger traces over my name, embossed in gold. I open the cover and read the inscription from James and Millie, written when I first came to live with them.

I turn to the book of Matthew and read through some chapters, like Tate asked me to do. So Peter walked on water to Jesus? I jot down a few notes and skit ideas.

"Katie?"

I glance up, my finger marking my spot, as my mom comes in. She sees what I'm reading, but says nothing.

"Are you hungry?" I ask. "There's some tuna salad for you in the refrigerator. And no kitchens were harmed in the making of your dinner."

She smiles and lounges by me on the bed. "That's nice of you." Her hand plays with a loose thread on my comforter. "I forgot your doctor appointment, didn't I?"

"Yup." I gauge her expression for anything revealing. Did she really forget? Was she on something and out of it? Was she wrapped up in work?

"Mrs. Scott is gonna have my hide. But I called and the doctor can see you next Monday." She rubs a parched hand over her face. "Remember when we lived in that one-bedroom apartment near Austin? And we'd watch *Gilmore Girls* together?"

"Yeah, those were good days." Minus the parties, the cracked-out strangers, the nights I'd spend alone.

She leans back and props her head on her hand. "We were kind of like them, huh?"

Yeah, except Lorelai wasn't psycho. Or on drugs.

"Katie, I would like things to work here. I'm trying . . . I really am."

"I know, Mom." I want to reach out for her hand. But I don't.

"I'm figuring this stuff out as I go. And I'm going to mess up a lot. I'm not the soccer mom type."

"I don't exactly see you in a minivan anyway."

Car lights flash into my room, and Mom jumps up. "That would be John. He's coming over to watch some stupid baseball game. He doesn't have cable."

No, but he has a job, and that makes him a winner compared to all the others.

As Mom gets the door, I get out the bread and tuna for them and PB-and-J for myself.

"What happened in here?" He points to the peeling and singed wallpaper around the stove. My eyes dart to Mom.

She joins me in the kitchen, wraps her arm around me, then pops a chip in her mouth. "Katie and I were just thinking about decorating." Her grip tightens. "It's about time some things around here get a makeover."

# Chapter Twenty-Eight

I DON'T JUST have butterflies in my stomach. I have acrobatic moths or bungee jumping bees.

Tate picks me up for church the next Sunday, and my mom waves good-bye from the door. Though I am confident in my acting abilities—and let's face it, I can command a stage—I have never had something I've written on display, up for public opinion. Or in this case, the judgment of twenty or so kids of the glue-eating age.

"Hey—" Tate swats my knee. "Don't look so stressed. We had a good run-through last night. Everything's going to be great. We've written a great script, and I'm a fabulous actor, so—"

I cut my eyes and clear my throat.

"All right, and you're not too bad an actor yourself."

"That's *actress*, thank you very much."

"Katie, you really are talented. I like how you brought some comedy to a passage that really isn't funny. The kids are going to eat that up."

I feel my cheeks warm and fix my gaze out the window, staring at pieces of this small town that still seems so foreign.

"So what do you want to do when you graduate? Study theatre?"

I open my mouth. Then shut it. "I really haven't given it a lot of thought."

"Are you serious? You haven't thought about your future? Your career? College?"

"I'm more of a day-by-day girl, myself." I punctuate my sentence with a playful wink. But inside the butterflies start a tango. How can I think about the future? Who knows where I'll be or what will happen to me. College was never even an option for me—until I went to live with the Scotts. Before them, graduating high school wasn't too likely. And now—I just want to figure out my place here in Middleton with my mom. Who has time to dream?

He pulls into a parking spot at the church, and by the time I grab my purse and script, he's opening my door. I take his outstretched hand and lift myself out of the car. I inhale just a hint of his tangy cologne, a smell that's becoming familiar to me, and feel a brief moment of calm. I can do this. I can totally be Peter for those kids.

The corners of Tate's mouth lift, revealing pearly white teeth. "You ready to walk on water?"

"I think I am." I return his smile. "But like I mentioned earlier, I will *not* refer to you as God before *or* after the skit."

"Oh, come on. Lunch is on me if you keep it up the whole day."

"You're lucky I'll even be seen in public with you." And we enter the building and head back to the children's area.

I change into my low-budget costume (a sewn-up brown sheet belted off with one of Pastor Jamie's ties) and meet Tate "onstage" in time to greet the first batch of kids to walk through the door.

I watch him call each kid by name, rough up one's hair, then give another little guy a piggyback ride. The kids are all over him—pulling on his clothes for his attention, showing spaces where teeth used to be, and telling stories about their weekend. And Tate, hanging on their every word, couldn't look more interested if he were talking to the president. Humming a happy tune, I join the group and help him greet the rest of the kids.

At ten o'clock, Tate welcomes everyone and begins his tale of Jesus feeding five thousand people. The kids' eyes widen as he holds up five loaves of bread and two rubber fish. In the role of Jesus, he builds on the Bible story, describing the disciples drifting in harsh winds on the lake.

I climb into Pastor Jamie's canoe and pretend to row. "Wow, it sure is windy out here. Sure is dark. I hope my hair isn't getting messed up." My body jerks in trembles, and the front row of kids giggle.

"Wait!" I cry. "What is that? *Who* is that? Do you guys see that man? He's walking on water."

"It's Jesus!" our crowd cries.

"Jesus," one kid yells, like I'm a total moron.

I stand up in the canoe, balancing myself with a paddle. "Jesus? Is that you?" As best as I can with my gimped ankle, I shake my legs, my knees knocking.

Tate raises his arm and unfolds his hand. His eyes burn into mine. "Take courage. Don't be afraid. It's me."

I chatter my teeth so hard, the back row ought to be able to hear. "Lord, if it is you, call out to me. Tell me to come out to you on the water."

*God, I feel like this is my own life. Like you've put me in this impossible situation—like Peter walking on water. I need you to make it okay for me too. Peter couldn't walk on water without you, and I can't do this—this new life—without you. I want to take my courage from you. Please reach out and get me before I go under. Please.*

"I'm right here." Tate's soft voice washes over me, snapping me back to the moment.

With one crutch, I climb out of the boat and step by tedious step, make my way to him. "Look at me!" I call out to the audience. "I'm walking on water! I'm walking on water! I'm—" My face falls. My head jerks down. "I *can't* walk on water!" And I slowly squat down, flailing my arms. "Help me! I'm drowning. Help me, Jesus!" *Please help me, Jesus.*

Tate meets me and my hand warms as he holds it. "I'm right here. I'm not going to let you go. Not ever."

I start to rise, my eyes steady on my cast-mate. "Don't let me sink."

"Where's your faith? Why do you doubt me?" And together we climb back into the canoe. As Peter, I bow my head and pretend to pray as Tate approaches the group and gives them some final thoughts on faith.

"No matter what situation you find yourself in, God's always there, hand out, ready to pull you through." He looks back over his shoulder, and I feel the weight of his stare. "He saved Peter. And he wants to save you." And he leads the kids in a prayer.

"That went great," Tate says, as he drives through my trailer park. "Loved the part where your knees knocked together. But I was a little afraid you were going to fall."

"Yeah," I laugh. "I might need to stay off my ankle this afternoon. All that rocking in the boat wore me out." He stops in my driveway and races around to get my door before I can protest.

"Hey, a group of us are going to watch a meteor shower on top of Stony Peak tomorrow night." He sees my look of ignorance. "It's a cliff top in Tuckerville. You should go with us."

"I don't know. I'm not really into meteors." Or cliffs.

"Oh, come on. These things don't come around every day. It will be something to remember."

Oh, I think I'll have plenty to remember from this time in my life. "I don't know. I was going to get some important stuff done tomorrow night—like file my nails. Or dust my mini-blinds."

"This astrological wonder is calling your name, and you know it. You can make a wish on it or something girly like that."

I shake my head and look toward the trailer where the blinds are all closed. My mom's car is in the driveway. She's supposed to be at work by now. "I'll let you know tomorrow."

"So Noah and the ark for next week?"

"Yes, but this time, I want to be the lead. I'll be Noah."

"I don't know if I'm ready to see you with facial hair."

I shut my door and eye the steps with dread.

"I'm going to help you up there, so there's no point in hiding behind the back of the house this time."

"You saw that?" I close my eyes and sigh. "All right, let's go." He grabs my purse and leads me up the stairs, talking to the cats like they're his long-lost friends.

"Blackie says you haven't gotten him that filtered water yet."

"It's on my list."

He stops at the door as I pull my key out. "Just make sure Stony Peak is on your list." And he hops down as I shut myself in.

"Mom?" No answer. I crutch it back to her bedroom and knock on the door. "Mom?"

The fan on her dresser blows across the room, sailing over her body and ruffling her washed out hair. Sprawled on the bed, she opens a bleary eye. "Whaddyawant?" Her mouth barely moves.

"Mom, you're supposed to be at work." I shove my watch in her face. "It's twelve-thirty."

"Don't feel like it. Call in for me, would you?"

"No." I feel her head. No heat. "What's wrong? Are you sick?" Dread settles in my stomach.

"Leave me alone. Shut the door." She yanks the sheet over her head.

"Mom—"

"Out."

I stand there for a moment, my heart heavy. My brain on over-drive. What do I do? Do I call the salon for her? Tell them she's sick? Do I let her take care of it? Do I call a doctor?

I call Millie.

Closing my bedroom door, I feel my burden lighten as soon as I hear her sweet voice.

"What's new with my girl? How are you?" Though I can't see her, I know she's smiling.

"Hey, Millie. Just . . . um, got back from church."

"What's wrong?"

"I think my mom is sick." I give her a vague description of her condition. "What should I do?"

"If you think she's sick, just let her sleep a while. If she's not better in a few hours, then you need to call me back." Millie asks a few more questions. No, I don't think she's thrown up. No, she isn't running a temp. Yes, her color looks fine. "It doesn't sound too serious. Maybe she just needs the rest."

Mom's been home every night this week, though. Why does she need any more rest? "Yeah, I'm sure she's fine. Just wanted to check with you."

"Katie, if she isn't up and around by this evening, we can come get you."

"No. We'll be fine. I'm sure it's nothing." I've nursed her through stuff before. "I can't wait to see you guys on the Fourth. You're still bringing Frances when you come and get me, right?"

"About that. Katie, I talked to your mom last week." I hear Millie stacking dishes in the sink. "She's asked that we cancel our Fourth of July plans with you."

"What?"

"She said she wanted to have you to herself on the holiday."

"No!"

"It's understandable, Honey. She is your mother, and she has the day off. She doesn't get many of those."

*Oh, she gets more than you know.*

"Katie . . . I know it's not what you wanted." Millie's voice lowers. "It's not what we wanted. But we'll get to see you for Chihuahua Days the next week. You can't miss that. Bobbie said we could have you all weekend. And you can spend all the time you want with Frances."

I rest my head on my desk and hot tears spill onto my cheeks.

"Katie?"

"I'm here." I rub my hand over my nose. "I gotta go. I'll let you know if anything changes with Mom." And I hang up.

I crawl onto my bed, curl myself into a ball, and lie there until the sun tucks itself in.

When I hear the front door open and the Cougar start, I don't even get up.

# Chapter Twenty-Nine

THE POUNDING ON the door shakes me from a dream Monday morning. I throw on a short robe and race to the door.

I look through the peephole. A woman who could be Iola Smartly's twin scratches her gray bun with her Bic pen and waits.

"Yes?" I say from my side of the door. I don't know this woman. Sure, she looks like a teacher on the verge of retirement, but for all I know she could be a serial killer. Her frumpy tweed suit could be her cover. Maybe she charms her victims—with efficiency and poor clothing choices.

"I'm Janice Holloway. I'm with Child Services of Norton County."

*Oh, crap.*

I crack the door and speak through the screen. "Yeah?"

"I have an eight-thirty appointment with Bobbie Ann Parker. Is that your mother?" Her eyes take in my morning attire. I know. The combination of the skimpy robe and the Aircast is mesmerizing.

"Yes. Bobbie Ann's my mother." But she's not here. And I don't think she's been since she took off last night. I never heard her come in, and I waited practically all evening. And no Pop-Tart laying out for me this morning. Guess I'll be canceling another doctor appointment.

"May I come in?"

"Now's not a good time." *Never* would be good. Come back nev-er.

The woman frowns sternly and steps closer to the door. "Are you . . ." She consults the file in her hand. "Katie Parker?"

Yes, but wouldn't I pay a million to be anyone else right now. "Yeah."

"I'd really like to come in, Miss Parker."

"My mom's not home right now. She's at work."

"Work? She was supposed to meet me here this morning. We have a scheduled visit."

"Um . . . I think work has been pretty hectic lately. They've been calling her in a lot." The work of a shampoo girl is never done. Lots of dirty heads in this town.

"Katie, might I come in for a minute?"

"I can't let you, ma'am. I'm not supposed to let strangers in the house," I say like I'm in first grade.

She pulls out some identification and holds it to the screen. "I would like to wait on your mother, if you please."

The screen door creaks as I open it wide, letting Mrs. Holloway into my living room. "I'm just going to change really quick, if that's okay." I don't wait for a response, but hop back to my room. It's everything I can do not to lock myself in there and jump out the window. Except the trailer's too high off the ground, and I know I'd sprain something else.

Thirty minutes later Janice Holloway and I still sit in the living room. By this time I have offered her a glass of water, a snack cake, and remote control privileges. She looks around the trailer and jots things down in her file.

Mrs. Holloway clears her throat and peers at her gold-tone watch. "I believe I will call her employer before I leave." She consults her file and punches in the number on her cell. "Can I speak with Bobbie Ann Parker? Yes, I know you're not open for business yet, but I was told she was there. It's important that I speak with . . . what? Oh. I see. Very well then. Good-bye." She slips the phone in her purse and regards me over tiny glasses. "Your mother is not there."

I stare at the floor, unsure what to say.

"Has everything been going okay here at home, Katie?"

"Yeah, sure. Great." Horrible. Lousy. I mean, I thought things were going to change. I thought we had a chance. But the last few days—I don't know. A few days ago my mom was reminiscing about *Gilmore Girls* and now she's AWOL.

"When was the last time you saw your mother?"

My eyes flit to the refrigerator where a bent picture of Mom and John hangs by a magnet. "T-today."

The caseworker stands up and smoothes her skirt. "You tell her I stopped by. This does not please me that she wasn't here." She hands me her card. "Tell her to call me as soon as possible."

I don't release my breath until the woman drives off. Then I close the door and sink to the floor. *Mom, what are you doing? Where are you?*

At noon Tate picks me up to take me back to his house to work on our Noah's ark script for Sunday.

"The first cross-dressing Noah." He taps the wheel to a Maroon 5 song. "I like it. Noah will be a little feminine, but maybe he's just metro, right? He's in touch with his—hey, are you in there?"

His hand waves in front of my eyes and I drag my concentration back to the present.

"You're a hundred miles away."

Don't I wish.

"You're not thinking about the smell of the ark or why they brought the skunks onboard, are you?"

I force a smile. "No, but I'll work on that. I'm all about getting into character."

He brakes at a four-way stop and swivels in his seat to face me. "What's going on with you? Anything you can talk about?"

My heart rips a little at his constant kindness. It's like he always knows the right words, the exact thing to say. Is this boy even human? "I'm good. Really." Then I apply fake smile number six. It's the one I usually reserve for moments when you have to say "Oh, what a pretty baby" and it's so ugly your eyes burn.

The street is empty and the Explorer doesn't move. The pastor's crazy son rests his hand on mine. "You know you can talk to me, right? You can tell me anything—well, not anything. I don't really understand feminine products or thongs, but I would still be willing to listen."

This drags a smile out of me. "I'm glad I met you, Tate."

He winks a crystal blue eye. "The ladies always are, Katie. The ladies always are." He jiggles my hand playfully then throws it back in my lap. "I can sit here all day long until you talk." He stares out into the barren street. "Probably gonna cause a traffic jam any time now, but I'm a patient guy."

"Would you mind . . ." I hate to ask. I really hate to get him involved and have him know my business. "Would you mind taking me by Sunset Salon before we go to your house? I need to check on something."

His intense gaze stays on mine for a moment before he responds. "Okay, then. Off to Sunset Salon we go." And with one last glance in my direction, he hangs a left and heads downtown.

I open my door before Tate even puts the car in park at the salon. "I'll be right back."

"Do you want me to—"

"No." I force myself to relax. "I'll just be a second. Stay here and keep the car cool." I don't need witnesses for this.

The salon door jangles as I enter, and a teenage receptionist greets me with a smile.

"I'm Katie, Bobbie Ann Parker's daughter." Her smile drops. "Is she here?"

"No, I don't think so." She holds up a finger to wait and slips off her stool. "Mom!" she yells to the back. A large woman trimming a poodle perm looks up. "Bobbie Ann's daughter is here." The woman nods, says something to her gray-headed client, and ambles my way.

"Katie, right?" I struggle to remember her name, knowing I met her on my first day in Middleton. "I ain't seen your mama."

"She's supposed to be here."

The owner plants her hand on her hip, and I read the name on her smock. Polly. "Girl, she was *supposed* to have been here the last three days. I ain't seen her since Friday."

"Friday?" The words pound in my brain. "No, she came to work Saturday. She was here all day. She even worked late."

Polly huffs through her nose. "Believe me, she wasn't here Saturday. I had to shampoo the clients myself, and we were backed up all day." She steps closer and I smell cheap, sweet perfume. "You tell your mama we've had enough. Last week she was late every day, always with an excuse about you and the doctor. But Saturday she just plain didn't show. And I don't have time for that. I run a tight ship, and anyone who can't pull their weight don't get to stay aboard." The owner swivels on a Birkenstock, returning to her curly-headed victim and permanently ending our conversation.

Even though Polly's daughter stares at me, the tears pool in my eyes. I look up and blink them away. Punching my crutch into the tile floor, I turn.

And there stands Tate. His expression dark, his mouth set. He lifts two fingers in greeting to the receptionist, envelopes me in his arm, and leads me out.

He starts the engine, cranks up the air, and turns the radio off. "Tell me." When the words don't come he reaches out and rubs my forearm. "Talk to me, Katie."

I lift an indifferent shoulder. "Nothing. Let's just go."

"It's not 'nothing'."

I roll my eyes. "I don't even know you, Tate. I'm not going to get into all of this."

"You know me."

I meet his penetrating stare. "Yeah, for a week." I study the set of his jaw and know he's not going to budge. "All right . . ." I run my hand through my hair and lean into the seat. "Last year my mom got arrested."

And I launch into the whole epic tale. I tell him about Sunny Haven Home for Girls, Iola Smartly, meeting the Scotts, my friends at In Between High. I tell him about finding God and finding my life in the spotlight of the Valiant Theatre. And I tell him about Charlie, and I try to describe Maxine, yet find there really aren't words to explain her.

"I knew there was a story to you," Tate says. "But I had no idea. You've got more plot twists than Harry Potter."

"Maybe you could just take me home now? I think I'm out of the mood to build an ark and save God's chosen people."

"Thanks for telling me. I hope you know it won't leave this vehicle—won't go any further than the Sunset Salon parking lot."

I give him a small smile. "I know." And I do. Somehow, though he's practically a stranger, I know I can trust this guy. God has blessed me with a great friend just when I needed one.

"Is there anything I—"

"No." I shake my head. "You can't help, but thanks." *Spare me your pity.* I've had more than enough of it in my life. "Let's just go."

"But you'll tell me—if you ever need anything?"

And with my reluctant promise to come to him for help, he backs the Explorer out and takes me home.

"Are you sure you're safe here?" Tate leads me up the last step of the trailer.

"This is not new to me. I've taken care of myself for a long time." Granted, I got used to the good life at the Scotts, where the line between parent and child wasn't so blurred. "I'll see you later. Seriously," I say when he hesitates. "I'll be fine."

"Mom?" My voice bounces off the thin trailer walls when I close the door. No answer. I head back to her bedroom, where, again, I find her sleeping. "Wake up, Mom." I shake her shoulder until she mumbles a protest. "Wake up."

"What?" she whines, her eyes still closed.

"Where've you been?"

"Work."

"No you haven't. I stopped by there today."

"Been working."

"You're lying." I stand there until she opens an eye. "The lady from Child Services came by today. Are you listening to me? Not only did we miss my doctor's appointment *again*, but you missed your meeting with the woman who decides if I stay or go." Her eye drifts shut. "Don't you care?"

"Get outta my room. Tired."

"Where have you been?" My voice raises, slightly desperate. I shake her again. "Where have you been? You're using again, aren't you?"

"No. Go away."

I swipe a tear away, not one of sadness, but anger. Frustration. "Sit up and talk to me!"

I flip on the light and jerk open the shade covering her window.

"Ow! Stop!" Her arms flail, and she covers her eyes. "If I get up," she slurs, "you're not gonna . . . like the consequences."

"Oh, really? What are you going to do to me?" I loom over her. "I can take you out with one crutch. You want to talk to me or do you want to talk to your parole officer?"

With a string of curses, she rolls over, her eyes bloodshot, glazed.

"Do you want me to call John? Your sponsor? Mom, you need help. *We* need help."

"I don't need help. I need sleep." She pulls herself up to a slumped, but seated position. "Don't you ever go to my work again. Understand?"

"You don't have a job. You haven't shown up in three days straight. Your job is gone."

"You're a liar. I was there yesterday." But she frowns in confusion. "What day is this?"

Does it matter? "Why did you tell the Scotts I couldn't see them on the Fourth of July?" I feel the hurt punch at my chest again. "You don't even intend to let me go to In Between for Chihuahua Days, do you?" I'm *so* aware of how stupid that sounds coming out of my mouth.

"I don't want you around them. They put ideas in your head. Those people aren't like us, Katie."

"Oh, you mean like they have jobs and don't roam the night like vampires?"

"See?" she bellows. "That's just what I mean. You will *not* talk to me like that in my own home."

"There's not going to *be* a home if you don't have a job. And the state won't let me live here if you don't pass your next drug test or home visit. And you have to at least *be home* for the home visit. That's kind of how that thing works."

"Shut up!" Her roar startles me. She throws the covers off and staggers out of bed, clutching the wall. "Get me a glass of water. Now!"

I hop backward on my crutches. "Why are you doing this?" I hate how pathetic I sound. "Why are you hurting us? Me?"

"You don't understand anything." A sneer distorts her ruddy face. "You don't know what it's like to be me."

"And what do you think it's like to be me? What do you think it's like to not know where I'm going to be next week? If I'll be in another state home?" I step closer and my voice shakes. "Do you have *any* idea what it's like to come home and find you passed out? Do you know what the first thought is that goes through my head? Do you, Mom? It's *I wonder if she's dead.*" I shake my head and sniff. "Do you know how it feels to have to look for vital signs on your own mother? What it's like to check for breathing while I hold my own breath?"

"I'm not dying, you little idiot. There is *nothing* wrong with me.

Did I ask you one time to check on me?"

I shake my head, vaguely aware of my dripping nose. "I need you to try. Can't you just try to get better? You've come this far. Don't go back. Please don't go back."

"I can't do this right now. I'm outta here."

"No!" I block the doorway with my body.

My vision becomes a blur as she tucks her head and plows into me. I fall backwards, my head slamming into the floor.

And I lie there, choking on a sob, as my mother jumps over me and bounds out the door, cursing my name, my existence, and things I can't even decipher as she escapes into the yard.

The Cougar peels out, tires screeching, rocks thrown against the trailer, and it disappears down the road.

My body and mind numb, I finally pull myself up and wait for my head to quit spinning. I lean into the doorframe and lay a hand over my racing heart.

And that's when I see it. My mom's phone.

I hop to the night stand, my whole body protesting. I scroll through the numbers until I find her boyfriend's name. The phone rings twice.

"John? This is Katie Parker." I drag air into my lungs. "I need to talk to you about my mom."

# Chapter Thirty

"KATIE, YOU CAN'T call the police on her."

I hold the phone to my ear and listen to John defend my mother. Like I'm the one who's got it all wrong.

"It's a relapse. It . . . happens."

"No! It doesn't just happen. Not when my life is on the line too. And the lives of others. John, she's on the road right now. She could hardly stand up on her own. Do you really think she's in any shape to drive? What if she kills someone?"

"I know you're upset—"

"Upset? Are you even *listening* to me?"

"You don't understand."

"Don't feed me that line. She's already tried. Look, your girlfriend's back on drugs. I thought you'd want to help. I thought you might know where she goes when she runs off."

He pauses. "It's not here. I wish it was, but it's not."

"Then where?"

"I don't know. Some friends maybe?"

"Who?" My hand clenches around the phone. "Think. Where would she go? Who would she be with? Look John, I know you don't want her in trouble, but there's a lot at stake here." You know, like my life. "I'm just trying to help her."

"I need you to trust me on this just once. Please, I'm begging you—don't turn her in. I'm getting in my truck right now. I'm going to drive around town until I find her. Then I'm bringing her back to my place to dry her out."

*And what about me?* I want to ask.

"You have to call me when you find her." I give him my own cell phone number.

"Only if I can have your word you won't call the cops. I know what I'm doing here. I've been there. And I really think she can pull it out. She's just relapsed. But she wants to be clean. She does."

I grind my teeth together. "Fine. But if she wraps herself around a phone pole or takes out some kids in a playground, I'm telling the world and anyone else who will listen that you stopped me from turning her in."

"Do you really want to go back to a group home? There's a lot of red tape involved in Child Services. It could be months before you're cleared to go back with your foster family. Are you prepared to risk that?"

I close my eyes and fight back a wave of panic. "No."

I hear his truck start in the background. "I'll be in touch."

* * *

BY THE TIME night falls, I'm no longer sad or scared.

I'm furious.

I've sat here all day long. Waiting. Waiting for my mom to return. Waiting for John. Waiting for the police to knock on the door and ask me to pick her up from jail. Or identify her body.

But Mom's not here and no one's called.

I reach for my phone, ignore my five missed calls from the Scotts, three texts from Maxine, and call Tate. "If the offer's still open to go with you guys to the cliff, I'd like to go."

Thirty minutes later, he's at my door. His crooked smile looks forced and his eyes are serious. "Rough day?"

I consider crumbling into him, but hold myself back. Once the tears start, they won't stop. I don't want to scare him with a total snot-dripping, puffy eyed, wailing melt down.

"I've had better. The talk shows were all reruns, so the day was kind of a drag."

He steps closer to me beneath the porch light and brushes his thumb under my eye. "I have two sisters. I know the look of carefully applied makeup to hide some major bawling. Did you get into it with your mom?"

I think of my sore butt, and my own mother stomping over me to get out of the house. "Something like that. Let's just go, huh?"

He chews on his lip as he looks me over. "She hurt you?"

I shake my head. "No." The pressure builds behind my eyes. Please, let's go.

"Where is she?"

I shake my head, my vision blurry. "I don't know," I whisper. "I need to get out of here for awhile, though, okay?"

"Katie, I don't think it's safe here for you."

I swat at a mosquito aiming for my arm. "I have guard cats." I look down at three curled up together asleep.

He doesn't smile. "My dad knows people. He could help. He could—"

"Our conversation doesn't go further than the Sunshine Salon parking lot, remember?" I stare at Tate. Hard. "You know nothing, and you say nothing. Please."

After a quiet drive, we meet the others at the downtown gas station. A few pile in with us, and another group follows in a Jeep.

Ashley and Tate discuss some people from school, and two other people I've never met carry on their own conversation.

I stare out the window and count the stars.

*God, you know how many stars hang in the sky. But do you know that I'm here—miserable? Do you even remember me? Did you drop me in Middleton and then move onto someone else? Are my problems too small for you? Because they seem gigantic to me. Overwhelming.*

"Ready?"

Tate's hand on my arm pulls me back to reality, and I see we're here. Wherever here is. I grab my flashlight and open the door. I lower myself down from the seat and reach for my crutches.

"Nuh-uh." Tate shakes his head. "Just stay put for a second."

I frown but obey. I really don't feel like getting out anyway. The night breeze blows on my face and suddenly I'm aware of how incredibly tired I am. I don't know that I've had more than four hours of sleep on any night I've been here. I've got more bags than Chelsea now—except mine don't say Coach. They say *I need about eight hours with a good, fluffy pillow.*

Tate opens the back hatch and passes off lawn chairs to his friends. Then he comes around to my side. And holds out both arms.

His smile is reluctant. "Okay, you're gonna hate this, I can already tell, but . . . um . . . I forgot to mention one little thing." His left cheek dimples.

I lift an eyebrow.

"You can't take your crutches up the hill. You'll never make it."

"Then why did you bring me out—*oomph*!" And before I can say "hand violation," Tate scoops me up into his arms. "Put me down!" I hiss. "I am *not* going to be carried like a baby."

"Yeah, I told you you wouldn't like it. See, I *know* you. Now, your job is going to be to hold the flashlight so I don't trip over something like a big rock because I *will* drop you and leave you for the coyotes. Or if I step on a snake because of your poor lighting skills, I will be forced to offer you up for a sacrifice. You think I'm a good guy, but no . . . I will totally make you take the venom before I do."

"Very funny," I say through gritted teeth. I jerk my head around, trying to gauge the reactions of his friends. They walk on, oblivious to us. "Ashley is going to think you're nuts."

"One, Ashley already knows I'm nuts. And two, it was her idea to invite you, and she—along with everyone else—would've known you couldn't maneuver the hill on your ankle, so just shut up"—he pulls me in closer with a grunt—"and enjoy the stinkin' nature."

As we ascend the hill, I wrap my arms around him and hold on tight. Eventually I lean my head back and stare out into the night.

"Um, Parker. The light." And I re-aim the flashlight on our path.

We finally climb to the top, and Tate sets me down, his breathing heavy.

I smirk down at him as he doubles over, hands on his knees, sucking wind.

"I don't feel sorry for you."

"When . . ." he gasps, "do you get off those crutches?"

If my mom had made the doctor's appointments, it could've been today. "Hopefully next week."

"Then that's when we should've scheduled this outing." He wipes his sweaty forehead and grabs two lawn chairs from his friend Jake. "Sit. It's going to be a while."

I shine the light on my watch. "How long?"

"The shower isn't supposed to start until midnight. We have a few hours. Did you leave your mom a note?"

"I don't think she'll mind."

Tate snaps his finger. "Jake, the backpack, if you please." His wrestler-sized friend heaves it to him, and Tate reaches in and pulls out a Coke for everyone. "And for you—" He digs further and presents me with a Diet Dr. Pepper. "Don't tell Ash. It's the only one I could find." He rests his hand on the back of my chair. "I thought you could use it more."

After Tate passes out two different kinds of cookies, everyone settles in and stares toward the sky. Voices are hushed as someone points out the Big Dipper, then later a shooting star. Much later, I stand up and hop toward the cliff's edge. I look out into the dark nothing below me, shining my flashlight on emptiness. Hollowness. I so relate.

"Girls who've had stressful days probably shouldn't stand that close to the edge."

I glance over my left shoulder and see Tate. The others are lost in a discussion about the loss of Pluto as a planet.

"I won't jump." Like I want to be buried in this cast?

"It's a big sky, isn't it?" His voice reverberates near my ear. His breath fans my neck.

I turn all the way around, inches from Tate's face. His eyes hold mine captive. I step closer. We're both right there, and I inch toward his mouth.

"Katie?" His hands on my shoulder stop me. It takes seconds to register it—rejection. I just got totally shut down.

I move back, my eyes wide. Hurt. My mouth opens, ready to blurt out some excuse. Anything.

Tate shakes his head and cups my face. "I'm not the person who can heal this for you. Right now you don't know what you want. You have a guy back home. You have a mom that's making you crazy. And what am I?"

I shake my head, mute.

"I'm your friend. And I'm a safety net right now. But I don't think I'm what you want—or what you need."

*Dear God, it would be so cool if didn't hurl on his shoes right now.*

"Tate, I'm—"

"It's okay." His hands fall away from my face and land at his sides. "Um . . . I know this is going to sound weird—"

*Oh, weirder than me throwing myself on you?*

The wind blows past us, and Tate tucks a flyaway strand of hair behind my ear. "Would you mind if I prayed for you—right now?"

I look up and blink back some tears. Hot tears of shame and humiliation. "Okay." I must be like a leper to him. What if he thinks I'm some sort of skank ho? Should I tell him I'm not? Should I say, "Hey, Tate, I am not the type of girl who tries to make out with the first boy I see whenever I'm on the verge of seeing a meteor. No, I usually reserve that for a lunar eclipse."

"Dear God, I thank you for Katie, for her friendship. It's come to mean a lot to me in a short amount of time. Lord, I know she's scared. And even though I don't know everything that's going on, you know every detail. And you hold her life and safety in your hands."

I close my eyes and think of Peter again, how he must've peed his pants—or his tunic—when he stepped out onto the lake, and especially when he started to sink. Tonight was definitely a sinking moment. *Dear God, things are just getting worse. I'm at the point of going under. Now when are you going to pull me back up? Is it too late?*

"Amen." Tate pulls me to him in a hug, which I don't return. Nope, I'm totally hands off. His chest rumbles with laughter, and he grabs my arms and wraps them around him. "Things are going to be okay, Katie."

"There's a meteor!" Ashley calls out and points upward.

I step away from Tate, unable to meet his gaze, and look toward the sky. He helps me walk back to the others, and I stand there, amidst their cheers and carefree smiles. And the first meteor zooms across the sky, a dusty tail streaming behind it.

Jake holds a lantern to his watch. "It was supposed to be here fifteen minutes ago."

"Nah. It's right on time." Tate catches my eye and a corner of his mouth lifts. "God's always on time."

# Chapter Thirty-One

MY MOTHER'S BOYFRIEND brings her home Tuesday during a commercial break of *General Hospital.*

I open the door as he helps Mom inside. She looks like a drowned rat. One who has tuberculosis or the plague. Her hair hangs in stringy pieces in every direction. Her face is as white as the crisp sheets at the Scotts' house. And she has mascara smeared down her cheeks like some lame attempt at goth.

When John returns from depositing Mom on her bed, I give him my fiercest glare. "Thanks for calling me and keeping me updated."

"I'm sorry. I've been busy. She didn't show up at my house until early this morning." He sits down on the faded couch, his fingers dancing a nervous beat on his knees. "Your mom's going to want to sleep for a while."

"What's she on this time?"

"Katie . . . she just made a mistake. It's over. The last thing she's going to need is you holding it over her head."

I narrow my eyes. "Interesting."

"What is?"

"How you think she's the victim here. You of all people should know better."

"I care for your mom a lot."

"I'm not really sure that's doing her much good." I release a ragged breath. "Where had she been? Who's her dealer?"

He runs his hand over his stubbled face. "I don't know that there is one. She just got her hands on some prescription meds, but it's over. It's not going to happen again."

*Dude, I'm sixteen, and you're more naïve than I am.*

"I'm tired." He stands up and pulls his keys out of his pocket. "I haven't slept since the night before."

I haven't slept since I got here.

"I can have her car brought out later."

"Whatever." And I walk to my room, leaving him standing there to let himself out.

I pick up my phone and scroll through the missed calls. None of them say Charlie. I left a message for him yesterday. Why hasn't he called me? We had a serious conversation to finish. And I could use a friendly voice right now. My fingers itch to punch in his number. *No, be strong. Don't chase him. Let him come to you.* Surely he wants more in a girl than a Gucci stuffed between her ears.

Dragging out my laptop, I sit on my bed and give Ms. Dillon's bonus point assignment some thought—my future. Where I'll be ten years from now.

> *Ten years from now I will be chasing my mother across Texas and any other southern state she can manage to run to. I will be answering phones from creditors, still making excuses to the neighbors, and holding off the landlord who wants his rent. I didn't have time for my senior prom, as I spent that night combing the ditches for signs of her car. And I didn't make it to my high school graduation because I couldn't remember what town I was in—we had moved so much. And of course, I didn't attend college because I didn't have time. I was too busy babysitting—my mother. And I* still *failed to get her roots touched up.*

I close the document just as there is a knock at the door. Probably John. Maybe he forgot another guilt trip to lay on me.

I peek out the kitchen curtains and groan as I see Janice Holloway from Child Services. This cannot be happening. I don't have the energy left to deal with this. But what am I supposed to say, "Sorry come back, my mom's sleeping off a big pill binge?"

As quietly as possible, I walk back to Mom's room. "Get up. Please get up. Child Services is here again." I shake her by the shoulder. "You have to get rid of them."

My mother blinks. "Not today. Don't feel good."

"Yeah, well *I'm* not gonna feel good if I get sent to a group home again. Mom, get up. Seriously. Tell them you're sick, but at least let them see your face."

"Tell them I'm at work." Her voice is weak, and I know she's useless right now.

"I can't say that. They know you don't work at the salon anymore."

"Tell them—" And the rest of her sentence becomes a groggy puzzle as she rolls over and goes back to sleep. I'm so glad everyone but me is able to catch up on their rest.

Janice Holloway pounds at the door, but I can't make myself answer it. Let her think we're not at home.

I creep back into the kitchen and stoop low so she won't see my face through the window. The portly woman, today dressed in a suit the color of Barney, talks into her cell phone for a few minutes before she stomps off the steps and drives away in a cloud of dust.

The rest of the week crawls by as Mom resurfaces to the land of the living and looks for a job. But without a high school diploma, her opportunities are always slim. Every day she comes back wearing a hound-dog face and no prospects. I go to the mailbox daily, knowing I will soon find a shut off notice from the utilities. I can do without a lot of things, but electricity—not really one of them. I spend my hours worrying about Mom, attempting more cooking, and keeping the trailer spotless. I figure if I can eliminate some of the stress at home, then her chances of falling back to the drugs are less. Though my cooking might actually generate more anxiety for her. Or at least heartburn.

Tate and I work on our script for our Noah's ark lesson through the week. Neither one of us says anything about my lips getting lost on Monday night, and Tate acts like nothing ever happened. I'm relieved things aren't weird, but yet . . . a girl would still like to know what goes on in the mysterious male mind.

By Sunday I shoot out the door before his Explorer even pulls into the driveway to pick me up. I leave my crutches in the trailer. The doctor at In Between told me I'd be off of them in a month, and thanks to my mom's inability to keep appointments, we're past the four weeks. But now it's kind of weird walking without them, even though I keep as much weight as possible on my good leg.

"How's your mom?" he asks, his hand shaking my knee—his trademark greeting.

I pull the seatbelt across my chest. "Better. She's been home every night since . . . well, since Tuesday."

"Have you guys talked—really talked?"

My laugh is bitter. "No. And when we do, we just fight. It's okay, though." I shut down the topic and crank up his radio. "It'll work out."

We change into our costumes, mine a Noah-like robe, and Tate's some weird-looking housecoat he brought, somehow thinking it made him look like Noah's wife. He looks more like an overfed housewife with way too much testosterone.

The kids laugh at my take on Noah, but as I glance out in to the rows, they sit on the edge of their seats and hang onto our every word. For the first time in a week, I feel my heart lighten. At least here, I feel a purpose. I know I'm doing some good. At home—I'm just taking up space and doing dishes.

Tate, still in his crazy outfit, peels off his wig and approaches the kids. He stands in front of them and speaks to them about faith, a reoccurring theme here at church lately. And in my own life.

"Noah didn't understand why he had to build an ark." Tate pauses until he has the attention of every wiggling child. "He just knew he had to be obedient and listen to what the Big Guy said. Sometimes the things we're supposed to do and the places God puts us don't make sense. But God doesn't need our approval. He just needs our willingness to do what he says."

Tate leads them into prayer and asks for a show of hands for those who want to learn more about Jesus and getting saved.

My breath catches as two boys raise their hands. Tate, his head still bowed, nods to them, then looks at me. His eyes hold mine, and my lips move into a giant smile. I feel like the arms of God are wrapping around me.

Tate finishes his prayer, dismisses the kids, then goes down on one knee to talk to the two boys. "Katie, we're going to need you over here."

With a singing heart, I join the group.

"Tanner and Cory want you to pray with us. We're going to pray the prayer of salvation with them."

The two boys lock hands. I place my hand in little Cory's, then hold out my other for Tate. He takes it and holds it to his heart for a brief second, his smile radiant as an In Between sunrise.

And we pray. And lead Cory Strickland and his best friend Tanner into the family of God.

* * *

"HOLD STILL!" I make my third attempt at wiping off Tate's drawn on eyebrows, but am giggling too hard to hold my hand steady. "What did you draw these things on with—a Sharpie?"

I sit next to him on the front row of the children's room, my own costume neatly folded away and in the corner closet.

His face jerks as he laughs. "And when your fake beard fell off and got stuck on your tunic?" He shakes his head. "It was like you suddenly sprouted some major chest hair."

"What about you tripping over your robe?" I punch his shoulder. "You just *had* to be my wife? You couldn't be a son? There were three to choose from."

"Yeah, that costume was uncomfortable."

"Nobody asked you to wear a stuffed bra."

He leans into me, as we laugh, shoulder to shoulder.

And that's how Charlie Benson finds me.

"Hey." The object of my In Between desire steps into the room, and I jump up.

"Charlie!"

"They told us we could find you back here."

Frances and Nash appear in the doorway and rush to me. They envelope me in a hug, and I squeal, jumping up and down on one leg. Charlie stands outside the circle.

"Oh my gosh! I had no idea! Where—?" I shake my head. "When? I mean, how—?"

Frances hugs me again. "When you told me you were going to this church, I wrote the name down. I thought we'd surprise you today with a visit and go to the service with you."

I look back toward Tate, who still sits in the chair. "Tate, this is my best friend Frances." Frances waves hello. "This is her boyfriend Nash. And this is—"

"Charlie." Tate rises and sticks his hand out. "You must be Charlie."

"Yeah. Good to meet you." Charlie's mouth might say good, but his face says the opposite. "Nice eyebrows."

"Oh." I chuckle and swab Tate's face with the washcloth again.

"It's okay." He locks his hand over mine, stopping my attempts. "If you help anymore, I'll be in danger of losing my real eyebrows." He smiles, his eyes taking in each one of us. "Well . . . I'm just going to get this stuff off and head to the sanctuary. It was nice to meet you all."

"The preacher's son?" Frances asks when Tate leaves.

"Yeah." But my focus is on Charlie when I answer. "We've been doing skits to tell Bible stories." I bring my attention back to Frances again. "It's the most amazing thing. It's so cool to use drama to tell a story from the Bible. It was Tate's idea. He loves those kids."

I sit between Charlie and Frances during the service. I write them each a few notes, completely unable to pay attention to the sermon. Tate sits across the aisle, but doesn't glance our way a single time.

I have so many questions for Charlie. What's his status with Chelsea? Where do we stand? Has he realized I am the sugar in his tea? The ketchup on his fries? We could make this work. We could. Like Tate said, if a guy likes a girl, distance won't matter. Doesn't it say something that Charlie made the drive this morning to see me? I think it does. I choose to believe it does. I shall have an ark-load of faith.

My head lifts after the invitation, and I roll my shoulders back in relief as a deacon reads the announcements then finally dismisses us.

We've just about escaped when Pastor Jamie steps off the stage to greet my friends. Tate joins us and makes the introductions.

"Glad to have you today. Come back anytime." His dad slaps Charlie on the back, then moves on to other guests.

Tate catches my eye and speaks low. "So I take it you don't need a ride home, right?" I shake my head. "Just wanted to make sure." He pats my shoulder and says good-bye to my friends.

"He's cute, Katie." Frances elbows me, watching the preacher's crazy son walk down the aisle. "We should set him up with some of our single friends. Would he be a good catch for Hannah?"

*I don't know. Would she be the type to throw herself at him? 'Cause he is so not into that.*

"Let's go eat somewhere." Charlie smiles finally.

We all pile into Frances's station wagon, and I direct them ten minutes out of town to a diner.

Charlie pulls out my chair for me at the metal table, and I take the moment to admire his sheer hotness. He's dressed in some Abercrombie khakis, a pink button-down shirt that sets off his tan, and some leather shoes I've never seen before.

"I liked your new church." Frances puts down her menu and fires off twenty questions. She and I dominate the conversation, filling in the blanks that text messages and hasty phone calls tend to leave. "Does the high school have a drama program?"

"I don't know." The waitress stops by, and I give her my drink order. "Mom hasn't enrolled me yet." Mom hasn't done a lot of things. "But I'm loving helping out with Sunday school. It's so cool to use my acting skills for . . ." I search for the words.

"For God?" Frances finishes, her face beaming.

"Yeah. Who would've thought God could use *me*?" I mean, what do I have that God could want? And second of all, I'm a brand new Christian, and I still can't find the book of Job without the index, (And hello, buy a vowel. Job totally needs an E on the end of it. Am I the only person this bothers?) It blows my mind that I could be useful to God. But after today, there's no denying it. I sip my iced tea and tell my friends about Tanner and Cory.

By the time Trixie, our waitress, jots down our order, the church youth group files through the door. Ashley is the first one to see me, and she waves and walks our direction.

New friends are introduced to old ones. I watch Charlie for any reaction upon meeting Ashley, who is the cutest thing in town, but he merely shakes her hand and smiles. He can resist her but not Chelsea? Boys are so weird. Even I think Ashley's hot.

"Hello again." Tate joins us and stands behind me, his hands perched on the back of my chair. "I'd say funny running into you guys here, but it's pretty much the only place to eat within fifteen miles." He leans over me, toward the table, and I inhale his light scent again. "I'd avoid the meatloaf."

The group filters out to their own table, and my eyes follow.

"Tate seems nice." Charlie stirs his tea.

"Yeah, they all are." Was that jealousy I heard? Could it be? Oh, perchance to dream. "Tate's been a really good friend to me. One of those people you meet and feel like you've known forever." Too much? Overboard? It's the truth though.

"Well, I'm glad you've found friends so quickly," Frances says. "That was my prayer for you."

Conversation turns to the latest happenings in In Between, including who's dating, who's broken up, and any other town news worthy of mentioning.

"And we've raised another thousand dollars to go toward Bubba's Big Picture." Nash nods, his chin-length hair covering one eye. "Only fourteen thousand more to go." He smiles weakly. "Totally doable."

"We have less than two weeks to go." Frances sighs, as the waitress serves our food.

"I wish I could be there to pitch in." I spare them the story of my mom banning all visits to In Between.

Nash volunteers to pray, and we bow our heads. "God, thank you for this day. For a great service. Thank you for Katie doing well and making friends. We pray you'd continue to guide her and strengthen her. And Lord . . . we pray for Chelsea Blake."

My head snaps up. *What?* How dare she intrude on our prayer!

"We know she and her family are having a tough time, and we ask you be with them and see them through. Give them peace and hope. Bless this food. Amen."

I raise my brows in question and Frances explains. "Since it hit the papers yesterday, I guess it's safe to mention that Chelsea's dad has been indicted for fraud. He's being held until the family comes up with the bail money. They're devastated."

"Chelsea's a wreck." Charlie slices into his fried chicken.

She's wreck as in, isn't that sad? Or as in, I give her my shoulder to cry on every chance I get?

"Well . . . uh . . ." My mind spins as I try to think of something to say. "I . . . er, that's too bad." Yes, that was the best I could do.

"We've been hanging out with her a lot lately." I can tell nothing from Frances's tone. "Just to keep her mind off her troubles, show her we care."

The mashed potatoes lodge in my throat. "Oh . . . good." I glance at Charlie, who concentrates on buttering his roll.

A few minutes later, Frances finally changes the topic. "When you come back and visit, maybe you can also do something about Maxine and Sam." She rolls her dark eyes. "Maxine is out every night with that . . . that Satan's spawn of a mayor. And Sam . . ." She looks to Nash, who finishes her sentence.

"The poor guy just mopes around town. You're not allowed to mention Maxine's name around him, but you know she's not out of his system. It's like they're both too proud to admit they've still got it bad for each other."

Frances pushes up her glasses. "Sam just wants to be appreciated though. He wants to know he's her main squeeze and that he doesn't have to jump through hoops to win her over."

My eyes roam to Charlie. I *so* relate. Sam and I are just victims in the cruel game of love.

I turn at the sound of loud laughter, and watch the Maple Street Chapel group make their way toward the door. Many of them wave good-bye, and Tate and Ashley walk our way, still chuckling over something. Their smiles are contagious.

"We wanted to invite you guys to the river. We're going over there about four o'clock, if you're still in town. It's a good time; Katie can tell you that. Even for a girl with one leg."

I lob a package of butter at Tate. "Can you stay?" I watch my In Between friends hopefully. Like stay forever?

"No, we have to get back as soon as we finish up here." Frances's face is full of regret. "My mom doesn't want me on the road after dark. This is my first road trip behind the wheel."

"Maybe next time when you're in town then." Tate's gaze drifts to me. "What about you? I could be at your house at 3:45."

I blot my mouth with my napkin and shake my head. "I'd better not. I think I need to stay in tonight and get some stuff done around the house." Plus I haven't been away from my mom this long all week. She's already been alone over four hours.

"Okay." His smile tilts. "But when supper time comes, you'll wish you had one of my special bologna sandwiches."

I'm still grinning when he and Ashley walk out of the restaurant.

The waitress brings our bills to the table, and before I can reach for my purse, Charlie grabs mine.

"I'll get it."

"No." My forehead wrinkles in confusion. "I'll get it." Though I have misinterpreted a lot of signals this week, I do know this is not a date.

I reach for the ticket, but Charlie intercepts my hand, holds it for a moment, then places it on the table. "Katie, I'm buying." His mouth pushes into a smile, and he actually makes eye contact.

"Okay," I concede. "But next time it's on me."

He nods. "Deal."

Outside I lift my face toward the warm afternoon sun and breathe in the Middleton air. Frances and Nash, chattering about some band member of the God Wads, walk ahead of us.

"Are you seeing that guy?" With his hand on my wrist, Charlie stops me.

*What's it to you?* I want to say. "No. Why?"

"You two just seemed . . . close."

I shield my eyes and look into his impassive face. "I guess we are." At this point I am sorely tempted to embellish. To tell Charlie that Tate won't stop asking me out, or that he sends me roses every day and dedicates songs to me on the radio. But I don't. "We're just friends. He was the first person my age I met in Middleton." I wait for Charlie's response.

He drops his head and contemplates the ground. "It bothers me."

My heart thrills at this. "Because I'm friends with a guy?"

He swings his attention back to me. "I don't know." His hand pushes through his brown hair. "I don't know anything anymore."

*Oh, boy.* Are we really back to that again? "Charlie, I can't wait forever until you figure it all out." I take a step closer. "Do you like me?"

"I'm here aren't I?"

"Just barely. You've hardly glanced at me since you've been here. And during lunch—did you even say two sentences?"

"I don't think things are ever going to be the same—with you in Middleton and me in In Between."

"I don't think that's what's changed. I think it has nothing to do with distance."

His brows snap together. "Of course it does."

"What were you going to talk to me about on the phone last week? You know, the last time you called me?" Did I mention that was a *week* ago? That doesn't exactly scream *my heart yearns for you.*

"You know . . ." He pauses, searching my face. "I think I have it all figured out—what would the best for both of us. Then I come here and see you again, and I remember how it used to be. How much fun we used to have. How easy you are to be with." His hands rub up and down my arms. "I miss that."

"I do too. But I don't want to date two of you."

"Tate?" He scowls.

"No, Chelsea. There can't be three of us in this relationship."

"She's different, Katie. I've given that a lot of thought, and I—"

"Charlie! We gotta go." Frances holds her car door open and watches us.

"What?" I prompt him. "What were you going to say?"

"Dude, we gotta hit the road!" Nash waves us over.

"We'd better go. We'll finish this conversation another time. Sometime when we're not surrounded by the smell of meatloaf and gravy."

I thought it was kind of romantic myself.

I sigh with resignation and nod.

Frances jabbers the whole way to my trailer, and my heart is already so heavy with missing her, I can't even focus on the thread of conversation. When she pulls into my drive, I blink at the pressure behind my eyes.

"Can we come in? I'd love to meet your mom." Frances throws Sally Ann in park.

I glance toward the house, painfully aware that Mom's car is gone. Where has she gone? Maybe it's just to the store. We do need groceries. But then again, maybe it's not the store. Maybe it's to a dealer's house. Or to an exploding meth house, and I'll see her on the evening news. Or—

"Katie?"

I blink at Frances's voice. "Um . . . Mom's not even here, and I'm sure the trailer's a wreck. Next time?" I echo Charlie's words and brave a glance at the boy beside me. The boy who was my science partner. Then my friend. Then something more . . . then nothing.

He rests his hand over mine—just for a second. "Next time then."

I take turns hugging my friends, nearly losing it as I pulled Frances to me. "We'll see you soon," she says, and I can only nod. "Oh! Before I forget, the Scotts and Maxine each sent you a care package."

Joy shoots through my heart, and I clap with childlike glee. "Lemme see!"

She goes around, opens the back hatch, and hands me a first box. "From James and Millie."

I dive into it. Some Gap tank tops, a new pair of flip-flops, some books, an iTunes card, and homemade chocolate chip cookies. Not even her soy tofu weirdo cookies—real cookies! Though I'm stuffed, I stick one in my mouth anyway. Ohhh . . . they taste like home.

"And this is from Maxine."

I stick my hand in the Hello Kitty gift bag and pull out . . . a signed picture of Brad Pitt? I lift questioning eyes to Frances.

She shrugs. "We were told not to ask any questions."

Fair enough. I rifle through the rest of the bag and find French truffles, a new *People* magazine, a pen that writes in disappearing ink, and a hundred dollar bill—wrapped up in five new pairs of Victoria's Secret panties.

"She said they were the latest and guaranteed not to crawl."

"Oh, it's great." I hug Frances to me again. "You guys are all great."

Charlie takes my packages from me and walks me up the steps. Swallowing back dread, I pull my house key from my purse.

"Thanks for coming, Charlie. It means a lot of me."

He hugs me again. Briefly. An altogether wimpy embrace. "That's what friends are for."

Friends. Right. *Thank you, Charlie Vagueness.*

I wave toward the car and say good-bye to Charlie again. Then step into the trailer, closing the door on my In Between friends. I peel back a curtain and watch their car from the living room window. Then I run to my mom's bedroom and peek through her window, staying there until there is nothing left of my friends to see.

They are gone.

Leaving me here.

In Middleton.

Because I am Katie Parker—a girl just born to say good-bye.

# Chapter Thirty-Two

"DON'T LOOK AT me like that."

I put the remote down as my mother walks through the front door. "Where've you been?"

"Do you know how sick I am of that question?" She pokes her chest. "I'm the mother. *You're* the daughter."

"*Hmm.* So you do know that. I wasn't sure."

"Don't smart off to me!" she roars, planting herself right in front of the TV.

"Did you get any groceries?"

"Get 'em yourself."

"Yeah, I'll just walk to the store." Fury courses through my every cell. "Maybe I could've, had you taken me to the doctor instead of going AWOL every time I had an appointment."

"Just shut up."

Though I've heard it a million times, I still close my eyes at her words. Millie and James would never talk to me like that.

She rubs her temples. "My head hurts. Get me some aspirin."

"Get it yourself."

"This is *my* house. You will do what I tell you to so long as you live here."

I stand up, throwing the remote on the couch. "Which won't be very long. At some point the Child Services lady is going to come back—and not to talk to you. But to take me. Is that what you want?

You ripped me out of the Scotts' house just to throw me somewhere else?"

"You've never wanted to be here. Admit it!"

"I wanted my mom back. I wanted things to work. I wanted you to have a job like a normal person. I wanted—"

"You are so judgmental. You get that from *them*, you know. Those *people* you lived with."

"Why?" I yell. "Because I expect you to have a job? As soon as I get rid of this cast, *I'm* getting a job. It's what people do—people who want to eat. Have you paid that electricity bill yet? The water?"

"It's about time you thought about helping out around here. Take, take, take, that's all you do. I can't do this alone, Katie."

"You can't do this *period*."

She jumps around the scarred coffee table, inches from my face. I smell the alcohol on her breath and automatically breathe through my mouth. "What do you want from me? I'm not perfect."

"I want you to be the mom who can at least remember a doctor's appointment. I want you to be able to get yourself to work so I don't have to pull out my old list of excuses for the landlord. I want you—" My voice breaks, and some of the anger seeps away, leaving mostly sadness. "I want you to love yourself *and* me enough to stay clean." I blink away the wetness pooling in my eyes. "Please love me enough to not send me back into the system. You don't know what it's like. I deserve better." I hear the whine in my voice and it's like acid in my stomach. "I can't go back," I whisper. "I can't go back to a group home for a single day."

My mom's body trembles, her breathing ragged. "I will try and find a job tomorrow."

"What have you been doing all this week?"

"Trying to find a job!" Her voice shakes the thin walls.

"You have to call the lady from the state. I can't put her off any longer. She left a message on the door Friday that you missed a drug test. You have to go take that."

Mom steps around me and sinks into the couch, her head in her hands. "I can't."

I swallow hard. "Why?"

"Because I just can't."

"You've got to start going to your support group meetings again. And talk to your sponsor. You have to get help. You're sabotaging your life." *And* mine.

"Just like that, huh?" She raises her face and laughs. "You got it all figured out, dontcha kid? You've got all the answers. Well, you don't know what it's like to be me."

I stare at her shaking hands, her red face. "No, I don't. I can't imagine. But you know what? This past year I learned what it is to be a kid—to be taken care of. To be loved and provided for. To not have to worry if I'd have anything for dinner or where I was going to get lunch money. To really be a kid and not the adult. Why can't we be like that? Why can't you just be the mom? *My* mom."

Mom digs into her pocket and pulls out her keys.

"No, don't go anywhere. Please. Just stay here tonight. I can't handle this anymore—this wondering where you are and if you're alive."

"Then don't worry about it. Did I ask you to worry?" She stands to her feet.

"Please don't go. We'll work on your résumé. We'll search online for a job."

"I don't need your help," she sneers, glaring down at me. "I'm going to John's. I won't be back tonight, so don't stay up and 'worry' about me."

"You're picking everything over me. John, the drugs . . ." I pull myself up and latch onto her shoulders. "When do I get to be a priority?"

"I don't know." She pushes past me. "But it ain't tonight."

"Please—"

My pleading voice stops her halfway out the door.

"Do this one thing for me. Don't leave me tonight." I see her eyes focus a bit more and know she's considering it. "I won't ask anything else of you. I'll make us some popcorn. We can watch some Lifetime." I smile weakly. "There's a new Tori Spelling movie on tonight."

My mom takes one step back into the living room.

Then her cell phone rings. She rips it out of her back pocket and checks the call.

"Don't answer it." I don't know who it is, but it can't be good. I'm sure it's someone who could never understand the value of a good Lifetime movie. Or a drug-free life.

"Uh-huh. Really?" Mom sticks her head back outside and waves. "I'll be right out." She stares at her phone. "Dang. Battery's going dead. Can I borrow yours?" A horn honks from the driveway.

"Who's out there?" I get up and look outside. Some guy sits behind the wheel of an old Ford truck. I can't see his face, but I can tell he hasn't shaved in this decade and he has hair longer than me. "*Who* is that?" Cause it sure isn't John.

"Just a friend. We go way back."

Like back to prison?

"Katie, I gotta go." She sticks her hand out and waits for my phone. "Come on." She sees the protest in my face. "I just need some air. I'll have your phone back to you tonight. I'll try to be home by nine. I will."

I have absolutely no reason to believe her. No reason to trust her anymore. Yet I hand my cell to her anyway. "Don't go through my numbers and call anyone."

Mom rolls her eyes then gives me a quick peck on my cheek. "Thanks."

"Mom?" She's pulling the door closed. "I love you."

The lines between her brows deepen. "Uh-huh. You, too, kid. I'll see you later." But she winks as the door shuts, and I know it's the closest to "Daughter, you are the light in my life and the reason I draw breath" I'm going to get.

I return to the couch, worn out as if I just finished a marathon and my nerves in shreds. I offer up a quick prayer for my mom's safety.

Three hours later I am mourning the loss of my phone. I have people to text! Family to call! Games to play. Could my life get any more miserable?

Yes, it could.

And it does.

The house goes dark.

And silent.

I curl my legs up on the couch and pound my head on my knees. No, no, no! This is *not* happening. I *knew* she hadn't paid that electricity bill.

Feeling my way to the kitchen, I locate a flashlight in a drawer. I hate the dark. I would never make it on *Survivor.* I would be the first one they voted off. In fact, I'd volunteer to be kicked off. I like my creature comforts too much. Like electricity, a soft bed, and food that doesn't make you want to grab a can of Raid.

I raise all the dusty blinds to let in the remaining light from outside.

Headlights set the living room all aglow, and I peer out the window over the sink.

Tate.

My heart picks up the pace. Do I let him in? He'll know we can't afford electricity. He'll know my mom is a total loser. But I'm bored. And I don't know when or *if* she'll be back. Total humiliation versus human contact. I don't know!

He raps on the door. I stay in my spot, motionless. Frozen. I can't let him in. I can't let him see me like this.

The small knocks turn into pounds. I close my eyes against the noise.

"Katie?" He bellows, his fists heavy on the door. "Katie, are you in there? Mrs. Parker?"

Oh, no. He's worried about me. *Go away! Shoo! I have attack cats. Don't make me sic them on you.*

I hear him descend the steps. *Whew.* I exhale my pent-up breath and take another peek.

Wait. What's he doing? He reaches into the back of his Explorer and pulls out a box. A cooler. He's getting out a cooler? *Um, not exactly a good time to tailgate, Tate.*

I move away from the window as he draws closer to the trailer again, still calling out my name. My neighbors are gonna be so ticked.

I hear the cooler hit the ground, and I frown.

Stepping away from the sink, I press myself to the back wall of cabinets. There's no way he can see me.

I gasp.

And my eyes connect with Tate Matthews—who stands on his Coleman cooler and spots me with his flashlight.

"Katie?" his voice spikes with fear.

"I'm okay!" I yell. "Drop your weapon." Okay, so now is not a time for flashlight humor.

"Open this door!"

*Dear God, what in the world have I ever done to make you mad at me? I clearly am being punished for something. Because I was born to Bobbie Ann Parker? Frankly, I think you owe* me *for that one. I would be willing to not hold it against you, if you'd just perform an eensy-weensy miracle and let this trailer floor swallow me whole.*

I wait.

*Not gonna happen, is it?*

With a cry of frustration, I propel myself into the living room, nearly tripping over my mom's shoes, and open the front door. But not the screen.

"Yes?" I say, all calm, as if I'm not standing with all the lights off, and Tate hasn't been shouting my name out like a war cry for the past minute and a half. "Were you just in the neighborhood?"

"Let me in." He shines his light into the living room. The beam zooms right and left.

"There are laws for that, you know." I gesture to his flashlight. "You can't just peek into a girl's house. People will think you're a perv."

"You have three seconds to open that door or I'm calling the police."

In one motion I unlatch the screen and fling it open. "No police."

He slips by me and steps into the living room, his flashlight still roaming. "Is everything okay here? I've been texting and calling you for hours."

I shrug a shoulder and watch the light dance on the worn walls. "Things are great. Why wouldn't they be?" Just because it's one hundred degrees in here since I'm too afraid to open the windows? And I'm nearly seventeen, and I'm still convinced the boogeyman exists and has waited all my life for the perfect opportunity to pay me a visit?

"Is your electricity out?" He shines the light in my face, and I swat it away.

"Ow! I'm blind! Watch the eyes, would you?"

"Answer me. What's going on?"

"Yes, my electricity is out."

"I didn't notice anyone else on your street in the dark."

Shame settles on me like an overstuffed backpack. "Yeah . . . um . . . not sure what the problem is." As in I'm not sure what the problem is with my mom not able to hold down a job and pay one stinkin' bill.

"Is your mom here?"

"Nope. She's out for a bit." Must get this boy out of here. "Hey, I'm really glad you stopped by, but I have things to do." I roll my eyes to the ceiling. *I have things to do?* Am I an idiot? Clearly unless it's things to do in Braille, I have *nothing* to do!

"Wait right here." And before I can work up a good objection, Tate is out the door and back again. "I still had my lantern in the back from last week at the cliff." He settles it on the coffee table and lights it up. "I'm just going to open some windows."

"Tate!" I must gain control of the situation. "It's okay. I'm perfectly comfortable in here." A bead of sweat drips down my cheek. "It's very . . . cozy."

"I could roast hotdogs in here." He flings open the living room windows, and a breeze swirls through. Okay, so it might have been a little bit stifling.

Tate lets in some air, then strides to stand in front of me. His hands clamp my shoulders. "Are you okay? What happened?" He peels a limp piece of hair off my forehead.

I stare into his fierce eyes. Then drop my head. "Momdidnotpaythebill."

"Take your hand off your mouth. I didn't understand a word of that."

"I said—" I hate my life. Can I be someone else? Just for one day? I want to be Hilary Duff or that girl from *Hannah Montana.* Except her dad totally needs a haircut. "My mom didn't . . ."

His grip tightens. "What? Pay the bill?"

I sigh and stare at the peeling linoleum. "Uh-huh." My head springs up. "But it's okay. I'm fine. No need to stay. It will be on tomorrow probably. We'll get it straightened out. She probably just forgot. I'll get it taken care of. I don't need lights. And sure, I'm missing a good Lifetime movie, but they show them over and over until you get sick of them and you're, like, could you please quit showing that same movie? I don't care if they do call it an 'encore presentation,' it's still a rerun, and I can only handle so much of the old cast from 90210, and—"

"Katie!" Tate gives me a little shake, and for the first time I see the beginning of a smile. "Come home with me."

"I'm not really that kind of girl."

He laughs and drops his hands. "I mean come have dinner with my family. Hang out with me and my sisters. We'll invite some other friends over. You can't stay here. You'll be completely in the dark soon."

"Thanks, I appreciate it. I do. But I need to stay close and wait for my mom." I don't know why, but I can't shake the feeling I need to be here when she gets back. And I want to see if she really is home by nine. "Was there a reason you stopped by—besides a really bad attempt at stalking me?"

Tate moves to the couch and sits down. I settle on the other end. "I started calling hours ago to see if you wanted a ride to church."

Oh. Sunday night church. Funny how a lack of electricity can make a girl forget these things. "I guess I'm not going."

"It's already over."

So's my life. "Well, it was nice of you to stop by, but—"

"Have you eaten dinner?"

Nope, haven't eaten since lunch. But since we're down to old candy, crackers, and juice there's really not any point in having an appetite.

"You can't stay here in the heat. Come back to my house. You can leave your mom a note, and I'll bring you back in a couple hours. She wouldn't want you to sit here alone in the dark."

*Oh, you'd be surprised.*

"I'm not going anywhere."

He scoots closer to me on the couch. "Clearly things aren't getting better with your mom. I'm worried about you. You can't live like this. Please let me call someone."

"No!" I clutch my hands in my lap. "You can't. You promised me. You have no idea what my life would be like if I get taken out of my mom's custody."

Tate nods, his jaw set. "I'm giving it one more week." He holds up a hand at my look of outrage. "If things don't get better, I'll talk to my dad. Not the police or anything—just my dad. He'll know what to do. If nothing else, you can bunk with my sister, Kari." A smile spreads on his face. "She's ten and likes to play Barbies. And she forces it on everyone she encounters."

"Well, as fun as the Barbies sound, it doesn't exactly work that way. I can't just go live with someone. You *have* to keep this to yourself."

"One week. That's all I can do. You're not safe here." He palms my right knee and gives it a shake. "Now, back to my original question, have you had dinner?" I raise a noncommittal shoulder. "Then if you won't leave the house, I'll have to fix you something here."

"You can't." My fear from his earlier words begins to dissolve. "My mom should be here in about fifteen minutes."

"So? Then I'll make both of you dinner." He gives me a nudge. "I'll be back soon."

"Where are you going?"

"The store."

"What for?"

Tate's eyes sparkle in the dim light. "Katie Parker, I'm going to prove to you there's more up my sleeve than bologna sandwiches and big biceps."

I smile at the crazy boy on my couch. "I always thought there might be."

# Chapter Thirty-Three

"CAN I INTEREST you in a drink, madam?" Two Dixie cups hang from his fingers. "I have a lovely vintage here that I think is just the thing." He pours Diet Dr. Pepper into my cup, swirls it, then holds it beneath his nose. "It's dark, it's bubbly, and best of all, should we decide to have a burp contest, this could push you to victory."

I stifle a laugh and take the drink.

And chug like there's no tomorrow. He lifts a brow, but says nothing. Only refills my cup.

"For myself, I'm more of a traditional guy." He pours himself regular Coke and takes a drink. "Ahhh. A very fine year." His skin glows in the light of the candles on the dining table.

It's nearly ten o'clock. Yet instead of worrying about my mother or counting the minutes, I'm totally caught up in this dinner. I've already reminded myself half a dozen times Tate only likes me as a friend—that was made painfully obvious. And I like Charlie Benson.

Don't I?

"Would you like some salad?" Using two plastic forks, he throws some in a bowl before I respond. "And for your dressing? You can have ranch." He holds up a lone bottle. "Or ranch."

"Oh, I must have the ranch."

"A very good choice." With absolutely no finesse, he squirts some onto my salad then places it before me. "Before we eat our greens, a toast." He lifts his Coke. "To . . ." He chews on his lip as he considers his words. "Good friends. A good meal. And my sincere hope the chicken doesn't make either one of us sick."

I clink my drink to his, savoring his playful smile and the burn of the Diet Dr. Pepper sliding down my throat.

After our salads, Tate brings me a fresh plate of chicken, a baked potato, and a small loaf of bread.

He gestures for me to take the first bite. "If you keel over, I'll know not to eat my own cooking."

With one eye on the chef, I cut into the chicken and lift a hesitant bite to my mouth. "Mmm. It's actually good."

He beams with pride. "All thanks to my super handy camping equipment—a grill and a little propane stove. Perfect for weekends at the lake, power outages, or when your mom won't let you get near the kitchen anymore." He leans over the table. "I've had a few mishaps."

That would make two of us. I tell him about my hamburgers that nearly brought the trailer down.

Thirty minutes later, still no mom. But I do have dessert.

"Whipped cream?" Tate holds out a can of Reddi-Wip over my bowl of strawberries and store-bought pound cake. "Don't answer that. You're a girl who appreciates the finer things in life. I can tell." He swirls the white stuff all over my bowl until it's piled high enough to lean. He places another strawberry on top. "Perfect."

"Have I thanked you for this yet?" I watch him over my fluffy concoction.

Tate stabs a piece of cake with his plastic fork and takes a bite. "No thanks needed." His hair is damp with the heat.

I set my fork down. "Yes, it is necessary." I watch him until I have his full attention. "I don't know what's going to happen in my life, Tate. I have no idea where I'll be this time next month—or even in a few days." I lower my head and wipe my mouth with my napkin. "But I hope you know your friendship has meant a lot to me. It's hard being the new kid, and I don't know that I've ever made a friend so fast as when I met you." All this honesty stuff is so embarrassing. I feel my face grow even hotter. "Anyway . . . thank you."

Tate's hand reaches out across the table. I stare at it. Once *not*-kissed, twice shy.

He wiggles his fingers in invitation, and I slowly place my hand in his. His fingers close over mine. My heart flutters, but I will the feeling away. He's a friend. Only a friend.

"I know things are going to work out for you. And no matter what," he squeezes my hand, "I'm here, okay? I want to be on the top of your call list when you need something." The candlelight dances on the wick and casts funny shadows on our outstretched arms. "You're an important friend to me."

Did he put the stress on the word *friend* or *important*?

"I'm going back"—I almost say *home*—"to In Between in a few weeks." Maybe. If I can escape. "You should go with me."

His expression doesn't change.

"Er . . . and Ashley and Jake. You know, the whole gang could go." That sounded a lot better in my head.

"Yeah, that would be fun. We'll see." Does he know he hasn't let go of my hand yet? Maybe the heat's getting to him. "So you'll keep me updated on your mom, right? I want you to call me tonight when she gets in."

"It's going to be late."

"Doesn't matter."

I pull away and stack his paper plate on mine. "I can take care of myself. I've been doing this for years."

"Well, that needs to stop." My head jerks up at his sharp tone. "One week. That's all I can do. And I want you to call me every day. And pick up any time I call." His features soften. "Katie, this is not a good situation."

"I know. But it's temporary. She'll get back on track." But as the words come out, I know I don't believe it.

"My dad has—"

"No."

Tate's eyes widen. "I was going to say my dad helps people out all the time with utility bills and other living expenses. It's part of the church budget."

"You can't tell your dad, Tate." Urgent fear pounds in my chest. "You can't. You know that will lead to other things—like me being sent away." I have no guarantee I'd get to go to the Scotts. It's just not worth it.

"But if I could swing it another way?"

"No." I cross my arms over my chest and pin him with my stare. "Absolutely not. *I* will take care of it."

"Okay, okay!" Tate scoots back his chair. "Let's talk about happier things for a while." I follow him into the kitchen as we toss everything into the trash. "How about I tell you about the time I snuck in the backseat of the car on my oldest sister's first date?" Tate leads me to the living room, and we settle back into the couch. "I was only ten."

At midnight, I cover a yawn, and my weighted eyes flutter. "You have to go home."

"I'm boring you into a coma, aren't I?" But he looks tired too.

I laugh and shake my head. "No, yours stories are great. Especially the one about setting the frogs loose in kindergarten. But it's late. I know you have to be home. The pastor's son *cannot* be hanging out alone with a girl in a candle-lit trailer at this hour. The deacons will have a fit."

"The deacons are my uncles."

"Go, Tate." I point toward the door with a tired grin. "Go home."

"I can't convince you to come back with me?" He holds up his hands. "Your virtue is safe. I won't stow you away in my bedroom or anything."

"Leave my house. I'm tired. As soon as I lock you out, I'm going straight to bed."

He stands up, and I follow him to the door. "You'll call me as soon as your mom gets home?"

I rub a knot in my neck and nod. "Yup. See ya."

"Okay. I know when I'm not wanted. I'm out." With one hand on the door, Tate stops. His eyes lock onto mine, and he pulls me close. Then closer.

I hold my breath.

His hand reaches out and eases toward my face. I'm frozen to the spot.

"You have just a little bit of whipped cream there." He flicks my nose. "Got it." And he shuts the door. "Call me!" he yells.

# Chapter Thirty-Four

BY TUESDAY NIGHT, Bobbie Ann Mason has lost any chances of getting a Mother's Day present out of me ever again.

She is still not home. It's been over forty-eight hours since she left, taking my cell phone *and* I discovered, the credit card the Scotts gave me.

I'm starving, I'm tired, and I'm furious. I've been eating stale graham crackers and rock hard marshmallows. But at noon today, something good happened. The electricity came back on. I know Tate is responsible. But when he came earlier to check on me, he acted as if he knew nothing about it. I can just tell by the look in his eyes he hasn't said anything to his dad (okay, I can tell by the fact that Child Services hasn't swooped in to get me), so Tate must've paid for our electric bill himself.

But I would cut out my tongue before I admitted we have no food in the house, and of course, I have no way to get to the store.

By the time dark falls, I'm settled into a good movie on TV. I can hardly keep my eyes open. I haven't slept in days, and I need a good Run for the Border. As I watch the murder mystery, I keep one ear for the door.

By the first commercial, someone pulls into the drive. Probably Tate again.

I don't bother getting up. I'm just too tired. And it's really hot in the house, even though the air has been blowing nonstop.

Then someone pounds on the door. "Katie?"

I frown and jerk to a seated position. I don't recognize that voice. Maybe it's someone with news of Mom. But what if it's Child Services?

I shuffle to the kitchen window and look out.

Rolling my eyes, I go to open the door.

And there stands John. He looks almost as bad as I do. His hair is a mess and he's shaking.

"Where's my mom?"

He charges past me. "Turn the TV on."

"It is on." *Einstein.*

"Turn it on a local channel. Try channel five."

I fumble with the remote, the hair standing on the back of my neck. "What's going on?" *Please don't kill me.* I hope this isn't his way of gaining entry into unsuspecting girls' houses. I will so ticked if they find my dead body tomorrow all because I fell for the line *turn the TV to channel five.*

A commercial for peanut butter blares to life, and a chubby kid smacks his lips and extols the virtues of a great PB and J sandwich.

"Turn it. Turn it!" John rips the remote out of my hands.

"Hey! Back off. What's happened? Tell me *now.*"

"Just watch." He keeps flipping the channels until a live news report catches his attention. "Watch."

Dread swirls in my stomach as I see a young journalist standing in front of the downtown pharmacy. "The two broke into the Middleton Pharmacy at nine o'clock this evening. They took petty cash, and a variety of pharmaceuticals such as Sudafed and cough syrup. Police have just released this surveillance camera shot of the event. If you recognize the man and woman or have any information, please call . . ."

The rest is a roar in my head. I struggle to focus as panic consumes me.

"Police say the woman has on a tank top that reads 'Born to Be

Wild' and a pair of cutoff shorts. Her face was covered with a pair of pantyhose."

I will never live this down. I know that's my mom. I know it. Not only did she rob a pharmacy, but she didn't even do it with class. She had hosiery on her head!

"The man, who looks to be in his forties, has long hair, tied back in a ponytail. He, too, had his face covered with a stocking."

*Jesus, take me now. Just call me on home.* My life has just been reduced to a bad episode of *Cops*.

The woman's rushed voice breaks through my tangled, swirling thoughts. "The man in question is considered armed and dangerous. As you can tell from the last frame of the security footage, he does have a weapon."

John shuts the TV off. The silence is deafening.

"Turn it back on."

"It's her, Katie." He paces the length of the living room. "Have you heard from her?"

"Have *I* heard from her?" No, I'm her daughter. Why would *I* hear from her?

"When's the last time you talked to her?"

I explain my last conversation with my mother on Sunday afternoon. "She left with some guy. Some long-haired guy. "Like the freak on the news. I clutch my head in my hands. I cannot believe this.

"I know that man. He came to our meeting two . . . maybe three times."

I raise my head, my eyes wide. "Are you going to the police?" Because I'm going to need to pack a bag. The state will come for me. And I'll spend the night, the week, the month with total strangers.

John runs his fingers through his hair. "No. I can't."

I feel a strange twist of relief, but at the same time, who *wouldn't* call the police?

"I can't the police on your mother. I know it's crazy, but I can't." He seats himself beside me on the couch. "I love your mother."

Make me gag. Do I really have to listen to this crap on an empty stomach?

"I thought she would rebound."

"Oh, she did." I quip. "Right back into her old lifestyle."

"I thought she could do it."

"Well, excuse me for throwing around blame, because it is all Mom's, but you didn't exactly make it hard on her to go back."

He shakes his head and stares at his hands. "I know." John jumps to his feet. "But I'm done. I have to look out for me now."

Yeah, I know the feeling. Stinks, doesn't it? I reach for the remote, and with a click, the news fills the screen again.

"Again, they are considered armed and dangerous. If you have any information, please call the police or this station immediately."

"Katie, you have to get out of here. They have to be so out of their heads. You can't be here if they come back. It's not safe." His tired eyes meet mine. "Do you have somewhere to go—someone to stay with?"

* * *

AN HOUR LATER, I throw my last suitcase in the backseat of Mom's old Cougar. The door creaks as I slam it shut, and I turn the key.

*God, help me. I have had just enough driving experience to pass my test—and we know that didn't go so well. Please help me get safely down the road. I have to get out of here. I can't stay here anymore. Oh . . . and help my mom. I guess.*

With Maxine's hundred bucks stuffed in my bra (sadly, there's still plenty of room), I crank up the air conditioner to max and crawl out of the driveway.

A half-mile down the road, I pull off to the side, open the door, and chuck my Aircast into a ditch. If Peter could walk on water, surely I can at least drive with this bum ankle. I cruise through a Mickie D's drive-thru and get a large Diet Dr. Pepper—no time to eat—and ease the Cougar back onto the open road.

And drive away from Middleton.

My eyes water, and I try to blink to ease the dryness. So tired. I am exhausted. I wonder if they've caught my mom. I left a note in the trailer so when the police do show, they won't think Bobbie Ann and her long-haired hippie have taken me.

I squint as I read road signs, and send up a prayer with each turn and exit ramp I take. Some of these road signs are just unnecessarily difficult. Like it's a big scam. They *want* you to get lost so you'll pull into a convenience store and ask directions—*and* load up on drinks, candy bars, chips, and nachos drenched in plastic cheese sauce.

Occasionally I see a landmark that looks familiar. Or maybe I just think it does. I pray it does. But what if I'm just driving in one big circle? I'm an hour and a half into this trip. What if on hour two, I take a turn and I'm at Middleton again? I will die. Just throw myself in the center of the four-way stop and let traffic have its way with me.

Except I think the Middleton four-way only sees about one vehicle an hour.

Which would be a little anticlimactic.

I rest my elbow on the door. Then my head bobs.

No! Must stay awake. Not much further. Maybe two hours or so, as slow as I'm driving.

With shaky fingers, I turn a knob and the radio blasts at full volume. I skip through some heavy metal, pass on some twangy country song about beer and tractors, and stop at the sound of some old Imagine Dragons.

The miles stretch out in front of me, and the dark of night—or morning—threatens to swallow up me and my car. My brain spins like a scratched CD, and the thoughts slam into one another. *What if the car breaks down? What will I do? What if they don't find my mom? What if the state comes looking for me? What if my mom comes looking for me? Will Tate worry about me tomorrow? What if he hears about my mom, and I'm gone? What if I lose this radio station and I have to listen to Frances's favorite—*

*KPOK, nonstop polka?*

At two a.m., I find an open gas station and pull over to fill my tank. I stare at the sign instructing me to prepay, and run inside as best as I can with one weak leg, and throw two twenties at the cashier. I sprint back out, my breathing hard and uneven. I don't want to end up on the news either—as a missing person. Who knows what could happen to me out here. There are some weirdos on the road at this hour. I catch a glimpse of myself in the rearview as the car fills. Okay, *I* look like a total weirdo. Ugh, my hair. It looks like I've been driving with my head. And makeup—there isn't a scrap left.

I rest my face on the steering wheel. Gonna close my eyes for a little bit. Just rest the peepers.

The pump shuts off, and my head springs up. *Wake up, Katie. Come on, you can do this.* I slap my cheeks and shake my head around. I just want to sleep. Maybe if I pulled around back and parked the car, I could take a little nap and then—

*No! I have to keep driving.* Must keep going.

And though I have four dollars change coming back to me, I peel out of the parking lot and join the truckers on the highway, my whole body rebelling at the fatigue.

Ten songs later, tears are flowing unchecked down my dirty face. I don't know where I am. Don't know where I made a wrong turn. Why didn't I buy a map? I can hardly keep my eyes open. *God, send me an angel. Send me some help. Send me a sign.*

And then I see it. My headlights shine on the beautiful green surface.

In Between, five miles. Exit 86.

I let out a whoop of joy and follow the road until it leads me into In Between. I pass by cow fields, the old water tower, Gus's Getcher Gas, Holly and Woody's video store. Strength surges back into my body, as I draw closer and closer to the Scotts' house.

I'm crying again when I pull into their driveway, but tears of elation and relief.

With the key trembling in my hands, I open the front door and step into the darkness. I take a moment to adjust to the blackened interior, my mind recalling exactly where everything is in this house. I inhale deeply, soaking up the smell that was my comfort for so many months.

And then wave after wave of exhaustion hits me.

My body is stiff, and my limbs cry out for rest.

On stumbling legs, I make it to the living room and tumble onto the leather couch. The jangle of a collar announces Rocky's presence, and I feel the familiar wet welcome on my hand.

"It's me, Rocky," I mumble. I tuck my hands under my head and close my eyes, drawing the safety of this place around me like the softest blanket.

And I smile at my last thought before sinking into unconsciousness.

*I'm home.*

# Chapter Thirty-Five

AT THE SOUND of muffled voices, I pry one eyelid open.

"Is she dead?"

"I don't know, Mother. Go get James."

"You go get him. I want to stay here with Sleeping Beauty. If she's dying, first dibs on her T-shirt collection."

Someone lets out an exasperated sigh over me.

"Fine. I'll be right back." Heavy feet stomp. "Jaaaaaames!"

I feel a hand on my face. "Katie?" A gentle voice calls from far away.

I can't seem to bring anything into focus. Images swirl in front of me. So tired. *Where am I? Please let me go back to sleep.* I think it's still dark. Must sleep more.

"Katie, wake up, sweetie." That's funny. Sounds like Millie. Obviously I'm dreaming. "Jaaaaaames!"

"Mother, for crying out loud, go get him."

"Maxine?" Someone thuds down the stairs. "Millie?" I smile at this voice. Sounds like my foster dad. *Welcome to my dream, James. Now go fix me some pancakes.*

"James, look—"

I try again to peel my eyeballs open at James's gasp. I'm so not dreaming.

"Katie? But—but how? Katie, wake up."

"I've been trying to nudge her awake for five minutes."

"Do you think she's on something?" The older voice hisses in a stage whisper.

The other two don't even bother responding. "James, I'm worried. Something's happened. We need to call Mrs. Smartly and find out what Child Services knows."

"Should we let her sleep?" James asks.

Yes, yes, let her sleep. She needs more sleepy time. More z's for me please.

"Katie, wake up." A soft nudge on my shoulder. "Mother, back up. You're going to smother her."

"Katie Parker, if you don't wake up right this instant, I'm telling James and Millie about the time you and I toilet papered the house of—"

And my two eyes pop open.

"Well . . ." Maxine pats my cheeks with a smirk. "Good morning, Sunshine." She throws herself on the small space left on the couch. "Now what in the green beans are you doing here?"

I try to sit up but my head is too heavy. "What . . ." I swallow and try again. "What time is it?" I look into the anxious faces of my foster parents.

"It's five." I continue to stare blankly at Millie. "In the morning."

I groan and try to roll over. Five? That means I've only slept a little over two hours. I feel like death. Like microwaved death. Like death dunked in skunk juice. Like death drug through the sewer pond.

"Talk later."

"I think we need to talk now." Millie brushes my hair back off my face. "Did you drive your mother's car here? All the way from Middleton?"

"Uh-huh."

"Does she know you're here?" James asks.

"Nuh-uh."

"Is the po-po after you?" This from Maxine. If I had the strength,

I'd roll my eyes.

"James, get her something to drink. Some water or some juice. Let's get this girl awake." A few minutes later my foster dad comes back with a glass of water. James clutches my shoulders and lifts me to where my head is propped against the armrest. I take the water and sip. My brain slowly begins to thaw, and the events of the last eight hours replay in my head like a bad movie.

"Oh, no." I shut my eyes against the images. "Not good." I hand the glass back to James.

"What's not good? Can you tell us what happened?" Millie rests a hip on the back of the armrest.

"My mom . . ." I shake my head, not sure where to even start. How do you describe chaos? How do you sum up disaster? "She was on the news last night."

"What for?" Maxine leans in.

I shrug a shoulder. "Robbery."

The room erupts into gasps and questions.

When the story is all told, I slide back to lie flat on the couch, utterly exhausted, as if I'd just lived it again.

"Why didn't you call us?" James's severe frown wrinkles his forehead.

"Mom has my cell phone." And then I remember another fact. "And your credit card. You're definitely going to need to cancel that." I hadn't even got to use it.

"Let's get her up to her room. James, why don't you carry her?"

"That's my room now!" But Maxine punctuates her outrage with a wink in my direction. "How come nobody ever offers to carry *me* to *my* room?"

"Because I'd be tempted to drop you." My foster dad gently scoots his hands under my limp form and cradles me in his arms. "Here we go. Up to bed now. We'll call Mrs. Smartly and she'll contact the people from the state."

"We're going to take care of everything, Katie. Don't worry about a thing." Millie's voice lulls me into a dreamy state as she chats all the way behind us up the stairs. "You just get some rest, and later, if you feel like it, we'll go to the Fourth celebration."

"Yeah," Maxine barks. "This year I'm going to prove to them I'm *not* a fire hazard. Every year I go, the firemen always hover near me. And I don't mean the cute ones, either."

James lowers me onto my bed, and Millie pulls the sheet, tucking it under my chin.

"Night." I yawn then smile up at three worried faces. "I missed you guys." And close my eyes. "Love you."

And fade to black.

* * *

WITH THE SUN shining on my face and the sounds of Maxine's hooting laughter from downstairs, I finally wake up at a few minutes shy of noon. I stretch my arms toward the ceiling, feeling like a totally new creation.

And then I remember my mom.

And the whole robbery thing.

And that I drove all night to get here.

But I am here. That's the important thing. I know James and Millie will take care of it all.

I jump into the shower and let the spray rinse away all the grim and all traces of Middleton.

When I walk into the kitchen, with a freshly scrubbed face and my hair in a damp ponytail, Millie is just removing something from the oven.

Ahhh. Cookies. I sniff in appreciation. I look at the baked goods, then quirk a brow in question.

"Yes," she laughs. "Chocolate chip cookies. The real kind. Not my gluten-free black bean and nut cookies."

"Yes!" I sidle next to her and help put the cookies on a rack.

"Are you hungry?"

"Starved." I don't tell her about the part that I haven't felt like eating in days. Not that there was anything in the house to eat anyway.

Millie scrambles up some eggs, fries three sausage links, and butters two pieces of toast, with a side of homemade strawberry jam. I sit at the bar and eat as she cleans the kitchen and puts in more cookies to bake. She looks like she could use a big breakfast herself. My foster mom has lost weight since I've been gone.

"So what have you heard?" I ladle on more jam.

A shadow steals across Millie's face. "They found the man in question, but not your mom. But they have positively identified her as one of the robbers. The police will want to talk to you. Are you going to be okay with that?"

I nod and swallow a bite of eggs.

"We talked to Mrs. Smartly, and she has contacted Janice Holloway and Child Services of Norton County. I think Mrs. Smartly is going to pull some strings for us and speed along the process of our getting you officially placed in our care."

I blanch and miss my mouth.

"No—" Millie holds out a hand "I mean you are staying in our care." Her mouth lifts in a warm smile. "We are *not* letting you go again. But I was referring to the paperwork that will need to be done to put you officially in our foster care."

Despite all the junk in my life, my heart lightens at this. Not that I doubted it, but it's still good to hear James and Millie want me. And they would fight to keep me here.

"Hey, Sweet Pea." Maxine sails through the kitchen and swats me on the rump. "You were snoring like an old man with sinus issues."

"I was not."

"The local lumber yard is quieter than you were." Maxine parks herself on the stool beside me. She glances at Millie, who has returned to the cookies. "I'm going to be needing your assistance."

I take a swig of juice. "With Sam?"

She purses her cherry-glossed lips. "He is seeing Mabel Doolittle, and . . . I feel we need to discourage this—for his own good. She ain't nothin' but a gold digger."

My head hurts as I roll my eyes.

"Well, she is. Sam not only has retirement, but he has a steady income from working at the Valiant. A penny-pinching floozy like Mabel would love to get her hands on him."

"I don't particularly care *where* Mabel puts her hands."

Maxine gasps and clutches her bosom. "Sam is caught in her web of deceit. He needs us, Katie."

"Maxine, this is about you. You have obviously *finally* seen the light, and now you want Sam back. Have you thought about the fact it's too late?"

She drums her manicured nails on the granite counter. "I am only acting out of concern for a friend. I was hoping you would value *your* friendship with Sam and do the same. Men are blind to the wiles of a crafty vixen."

"Yeah, but enough about you."

She bumps me with a hip and nearly sends me to the floor.

"Speaking of men . . ." Maxine waggles her perfectly arched brows. "Tell me about this Tate character you *befriended* in Middleton."

Tate.

Oh, my gosh. Tate. I forgot about him. He must be wondering where I am by now.

"Can I borrow your phone?" I stand up. "I need to make a call."

Millie turns around at my sharp tone. "Mine's on the table over there." She gestures to the breakfast nook.

"I have to call Tate and tell him I'm okay. He's been stopping by the trailer every day to check on me." What was his number? I wish I had my own cell phone. Was the last number a seven or a nine? *Think, think, think.*

I punch in the number that first comes to mind.

Some old man answers. I hang up.

I try another variation.

"Heavenly Days Funeral Parlor." Nope. Definitely not him.

My breath whooshes with relief when Tate answers on the third try.

"Tate? It's me."

"Katie?" His sigh fills my ear. "Where are you? Are you okay?"

I hold the phone between my ear and shoulder and walk out to the back porch. His voice brings a smile to my face. "I'm fine. I guess you know my mom . . . um . . ."

"Yeah, yeah, I know. I'm sorry. Where are you?"

"I'm in In Between."

"I've been worried sick about you. I didn't know if you were with your mom or if something had happened to you." He pauses, his breathing heavy. "So many things were running through my head."

"I'm sorry. I had no way of getting in touch with you."

"You could've come by on your way out of town. I would've driven you to In Between." Now his voice sounds angry.

"I'm so sorry. I had to leave immediately though. And it was late—I couldn't just barge in on you and your family. When I saw my mom on the news, I just reacted. But I'm safe. And I'm home."

"They haven't caught your mom yet."

"I know." Which does send the occasional prickle of fear down my spine. "She's messed up. I couldn't help her."

"It was never your job to help her." The sting is gone from his voice. "I'm glad you're okay. I've been praying like a madman for you."

I give him the house number. I remind him about the date auction next week. "You guys should come up for that. Should be a great time. Chihuahua Days are quite the thing, I hear."

I can hear his smile. "Who could pass up something called Chihuahua Days? I'll ask Ashley and Jake and see if any others want to go. I have a feeling we haven't truly lived until we've experienced it."

Actually you haven't truly lived until you've seen your mother on TV robbing a pharmacy. Now *that's* a good time. "Yeah, it would be nice to see you . . . and the gang."

"I'm so glad you're okay. Everyone here will be very relieved."

"Thanks." I gaze at the familiar backyard. "Thank you for everything. You were my Middleton best friend."

. . . And awkward silence.

"Anyway," I rush. "Tell everyone hello and thanks for the prayers. I better get back to my family."

"Take care of yourself, Parker."

"I will. I'll miss . . ." Hundreds of words dangle on my tongue. "The Sunday school kids."

"There won't be another Noah like you."

# Chapter Thirty-Six

THE WORLD IS right again. Well, except for the giant detail of my AWOL mother.

Millie convinces me to keep my presence in In Between a secret until we can surprise everyone at the Fourth of July celebration. And when Frances spots me, she squeals like a bottle rocket.

We hug like long-lost sisters. "Oh, my gosh! I thought you weren't coming!"

My smile stretches so wide, my cheeks hurt. "I'm here."

"I can see you're here!" Frances says.

"No, I mean, I'm here to stay." Questions flash in Frances's dark eyes. "My mom got into some trouble." I look at the other churchies now flocking around us and give her that secret look only a best friend could decipher. "I'll fill you in later."

"Where are your crutches?"

"Millie twisted some arms and got the doctor to see me this morning. I don't ever have to see the crutches again." Those poles of evil. "And the Aircast is gone. I just have to do some therapy exercises and start getting in the habit of using my ankle again."

"Hi, Katie." Charlie's gray eyes sparkle. "Did I hear you say you're home for good?"

"Yeah." I search his tanned face. "Can you handle that?"

He pulls me into a hug. "I think I'd like to try."

"Welcome back." I pull away from Charlie and find Chelsea

standing to my left, her blonde highlights overtaken by her natural light brown shade. She fumbles with the strap on her purse, oddly nervous.

"Hey." My greeting comes out more like a question. Chelsea looks like I felt last night—like she spent the entire evening in the spin cycle of the washing machine. Circles hang beneath her eyes and her chin no longer sits at such a high angle. "Is this your sister?" I point to the mini Paris Hilton beside her, decked out in a flouncy dress and layers of costume jewelry.

"Yeah. This is Cassidy." The younger version of Chelsea bestows a toothy grin on me and clings to her sister. I notice Cassidy's shoes are on the wrong feet, and wonder that Chelsea would let her out of the house with that fashion violation. "We're going to walk on and get Cassidy something to drink, but I wanted to tell you . . ." Chelsea's intense eyes seek mine, as if she's on the verge of saying something profound. She blinks. "Um . . . I just wanted to tell you it's good to see you."

"Right," I say to her retreating back. "Good to see you too." Then I zoom in on my friends. "*What* was that about? She looks terrible. Is she sick?"

An awkward silence descends. "She's had a really hard time lately. Since her dad's in jail, her mom has pretty much fallen apart. All she does is stay in her room and cry, so Chelsea's had to take over since her older sister moved away to college. She sees after her younger sister."

I can tell Charlie is waiting for me to say something catty. But I don't. I'm not into kicking girls while they're down. Even if they've never been nice to me a day in my life just because I didn't carry a Fendi bag or have the right kind of jeans. And just because she made me feel inferior all the time and reminded me at every opportunity my mom was in prison, I won't throw it back in her face.

But it's dang tempting.

I spend the rest of the night running between my foster family and my friends. I can't get enough of either one. But when darkness takes over the In Between sky, I park my chair with my friends.

Charlie comes back from a trip to the concession stand and hands me a Diet Dr Pepper and sets up his chair next to mine.

When his arm settles on my armrest, I look into his eyes. But I'm not sure what I see. Not sure what I *want* to see. I know it's going to take some work to get back to the easy friendship we had. And I know we need to build that back up in order to move on to anything more.

My friends scoot and make a spot for Chelsea and her little sister. Charlie's ex-girlfriend sits in front of him, holding Cassidy on her lap. And Charlie's gaze strays to Chelsea, like he's afraid she's going to break into a million pieces any second.

The first of the fireworks explode into the sky, sending swirly red, white, and blue lights streaming down. The crowd gasps in delight. As a balmy breeze wafts over me, I sink deeper into my chair, lean my head back and just take it all in. There's nowhere else I'd rather be.

A small band plays patriotic music in a nearby gazebo, and I find myself getting all misty-eyed. Tonight is my declaration of independence too. I'm free of my past. Free of my mother and her legacy of substance abuse and a life of no possibilities. And I'm free of the guilt that has been with me since I landed in In Between and tasted the good life. This is where God has planted me, and I know I was born to thrive here. My mom made her own life choices, and I don't have to feel guilty for rejecting her life and instead embracing what God offers me with the Scotts. Family isn't about genetics. It's about the people who love you. And I am not letting them go again. They need me too much.

A flag bursts overhead and my mouth drops in awe. I actually haven't been to too many fireworks displays. I didn't know they could do all this. It's amazing.

Next to go up with a bang is a group of lights supposed to look like Uncle Sam. I squint and stare harder. It actually looks more like a bear with a Mohawk.

I smile as various Fourth of July greetings light the night. The crowd reads them aloud, one word at a time. "Happy . . . Fourth! . . . God . . . Bless . . . the . . . USA!"

More words pop and we call them out, piecing together a curious sentence. "Sam . . . Needs . . . a Real . . . Woman . . . "

*What?* The group around me dissolves into laughter and questions. I say nothing. Instead I scan the crowd and see Maxine sitting with the Scotts, her eyes glued to the sky. A sly smile hangs on her face.

My eyes bulge at the next message.

"Rebuke . . . Satan."

"And . . . Mabel . . . Doolittle."

I see Millie lean over and say something in Maxine's ear. My foster grandmother only shrugs.

Chuckles fill the field we've gathered in, and tongues go to wagging as the evening erupts into a light display that puts all the rest to shame. I resist the urge to cover my ears, but know I will hear the loud booms even when they stop. And part of me hopes they never do stop.

But the magic of the fireworks draws to a close, and all of In Between stands up and claps.

"Hey, kids." Buford T. Hollis walks by, his arm around his short wife.

"Buford, we've got a lot planned for Chihuahua Days," Frances says. "We're going to save the drive-in yet."

"Next Saturday night is the deadline. I won't fight anymore after that. We have to accept defeat at some point."

Fire lights Frances's eyes. "We won't have to, Buford. Bubba's Big Picture is not going down."

"Thanks, kid." He tussles her dark hair. "You're my favorite."

After some final hugs to friends, I gather up my chair, but Charlie takes it from me. "I'll carry it for you. Just lead the way." My heart warms just like the good old days. But then he stiffens beside me. I follow the target of his stare.

"Hey, Chels." Jordan Landers, co-captain of the cheerleading squad, but number one leader of her own snotty posse.

Chelsea's face is a blank mask. She draws her sister in closer. "Hey."

"Is your dad here tonight?" This from Chelsea's one-time running buddy, Caila.

"Oh, wait. No, he's in jail. Oops!" Jordan giggles behind her manicured hand.

"You can't talk to her like that." The words launch out of my mouth like a rocket.

Caila parks a hand on her hip. "Oh, yeah?"

I step in close and loom over her, drawing up to my full five-foot-nine. "Yeah." My head bobs with attitude. "This"—I jab a finger in Chelsea's direction—"happens to be our friend. And unless you want me to stuff you in your little *fake* Kate Spade bag, you probably ought to consider leaving." I arch an eyebrow. "My mom did time too. And I learned a *lot* from her."

"Come on, Caila." Jordan pulls her friend to safety. "They're *so* not worth it."

"This is an original!" Caila clutches her purse to her chest as she walks away.

"Not fake?" I call out. "Oh, I must've confused your personality with the bag. My mistake."

Cassidy's bottom lip trembles, and I feel the punch of her pain all the way to my toes. Chelsea picks her up and holds her close, whispering words of comfort and stroking her hair.

Charlie's gaze wanders to me, and I can see his struggle so clear it might as well be scrolling across his forehead. "It's okay." I reach for my chair. "I need to go find my family."

He doesn't smile. "I'm just going to take her home and make sure everything's okay."

I lay my hand on his arm. "It's okay, Charlie."

And it is.

But Maxine? Not so fine. That woman is in *so* much trouble. I shout out a round of good-byes, and make my way toward the Scotts. Maxine sits in her chair, her legs crossed, and she files a pink nail, as Millie and James take turns lecturing.

"That was embarrassing, Maxine. Rebuke Satan *and* Mabel Doolittle?" James rips off his glasses and massages his forehead.

"Mother, how do you think Mabel felt when she read that?"

Maxine shrugs. "I assumed she was illiterate."

"Let's go." Millie slings her purse over her shoulder. "I won't be able to hold my head up in town for a month. And I was *just* getting over the last incident."

I walk beside my foster grandma. "Last incident?"

She rolls her blue eyes. "Yeah, a couple weeks ago I invited some of my girlfriends over to have a party in the yard."

"So?"

"Millie didn't think a group of senior citizens zipping down a Slip 'n Slide in our bikinis was appropriate."

"Still, Maxine. That was crazy."

"I have a right to bare arms! And legs. And my belly button ring. And—"

"No." *Ew.* I try to shake the visual out of my head. "I meant tonight. Kind of not cool."

"I'm losing him, Katie."

"And you thought an ominous warning in squealing fireworks would bring him back?"

"I don't know what I thought." She grabs my hand and we stop. "I need help."

"Yeah, mental help."

"Would you focus!" She rips lip gloss out of her pocket and daubs it on. "I have a few more ideas."

"Moving on to Plan B?"

She smacks her lips. "Oh, I think we're probably on Plan Q at this point."

"And what do you need from me?"

A wicked gleam lights her face and instantly fills me with a familiar unease. "What do I need? Whatever would make you ask such a thing?"

# Chapter Thirty-Seven

"SO YOU'LL DO it?"

I lower my *People* magazine to glare at Frances, and at that exact moment, a Chihuahua linebacker cannonballs into Charlie's pool, the spray leaving no part of me untouched.

I shake out my magazine and wipe down the article on actresses who don't believe in plastic surgery. It's a very short piece of journalism. "Frances, I told you last night, I just got back into town. I'll help in other ways, but I don't think I want to strut my stuff down the runway and let In Betweenies bid on me like I'm cattle or something."

"I invited your friend Tate."

I almost swallow my gum. "What?" Great. Now he's been invited by me *and* Frances. What if he thinks I'm stalking him?

"Yeah, called the church and left a message for him. Haven't heard back yet. Wouldn't it be cool if you were on stage, and there was a bidding war for you?" Frances sighs as she reapplies sunscreen.

"Yeah, really romantic," I deadpan. And so not possible. Tate and I are just friends. And I'll probably never see him again anyway.

"Romantic? Whatever. I just meant it would be good for profits." She adjusts her bathing suit top then waves toward the pool entrance. "Chelsea's here."

My eye roll is automatic, born out of habit. But one look at Chelsea has me tamping down remorse. That girl is seriously down. The golden child scans the crowd of churchies for a familiar face. I can almost feel her discomfort from where I lounge in a far corner.

"Maybe you should go ask her to sit with us." I cannot believe that came out of my mouth. Sometimes my random acts of maturity nearly give me whiplash. So unexpected.

Frances lowers her oversized sunglasses down the bridge of her nose. "Are you sure?"

I shrug an oily shoulder. "Sure. Why not."

My best friend scampers over to rescue Chelsea and brings her back to our spot. Though Charlie's in the middle of a mean game of pool football, I know he's watching. Just like last night at the fireworks show, his worried eyes follow Chelsea. And then he's tackled and shoved below. I smile as he comes up sputtering.

Chelsea sets down her beach bag, but hesitates to lay down her towel in the only empty spot—beside me. I move my flip-flops, a clear invitation for her to settle in.

Frances makes small talk with Chelsea, who has yet to make eye contact with me. This girl is so weird. I cannot figure her out. Yes, her dad is doing time. But is there video footage of him wearing pantyhose and robbing a drug store? Is he MIA? Um, no.

One hour and two Gatorades later, I grab my sunscreen and squeeze. Nothing comes out but fart noises. "Shoot. Frances, do you have any—"

A new bottle is slapped into my hand. I look at my donor—Chelsea. She doesn't smile. "Borrow mine."

"Thanks. If I get a sunburn, Millie will freak. She thinks I ought to be out here in a long sleeved shirt and gigantic garden hat anyway."

"I have plenty of sunscreen. I'm a little obsessive about keeping it on my sister when we go to the In Between pool."

I blink. Chelsea Blake at the public pool? She probably had her own cabana boy at her gigantic house, and now she's paying three bucks a swim like the rest of us commoners? Wow.

"And I always carry extra because if you run out at the pool, it's like four times what you'd have to pay at Wal-Mart."

*Who are you and what have you done with Chelsea?*

"Um . . . yeah. That's definitely a rip-off. Like movie popcorn." I smile and watch as Chelsea's mouth slowly works itself into a grin.

I hand the sunscreen back, and Chelsea hesitates as she takes it. "Katie?"

I flop onto my stomach and tilt my head toward where she sits on her towel. "Yeah?"

Chelsea bites on her pink lip. "I . . . I . . . uh . . ." The apples of her cheeks glow red, but it has nothing to do with the intense heat. "I wanted to say thank you." Her eyes survey the area, then she leans in closer. "Thank you for standing up for me last night. You were the last person I expected to have my back."

"Yeah, well, those girls were hideous to you. You don't need to take that crap, Chelsea. You have to stand up for yourself—especially if your sister is around."

"I know." But she doesn't look convinced.

"Is that the first time that's happened?"

"No, but the first time they've come after me in front of others." She shakes her head, and I marvel at her messy ponytail that couldn't be more perfect. "I thought they were my friends. Ever since we lost everything . . ." She looks away.

"Your friends dropped you when all this happened?"

"Yeah." She reaches into her bag and pulls out some lip balm. "Guess they weren't really my friends."

A snooty remark about the quality of her so-called friends bubbles to the surface, but I ignore it. "You don't need them then."

Chelsea tries to pull off a smile, but it doesn't work. "Right."

"You've got plenty of friends around here." Okay, not quite. But she could work on it. We're a decent group. I think as soon as people see Chelsea's a little more humble, they'll warm up to her.

"Would you like a Perrier?" Chelsea holds up a fancy bottle.

Well, we couldn't expect her to change overnight, could we?

"Hey, ladies." I squeal as Charlie stands over me, dripping. "You're not getting into the pool? Afraid to get your hair wet?"

"Oh, is your little boy's game of catch over?" I look up through dark sunglasses. "I'm surprised there's any water left in the pool after that dunk you took. It looked like you inhaled it all." I hold back a smile and return to my magazine.

"No water in the pool? Hmmm." Charlie lunges and tosses me over his shoulder. "We'll just have to test that theory."

I squeal and squirm, but his hand is locked tight on my legs. "Put me down! Do *not* throw me in there, Charlie Benson. You do *not* want to do that. I—"

And the rest of my sentence is lost beneath the surface of the blue water, as I plunge to the bottom.

I shoot back up, gasping. Charlie stands at the edge, his arms crossed, a look of victory on his face.

"Any water left in there, Katie?"

I pull the hair out of my eyes, and swim to the ladder near him. "I hope you sleep light." I pull my body up the first rung. "Because there will be revenge. When you least expect it, Charlie Benson, I *will* be there. I'm gonna haunt you like the smell of sweaty gym socks."

Charlie laughs, pulls me out of the water, and follows me back to my lounge chair. Everyone on that side of the pool laughs, and I can't contain my own chuckle. Though I'm a little uncomfortable with him walking behind me. Seriously, what *is* it with girls' bathing suits? They get the least bit wet and it's an automatic wedgie. And usually not the kind that works itself out—the serious kind that requires extraction. Guys have no clue at our torture.

I flop onto my chair butt-first and drape a towel over me. Charlie sits at my feet. His mouth tightens at the corners, and he plays with the handle of my bag. He focuses on a spot between Chelsea and me.

"Hey, tell Katie she needs to sign up for the date auction," Frances calls out to Charlie, and my eyes widen.

"No. Not gonna happen," I say to let him off the hook. Awkward.

"What's this about Katie not volunteering for the date auction?" Nash joins us and parks himself next to his girlfriend.

"I *am* volunteering. I'm just not going to be part of the auction." My face flushes pink. "It's not that I don't want to. It's just the bidding on me would get out of hand. Yeah, fights would break out. Boys would give up their college savings for that one date. I couldn't have that on my conscience." And if Charlie didn't even bid, I'd cloister myself up in my house for the rest of my miserable life.

"You should do it, Katie."

I try to read Charlie's expression, but it reveals nothing.

"We've got space for you, too, Chelsea," Nash says, and inwardly I groan. Wonderful. That's so fair. It's like having me strut the runway with Gisele or Kate Moss.

"It's for a good cause," Frances emphasizes, but I get the chastisement in her eyes. She puts the squeeze on. "Chelsea?"

"No, I don't think so." Her face has returned to the sad look she wore when she came in.

"You know we won't let your friends do anything to hurt you." Charlie's voice is all comfort.

"Ex-friends, and now is just not a good time."

"You'd be helping to save the drive-in." Frances is not backing down. She pinches my arm and shoots me a look that says, *Just go with it.*

"Um . . . yeah. Buford Hollis really needs our help, Chelsea. Come on, I'll do it if you will. We'll show In Between what hot looks like." *Or you will. I'll just follow behind you and try to bring in more than fifty cents.*

Charlie flexes his arms. "Wow, my hands are just itching to toss someone else in the pool." He leans in toward Chelsea. "Sure you don't want to be in the date auction?"

She shakes her head, her eyes downcast. "It really isn't a good idea."

Charlie gets to his feet and sighs deeply. "I was afraid you were going to say that."

He reaches for her, and with a yelp and a giggle, Chelsea jumps up. "Okay, okay! I'll do it." She laughs and brushes a tendril of hair off her cheek. "Sign me up."

When Frances drops me off at the house a couple hours later, I know between the two of us, we are totally smelling Sally Ann up with our potent B.O., a mix of sweat, chlorine, and multiple brands of sunscreen. I hold the car door open and peel my sticky legs off the seat.

I tell my friend good-bye and head up the sidewalk.

"Katie?" Frances leans out the passenger side window.

I walk back to the car.

"Thanks for helping us persuade Chelsea to help out with the fund-raiser."

"Um . . . sure." It's going to be loads and loads of crazy fun. People bidding on me, me basing my self-worth on the dollar amount I bring, and then watching people hold onto their checkbooks until Chelsea, the beauty queen comes out.

"You have no idea what she's been like lately. She's just now starting to show signs of coming out of it. She feels like she has nobody."

"Glad to help." And I wave good-bye to my friend and walk into the house, my shoes squishing all the way.

A note stuck to the fridge tells me that Millie is at the theatre, Maxine is at karate, and James is, of course, at the church. Just me and Rocky, the slobbery wonder.

I reach in the fridge and claim a bottle of water.

When the phone rings, I pick it up, untwisting the lid on my drink. "Hello?"

Silence.

"Hello?"

"Katie?" My heart jumps at my mom's voice.

"Mom? Where are you?" I hear cars zoom in the background.

"A payphone."

"Where?"

"It doesn't matter. Listen, I need some money."

*I'm fine. Thanks for asking. Yes, after you left me stranded, I did survive.* "I don't have any. Where are you, Mom?"

"Why—so you can turn me in? I don't think so. But I could be close enough to meet you if you could get me some cash. It's important."

Important is such a relative word. I would think *I* was important. "I don't have any way of getting you any money. You have to turn yourself in. This is crazy. The police are looking for you."

"You think I don't know that? Things just got . . . out of hand. I need your help."

"You need help, but there isn't anything I can do for you."

"So that's it?"

I can hear my own heartbeat. "I guess that's it."

"Katie, if you can't get me money, at least don't turn me in. Don't tell anyone I called. Do you hear me? I'm your mother." And for a minute she sounds normal. And my heart breaks. "I'll turn myself in soon. Let me be the one who goes to the police. You don't want that on your conscience."

I rub a hand over my face and try to think.

"Don't call the police. Don't tell anyone. Do this one thing for me."

And the line goes dead.

* * *

NOTHING ZAPS YOU more than the sun. Well, maybe stress. And I've been exposed to both. When the family gets home, I say nothing about the phone call. And I lug the guilt around all evening like an overstuffed gym bag. After pretending to watch the evening news with James, I collapse into my bed.

When a flashlight is shoved in my face an hour later, I'm still awake. "*What* is that?"

"Get up." Maxine towers over me, completely dressed all the way down to her knee pads and biking helmet. This is *not* a good sign.

"Go away, Maxine. It's after eleven o'clock. I'm tired. I still haven't caught up on my sleep, and you reek of trouble."

Maxine sniffs her pits. "I need to change deodorants."

"Get that light out of my face and go away."

My foster grandmother kneels beside my bed, her face inches from mine. "Sweetheart, Sugar Bear, Honeydew—"

"I have sensitive gag reflexes . . ."

"Toots, I need some assistance. I have had a long heart to heart with my Lord and Savior, and I know what I need to do."

"Go back to bed."

"And that ain't it." She pushes on my shoulder and shakes me. "Open those peepers. There you go. Now listen up. It has come to my attention I may have acted a little too hastily in giving Sam the boot a couple months ago. I have seen him about town with his new woman—Mabel Doolittle—" Maxine pauses to let the name roll of her tongue like soured milk. "And Sam looks terrible. Katie, I fear he's in a bad way, and by cutting off my love from him, he just isn't thriving." Maxine nods. "He needs me. So we must save him."

I yawn. "So you're willing to sacrifice yourself to save him."

"Exactly."

Crazy, thy name is Maxine Simmons. "And what is it you propose to do? In the dark. At eleven o'clock. While James and Millie are in bed."

"We're going to Sam's house."

I sit up. "What? I'm not going over there. Let me guess, you want to do some breaking and entering and leave love notes all over his house while looking for clues about the seriousness of his relationship with Mabel?"

Maxine tightens her chin strap. "I hadn't thought of that." She shakes her head. "No, what I want to do is just go over there and surprise him with—" Her eyes dart away.

"Yes?"

She clears her throat and coughs. "Love sonnets."

"Love sonnets? You Maxine Simmons, want to woo Sam Dayberry with love poetry? And you honestly think going to—" I close my eyes and pray for patience. "You think that's going to work, don't you?"

Maxine flings the blankets off my bed. "Of course it is. Sam's a theatre person like you. He's into all that Shakespeare and stuff. Get up, Parker. We have a date with destiny. A rendezvous with romance. A par-tay with poetry."

"I can't just leave the house without James and Millie's permission."

"You're with an adult."

"Not a sane one."

Maxine whops me with a pillow. "They'll never know. We'll be back within the hour."

"*You'll* be back within the hour. I'm staying right here."

"If you don't get up, I am ratting you out and telling Millie where you and James stash the contraband snack food."

I gasp. "You wouldn't."

"Try me. I would gladly suffer through months of endless tofu with no break in sight, just to secure your help."

I stew over this. She knows she has me, that hag. James and I need our junk food stash like we need air. It's our oasis away from Millie's organic, soybean world.

"If we get caught, you are taking the full blame for this."

Maxine holds up her right hand. "I promise."

"And no throwing me under the bus this time and telling James and Millie I was sleep walking, and you were just following me for my own protection."

"I will never use that excuse again. We'll leave them a note just in case."

"I suppose you expect me to drive?"

"Amateur!" Maxine's cackle rattles my frazzled nerves. "No, that would make too much noise. We'll take my bike." She hands me my helmet, a violet number she purchased for me some time ago. "Get dressed. I'll not have you roaming the streets all indecent."

I open my mouth to retort, but decide it's not worth the energy.

Maxine and I slip outside, where her bicycle built for two, Ginger Rogers, waits for us under the porch.

I throw a leg over. "You're going to have to do most of the pedaling. My ankle isn't up to much of a workout yet."

She turns around and stares at the top of my head. "Ahem."

With a super deluxe eye roll, I smash my purple helmet over my hair. "Start pedaling, Granny."

Using mostly my good foot, I help Maxine push the bike through town. We sail through Main Street with her headlight beaming. We meet no cars, but do get some strange looks from a bleary eyed cow or two.

"Lean!" Maxine hollers, and we tear through a few yards, only to come to a screeching, grass-throwing halt in Sam's backyard.

My foster grandmother's gulps as she contemplates Sam's darkened bedroom window on the second story of his brick home. "My, it sure is hot out here tonight. Is it hot out here to you, Katie? It's just unseasonably warm." She fans herself with a hand.

"Actually I was wishing I had brought a jacket." My teeth hold down my top lip so it doesn't escape in a smile. "Let's get this over with. I'm missing my beauty rest."

Sweat beads at Maxine's temples below her helmet. "I—I just need to practice a bit. Give me a second." She takes two steps away from me, pulls out a piece of paper from her denim capris, then turns her back. I hear a mumble of words. "Love thee like . . . No, no. I need thou like. Drat! You are so fine, dawg. No!" Next come vocal warm-ups. "Mi-mi-mi-mi-i-i-i!"

"Maxine?"

She jumps and clutches the paper to her chest. "What? Can't you tell I'm in the zone?"

"The psycho zone?"

"No, the inspired, totally poetic zone." She sniffs. "You wouldn't understand."

"Maybe we should just go home." Before the police cruise by on their nightly watch and catch two idiots creeping around an old man's bedroom window.

"No." She motions me over to her. "I can do this. Why don't we pray?"

I stomp my foot and hiss. "You want to *pray*? About *this*? About our sneaking out of the house at midnight to recite *poetry*?"

Maxine lifts her chin and stares up into the night. "Dear God, help me shun this doubter."

"Fine." I bow my head. "Just do it."

"That's a great attitude. Very holy." Maxine lowers her head and takes a deep breath. "Dear Lord. First of all, forgive me for sneaking an extra six cookies after dinner and taking more than my share."

"Get on with it."

"And forgive me for telling Martha Culpepper her new hair cut looked good, when we both know it looked like a porcupine ravaged her head."

"Maxine—"

"But God, right now I want to ask for your hand of favor. Lord, I do need some help, I admit that. I let a good man go, and I know it's only through your grace and my fabulous bod, that I'm going to get him back."

My neck constricts in a cramp.

"God, help me to be all poetic and rhyme-y. Let the love words just roll off my tongue without me puking on the petunias. Amen." She squares her shoulder and walks toward his window. "Grab some rocks."

With a huff that could be heard in the next neighborhood, I traipse through Sam's landscaping and pick up some pebbles for Maxine. "Here." I drop them in her hand.

She lobs one at his window, high above her head. And misses. "Nope. I'll try again." The second one produces no results. Neither does pebble number three or four, which hit the side of the house. "Hold this." Maxine shoves her paper in my hand and scans Sam's yard for more ammunition.

She returns and tosses another rock toward his window. It hits the gutter and bounces off, beaning Maxine right on the head. "Ow!" She rubs the top of her helmet and then gathers all her rocks into one hand, winds up her arm and lets them fly.

*Crash!*

I wince at the sound of shattered glass and move out from under the window.

"Dagnabbit!" comes Sam's throaty yell. "What in blue blazes?" His room lights up and his bald head appears. "Maxine?" He rubs his eyes. Probably thinks he's in the middle of a nightmare. "Maxine, is that you?"

She freezes. Her eyes jerk to mine.

"Go!" I whisper, shooing her toward the light. "Go!"

"Uh . . . uh . . ."

Oh, not good. I unfold her piece of paper, and run and stick it in her trembling hands.

"Katie?" Sam calls.

I ignore him and run back to my spot a safe distance away. "Speak, Maxine!"

Her round eyes skim her notes for an uncomfortable amount of time before she clears her throat, looks up at the window and begins.

"Sam, I have something I wanted to say to you."

"And you couldn't have done it *without* breaking my window?"

She turns toward me again. I nod rapidly and give her two thumbs up. Oh, this is hideous. Absolutely hideous. It's like the time in third grade when Ryan Tillman wanted me to be his girlfriend, so he gifted me with a dead, bloated frog.

Maxine tries again, her voice unsteady. "I have made a lot of mistakes, Sam. But tonight I only have this to say." She steps closer to the house and shouts up to the second floor. "Here's why I want Sam to be my sweetie. Took him for granted, but now I think he's oh-so . . . um . . . neatie."

I cover my eyes. I can't watch this.

"He's got wrinkles and doesn't have much hair. He won't see my plastic surgeon, but I guess I don't care."

If only I could cover my ears.

"His coveralls usually clash with my clothes. When we dance, he steps all over my toes. He dates old bags, hussies, and tarts. And here I thought he had more smarts."

Oh, to be home in bed now.

"If he came crawling back, I would smile. And let him stay at least for a while. Don't need no fancy gifts, just maybe some kisses. With a little sweet talk, might convince me to be his missus."

Her voice grows in strength and volume. "He's dashing. He's daring. He's so supah fly. We have that in common, my Sam and I. You, Sam, are my one and only cutie. I love you for your kindness, your smile, your old geezer booty."

I open my eyes and watch Maxine's face, tight with uncertainty, fear, and maybe a little too much BOTOX. Sam glares down at her, his arms crossed in disgust.

"Maxine hearts Sam, the whole world would agree. Now when will that baldie get down on one knee?" She drops her paper and stares at her man.

Moments tick by. The cicadas chirp in the distance. I swat a mosquito on my arm.

"Well?" she hollers. "Are we gonna get married or what?"

"Married?" Sam yells through the hole in his window. "You tossed me out like stinky trash, Maxine Simmons. You dropped me one too many times."

"You need me, Sam. That old bat Mabel Doolittle is no good for you."

He gestures toward his window. "And you are?" Sam shakes his head. "Go home. Take your granddaughter home and get her to bed."

Maxine's bottom lip quivers for just a split second before she recovers. She pulls herself up tall and turns on her heel. "Very well. I can tell when my art is wasted. Let's go, Katie."

I climb out from the shadows, and we settle back onto the bike.

Maxine wordlessly steers us out of the yard and onto the street. Sharing in her defeat, I help pedal.

But when I look back, there's Sam.

Still at the window. Watching his old flame ride away.

# Chapter Thirty-Eight

"HAVE YOU HEARD from your mom?"

I nearly drop the phone as I listen to Tate's voice come through my new cell. "No. What would make you ask that? Of course not."

"Hey—no reason. Just checking on you." I take some deep breaths and wait for my heartbeat to still. "Are you doing okay?"

"Yeah. I think so." Except for nearly jumping out of my skin just now. "As long as I focus on all I've got here in In Between." But occasionally my mind drifts to the fact my mom is a felon on the loose, and she couldn't love me enough to make it all work. But then I remind myself that she's not me. And I'm not going to be her. Ever.

"Some of us in Middleton miss you."

What does that mean? "And I miss . . . Middleton." Take that. "So how is Sunday school?"

"Not the same since you've left. I recruited Ashley, but she's a little monotone."

"So Frances mentioned she invited you to Chihuahua Days."

"Yeah, I don't know if I can make it. I do have a friend who lives near In Between I've been meaning to visit, but he might be too busy for me next week."

I swallow disappointment. "You don't want to miss a celebration of tiny dogs." I hear Millie call me from downstairs. "I'd better go."

"Hey, Katie?"

"Yeah?"

I can hear the smile in his voice. "Am I still your Middleton best friend?"

"The one and only." And with a goofy grin on my lips, I run downstairs and join Millie in the kitchen.

As soon as I see the box of take-out pizza, I know something is wrong. Millie doesn't order pizza. She makes pizza. And it usually includes weird vegetables and things that are so healthy they're practically dug straight out of the garden.

I open the box and sniff. Pepperoni with extra cheese.

"What's for lun—" Maxine skids across the kitchen floor in her ballet flats. "Oh." Her eyes narrow. "Pizza? *Real* pizza?"

Millie sets three plates on the bar. "Let's eat."

But nobody moves.

"No tofu sprinkles?" I ask.

"No."

Maxine cocks an eyebrow. "No soy cheese?"

Millie shakes her head.

I pull out a stool and sit down. "What's going on?"

My foster mom flops a steaming piece on a plate and slides it my way. "Have you heard from your mother?"

"What?" Is this the question of the day?

"The police are tracking your old cell phone. Your mom's still using it—or someone is. There's no record of her calling this house, but they think she's not too far away from here. There's a good chance she'll contact you, if she hasn't already. Do you know anything?"

I take a bite, and even though it burns my tongue, I continue to slowly chew, buying some time. "I know nothing." And that's true.

"You haven't talked to her?"

"I . . ." I can't turn my own mother in. Can I? I shake my head "I don't have any idea where she is or—"

Millie pulls a Diet Dr. Pepper out of the refrigerator and places it at my elbow. This is serious. "I know she's your mother, sweetie, but you have to help the police if you know anything."

"Millie, I haven't seen anything of her since she left me in Middleton."

My foster mom considers this for a few long, agonizing seconds before she nods. "Okay. But Katie, your mom . . . she could be dangerous. We don't know what kind of influence she's under. Under no circumstances are you to meet with her. And if she calls, you need to alert one of us as soon as possible."

*In other words, Katie, be afraid of your mom.* So uncool.

Maxine covers a yawn and climbs onto the stool next to me. "So sleepy."

Millie passes her mother a plate. "Must be that kind of day. When I stopped in at the Valiant earlier, Sam could hardly keep *his* eyes open."

Maxine chokes on a bite. I whack her on the back until she slaps my hand away.

"Did he say what was bothering him?" I ask, and Maxine kicks me in my good ankle.

"He said it was nothing. Just a varmint causing a ruckus in the middle of the night."

I study my fingernails. "Sam should've called animal control. They could've shot it for him."

"Uh-huh," Millie agrees. "Or tranquilized it and hauled if off."

Maxine's head turns slowly until her eyes are level with mine.

"Problem?" I droll.

"Nothing that can't be fixed."

Not with my help. Nope, I am out of the Maxine-helping business.

"I'm going back to the Valiant to finish getting it ready for Chihuahua Days next week. Friday evening we'll have community bingo. And the date auction will be onstage Saturday, of course. That sounds like fun, doesn't it, Mom?"

"Bingo? Whoopee."

"I take that to mean you won't be helping Katie and me set up today?"

"Nope." She swigs from her root beer mug. "I have . . . work to do."

A pepperoni falls out of my mouth. "What kind of work?"

"Secret old lady stuff."

The worst kind of stuff there is. "Just make sure you don't break anything." My voice drops. "Again."

* * *

ON THE WAY to the Valiant, my eyes scan the town for signs of my mom or the truck I last saw her in. I'm so sick of this constant state of nervousness, like she's going to jump out and scare me any moment. I just wish the police would find her so I wouldn't have to worry about it.

Or she'd do the right thing and turn herself in like she said.

"Wow, the place looks great." I haven't been in the Valiant since I left last month, and if I needed any more assurance that I'm truly home, this theatre is it. The familiar smell hits me and I inhale deep like it's expensive perfume.

"We got a local artist to design all the Chihuahua décor." Millie leads me toward the stage. "And we're still working on the backdrop for the date auction. I thought we'd just clean up today, get all the dust out and polish everything 'til it glows."

I walk backstage to get the supplies to shine the wooden portions of the theatre seats.

I find Sam, his head stuck in between two shelves, mumbling beneath his breath. "Silly, frivolous, prideful—"

"Sam?" I tap him on the shoulder.

He shrieks like a girl, rips his cap off his head and clutches it to his chest. "Wh-what do you want? Oh, it's you."

"Hello, to you too."

He puts his cap back in place. "Sorry. Just a bit on edge today." His face changes and he jabs a pointy finger toward me. "What do you have to say for yourself, young lady?"

"Um . . . I need the wood polish?"

"Oh, sure." He digs into the closet and produces it. "No! Blast it! That's not what I mean, and you know it. What in tarnation did you think you were doing last night? I thought you were a smarter girl than to get up with Maxine in the dark of night and go riding through town."

"Sam—"

"Don't give me those puppy dog eyes. It won't work. I know you're not the one responsible for breaking my window, but your presence there last night says you encouraged Maxine's harebrained idea."

"I did not encourage it. I didn't really know for sure what she was up to."

"Maxine's ideas are crazy in the best of conditions, but any of them that require the cover of night are absolutely insane. You don't have to be an honor student to get that."

"I did have to take a summer school class—"

"Don't sass your way out of this. It's dangerous for two girls to be out at night like that. And I assume James and Millie didn't know?"

I snort. "Um, no."

"I couldn't sleep at all last night for worrying if you two had made it home all right."

I grab the supplies out of his hands. "You were worried about Maxine?"

"No. A pack of wolves could've carried her off, and I wouldn't have cared. But I did worry about you."

I focus on the twitch at the corner of his eye. "Sam Dayberry, you're lying."

"You haven't been off your crutches long. I was concerned that all that pedaling—"

"You weren't just worried about me." I step closer. "You still care about her. You were up all night because you thought about what she said."

"Thought about what she said?" He slaps his knee. "That's a good one. Would that be the line where she said I needed to see a plastic surgeon or the line in which she mentioned I needed to crawl back to her?"

Hope pumps through my veins. "You know perfectly well it's not about the words. She did that—for you. She humbled herself and read you *poetry*. Homemade poetry. She doesn't even *like* poetry, but she knows you do."

Sam's face pinkens, and he studies his old, black shoes.

"You have to give her another chance."

"She's out of chances!"

"Is she?"

"She's fired up because I'm seeing Mabel Doolittle. That's all this amounts to. She doesn't want me, but she doesn't want anyone else to have me either."

What girl hasn't felt that way?

"I don't think that's it this time. I really don't. You should have seen her last night after we left your place. She was . . . speechless. Withdrawn. Sad."

Sam blinks a few times. "If she was sad at all, it's because she knows I'll send her the bill for my window replacement."

I grab a few more rags from the closet and shut it tight. "That's not it, and you know it. She's changed, you know. Maxine dumped you so you'd pull out the big guns and woo her back. It blew up in her face, and you called her bluff and let her go. And now that she knows what she's lost, she wants you back."

"Katie, I'm too old for this reality-show dating stuff. I'm not the Bachelor."

"You're a hot commodity in this town among the senior ladies.

But only one of them wants you bad enough to ride across town in the dark and yell in verse, right?"

He rests his chapped hand on my head. "Get to work, girl. Millie will be looking for you."

"Give it some thought though, okay? She loves you. She just doesn't know how to tell you. You're like a bad cold she can't shake, but she's finally realizing she doesn't *want* to shake it. She *wants* to be sick." That didn't come out quite right.

Sam quirks a brow, and his tired eyes look away.

But not before I see something glimmer there.

# Chapter Thirty-Nine

JAMES WINKS AT me from his seat when Sister Shonda Leon takes the stage for her solo. The Bible may say make a joyful noise, but my foster dad and I decided some time ago we're not sure the Lord had heard the likes of Sister Shonda yet. She could pierce an eardrum with one note. And I laugh to myself because behind James's kind, pastoral expression lurks a man praying for mercy and earplugs.

I watch Maxine pretend not to stare at Sam Dayberry and the frumpy woman sharing his pew, and I try *not* to notice Charlie occasionally peering at Chelsea Blake. And in the middle of taking notes during James's sermon, I feel an occasional twinge of homesickness for a little church in Middleton and twenty snotty nosed kids. And one blond-haired boy who carried me up Stony Peak toward the sky.

Charlie's arm rests on the back of our pew, and as I sit next to him, I wonder what's in his boy's brain. Does he want Chelsea back? What exactly does an arm behind me mean?

After the service the churchies pile into cars and trucks and head over to the Burger Barn for lunch. I have no idea where Charlie and I stand or where I even want us to stand, but I *do* know I want a chocolate shake.

I order and sit at a table with Nash, Frances, and Charlie. Two seats are left open, and when Hannah comes through the door with

Chelsea, Frances waves them over.

"Katie," Charlie whispers in my ear. "Are you okay with Chelsea hanging out with us?"

"Yeah. Why wouldn't I be?"

"I . . ." Charlie struggles with an answer. "I don't know. I know she wasn't your best friend before you left."

I rest my hand on Charlie's. "She's *your* friend. I get that, and I'm fine with it. And you're right—she really does need people right now."

His fingers clasp mine. "Thanks. It's important."

"I know." And I pull my hand away when the girls sit down.

The Burger Barn doesn't serve it up speedy like McDonald's, so while we wait for our orders to be called, I head for the ladies' room.

When I come out of the stall to wash my hands, Chelsea is there, applying lip gloss in the mirror.

"Hey." She wears less makeup than she used to, but the girl is still disgustingly beautiful. And I want to hate her for it.

"Hi." She laughs nervously. "I don't know why I do this—put on lipstick before I eat. It's stupid, I guess."

Yeah, it is. "You never know who might walk into the Burger Barn though. It's best to be totally prepared. It's our job as girls to look as fetching as possible at all times." Am I rambling? I think I'm rambling.

"Katie—" She fixes a bra strap that peeps out of her sleeveless top. "I'm sorry for the way I treated you . . . you know, before. I judged you on everything but what actually counts."

I catch a glimpse of myself in the mirror and force my hanging mouth to close.

"I've learned a lot in the last few weeks—more than I cared to. But I know I was a total snot to you because of where you came from and your mom. And now that the shoe is on the other foot—"

*Would that be a Manolo Blahnik or a Jimmy Choo?*

"—I understand how you felt. I can't change what my father did any more than you can change your mom's mistakes. But I know I don't want to be like him—probably anymore than you want to be like your mother." Her hollow laugh echoes in the small bathroom. "Most days I don't even want to be like *me*."

"Chelsea, you're a good person." *Don't smite me, God.* This is a well-intended lie. And one day it will be true. I hope. "You have to quit walking around like you're a nobody. I realize the people you're hanging out with lately aren't up on all things *Vogue* and *In Style*, but they're sure not going to throw you overboard and laugh in your face when things get rough."

Her glossy lips form a smile. "You're right. It's just hard. I snubbed you guys for so long, and now I've basically come crawling back, hoping you'll be my friend."

"And have you been disappointed so far? Have these guys let you down?"

"No." She washes her hands and reaches for a towel. "And I wanted to tell you I'm sorry I tried to steal Charlie away from you—before you left."

*Oh, you did? I hadn't noticed.*

"When he and I broke up I realized he was my only true friend. After my dad's scandal, my other so-called friends scattered. And I realized—I was just like them. But not anymore. I want you to know Charlie and I are just friends. But Katie, I need his friendship right now. I know I don't deserve it, but I need it."

She says that like she thinks Charlie and I are a couple. "It's not about deserving it." I feel like I'm talking to a reformed member of the *Mean Girls*. "That's what friends do." They're more than shopping buddies. "Charlie's a pretty amazing guy, huh?"

"I didn't realize how much that was true until the last month. He's seen me at my ugliest and still he's right there."

"Yeah—that's Tate." What? No! "I mean Charlie."

* * *

"WHAT HAPPENED TO you?"

I nearly drop my bowl of ice cream as Maxine enters the living room where I sit with my foster parents watching a movie. Her hair looks like a pack of monkeys pounced on it. There's a run in her hose I could stick my hand through, and she's rubbing her knuckles.

"I broke up with the mayor tonight."

"Are you okay?" I ask, as Maxine hobbles to a chair, noticeably shy of one shoe.

"Oh, I'm fine. The old feller got a little handsy in between dessert and my good-bye speech, and—"

James mutes the TV. "He did all *that*? I'm going over there to talk to him."

"Oh, sit down, toots. Just had to walk home. Took a few shortcuts, got hung up in a barbed wire fence or two. Chased by some dogs. No biggie. The fence did most of this, but I took care of our mayor."

Millie scoots to the edge of her chair. "What did you do?"

Maxine flexes her fingers. "I'm not a black belt for nothing."

Millie frowns. "Actually you're *not* a black belt."

"I'm a kick-some-tail belt. I totally went ninja on that dude."

"I cannot believe that creep," Millie seethes. "James, you should pay him a visit tomorrow."

"Well . . ." Maxine stretches wide and drags out a long yawn. "It's so late. I think I'm going up to bed. Shouldn't you be getting to bed, too, Katie? A growing girl needs her sleep."

I glance at the clock. "It's seven-thirty."

"Oh." Her face falls. "Is that all? Okay, I guess I'll go up and take a nice, hot bath and scrub the paw prints off. When you come to a commercial, you can come up and keep me company."

"It's a DVD."

Maxine purses her lips. "When it gets to a boring part, meet me upstairs. I have a friend who has a problem, and I wanted to tell you about it." Her eyes laser into mine.

"You can tell me about your friend tomorrow."

"My *friend* wants to solve her problem *tonight*."

"If this is about the fact Linley's Department Store doesn't carry Betty Lou's brand of Velcro shoes—"

"Meet me upstairs in ten minutes!" Maxine blasts through clenched teeth, then smiles like a homecoming queen for James and Millie. "Ten minutes," she hisses in my ear. "Or else I feed all your Victoria's Secret underwear to Rocky." And she turns on her one heel and limps out the room.

Eight minutes later, I race up to my room. A cleaned-up Maxine sits on my bed, petting Rocky. "Good timing. Sit."

I slam the door behind me. "This had better be good. I'm missing a movie."

"So?"

"With Matthew McConaghey."

Maxine's eyes twinkle in appreciation. "Nice." She waves a hand. "Anyway, we have work to do. Though my poetry reading stunk it up, I still have a few tricks up my sleeve."

"Would that be the sleeve you lost on the barbed wire fence?"

"Rocky, how many pairs of bloomers can you fit in your mouth at once?"

"Okay. Just tell me what you're going to do."

Maxine smiles sweetly. It gives me chills. "What *we're* going to do, Sweet Pea. Now listen close. In that bag over there is a giant canvas sign I made."

I pick up the bag and unfurl the material, laying it out on the floor. "Maxine loves Sam *Dew*berry?"

"It says Dayberry. The paint just ran a bit. Now while there's still a little bit of light out, we need to go hang this."

I'm afraid to ask. "Where?"

"On the water tower, of course."

"I'm not climbing that thing! It's a million years old. It's bound to tip over or cave in."

"It withstood the tornado last spring. I think it can take two girls standing on it." Maxine refolds the banner. "Now all I need you to do is climb up the water tower with me and help me hang it. Then we'll climb right back down. It's easy. This can't go wrong. There are no windows to break. It's foolproof."

"It's desperate, though."

"And these are desperate times!" she cries. "I'm running out of options here. Helen Shelby says she saw Sam treating Mabel to a double dip at the Burger Barn this afternoon." She stamps her foot. "A *double* dip! *That* is serious."

"Vanilla or chocolate?"

"Does it matter?"

"I honestly don't know. I'm still trying to figure out the double dip thing."

"I will run this bag outside and prepare the bike. Meet me in the living room in two minutes. Go!"

Rolling my eyes all the way, I slink back to my seat in the living room and tune into the movie.

"Katie, dear!" Maxine calls from the doorway.

"Yes?" I feign innocence.

"It's such a nice summer night. How about a bike ride before it gets dark?"

"I'm watching a movie."

Maxine pops her gum and steps into the room. "I said how about a bike ride?"

James and Millie eye us warily.

"I'd love a bike ride." My voice is as flat as a deflated balloon. "It would be oh-so refreshing and enjoyable. Thank you, Foster Granny."

With some lame excuse about needing exercise and finishing the movie another time, I follow Maxine outside to the driveway where once again Ginger Rogers awaits.

"You call me Foster Granny again, and you're going to wake up one morning with all your bras in the freezer."

"You do and I'll string your girdle collection up the city flagpole."

Maxine reaches around her seat on the bike and swats my knee. "And away we go!"

It's a short ride to the In Between water tower, and thankfully all the good citizens of the town are tucked away on this Sunday evening. Because I do *not* need witnesses for what is about to happen.

"You grab the bag." Maxine puts the kickstand in place, and we begin our ascent up the steel rungs to the top. For every step I climb, I think of another reason why I shouldn't be doing this. By the time we get to the top, I'm up to one hundred and twelve, and my bad ankle throbs like a smashed finger. Millie would *kill* me if she found out about this.

*Ick*. It's nasty up here. This thing looks even worse up close than it does from the road, and I didn't think that was possible. "It's like a bird haven." I point to a few nests and the splattered floor of dried bird poop.

"Aw, look. Babies." Maxine coos over a cheeping nest.

"Yeah, precious. Let's get this over with before we get arrested."

"For what?" she scoffs. "Beautifying a landmark?" She walks across the lookout area and paint flakes off with her every step. "Okay, help me out." Maxine unfolds the banner and the slight breeze makes it dance.

I dig in her bag and get some plastic ties to anchor her giant love note to the railing.

"Ow!" Maxine jerks back. "What was that?"

I look up to see fluttering wings in the distance. "Probably a bat. It is getting dark."

She casts a worried glance toward the horizon, but lifts up her end of the banner and we attach it to the rails. "It looks pretty good. I think it's just a bit—" A bird dive bombs Maxine's head. "That thing pecked my helmet!" She waves her hands in the air to swat it away.

"It thinks you're bothering the nest. Come on, let's get out of here."

"Just a few more seconds." Her eyes plead with mine. "It has to be perfect, Katie."

I sigh. "Fine." But I squint in the diminishing light for any more psycho mama birds.

"That lower corner will not stay down. I'm just going to lean over the railing a bit and smooth it out."

"Maxine—"

"I'll be fine. See, I'm holding on. Nothing gonna—

"Maxine! Don't move. Don't—"

I watch in horror as two mama birds zip through again and plunge straight for a new target. Maxine's butt.

"Almost got it. Just a little to the—*aughhhh*!!" As soon as a beak hits butt, Maxine flips over the railing.

I scream in terror. I can't look!

I must!

I look over the edge, and there the banner hangs length-wise—with Maxine dangling from the end.

"*Hellllp meeee*!"

*Oh, dear God, please don't let her fall. Let these plastic ties hold the banner to the rail. And I hope her arm muscles—which only get used when she picks up her two-ton purse and lifts the remote—can continue to hold on. Help!*

Think! What do I do?

"Call someone! Get me down from here!"

"Maxine, grab onto the rungs." I pull out my phone.

She reaches out and latches onto the ladder with all she's got.

"Now climb down!"

"I can't! I'm scared of heights. Just call someone!"

"Yes, I'd like to report an emergency. I'm at the In Between water tower. No, *on* the water tower. My grandmother is hanging from it. From what? Well, she made this really sweet banner for her—"

"Skip the details and get me some help!"

"You can be out in a few minutes?" I say a few more prayers as I shut my phone. "They're sending someone."

"You should climb down in case I fall."

My brow beads in sweat. "Well, I don't think you're heavy enough that you'll tip the water tower."

"No, you pigeon-brain! In case I need you to catch me."

My brain creates a visual of that. And it ain't pretty. "Um, yeah, I think I'll just stay up here."

A familiar sound of a siren echoes in the distance, and I begin to breathe again when the red fire truck pulls in next to the tower. The police follow.

A few men jump off the fire truck. The captain pulls off his hat and peers northward like he can't believe his eyes. "Maxine loves Sam *Dew*berry?" he reads.

"Dayberry," I correct—then wonder why.

Maxine says nothing. Just hangs from the rungs.

"Raise the ladder, boys!" And within a minute the captain is scaling the extended ladder. He reaches for Maxine. "You're going to have to trust me and—*oomph*!" Her legs clench around his waist and the rest of her body follows. "Hey, didn't you teach me in Sunday school when I was a little boy? About twenty-five years ago?"

"Just shut up and get me down. Save now. Yak later."

"I'll meet you on the ground!" I shout. Dodging bird nests, I walk across the water tower and ease myself down.

The police officer waits for us at the bottom, his arms crossed, his mouth set. "Mrs. Simmons, why don't I drive you home?"

"Oh, no." Maxine's voice shakes as the fireman carries her to the safe ground. "I prefer to ride my bike. Such a lovely evening."

"Um, ma'am, could you maybe peel yourself off of me now?"

Maxine's unfocused gaze takes in her rescuer. "My hero."

"Just doing my job, ma'am." He coughs and shoots a look at the policeman "Though a weird one."

"Maxine, get off the fireman," I snap.

"Mrs. Simmons, you and your friend here need to get in the patrol car. I'm taking you home."

"Young man, you do *not* need to talk to me like I'm crazy. I am a victim here!" Maxine gains some steam as her head clears. "I was attacked by a crazed bird!" She points to the tower. "That is a serious problem that *must* be taken care of immediately! Now unless you want to hear from my attorney, you will see to the bird matter and let me go about my business."

"Mrs. Simmons?" Officer Friendly cracks the gum between his teeth. "You can take a ride to your residence or you can take a ride downtown."

"A ride home would be nice. Thank you."

I can't even look at my foster parents when they open the front door.

"Hello, Officer Creech."

"Pastor Scott—" He pushes us into the porch light. "I believe these two belong to you."

# Chapter Forty

IF YOU WANT to see time stop, get grounded. I have spent the slowest week of my life without television, without my phone, without fun—all because of Maxine's water tower acrobatic show.

"You can quit huffing and puffing over there. I know you're mad at me. And I know you're sick of stuffing these Chihuahua piñatas." We've been working all week on this Chihuahua Days stuff, and this morning I'm grateful I'm officially ungrounded, and in eight hours the festivities will start and be that much closer to being over.

I glare at my foster grandmother, my hand stuck halfway up a Chihuahua's—well, never mind. In a place totally inappropriate for candy, in my opinion. "Hand me some more gum."

Maxine slides a bag across the Valiant stage, where we sit, surrounded by stupid dog decorations. I mean what kind of people celebrate a dog? Seriously, aren't there better things to celebrate?

Sam walks down the aisle of the theatre, his hat low over his eyes. He stops in front of me, his back to Maxine. "Do you need anything else? I'm about to go into town and hang some of these from the light posts."

"No, we don't need anything." Maxine answers, then shifts awkwardly. "We don't need anything from you at all."

I bite my lip and stare straight up into the fly space.

"Well, I don't believe I asked anyone but Katie if they needed anything." Sam doesn't take his eyes off me.

"Maybe Mabel Doolittle needs something."

"Maybe she does."

"Maybe she needs a big piñata stuck straight up her—"

"Can it!" Sam makes a strangled sound and whirls on Maxine. "You don't care about anyone but yourself, Maxine Simmons."

"I care about you, you old coot, though Lord only knows why." She grimaces and curls her legs beneath her.

"Would you like to repeat that—maybe in a couplet or a sonnet?"

Maxine gasps and her hands fly to her chest. "How dare you mock my . . . my art! My poetry! The words of my heart."

"You think rhyming sweetie with neatie is *art*?"

Maxine jumps to her feet, her arms swinging. Then immediately moans and clutches herself in pain.

"Maxine!" Sam leaps onstage and rushes to her. "Maxine, what's the matter? Are you hurt? Is it your heart?"

She lunges for her piñata and hurls it at him, yelping all the way. "Get away from me. There's nothing wrong with my heart—especially now that I know for sure I no longer love you!"

"What is *wrong* with you?" Sam's hands fly over Maxine, determined to get to the source of her angst. He looks to me for help, but I just shrug. I am so staying out of this.

"*You're* what's wrong with me. Now take your mitts off of me. Your handsiness may be acceptable to Mabel, but I am a woman of integrity—not some trollop!"

I turn my head in a desperate attempt not to giggle. But when I regain my composure, I see Maxine limping off the stage, her hands balled into fists.

Sam takes off his hat and wipes his forehead with a handkerchief. "*What* was that about?"

Enough of these games. I thought that was what high schoolers did. "Her whole body is bruised."

Sam's expression grows fierce. "I will tear that mayor apart from limb to limb! I—"

"No, Sam." I walk toward him. "You had to have heard about Maxine hanging from the water tower last Sunday night. Everybody in town was talking about it."

His eyes roll beneath bushy, white brows. "Might've heard something about that. But people talk about Maxine all the time. I didn't pay much attention."

"She climbed up there to hang a banner—for you."

"For me?" He considers this. "I thought it was just another stunt to get the attention of the firefighters. She does love a man in uniform."

"Just one in particular." I smile and dust some piñata confetti from Sam's overalls. "Do you really want to spend the rest of your life without her? There's only one man she'd dive off a water tower for." And I leave him standing beneath the stage lights, alone with his thoughts.

* * *

I CAN'T CONTAIN my yawn as I place a marker on B12. I've never liked bingo. I never win, but I always sit by someone who does.

"Bingo!"

Nash and I swap a look. This is Frances's sixth victory for the evening.

He shakes his shaggy head. "I give up."

Frances claps her hand in glee and runs up to the front to pick her prize.

"Katie, are you okay? You seem a little down tonight."

I clear my bingo card and answer Charlie. "No, I'm fine. Just tired from all the prep work this week, I guess. It may look easy to put on a celebration in honor of the mighty Chihuahua, but it is not." And Tate didn't show. I know he would've found a way to make bingo fun with all his crazy ideas. He made everything fun. Even spectator volleyball. I miss him—his friendship that is.

I scan the room again. "Chelsea couldn't make it tonight?"

"No, she had to babysit her sister."

I look at Charlie's totally cute face. Would I be willing to write stupid poetry for him? Would I brave bird poop and scale a water tower? We have been through a lot together.

I yawn again and feel my eyelids droop. We've been at this for hours. How much more torture can I take? I just don't have the attention span for this game. It's like I need two of me—one to listen and one to pay attention to my card.

"Come on." Charlie puts his hand on my back. "I'll take you home. You're about to face plant in your bingo chips."

"But this could be my winning game."

"I wouldn't put money on it."

"Fine." I sigh and stand up. "Good night all. I will see you in the morning for the pancake breakfast in the fellowship hall." Even the church has decided to donate the proceeds to the drive-in fund.

"Be there at six-thirty!" Frances reminds me.

Those better be some dang good pancakes.

I follow Charlie out of the Valiant into the parking lot. Even though it's close to eleven, the town is all lit up and wide awake for the weekend celebration.

He opens my door and I climb inside, content to melt into his seat and close my eyes for a second.

"You've really been working hard this week." He starts his truck and a local radio station blasts a report of events in town.

"Yeah, well, you do the crime, you do the time."

Charlie laughs. "Wish I had a picture of you two on the water tower."

I chuckle myself. "It was crazy. Life with Maxine is never dull."

"Any chance she and Sam will get back together?"

"I don't know. They kept their distance tonight. And he still sat with that Doolittle woman."

"Sometimes it's hard to know what you want."

I wave at some people walking home. "But sometimes what you want is just right there, you know? Like it was there and you didn't realize it until it was too late."

Charlie glances at me in the darkened truck. "I hope by the time we're their age, we have this stuff all figured out."

He pulls into my driveway and walks me to the door, his hand at my back.

I stop beneath the porch light, where it glows on me like I'm center stage. "Thanks for the ride." I smile up at him, waiting to see what he does. What he says. We're on the verge of a moment here, but . . . a moment of what?

Charlie exhales deeply, like there are thoughts trapped in his head. "Katie?"

"Yes?"

"Did anything happen between you and that Tate guy while you were in Middleton?"

My heart lurches in a painful beat. I think of that embarrassing night on the cliff top. "No. Definitely not." What had I been thinking then? I could've ruined that friendship. "Did anything happen between you and Chelsea while I was gone?"

His steady gaze meets mine. "No."

Okay then. Not sure what this means except that neither one of us has seen any lip action.

Charlie inches closer. "Do we try to pick up where we left off?"

"I don't know. That wasn't exactly a good place."

"I'm up for trying it again if you are."

Is it me, or did he just say that in the same tone I would use when confronted with one of Millie's carrot soufflés?

"Do you always get this romantic during Chihuahua Days?" I drawl.

He pulls me to him and locks me in a warm hug, his head resting on mine. "Must've been all those corn dogs I ate."

"Might've been the puppy paw chicken nuggets." I lean back in his embrace and look up. His face draws closer to mine. Closer. His lips part.

"Charlie—"

"Yeah?"

I swallow. "I don't think I'm there quite yet."

He stops. Considers this. "You know what? I'm not either."

With a quick hug good night, I head back into the house, not sure whether to feel rejected or comforted by the fact Charlie wants to take things extra slow. I mean, it's one thing for me to say, "Let's build this friendship back up." But no matter how I feel, he should be thinking, *I cannot live another day without you!* Right?

I think I've seen too many Hilary Duff movies.

I call out for my family, but get no reply. James was working a dunking booth and Millie had duty at the Valiant. I guess I beat them home. Rocky's out in the backyard, and who knows where Maxine is. Hopefully not hanging off another In Between landmark.

On heavy legs, I carry myself up the steps and into my room. I head straight for the bathroom and wash my face.

With a toothbrush dangling from my mouth, I open the bathroom door and—

"Mom!" My toothbrush falls.

There on my bed sits Bobbie Ann Parker.

I take a step back.

Her bloodshot eyes follow me.

"Hello, daughter."

"Wh-what are you doing?" She smiles, and I rub the chill bumps on my arms.

"I wanted to see you."

"Mom . . ." My brain races for the right words. What *do* you say when your criminal mother sits right in front of you? "You can't be here."

"Why?" She stands up. She looks gaunt, thin. Like she's lost ten pounds since I saw her last. "I wanted to make sure you were okay."

I'm definitely on alert now. The woman who left me alone for days without electricity and food would not come track me down in In Between to see if I was doing well. "I'm fine. The Scotts are taking good care of me."

"Of course they are. I *knew* you'd come back here."

"Did you expect me to stay in your trailer?"

"It was never good enough for you, was it?"

"Of course it was." I shake my head in disbelief. "You left me. You took off with that guy and just left me. I had no food. No electricity." My voice grows stronger. "Do you remember that? Why *wouldn't* I come back to the Scotts?"

"How can you pick them over me?"

"You robbed a pharmacy!" I yell. "You made the choice for me!"

"I needed some medication!" she shrieks back, stepping forward. "You don't know what my life is like."

"And you don't know what mine is like. And why? Because you're never around!" Fear is replaced by anger—burning, fiery anger. "All I ever wanted was for you to love me. And *want* to take care of me. You always made me feel like a mistake. Like I was just something in the way. You took care of those stray cats more than you did your own daughter."

My head snaps as she slaps my face. "Don't you dare speak to me like that!"

I clutch my face and taste blood on my tongue. "You need to leave." I will not cry. I will not show fear. *God, help me. Get her out of here.*

"I'm not leaving until I get what I want."

"Your car? The police will find you in a second in that thing."

"I don't need a car. I got my own ride." Her glassy eyes dart around the room. "I need money. Cash. And you're gonna get it for me."

"I don't have any money."

"You're lying!" I flinch at the force of her voice. "You're lying, and I know it. These people have money. If they don't, then they have stuff I can sell to get money. Either way, you're going to lead me to it."

"Mom," I whisper, my voice, my heart broken. "Just leave. Turn around and walk away. You're only making things worse. I don't want to call the police. Don't make me be the one to turn you in." *You're killing me.*

"You can't call the police. I cut the phone line. And I still have your cell phone." It doesn't even occur to her that I could get a new one. "Besides what kind of daughter would you be if you turned your own mother in? I would *never* forgive you for that." She reaches out a spastic hand and pats my red cheek. "You didn't tell anyone when I called last week, did you?" She shakes her head and answers her own question. "And you ain't gonna tell anyone about this visit." Her fingers move to my hair and tighten. "Just tell me where some money is, and I'll leave."

I take a deep breath, my options scrambling through my head.

"Tell me!" She jerks my hair, and it's everything I can do not to throw her into a choke hold like I learned in PE this year. But this is my mom. I . . . I just can't. I have to get her out of here. And quickly.

"In . . . in the kitchen."

Mom's eyes narrow and she struggles to focus.

"There's a cabinet over the sink. Inside—there's a sugar jar. If you open it, there's cash. It's where they keep their grocery money."

"How much?"

"I don't know. Two hundred maybe?"

Mom runs a bruised hand over her face, then releases me with a shove. "I'll be right back. If that money isn't there—I'm coming back for you. And you *will* regret it."

"It's there. Just take it and leave. The Scotts are due back any minute. You have to get out of here."

My mother walks backward to the door, her eyes never leaving mine until she leaves. I hear her clumsy feet on the stairs.

And I reach into my pocket and pull out my cell phone.

My hands tremble, and I fumble with the buttons.

I shut it.

This is my mother. My only family. I can't do this to her.

I squeeze my eyes shut and mumble a quick prayer. A plea with God.

And the word *amen* is no more out of my mouth, than I see James and Millie in my head. And Maxine.

Bobbie Ann Parker is *not* my only family. Family doesn't do this to someone. A mother doesn't hurt her child.

"I need the police here immediately. I have an escaped criminal in my house." My throat convulses around a lump of tears. "It's my mom."

# Chapter Forty-One

THE BEDROOM DOOR slams against the hinges as my mom pushes her way back in. "Do you think I'm stupid? There's no money in there."

"Mom, you're not in your right mind. Don't do something you're going to regret."

"I regret listening to you." She raises her hand to strike me again, but this time I'm ready. I catch it mid-swing and hold it right, giving just a little twist. With my eyes I dare her to push it.

"They do keep money in there. Maybe they used it this week." I don't know. Grounded girls don't get to go to the grocery store.

"You're a liar."

"And you're strung out."

"You think you're so smart," she sneers, then pushes away from me. I stumble back into the wall. "Find me some credit cards."

"You took the only one I had. The rest are with James and Millie—who should be here any time."

"Then find some jewelry." She advances on me again, grabbing my bedside lamp. "Go."

I know Millie has a jewelry box in her room. She has her first wedding set in there and a ring her grandmother gave her. I can't stand the thought of my mom's dirty hands on them. "No."

Her face is flushed red, and her lip curls. "What did you say?" The lamp shakes in her hands.

"I said no. I'm not giving you anything of the Scotts."

And the woman who brought me into this world, who took me to my first day of kindergarten, who would sit down and watch *Gilmore Girls* with me, goes ballistic. She leaps for me, fists swinging, spit flying out of her mouth, shrieking like a madwoman.

I close my eyes as she approaches, put my hands in front of my face, and get ready to take her down.

And then I hear a sound that I would never have called beautiful. A police siren.

My mom freezes, her eyes frantic. She drops the lamp and runs from one side of the room to the other. She darts to the window and looks out. Then looks down.

"You can't jump."

"Shut up! Just shut up! How could you do this to me?" Her words are darts into my heart.

She makes a leap for my door, but I throw myself in front of it. She reaches around me and claws for the knob.

I hear the heavy stomping on the stairway, and that's when I let her go.

And dissolve onto the floor, my head on my knees. Breath ragged. Shaking limbs. Choking sobs.

I block out the sounds of struggle and commotion below. I hear my mom scream, and I cover my ears like I'm four. And I stay that way, with my arms wrapped around my body, rocking back and forth until the noises stop.

And then gentle arms are wrapping around me.

James.

"Katie? Katie, are you okay?" He takes in the destroyed bedroom. "Talk to me."

"I'm fine. I'm okay."

Millie's kneels beside me. "Did she hurt you?"

I swipe my eyes. "No." I shake my head, at a loss to describe the last ten minutes. "Did she—Did they get her?"

"Yes." Millie pulls the hair away from my face, then her eyes widen as she discovers my cheek. "Did she—"

"It's nothing." I brave a half-smile. "She's so out of it. She wanted money."

"And you called the police?" James asks.

"Yeah. I called the police on my own mother." Do they make Hallmark cards for this?

Millie grabs my chin. "You did the right thing. Do you understand me? There's no telling what could've happened or what she would've done, Katie. You are a brave, courageous girl, and we love you."

The tears flow again, and I sniff before I drown in my own snot.

"We are *never* letting you go. Do you hear me? Never." Millie pulls me into a hug. "I'm so sorry we weren't here to protect you. We should've never left you alone until your mom was found."

We all jump at the knock on the door. A policeman enters. "We've got Mrs. Parker in the car. She's not going to hurt you anymore."

*   *   *

AT TWO A.M., I lie awake and relive the night's events. The policeman said my mom wouldn't hurt me anymore, but that wasn't exactly true. At some point maybe I will get over my guilt of turning my own mother in. But not for a while. At some point I will not relieve the past few months and try to figure out something I could've done to save her. But not for a while. And at some point I will be able to write her a letter and tell her I still love her.

But not for a very long while.

# Chapter Forty-Two

I SLEEP RIGHT through the pancake breakfast.

When I slink downstairs, rubbing my eyes and yawning, Millie sits in the breakfast nook, sipping coffee.

"Good morning." I head to the fridge, but she beats me to it.

"Just sit down. I'll fix you a good breakfast."

"Millie, I'm really not in the mood for a tofu scramble this morning."

She smiles and ushers me to a seat at the table. "How about waffles?"

"*Real* waffles?"

"Though the preservatives are against my better judgment . . . yes." Pots and pans rattle as she gets out her supplies. "Did you get any sleep?"

"Not much. You?"

"No. James and Mother are at the pancake breakfast. I hope they do well."

"Yeah, Frances is counting on it." And I am too. I don't think anyone in In Between but the mayor wants the drive-in to shut down. "The fund isn't anywhere near what it will take to save Bubba's, though."

"You never know what could happen. Don't count it out yet."

We talk some more about my mom and last night. But talking can only do so much. It's going to be a long time before the images of the past few days aren't stuck with me like a bad tattoo.

"Well, look who woke up." Maxine flounces into the kitchen an hour later. She gives me a loud smooch on my cheek. "I've got just the thing to cover up that bruise on your face. Can't have you taking the runway all multicolored."

"I was thinking of calling Frances and telling her I'm not going to do it."

Maxine feigns shock and collapses into the seat beside me. "What? And break the heart of every boy in town? I don't think so."

"I just don't feel like it. And I don't think my twirling around the stage is going to send the drive-in fund over the top."

"Katie, this town needs you. And your little brainiac friend needs you. She will flip her neurotic lid if you bail now."

"I don't know. I'll think about it."

* * *

BY FIVE O'CLOCK my face hurts. Not from my mom's hand, but from Maxine's.

"No more makeup, Maxine. Seriously, back away." I shove her big powder puff away for the last time. "I can't believe I let you talk me into this." It's like all the adrenaline from last night short-circuited my system, and now I'm just drained. I want to crawl into bed with a good book and stay there for a few days.

"Pucker up, Sweet Cheeks. You need some gloss on those lips."

"I look like a pageant reject. Enough makeup." I sidestep my foster grandmother and slip out of the bathroom. "Let's just go."

James whistles as I descend the stairs. "Do you want to drive?" He holds up the keys.

I pluck them from his fingers and wait for the family in the car.

As James and Millie chatter in the backseat, Maxine keeps me company in the front, belting out a Justin Timberlake song. "I'm bringing sexy back!" I listen to her off-key warble for a full minute before cranking up Millie's radio.

At the Valiant I say good-bye to the family and make my way backstage, where everyone is to meet. When I see Frances, she instantly pulls me into a death-grip hug and demands a recount of last night. I give her the short version.

"Katie, I know last night was hideous. And I'm really proud of you for going through with the date auction. This is probably the last thing you want to do."

It was the last thing I wanted to do *before* my mom made a guest appearance. "I'm fine." I step away from my best friend.

"Let's just pray we get enough money. This is the last fund-raiser, and you know the mayor has the wrecking crew ready and waiting."

Chelsea weaves through the throng of girls and greets us. Her smile is hesitant. She still doesn't get she's pretty much one of us now. No matter what she was like before. Her slate's been wiped clean. Her super snotty slate.

"Hi, girls." She looks like a movie star in her bohemian sundress and oversized earrings. And if I'm not mistaken, those are new highlights. "This is nerve-wracking, isn't it? I mean to go out there and wait for someone to"—she makes a disgusted face—"bid on you."

"But it's all for a good cause," Frances defends. "The date is all paid for and donated by local businesses, so it should be a good time no matter who you end up with."

Chelsea and I look at each other and giggle. "Yeah, right." I can see the dorks counting their change for me.

Frances consults a clipboard. "Chelsea, you're up third. So you've got about ten minutes."

I check my name on the list, and see I'm pretty far down toward the bottom. "I'm going to go see if Sam's here." I also saw Mabel Doolittle's name on the list. What if he bids on her? He can't! Maybe if I talked to him one more time.

When I walk out into the theatre, I notice the seats filling up quickly. Yup, many, many people in here. My own little dress suddenly feels too tight. All these people will be staring at me. Saying things like, "Oh, that girl's not worth more than five bucks." Or "She comes with a month's free video rentals." It's a little humbling to know part of your allure is that you're a package deal with a few DVDs and an all-you-can-eat plate of pork chops at Ida Mae's House of Vittles.

I make my way through the crowds and breathe in some fresh air in the less crowded lobby.

"Do not bid on her."

I freeze, but don't turn around.

"Seriously, spread the word. Do *not* bid on Chelsea."

I step behind a large man and peek around him. Chelsea's former friends break from their circle and spread out, catching anyone from In Between High they can find.

Her ex-best friend Jordan Landers snickers with another girl. "I want total humiliation. Nothing less." And she struts away.

"Katie!" Charlie waves from across the room. With his quarterback's skills, he works the crowd and is at my side in no time. "They're starting. Come on." His eyes linger on my face. Then my outfit. "You look great, by the way."

I smile distractedly as he leads me through the doors. "Thanks. But Charlie—"

A select group of the Chihuahua marching band plays a slow song as Frances welcomes everyone to the date auction. She explains the rules and everyone applauds.

"Charlie, I need to talk to you."

Hannah glides onto the stage against a background of tacky dog decorations and an arch of ivy. Frances reads off various facts about our friend. "Hannah likes ice cream, puppies, and yodeling."

The bid climbs until it reaches sixty-two dollars. "From gentleman number . . ." Frances squints into the crowd. "Forty-seven."

Hannah peers into the crowd, but is ushered off before she sees her date.

"And next we have the lovely Mabel Doolittle." Mabel waddles out in a matching polyester blouse and skirt, an outfit that probably saw better days when Madonna dominated MTV and Regan was in office. She turns an awkward little circle as the crowd claps.

"Do I hear ten dollars?" Frances nods. "Do I hear twenty?"

I see Sam Dayberry's hand slowly rise. Mabel smiles.

"What about thirty?"

Again Sam bids. His hand may be saying yes, but his face sure isn't. My heart races with hope. He looks miserable! Excellent.

"One hundred dollars!"

A wave of murmurs passes through the audience as we all swivel our heads to the new bidder.

"One hundred dollars for the beautiful Mabel Doolittle." The mayor stands and holds up his number. His eyes dare anyone to bid against him.

"Can anyone beat one hundred?" Frances asks. "And the date goes to"—she forces the words out like rotten meat—"the very same mayor who condemned the drive-in." And he earns a polite golf clap.

"Next up is a lovely, soon-to-be junior from In Between High, Miss Chelsea Blake."

"Charlie—" I tug on his sleeve. He is captivated by the sight of her, but after another tug, wrenches his eyes away from the stage.

"Yes?"

"Remember some time ago when you told me Chelsea needed you?" He nods blankly. "You were right. She does. She needs you now." I fill him in on what I overheard in the lobby. "Charlie, that's the girl who should get your bid tonight."

"What about you?"

I shake my head.

"We're not going to happen right now, are we?" he whispers.

"I just think she needs you more."

"She and I really are just friends." He stares at his hands. "But she's changing, Katie."

"And you like this new Chelsea." I can see it in his face. "It's okay." I shrug and grace him with a smile. "I just dated you because you're the captain of the football team."

"I knew you were a user." He laughs and places his warm hand over mine. "Thank you."

Somehow I know Charlie and I will revisit the relationship issue again. It might be next week. . .or it might be years from now. There's just something about that boy.

Frances opens up the bids.

"I guess I'll start my bidding," he says.

I stand up and toss him a wink. "She's totally worth it. She comes with a double cheeseburger combo meal."

And so I walk back to take my place behind the curtain. Alone. Knowing there is now a really good chance no one is going to bid on me and make all my date auction dreams come true. I will stand there onstage. One girl and her pork chop package. Rejected. Maybe James will take pity on me. Of course, then I'll be the girl who was so pathetic her foster dad had to cough up some bucks.

After three more girls and one senior citizen who went out in a walker, Frances calls my name. I instantly want to hurl.

I step into the spotlight and pray I don't fall on my face. My best friend reads some facts about me. I'm thankful she leaves out things like *Katie likes to follow mad old ladies up decrepit water towers. She also can frequently be seen on the back of a tandem bicycle named Ginger Rogers. And in her free time she enjoys getting grounded and feeding her soy burgers to the family dog. Can I get five dollars? No? How about a dollar? Great! Thank you boy with the pocket protector . . .*

A voice in the back starts the bid at twenty bucks. Not bad.

Then I hear thirty. But even the lady on the walker got thirty.

My eyebrows rise at fifty.

But when the bidding continues all the way to one hundred and twenty-five, I lose my plastic smile and paste on a real one. *Whoever you are, thank you for saving me from total humiliation.*

"One hundred and fifty." I scrunch my eyes, desperate to see who the voice belongs to.

And then I gasp. And my heart thrills.

Out of the shadows walks a boy I knew in Middleton. The boy who showed me a meteor shower when it was the last thing I wanted to see. Who let me be Noah while he dressed like a girl. And fixed me dinner when I was without electricity. And without a mother.

"Going once . . . twice . . . gone! Our winner is number ninety-four." And I smile at Tate Matthews, the guy who just won himself a pork chop dinner and saved my dignity.

* * *

WHEN THE DATE auction is over, I run out into the lobby. Where Tate stands—patiently waiting.

He's such a sight for sore eyes, I want to throw my arms around him, but I resist.

He does not. He clasps me to him, and I inhale his familiar cologne. "I've missed you, Parker."

I smile and step back. "I missed you too." He opens the door, and we walk out into the night air and toward the theatre grounds, where music has been playing all night. We join the crowd listening to a brass quartet as they finish up their set. "I didn't think you'd be able to make it."

"I'm staying with a good friend. Do you know him? He's providing some of the music tonight."

I follow the direction of Tate's pointing finger and see Brian Diamatti holding up his bag pipes. He waves enthusiastically.

"Is that a kilt he's wearing?"

"Yup." Tate grins. "And that's the girl he bid on."

Hannah walks toward Brian and hands him a water. Her eyes are just as starry as her new skirted friend's.

Tate leads me to a large oak tree, and we stand beneath it, under the glow of paper lanterns. "I heard about your mom. Are you okay?"

That is just the question of the night. I've heard it a hundred times. "Yeah, I'm totally okay." He slants me a look. "Okay, not *totally* okay, but I'll be fine."

His hands move to my shoulders, and he guides me under a light. "Is that a bruise on your face?" His thumb brushes over it.

"It's nothing." I blush and shrug.

"I'm sorry that happened to you." His voice is warmer than hot caramel topping melting on ice cream.

"It happens." That was totally lame.

"But it shouldn't happen to you."

"Tate, thanks for coming tonight. It was an incredibly nice thing to do. I really appreciate the donation. It will help Buford Hollis a lot."

"I didn't do it for the drive-in."

"You didn't?"

"That night on the cliff—"

*Oh, you just* had *to bring that up, didn't you?* "I'm really sorry. It was the stars and the moonlight, and I'm all confused. Or I was confused. But now I'm not because I told Charlie he should bid on Chelsea, and then he did because deep down he wanted to anyway, and I—"

"Katie?" Tate's hands frame my face. His gaze roams over the blue and purple spot on my cheek then back to my eyes.

"Yes?" I breathe.

"You started something that night on the cliff." He pulls me to him. "And I'd like to finish it." Then his lips lightly brush mine, and I surrender to his kiss as a bagpipe honks in the distance.

"Tate?" He raises his head and smiles down at me. "How are we going to make this work?"

He tweaks my nose. "If a guy likes a girl, distance doesn't matter. I'm game if you are." Tate releases me only to hold his arms out. "I think they're playing our song."

I glance toward the stage, where Brian Diamatti is getting down on his bagpipes, playing something that sounds like a John Mayer song.

One hand goes to my waist and the other he clasps in his own. "Totally my favorite song." And he hums along, with his chin resting on my head.

"What is it?"

"I have no idea."

# Chapter Forty-Three

THE END OF Chihuahua Days is signaled by Brian Diamatti's rousing rendition of "The Star-Spangled Banner." Or maybe it was "Friends in Low Places." Hard to tell.

The mayor takes the stage. "My fellow In Betweenites."

I prefer In Betweenies.

"The time is now eleven p.m., and our celebration must come to an end for yet another year. It has been a grand time. One of fellowship and good memories."

And disgusting amounts of dog-shaped funnel cakes.

"As you know, citizens, tonight was the end of the deadline I so graciously extended for Buford T. Hollis and the Big Picture Drive-in. Miss Vega, if you would, please take the stage and announce the grand total of *our* fund-raising efforts."

Frances climbs the stairs to the stage, a somber expression on her face. This is not good.

She grabs the microphone and it squeals in response. "Good evening." She sighs and it resounds through the large speakers. "We needed to raise approximately twelve thousand, eight hundred and seventy-two dollars tonight. The town really came together. The Big Picture is more than just an old drive-in. It's a piece of our history. Some of you have grandparents and parents who saw movies in the Big Picture's glory days." Frances opens a piece of paper. "I am saddened to say we didn't raise enough money."

The crowd groans.

"But I would like to present the money tonight to Buford Hollis, and if he chooses, he can add to it and hopefully keep the drive-in open."

Buford, in old bib overalls and a wife beater T-shirt, lumbers onstage and joins his little champion. He smothers her in a bear hug and wipes away a tear with a meaty hand.

"Buford, tonight we present you with a token of this town's love and support—seven thousand dollars."

After a polite but disappointed round of applause, Buford presses his face a little too closely to the mic and speaks. "Y'all are my friends and my neighbors. And I've enjoyed the last fifteen years of running the Big Picture. But I'm sad to say it's not enough. I will surrender the property tonight to the mayor and the money will be donated to the school."

The audience mumbles and begins to move away from the stage. The night is over. The life of the drive-in—over.

"Wait!" Sam Dayberry shoves through to the front. "Wait." The crowd stills and turns to the Valiant caretaker. "Could a person buy the Big Picture?"

The major barks. "No, it's too late. It's—"

"Yes!" Buford nods his head, his Cowboys cap bobbing. "It's been for sale for years. Never even had a looker."

"We are minutes away from closing this deal." The mayor jerks the microphone from Buford. "I have been more than patient. More than lenient. It's time to embrace progress!"

"What would it take to buy that drive-in?" Sam calls out.

Buford throws out a number that makes my eyes bulge. The people of In Between prepare to walk away.

"Sold!"

The air stills. The cicadas even stop to listen.

"What?" the mayor croaks.

"Sold." Sam joins them onstage. Using Buford's back, he scribbles out a check and rips it out. "You'll need to wait 'til tomorrow to cash that," he whispers. Then Sam turns toward the shocked stares of the people of In Between. "What? I used to work for a little company called Macintosh."

And the night air fills with shouts and cheers. Backs are slapped, babies are kissed, and good friends are hugged. My eyes tear up as I see the joy radiating from Frances's face. Her dream came true. The Big Picture will be saved.

"I . . . um . . ." Sam adjusts the microphone to his height. "I will need a business partner for this though. I'm just the backer. I don't know how to operate a drive-in." He searches the crowd until he finds just the face he's looking for. "Maxine Simmons . . . I've made a lot of mistakes."

My foster parents push Maxine toward the front. Her mouth is frozen in an O.

"I don't want to go into any more ventures without you," Sam continues, taking his hat off his head. "I need your help for the Big Picture. It will need your woman's touch. Your way with . . . popcorn. Well, no . . ." He shakes his head as if to clear it. "The truth is I don't know anything about . . . er, ticket sales. Dagnabbit! I love you woman, and I want you to marry me."

Sam descends the stage steps two at a time and walks toward my foster grandmother, who still stands in a stupor likes she's been hit by lightning.

We all surround them, desperate to hear the rest. Tate takes me by the hand, and we inch in close.

"Maxine, the drive-in isn't the only thing I won't know how to do without you. I don't know how to do life without you. I've been a mess. And though you drive me nuts, and you get into trouble. And I mean big trouble."

"Amen!" someone shouts.

"Me and my chicken truck can testify!"

Brian Diamatti begins to softly play "I Will Always Love You" on his bagpipes as Sam bends to one knee. "Though you are trouble with a capital T, and the entire police force in In Between and the surrounding counties know you by name and Social Security number—"

"Get on with it, baldie." Maxine pops her gum, her expression bored. But her telltale hands shake.

"I want to know if you'd do me the honor of marrying me and running my snack bar for the rest of my life."

Maxine throws herself at Sam, planting kisses on each of his scruffy cheeks. "I do! I will! I shall!" She hugs him close. "I think this moment calls for some poetry."

* * *

A FEW HOURS later, I fire up my computer and sit my tired body down.

And I complete my long-expired extra credit assignment for Ms. Dillon. Six pages later I come to my finale.

> *I don't know where I'll be ten years from now. But I know I will be loved by the family God created for me. And maybe they are a little crazy. But they are mine.*
>
> *In a decade Millie will be cancer-free and hopefully tofu-free, as well. James will still be a rock star of the pulpit and a closet* American Idol *fan. And I hope by this time their daughter, Amy, realizes what amazing parents she has and cleans her life up. I look forward to Christmas dinners where every chair is filled.*
>
> *Sam will no doubt be tired and worn from chasing after Maxine and keeping her out of trouble. Or jail.*
>
> *And me? Millie says I'm going to college, and I think she just might be onto something. But James says Broadway might be calling my name. He might be right too.*
>
> *My youth pastor once said that God has a plan for me, a plan bigger than anything I could ever come up with . . .*

"Sweet Pea, turn off that light. We have a wedding to plan tomorrow. Gonna get me one of those Vera Wanger dresses." I smile at my foster grandma. She fluffs her pillow and grins back.

My eyes scan my computer screen, and I highlight the document—every word of my future.

And I hit delete.

Because you know what? I don't know what's in store for me. But God's done pretty good by me so far. I think I'll just let *him* write the rest of my pages.

# Chapter Forty-Four

MAXINE FASTENS THE last of the thirty buttons on the back of my maid of honor dress. "You look smashing, Toots."

I glare at my foster grandmother in Bubba's bathroom mirror. "I look like an overstuffed prom queen from 1986. You *promised* me there wouldn't be a butt bow."

Maxine cackles and swats me on the tush. "Don't think of it as tacky. Think of it as a highlight on one of your finer features."

"I still think it would look better in the trash can."

The bathroom door swings open and Millie pops in. Her straw hat bobbles sideways revealing a bald, but healthy head. "Come on, ladies. It's time."

Maxine shivers like a wet dog. "Oh, glory! I'm so nervous. I am so pee-my-pants nervous." She clutches me. "I don't think I can do this. I'm too young to get married."

"Mad Maxine, there's no one else on this planet who could get me in a lima bean–colored pouffy dress but you. Just you." I place my hands on hers. "You are my grandmother, and I love you." I watch a tear trickle down her cheek, and I lean in, touching my nose to hers. "But if you don't march yourself down the aisle to where Sam is waiting for you beneath one big movie screen, I will drag you out myself. By your overly processed, bleached-blonde roots."

She inhales deeply. "Do you really think I can do this? This marriage stuff?"

"By the G.O.G, baby." I smile and pat her too-smooth cheek. "The G.O.G."

## *Can't Let You Go*

A Katie Parker Production Novella

Summer 2014

Katie Parker is now a twenty-three year-old college graduate, fresh from a year of performing on the great stages of London. When she runs into old flame Charlie Benson in the airport, both of them are bound for In Between, brining their baggage and more secrets that can be stuffed in an overhead bin. A flight mishap throws the two together, and Katie finds she can't escape Charlie when she returns to their small town. But does she even want to? Katie's returned to mend a broken heart and figure her life out, but when she discovers what has really brought Charlie back to town, she's thrown in the middle of an all-out battle.

Can she risk her heart again for a guy whose kisses make her weak in the knees, but whose secret could destroy all that she holds dear?

## Chapter One

"What do you mean my bags aren't here?

I lean over the counter at the O'Hare airport, fresh out of patience and smiles. The TSA employee's fingers clickity-clack on his keyboard, his generous brows knit together like an escaped wooly worm.

"I'm sorry, Miss Parker. Something apparently went very wrong, and your luggage seems to be on a flight to Reykjavik."

"This is unacceptable. Who goes to Iceland?"

"Apparently your bags do."

I want to slap my hand on the counter and yell until Mr. Brows makes this all okay. Because I just can't handle one more catastrophe. My bottom lip quivers, and I hear the pitiful words tumble from my lips. "My whole life is in those bags."

"Surely not everything," says a voice behind me.

*That voice.*

One I haven't heard in years, except in my dreams of home and heartache.

I turn around, pushing my tired, limp hair from my flushed cheek. Suddenly all the exhaustion of a ten hour flight evaporates, the weeks without sleep, the homesickness. All that I left behind in London. "Charlie Benson." His name comes out of my mouth like a sacred whisper as he stands there smiling.

I immediately burst into tears.

"Hey," Strong arms wrap around me, and I'm taken right back. My head pressed to Charlie's chest, I inhale his achingly familiar scent, and I'm no longer this broken, exhausted twenty-three year old, who just spent a year studying abroad, the pieces of my heart, my only luggage that followed. I'm sixteen, back in my hometown of In Between, dancing with one sweet Charlie Benson on my back porch underneath the Texas stars.

"How are you here?" I dash at the tears and take a much-needed step back. I take in the boy before me. Can I even call him a boy? He stands tall, shoulders broad, as if now carrying not just muscle, but some of the world's responsibility. With his dark dress pants, white button down, and navy tie, Charlie looks all man. And a professional one at that. "Are you traveling for work?"

"I live in Chicago now. Got out of a meeting only minutes ago. I'm on my way to In Between. You?"

I gesture to the desk. "I was trying to track down my luggage. I flew in from Paris, but had a terrible layover. I'm finally headed home as well." To my mom and dad, my crazy grandmother, to people who love me.

"You were studying in London this year, right?"

*Don't think about it. Don't think about it.* "Yes."

"My mom keeps me updated on In Between. She said you were in some plays on the West End." At my nod he smiles. "She says you're kind of a big deal."

Glad someone thinks so. "Just lucked into some good roles, I guess."

"*Flight 247 for Houston will now begin boarding our first class passengers. . .*"

Rain pelts the wall of windows at the gate, and I wonder if the crew has noticed.

"Are you on this flight?" he asks.

"Yes, you?"

"Yep." He reaches out, runs his hand down my arm, his head tilted just so. "Are you sure you're okay?"

"What, me? This?" I gesture to my mess of a face. "Jet lag, you know? And then the airline losing my stuff." I give a laugh so genuine, the Academy should FexEx me an Oscar. "I'm sorry. I'm a little homesick, and when I saw you—" I shake my head and smile. "I guess you were just a sight for sore eyes."

His lips tip in a grin. "Last I heard you were engaged."

Another announcement for our flight cracks across the speakers, but it sails over my head. "Wow. Word travels fast."

"You can't beat the small town communication system."

"You mean my grandma?"

His laugh swirls around me, settling somewhere in the gray recesses of my heavy heart.

The garbled voice comes across the speakers again.

"Time for me to board," Charlie says. "Where are you sitting?" He holds out a hand for my ticket, and I fumble in my bag to find it.

"It's here somewhere." I dig through the outer-pocket, coming up with a nail file, half a Snickers, two pieces of gym, and ten wads of used Kleenex.

"Hey." He steps nearer. "You're shaking."

I shrug and continue digging. "Fatigue."

He takes my worn leather messenger bag, looks in the middle compartment, his eyes never leaving mine, and pulls out my ticket. "You're still afraid of flying, aren't you?"

The things people remember. One senior class trip to Miami Beach with me trying to storm the cockpit demanding two forms of identification from the pilots, and everyone thinks you have a full blown neurosis.

Please. I've grown up since then.

*"Final boarding call . . ."*

"It's been incredible seeing you today." Charlie pulls me in for a hug, and I just breathe him in. The warm, the familiar, the safe. "We have more catching up to do," he whispers near my ear. "Are you going to be okay?"

"Definitely. I haven't had a flying meltdown in such a long time."

It's been at least three hours.

Clutching a water bottle and my wrinkled ticket, I follow Charlie as we board the sparsely populated plane. He stops off in row seven, while I schlep to the very back of the cabin. Next to the bathroom. How these odiferous seats don't come with a discount is beyond me.

I squeeze my bag in the bin above me, then settle into the window seat, hoping the two empty seats on my right remain that way. Buckling in, I check my phone one last time. I quickly respond to a text from my mom, two from my dad, and five from my grandma that consist of nothing more than her fish-lipped selfies with the message "My face misses yours!"

And then there are those voicemails I immediately delete.

Fifteen minutes later, we taxi down the runway. I sit in my blissfully empty row, push my breath in and out, and pray to the Lord Jesus to spare me one more day. I'm not afraid of what comes after death. I'm just a little terrified of the actual dying process. Especially if it involves crashing, flames, and wasted drink carts.

I'm just promising the Holy Father my favorite mascara and first born when a shoulder bumps mine, as someone throws himself into the seat beside me. I continue to whisper my beggar's prayer when a hand covers my clenched fingers.

I look up.

Charlie smiles. He brushes my damp hair from my face like he's done it a million times before. His strong hand pulls one of mine into his. And he just holds it.

"I'm not afraid to fly," I say.

"Of course not." He gives our fingers a squeeze. "It's the fatigue."

Thunder cracks outside. "Do you think it's safe to fly?"

"I do."

"But I read this report that when it storms, your statistical chances of—"

"It's perfectly safe."

"But sometimes lightning can be magnetically attracted to the wing and—"

"Nearly impossible."

"And then there's the possibility of—"

"Katie?"

My heart beats wildly, and my bones ache with exhaustion. "Yes?"

His gray eyes hold mine. "I won't let anything happen to us."

"Promise?"

With a smile as safe as church and sweet as sun tea, he slowly nods. "Always."

# Chapter Two

I was practically raised on the streets. By twelve, I had a rap sheet, knew how to steal to eat, could pick a lock with just paper clips and spit, and could deflect the advances of my druggie mom's boyfriends with one well-placed knee.

I was fearless.

And now here I sat in my cushy, cramped plane seat, a half hour into the ride, tremoring slightly, and noticing I'm still clutching Charlie Benton's hand like it's all that's holding us upright.

I let go and give a small laugh. "Sorry." Nothing like reuniting with an old friend by welcoming them into your neurotic phobia. "Takeoffs make me nervous." And the part that comes after—the whole driving in the sky thing, hanging by clouds, winds, and various gravitational whims. His piercing gray eyes soften, and I remember all the times as a teenager I'd stare into them, sure there was a God, and He had baptized this boy with a benevolence of genetic blessings that resulted in one beautiful, intelligent boy who had routinely taken my breath away.

"I love to fly," Charlie says. "I've put in a lot of miles in the last year. I love the rocking of the plane, the hum of the engine. Some of the best sleeping conditions."

"Right." I would have to be drugged unconscious. "So tell me about your job." Charlie had gone to college in Chicago, leaving the town of In Between, while I had stayed behind, doing junior college, then university.

His gaze leaves mine, and he looks down the aisle toward the flight attendant pushing a cart. "Nothing exciting. I interned for this company my senior year. They hired me right after graduation."

"What do you do?"

"I'm very entry level," he says. "I'm kind of a glorified paper pusher right now."

"I know that won't last long. What company did you say you're with?"

"Would you like a beverage?" The flight attendant brings her silver cart to a stop by us, her red lips smiling.

I request a diet soda, and the woman pops the top on the can and pours it over ice.

"You probably want to give her the whole can," Charlie says. "I think Katie here could use the stiff drink."

"Would you like me to pour in some complimentary tequila?" the flight attendant asks.

I nod vigorously. "Yes, please."

"I was just kidding." She laughs and pushes her cart down the aisle.

More cruelty delivered mid-air. Thanks, lady.

"You're fine," Charlie says. "The hard part is over."

"Maybe you could keep talking." I snuggle my side into the chair, facing my old friend. My old boyfriend. "Keep my mind off our imminent doom."

He laughs. "Tell me about you. You haven't been too present on Facebook the last year. Hard to tell what you've been up to."

Images of the last six months flash through my mind. Some of them amazing. Some of them. . .not worth thinking on. "I finally graduated." I take a bolstering swig of diet soda, enjoying the way it burns going down. "Then I got selected to go work in London." Had that been a blessing or a curse?

"My mom said you were in some pretty impressive productions."

I'd forgotten how intense his gray eyes could be. So focused, like I'm the only person he wants to be talking to. Those eyes were older now, still full of mischief, always reflecting an intimidating intelligence, but now there was something more looking back at me. Something darker, maybe a little bit heavy. Like Charlie Benson might have some sadness and secrets of his own.

"It was an unforgettable experience," I finally say.

"And now you're back for a visit?"

"Yes." I leave it at that, clutching my arm rest as we hit a few bumps of turbulence. "And you? What's bringing you back?"

He lifts his drink and absently swirls it, studies the dark contents. "I want to check on my dad. Spend some time with him."

"I thought he was in remission." My mom had told me last year when Charlie's dad had been diagnosed with liver cancer. The whole In Between community had rallied around the bank president with prayers, well-wishes, and many a foil-covered casserole.

"He is. And things are looking good." Charlie looks past me and out the window over my shoulder. "My company gave me some time to come home and be with my family, so I took it."

I want to ask more, but one turn of mercy deserves another, and I let it drop. God knows I don't want to talk about what's really dragging me back to In Between, and given the set in Charlie's jaw, this topic is not a welcome one.

"You dated that Tate guy for a few years," Charlie says. "What happened to that?"

The plane makes a sharp jerk to the right, and I slap my hand on Charlie's. I frantically look around, but neither of the flight attendants seem concerned. The person across from us reads a *People*, while the couple a row ahead amiably chats.

"Um. . ." *It's okay. We just hit an air pocket. Calm down.* "Tate, yeah. He's now a missionary in Uganda. We're still friends." High School Love Number Two and I had simply moved in different directions.

Lightning cracks outside, and I jump as it feels close enough to touch us. Charlie's fingers slid back and forth over mine. "We're fine," he said as the plane dipped, sending my stomach to my feet. "Just a storm."

And just how many more of those did I have to endure?

I look at my hand captured in his, and I knew Charlie was just being nice. That's just who he was. But the rhythmic strokes of his fingers calmed my frayed nerves as nothing else had on this voyage home.

The plane began to shake and rattle like the busted glove compartment on my old Toyota. Only I couldn't turn up the radio, sing my car solos, and drown out the noisy vibrations.

"Why do you think we didn't work out?" I ask.

Charlie doesn't startle. Merely lifts a dark brow as he inclines his head closer to mine. "Where did that come from?"

"Was it me?"

"I—"

"Is there something about me that pushes guys away? That asks to be dumped?"

His hand on mine stills just as a flight attendant gives a staticky report. "Ladies and gentlemen, the captain has turned on the seat belt sign. We're hitting a brief patch of turbulence with this storm, but we'll be out of it in no time. Food and beverage services will be resumed as soon as we get the all clear."

"That can't be good, right?" I sit up as straight as my seatbelt will let me, frantically taking in every detail around me—the location of the flight attendants, the body language of fellow passengers, the reassuring presence of the wings that still seem to be blessedly attached.

Charlie pours more drink into my icy cup. He's probably regretting sitting by me. He probably wishes I'd drink my diet soda and happily pass out in a carbonated coma, so he could go back to his own seat and read his *Wall Street Journal* or whatever it is a calm, brainiac would read.

I need medication.

"Here, eat some of these." Charlie reaches into the leather bag at his feet and pulls out a box of M&Ms.

I snatch them out of his grip and down a handful. I chew vigorously, savoring the sugar and chocolate on my tongue. What if this is the last time I taste such heaven?

The plane, deciding the shaking was just its opening act, brings on the full-on quaking, jumping up and down like a Pentecostal with the Holy Ghost. My butt gains some air, and I turn my frightened gaze to Charlie. "What's happening?"

"Turbulence." He lifts a shoulder in such a lazy fashion, you'd think he didn't notice the way his hair bounced on his head from the aeronautical shenanigans. "You were asking me why we didn't work out."

"I was?"

His smile is soft, slow. "Why do you think we didn't make it?"

I tighten my seatbelt, trying not to wonder at the age of it. "Because you had your eye on some blonde Barbie who I could never compete with."

"That's not true."

"That you didn't have your eye on Chelsea Blake?"

He has the decency to look guilty. "That you couldn't compare. You were prettier and smarter than her any day."

Men in shimmy-shaky planes will say anything. "But you dumped me to go after her."

"I believe it was a mutual break-up."

"Because I knew what was coming."

"It was you I took to the senior prom." He squeezes the hand he's still holding and gives me a look that zings right to my weary core. "And you and I spent most of the night camping with on a blanket under the stars."

"At the lake." He'd built me a fire, made a pallet on the rocky ground, tucked me into the crook of his arm, and pointed out every constellation he could find in that April sky while I rested my head on his chest and listened to the crickets and the cadence of his heart.

Then we graduated. And Charlie Benson, of the lingering kisses and spell-binding astronomy, had moved away.

Rain and wind battle outside my window, and I utter a quick litany of prayers. Prayers that beg for calm skies and fifty more years of life.

"Guys don't stick around though," I say, watching a bolt of lightning slash the sky. "Eventually they find someone else, something better."

He leans close. "Is that what you really think? That you weren't good enough?"

"It's hard to argue with history." I hold up a hand to stop him from interrupting. "I'm not trying to be pitiful. I just want to get to the bottom of it. I'm tired of making mistakes, wasting my time." Being tossed out, left behind.

The plane takes a leap north then dips back down. My breaths catches in my throat. "I want off this thing," I say. "I want off this thing right now."

"Please put your seats in the upright position," announces the flight attendant. "Return your tray to its proper place."

The pilot takes his turn next, giving instructions and saying God knows what (probably Last Rites). But I can't hear a thing for the rising noise around me. An overhead bin to our left flies open and a bag torpedoes into a grandma and her knitting needles. Somewhere up front a baby wails. Nervous chatter gathers like tornado winds.

"What's the pilot saying?" My heart beats a crazed staccato, and I want to both cry and laugh at the insanity of it all.

"He said to stay calm that we'd be out of this storm soon." Charlie takes quick stock of the situation around us, then turns his attention back to me. "You were telling me why you broke my heart our senior year."

"I did not."

I expect him to smile, to follow up with a joke.

But Charlie says nothing.

He captures my other hand, prying my fingers off the arm rest, then pulls me closer, resting his forehead on mine. "I don't think you remember the events of those last few months accurately."

I swallow then lick my trembling lips. "You left." Just like they all do.

"I cared about you."

"You had a funny way of showing it."

"Katie, I—"

His words die as light and fury explode around us.

The flash of lightning.

Screaming.

Fire.

Falling.

Plummeting.

Spinning.

Screaming.

My world goes dark as Charlie throws his body over mine. "We've been hit," he yells in my ear. "Hang on. Just hang on to me."

I can't breathe. Can't drag in enough breath.

*Please God, save us.*

I utter the plea silently.

Aloud.

"Charlie?"

"I'm right here. I'm not letting you go."

His arms encircle me and hold my tight. He mumbles words of assurance, broken prayers, and other utterances the terror swallows whole.

"Charlie?" I shove off his hands, his body. "Charlie!" With all my strength I push him away, only to grab his face, his stubbly cheeks in the palms of my hands.

He finally lifts his head, his eyes wide, unfocused.

"I love you, Charlie." I pull his face to mine, blocking out the shrieks around us and the spin and tilt of death. "Do you hear me? I never stopped loving you."

"Katie, I—"

Then I press my mouth to his, holding Charlie Benson to me, knowing these lips will soon draw their last breath.

And I don't want to waste these minutes, seconds.

Then Charlie Benson's kissing me back. His lips cover mine. His hands cradle my head.

The world spins.

The plane falls.

And I just hold on.

"I've got you," I hear him say again. "I'm not letting you go."

And after all these years, I believe him.

Just when it's too late.

# About the Author

Four-time Carol award-winning author Jenny B. Jones writes romance with equal parts wit, sass, and Southern charm. Since she has very little free time, she believes in spending her spare hours in meaningful, intellectual pursuits, such as watching bad TV, Tweeting deep thoughts to the world, and writing her name in the dust on her furniture. She is the author of romantic comedies for women such as RITA finalist *Save the Date,* as well as books for teens, like her *A Charmed Life* series. You can find her at www.JennyBJones.com or standing in the Ben and Jerry's cooler.

CPSIA information can be obtained at www.ICGtesting.com
Printed in the USA
LVOW07s1835090316

478458LV00007B/896/P